WHEN
I'M
GONE

OTHER TITLES BY EMILY BLEEKER

WRECKAGE

WHEN I'M GONE

A NOVEL

by Emily Bleeker

LAKE UNION
PUBLISHING

Published by Lake Union Publishing, Seattle

www.apub.com

Amazon, the Amazon logo, and Lake Union Publishing are trademarks of Amazon.com, Inc., or its affiliates.

ISBN-13: 9781503953383 (hardcover)

ISBN-10: 1503953386 (hardcover)

ISBN-13: 9781503951457 (paperback)

ISBN-10: 1503951456 (paperback)

Cover design by Shasti O'Leary-Soudant / SOS CREATIVE, LLC

Printed in the United States of America

First edition

*To my children, who believe in me far more than I ever
dare to believe in myself*

JANUARY

CHAPTER 1

It was a beautiful funeral. How could it not be? Natalie planned the whole thing, and she always had a knack for entertaining. Luke and Natalie had visited the funeral home together, but Nat did all the work. From the donation basket for the National Cancer Society to the personalized video messages playing on a loop in the foyer, it was probably the funeral of the year in Farmington Hills, Michigan.

Luke pushed the button on the garage door remote and pulled in to the left of Natalie's tan minivan. They glided over the familiar double bump that meant they were home, and the kids shifted in the backseat.

Luke checked on Will in the rearview mirror. His eyes were red-rimmed and wet, again. Fourteen is a rough enough age without dealing with losing your mom. He hadn't reached the "I've run out of tears" stage yet. Teenagers must have extra tears because of all the hormones.

Luke was in the "dried-up" stage, and it was almost worse than sobbing uncontrollably. At least when you are crying, no one makes comments about how well you are taking this or how relieved you must be that she's in "a better place." What they don't know is this: appearing okay is a lot easier than actually being okay.

May picked up her head slowly, as if it weighed twenty pounds. "I'm hungry, Dad. What's for dinner?" Sometimes Luke wondered if May was a teenage boy and not a nine-year-old girl.

Will sighed. "We ate at the funeral, May. Dad doesn't have time to—"

"It's okay, Will." Luke held up one hand. "Grandma Terry put some meals in the freezer. If May's hungry, I'll make dinner." Natalie's mom left right after the final chorus of "Amens" at the funeral. Not a surprise. She'd never been a big Luke fan. He was ready to walk into the house without feeling her stony eyes on him, as if she thought he'd willed Natalie to have cancer.

"You guys go in. I'll get Clayton."

May and Will unclicked their seat belts. "Did you bring home any of those chocolate pretzels from the luncheon? Those were good." May shoved her little face between the two front seats. Her upturned nose was her mother's, her eyes were Luke's, and her smile was some amazing fusion of DNA from the two of them.

"God, don't act like this was some birthday party you went to," Will said as he pushed open his car door and then slammed it so hard the car tilted. This was new, the anger.

"I'm sorry, baby, he doesn't mean it," Luke reassured May. He should be scolding Will for the way he treated his sister instead of making excuses, but he didn't feel like fighting. May shrugged and opened the door Will had slammed in her face. "Grandma put some snacks in the cabinet under the island. You can have whatever looks good."

"Thanks, Daddy." May scooted to the edge of the seat and hopped out of the car.

Will's anger was new but it wasn't surprising. Luke had suffered through several bouts of anger starting on the day Natalie came home from her three-month checkup. They had lived through the first three months of remission in a state of joy and nervous optimism. The day after her clear scans Natalie stuck a magnetic yellow ribbon on her car, and three months later her hair had finally grown in enough that she didn't have to deal with looks of pity when they went out in public. During her shift at Relay for Life, she wore a purple T-shirt with SURVIVOR printed across the front. She was in remission, damn it. But Dr. Saunders took it all away three months later with a few scans and a blood test. Yeah, that's when he was angry.

Luke pulled his car keys out of the ignition and slid them into his pocket, flinching as his knuckles brushed the fabric of his pants. The only way he knew how to deal with the anger and not lose control was with his punching bag in the basement. Next time he'd do a better job taping up, but for now the pain was a welcome distraction.

He opened the back car door with a quiet pop, and took a second to watch little Clayton sleep. His lips arched into a perfect cupid's bow, his almost invisible lashes brushing the tops of his cheeks. *Why are little kids' cheeks so temptingly kissable, especially when they are sleeping?* When he unclipped the buckle across the three-year-old's chest, Clayton's eyes fluttered open.

"Daddy, are we home?"

"Yes, honey, we're home. Let's get you in some pj's." Luke mashed the orange button with this thumb, unlatching the last two buckles and freeing Clayton.

"I love you, Daddy." Clayton put out his arms and leaned forward, his lanky little body sloughing out of the chair easily and sagging into Luke's arms, where he closed his eyes and fell back into his deep slumber. Luke breathed him in. He smelled like little boy sweat and Cheetos dust—Cheetos being the only way Terry kept him quiet during the memorial service. No, Luke wasn't angry now, just sad—sad in his chest, in his bones, and pretty much in every single part of his body.

Luke approached the steel door leading to the house, his arms full of sleeping little boy. It was open a crack so he pushed it with his elbow, squeezed through the minimal opening, and kicked it closed. His footsteps echoed in the empty hallway, usually full of backpacks and kids' shoes heaped precariously in baskets. He'd always hated those baskets before, spilling over with shoes, shoes that tripped him up as he headed in from work. Now he missed them and those ordinary annoyances of life.

Before she left, Natalie's mom had cleaned the house, top to bottom. The front room stood empty. The hospital bed, piles of magazines, and stacks of half-full water bottles—all were gone. The TV they'd rigged to hang in the corner by the front window was missing. An electrician came yesterday before the viewing and set it up in the basement, along with a new game system that Terry bought, as though it could make the kids forget that their mother had died. Now, the room where his wife took her last breath looked like any other formal living room: off-white furniture on tan carpet and family pictures on the wall.

At least it smelled the same, vanilla and cinnamon. There had to be some scented something somewhere pumping the smell through their vents. He'd better figure it out soon, because one day it would go away and home wouldn't smell like home anymore. Annie might know. As Natalie's best friend, she'd be the most likely to be aware of all those little tricks.

Luke took in a deep breath, the spices in the air filling his lungs as if they could give him nourishment. With Will moping in his room and May rummaging around the kitchen, it almost felt normal in here. It was nice to be alone in the house without all the generous but awkwardly helpful family and friends. Now he could lounge around in his sweats without wondering if the hole in the rear revealed too much of his boxers.

Clayton was growing heavier by the second, and Luke's knuckles and forearms burned from his late-night boxing session. He turned to the stairs, praying that the sleeping child wouldn't wake up before he could get him in bed. As he stepped away from the empty, echoing entryway, his foot slipped on something, sending him off-balance and threatening to make him fall. With a lurch, he steadied Clayton's body out of a desperate desire to avoid the screaming that would accompany a fall. Luke glared at the simple rectangle of colored paper that had almost tripped him.

Normally a piece of loose paper on the floor would be a runaway homework page or a carefully drawn art project set free by a fallen refrigerator magnet. *Another condolence card,* Luke thought as he crouched down. Clayton stirred on his shoulder. Luke pinched the stiff envelope between his fingertips and held it up to the slash of light shining in from the front porch.

"To Luke" was scrawled across the front in looping black letters. The *L* looped at the top and side; the *K* was petite and slanted. Luke bit his tongue—it was Natalie's handwriting. The familiar burn of tears pricked the back of his eyes.

Where did this come from? Luke glanced around for a clue as to how a letter from his dead wife was lying in the middle of the entryway. His eyes rested on the brass flap on the front door. The mail slot. Natalie had picked out that stupid door when they built this house ten years earlier. Then, after one freezing Michigan winter, she'd asked him to seal it off. He'd never gotten around to it. Not in nine years. And now his dead wife was communicating with him through the slot.

No. Of course she wasn't. Luke shook his head and tucked the card into his suit-coat pocket. Whatever this was, it wasn't a letter from *dead* Natalie. When people die, they don't send letters through mail slots, they don't even go live in some magical place called heaven, they just die. Someone was messing with him.

May ran out of the kitchen as Luke's foot hit the stairs, still in the black knee-length dress she'd worn to the funeral.

"Dad, can I have this granola bar?" She held up a shiny silver package. "Mom always said no sugar before bedtime, but I thought maybe this once?" May had this way of casually bringing up her mother that punched Luke in the gut. How could she be so strong and he so weak?

"Sure, honey." Then, feeling a little guilty, he added, "Grab a glass of milk with it too, okay?"

"Uh, Dad? I can't pour my own milk. It's too heavy. I always spill." She put the end of her shoulder-length brown hair in the corner of her mouth, a habit ever since her hair was long enough to reach. Natalie had thought it was a soothing mechanism, but it still grossed her out. Luke chose to ignore it; May could use a bit of comfort right now.

"I'll send Will down to help you."

"He's not still mad at me, is he?" She pulled the wet strand of hair out of her mouth and tucked it behind her ear. Luke shuddered. *Okay, maybe it is really gross.*

"No, hon, he's not. He's sad, and sometimes sad comes out as mad."

"Hmm. Okay." She shrugged her shoulders and ripped the package open between her teeth before walking back into the kitchen.

"I love you," Luke called after her.

"You too!" she shouted back over her shoulder.

◆ ◆ ◆

After getting Clayton down and coaxing Will into helping his little sister with a snack and bedtime, Luke tossed his suit coat on the bed and yanked off his belt with a snap. He could wear the belt again, he decided, but not the suit. How can you wear a suit you wore to your wife's funeral without remembering . . . everything? He retrieved the suit bag from the closet and quickly hung the coat inside. A flash of blue in the pocket caught his eye.

The letter. He'd forgotten, or maybe he'd made himself forget. It looked like Natalie's handwriting, and because of that, he grabbed the letter and let the suit bag fall to the floor along with its wooden hanger. He ripped the envelope open by sliding his finger under the flap. A folded sheet of spiral notebook paper slid out. Well, that confirmed it.

No one but Natalie would write letters to her widower in a fifty-cent spiral notebook and rip it out without cutting off the fringe.

Luke threw the empty envelope on his bed but paused when he caught a glimpse of himself in the mirror across the room. His dusty-blond hair was still carefully combed in a part, tie knotted at his throat. He looked neat and tidy, ready for a job interview or big presentation at work. The only sign of how devastating this day had been was a coating of straw-colored stubble on his chin. It didn't feel right that he could appear so put together on the outside when he was falling apart on the inside. Luke quickly untucked his dress shirt, loosened the knot on his tie, and ran a hand through his hair till the part disappeared.

There, much better, he thought, reassessing his reflection.

He couldn't put it off any longer. With shaking hands, Luke sat on the edge of his bed, his back to the mirror, and unfolded the spiral notebook paper. At the top, written in what was undoubtedly Natalie's handwriting, it said: "The day I'm buried." Underneath was a block of writing, the looping letters so familiar it was like she was whispering in his ear as he read.

> Dear Luke,
> Or maybe I should say "Dearest Luke" or "To my loving husband, Luke," or I could go casual and say, "Yo, Luke!" I'm not sure how a dead lady addresses her husband. If you're reading this, I'm probably dead. Or you're snooping around my stuff, found my private journal, and decided to read it. Which, if that's the case, shame on you! But I'm guessing I'm dead, because you're not really the nosy type.
> First let me say—I love you. I love you and our children more than I could ever write in words. The idea that you are living and I am not makes me want

to throw up, like when we had that horrible stomach flu right after Clayton was born. It makes me angry and jealous and a bunch of other really ugly emotions. So, before I get all mushy on what has probably already been a supermushy day, I'll leave it at this: I didn't want to leave you.

I feel pretty melodramatic writing you a letter to open on the day of my burial. According to Dr. Saunders I have a pretty decent chance of beating this thing, but you know me: I don't trust doctors. No harm in starting this journal, you know, just in case. I've always wanted to try my hand at writing; maybe this will be my first step toward finally writing the novel dancing around my brain for the past ten years. They say write what you know, right? Apparently I know cancer and we are *not* friends.

First day of chemo tomorrow. I'm so nervous. No, it's not about the hair thing even though I know I whine about it enough. I'm less worried about losing hair and more worried I'm going to lose myself, become one of those hollow chemo patients I see sitting in Saunders's waiting room, skin and bones. Today there was a girl who threw up right there in the waiting room after her treatment. It was probably one of her first times because she still had her hair, or maybe it was an awesome wig. Note to self, ask where she got her wig.

You want to know the worst part? The nurses acted like it was no big deal, like cleaning up vomit off the waiting room floor (and walls and chairs) was normal in an oncologist's office. Come to think of it, there's no carpet in Saunders's offices at all. Maybe they had to hire steam cleaners one too many times so they decided linoleum was more cost-efficient?

Anyway, enough about that. I'll let you know how it goes tomorrow. Tonight I hope you give our kids an extra hug and kiss from their mother. I don't think you should tell them about this yet. It can be quite scary to think your mom is writing you from heaven . . . or wherever I am. I know when Tangerine went belly-up in the fishbowl, you told the kids, "When you die, you die." I'll be honest—I thought it was a bit cruel. I wonder if you think I'm gone forever now? Worm food, fertilizer, pushing up daisies, taking the big nap. Well, wherever I am, I love you. I miss you. I'll write again tomorrow.

Love,

Natalie

Luke smoothed the creases in the page against his thigh. He didn't know what to think. Reading the note, he heard her voice in his head, just like she was sitting next to him. He thought it would make him sad, but somehow, it didn't. The letter made him feel warm in his midsection. It made him want to hang up the suit instead of burn it.

He folded the paper carefully along the already-formed creases, put it back in the envelope, and placed it on his pillow. It looked like it belonged there. Natalie was always doing thoughtful things like that. Once she even wrote him a love note in black ink on the banana she put in his lunch. At the time Luke had thought a love note via banana was the strangest message delivery method ever. Until today. Writing letters from beyond the grave was far stranger but also—wonderful. Could there really be another one tomorrow? The idea almost made him smile.

Maybe he'd revisit the suit issue another day. He finished changing into his holey sweatpants and a long-sleeved T-shirt, wondering if he'd get any sleep tonight. Grief seemed to chase away the comfort of sleep, and he longed for a night where he could drift off into a blissfully unaware dreamworld, where life was potentially weird but definitely less paralyzing. His doctor had prescribed him a sleep aid, but Luke was almost used to the insomnia by now.

He finished hanging his dress pants and suit coat on the oversize wooden hangers they came on and worked the garment bag over them until it zipped closed. He eyed the spot where he usually hung it, toward the front of the closet right before his short-sleeved work shirts. If he was going to keep the suit, it couldn't stay there at the front of the closet, where he'd see it every time he got dressed or grabbed a pair of shoes. It would have to go to the back, where, after some time, he might even forget about it. He rushed boldly to the back of the walk-in closet, his back to Natalie's side, where her dresses and blouses hung undisturbed, unaware they no longer had an owner to wear them.

Currently, the last item in his closet was a black, oversize Hawaiian shirt with bold red flowers plastered across the chest. Luke prodded the shirt forward to make room and placed his suit in the resulting gap. When the metal hook hit the rod with a clank, a white piece of fringe from the notebook paper fluttered to the carpet like snow. Luke watched it fall in awe, like it was the first snow of the season. But as soon as it hit the carpet, he snatched it up quickly as though it would melt. Holding the stray scrap of paper in his palm, Luke settled to the floor and leaned against the pliable wall of Natalie's clothes. Her familiar scent of fabric softener and lotion engulfed him as he studied the piece of fringe.

The letter didn't take away the hollow place inside him that burned like an essential internal organ had been removed, but it did do something else. For the first time in months, he didn't dread the sun coming up in the morning because there might be more. Isn't that what she said? She'd write more?

Lately Luke had given up on hope, finding it an utterly useless exercise that left him with nothing but bitterness. But tonight, as he imagined another blue envelope slipping mysteriously through the mail slot on his front door, something like hope stirred inside him again. Luke picked up the fringe between his thumb and index finger, rubbed it gently, and whispered, "Thank you."

CHAPTER 2

Clayton was up before the sun. Luke brought him in his bed and clicked on a show. That quiet time lasted only about twenty minutes. Then the demands started.

"Daddy, milk."

Luke sighed. "Milk, please?" Natalie had a thing about politeness with the kids. Guess he should try to keep things up to her standard.

"Okay. Daddy, milk please?" Clayton lisped, his pleading three-year-old eyes taking up half of his face. How could he say no now?

By his third trip to the kitchen, there was still no noise from the two closed doors in the upstairs hall. It was nearing 11:00 a.m., and Luke was starting to wonder how long he should let them veg today. All day sounded like an excellent idea.

He dragged his feet down another set of stairs. As he peered over the railing, something blue caught his eye and left a lump in his throat. He slipped his hand into his robe pocket, fingering the letter he'd found on the wood floor last night. It was still there, the frayed edges of the notebook paper his constant comfort for the past twelve hours. One letter would've been enough, or so he'd thought until he saw the newest blue rectangle, half-hidden by the bills and condolence cards from the daily mail delivery. Now all he thought about was more, more of Natalie and her comfort. When Luke thought about it that way, he was sure he could never have enough.

He raced down the stairs, jumping off the last two, his bare feet hitting the wood with a slap. The sun, reflecting off a new powdery coating of snow outside, poured in through the tall, skinny windows framing the door. Luke rubbed his eyes with one hand as he shoved all the other letters aside and snatched Natalie's envelope with the other.

His name was scrawled on the front, this time with their address and a stamp. No return address. Postmarked: Farmington Hills, MI. Luke flipped the letter over; "DAY 2" was written in bold letters on the back. Without any attempt at neatness, he poked a finger under the flap and ripped. Peeking past the jagged opening, he peered inside. Another piece of folded notebook paper with the fringe sticking up like it was beckoning him to take a look. Luke unfolded the letter greedily.

The front of the page and half of the back was filled with her hand-writing. Stumbling to the stairs, he collapsed on the second to bottom step, shifting back and forth to fit on the narrow seat. There was no time to savor this letter. He had to read fast, before Clayton noticed him missing and before May and Will showed their faces.

Natalie was right; it wasn't a good idea to share the letters with the kids now. It was the wrong time for them, but also the wrong time for Luke. He wasn't ready to show anyone the letters yet, though he wasn't sure why. Maybe it was because some of his favorite times with Natalie were the ones they'd spent talking, just the two of them, processing the day and life and the kids. He didn't know how to do it alone. The paper crinkled in his hand as he began to read.

DAY 2

Dear Luke,

Okay, so chemo officially stinks. I can't write much today; I feel like I have the stomach flu, got hit by a car, and was secretly drugged with sleeping pills, all at the same time. And unless all those things happened without my knowledge, it must be the chemo. It makes sense because chemo literally *is* poison. Dr. Saunders keeps saying it's good poison. Now that's an oxymoron if I've ever heard one.

I need to sleep, but I hope you get this letter in time to do something today. I know I'm dead and all, but that doesn't stop me from asking you to do crap for me. It only stops me from nagging you about it until you get it done.

Would you make the kids pancakes? I know breakfast is not your thing, but trust me, some mornings (like the morning after your mother's funeral) nothing tastes as good as hot pancakes made by someone you love. Not the cardboard box kind though. You've got to use *my* special recipe pancakes. I'll write it out on the back since it's all in my head. *Oh!* Don't forget, May likes hers with a chocolate chip smiley face. She won't eat them without it.

Here's a crazy idea—maybe you could try one for once.

Kiss the kids. I love you and miss you.

Love,

Natalie

Luke flipped the page over, hoping to find another message from Natalie, but instead there was a recipe. It looked pretty simple. For the past few weeks someone had been here to make meals for the kids, or folks had dropped prepared dishes off in Tupperware containers. Luke could barely eat them though. Even during those last three months when they knew the end was coming fast, Luke leaned heavily on boxed cereal, mac and cheese, and plenty of bananas and carrot sticks to let Natalie know he was attempting to be healthy. Now the pressure of making sure the kids were fed three at least semihealthy meals a day was all on him.

"Daddy! I need milk!" Clayton shouted from his bedroom, and it echoed through the two-story entry. So much for politeness. A door opened in the upstairs hall.

"Dad, Clayton is yelling. I was trying to sleep." Will's voice dragged, and Luke wondered how late his fourteen-year-old had been up last night.

"I'm grabbing him a drink, then I'll make breakfast. Pancakes sound good?" Luke folded the letter as he spoke, put it back in the envelope, and added to the other one still in his pocket.

Will leaned over the railing, his bed-head hair sticking up in almost stylish brown spikes. He looked like his mother, even had her little lisp that came out when he was tired or distracted. When Will was little, Luke was always a little jealous his son didn't look more like him, but now he was glad. He wished all the kids took after Natalie because seeing those little parts of her live on in them made Luke miss her a fraction less.

"Dad . . ." Will hesitated. "You don't make pancakes."

"Well, I'm going to try." Luke walked up the stairs to his son and placed a hand on his shoulder. "I'm an engineer. If I can design cell phones the size of a credit card, I can certainly follow a simple recipe."

◆ ◆ ◆

It was almost noon by the time Luke found all the ingredients on Natalie's list. Will gave up on the hope of pancakes at about eleven thirty and ate a bowl of Cheerios before disappearing back into his room. But May was loyal. Once she heard sounds in the kitchen, she vowed to not take a bite of any food until a pancake stared up at her. Luke was touched by her devotion but also a little concerned the poor child would starve to death before an edible pancake landed on her plate.

He frowned at the lumpy mix of milk, white vinegar, melted butter, and eggs. According to Natalie's directions he was supposed to pour it into the dry ingredients and stir till still slightly lumpy. He sniffed the mixture; it smelled like Windex and eggs. No way he was doing this right. He was about to dump the semicongealed off-white muck into the flour when the door to the garage opened and closed with a slam.

"Hello, Richardson family. Anyone here?" Annie called. "I waited as long as I could."

For the past three months, Annie came by every morning at 8:30 a.m. For a while she pretended she'd happened to be in the middle of a run and thought to stop by. When the heavy snows came on in the first week in December, she started showing up in her minivan. Natalie and Luke pretended not to notice. When Natalie couldn't get out of bed anymore to answer the door, they gave Annie the garage code. Apparently her morning visits hadn't expired with Natalie.

She came around the corner in an ankle-length winter coat with snow on her shoulders. "Oh my gosh, it's cold out there."

Great. A real person. Luke made sure his robe was tied tight enough to hide his "hole in the butt" sweatpants that horrified Natalie's mom so much. Will and May weren't in much better shape. Luke wished he'd at least gotten them dressed and had them run combs through their hair. Instead, Clayton lay half-asleep in a sugar coma on the couch from all the "stay quiet" lollipops. Rainbow-colored drips decorated the collar of his airplane pj's.

"*Annie!*" May jumped up from her spot in front of the TV and sprinted toward Annie, nearly running into the half wall separating the kitchen from the family room. She was still wearing an off-white flannel nightgown, her hair frizzed around her head like a dandelion poof. The kids were a mess. Then again, if anyone could understand, it would be Annie.

"Hey, girl." Annie let out a big "*oooff*" as May threw her boney little arms around her neck. "How's your morning going?"

"Fine," she said as Annie lowered her to the ground. "Daddy's trying to make pancakes."

"Try is the operative word in that sentence," Luke mumbled.

"Well, I think you're pretty lucky to have a daddy who wants to make you pancakes. Even at," she pulled her phone out of her coat pocket and glanced at the screen, "noon. Breakfast for lunch sounds fun. What can I do to help?"

Annie's bobbed blonde hair bounced as she pulled off her beret-style hat and tossed it on the counter. Under her massive purple coat, she wore a long-sleeved running shirt and yoga pants. Could she really still be trying to sell the idea she'd stopped by on her run? Natalie would've made a joke. It would've been funny. Even if he didn't know exactly what she would've said, the idea still made Luke smile and get a choking feeling in his throat. He swallowed and held out the curdled mess he'd been stirring.

"Do you know anything about this?" His lips were pinched together as he remembered the smell.

"Oh my God. Is that Natalie's secret pancake recipe?" Annie rushed over, taking in the ingredients on the counter. "I've begged her for the recipe for years. Did she really leave it for you?"

"Yeah, it's right there." He pointed to the letter propped up on the counter. He was trying to keep it far away from the mess of flour and liquids.

"Can I look at it?" she asked as she snatched the paper off the counter. Her light eyebrows pinched together as she scanned the page. Luke watched her soak in the looping lines of Natalie's handwriting and the tears gathering in her eyes as she read.

He hadn't really considered how hard this must be on Annie, to mourn for a lost friend. At least when you are a widower, everyone expects you to be sad. Annie had loved Natalie like a sister, yet she was expected to go on with life as though Natalie meant no more to her than the checkout girl at the Wal-Mart.

Though they were as close as sisters, they looked anything but. Natalie had been a short brunette who never let a jeans size get in the way of enjoying brownies or skipping a day of cardio. Besides, she'd always insisted she didn't have strong enough cheekbones to pull off superskinny. Luke didn't mind; he thought her curves were plenty sexy and her self-confidence even more so. He'd rather have a woman who wore a size ten but wanted to make love with the lights on, than a size two who hid in the shadows.

Annie, on the other hand, was fair, sinewy, and a head taller than Nat. She liked her morning runs and green drinks but mostly because she sat at a desk all day transcribing medical documents. When Luke and Nat doubled with Annie and her husband, Brian, it always made Luke feel uncomfortable the way men's eyes would follow Annie around a room. Brian didn't seem to care; he had a natural self-confidence Luke secretly envied, and Natalie rolled her eyes, so Luke learned to ignore it.

But it didn't matter to Natalie and Annie what they looked like. The two women meshed from the moment they met at a PTO meeting when Will was in kindergarten and Annie's son was in fifth grade. Annie's face was streaked with tears by the time she lifted her gaze from the handwritten recipe.

"She was such a stinker." Annie sniffed and wiped her nose with the back of her hand. Luke tried to rip off a paper towel, but it caught on the roll and shredded in his hand. Annie took it anyway and blotted at her eyes. "Thanks." She cleared her throat with a tearful kind of a chuckle. "Do you realize this is the exact recipe from findyourrecipe.com? Word for word. She always made me think she had some special ingredient."

Luke snickered, swallowing hard again. "So this bowl of disgustingness makes sense to you?"

"Yes." She squinted. "If you followed the directions right, you made buttermilk. Congratulations."

"You're telling me I could've bought the stuff?" He poured it into the flour mixture, where it made a plopping sound.

"Yup, right there in the dairy section." Annie laughed, crossing the tile floor to the fridge with the note in hand. "I'll hang this up here if you're finished with it." Reaching toward the magnets covering the freezer door, she froze. "Oh my God, Luke, did you see this? On the back?"

Goosebumps developed on Luke's forearms. He'd forgotten about the letter. That was private. Without thinking, he raked his hands over his dark-blue robe, leaving off-white streaks across his chest.

"Yeah," was all he could think of to say. He wanted to take it back, to hide it away and make her forget she ever saw the intimate message on the other side of the paper, but it was too late. She was already reading.

"Where did you get this?" She held it up, her voice shaking almost as much as the paper in her hand.

He shrugged, trying to play it off as no big deal. "It came in with the daily mail."

"But it says day two," Annie said, her voice getting squeaky and high-pitched. "Where is day one?" Her forehead wrinkled, her eyebrows furrowed, and her breathing grew rapid.

Luke could see Annie's pulse pounding on her neck from across the room, but he didn't want to answer any questions. Usually a rational-minded engineer, he was avoiding the inevitable questions that would follow. Who? Why? How? Right now he just wanted the letter back in his pocket.

"I have the first one." It only took two giant steps to close the space between them. "But these are private, Annie; I'm sorry. I know you two shared everything, but I need this to be my thing with Natalie." He put his shaking hand out. "It's all I have left."

Standing this close to Annie, he noticed her red-rimmed eyes had dark circles smudged underneath. She hadn't slept in a few days, he was certain. Natalie had always said her best friend was an expert at appearing to be okay. He'd never understood what she meant until today. The letters might help her too, but he didn't even hesitate. Though it might be selfish, this was nonnegotiable. Natalie's letters were for him and him alone. His hand remained open between them.

"I'm sorry. You're right." Annie passed him the letter with a deep, quivering breath. She nodded, her eyes filling with tears. But she didn't actually cry, which was a relief to Luke. He didn't know how to comfort any more people. Hell, he was doing a lousy job comforting his own children. Annie wasn't missing out on anything.

He considered patting her on the shoulder until he noticed how close they were standing, foreheads almost touching, Annie's breath rustling the hair over his ears. He stepped back across the invisible line married people wear around them when spending time with the opposite sex, folded the letter protectively, and put it back in his robe pocket.

"I . . . I'm sorry," Luke said gently, stumbling over his words. "It's just . . ."

Annie's lips turned up in a half smile as she brushed invisible tears out of the corner of her eyes.

"No worries." She took a deep breath and wiped at her nose with the paper towel fragments, then glanced around the kitchen. "Let's get these pancakes cooking, shall we?"

Luke let out the breath he'd been holding. "All right. Let's do this thing."

When Annie turned her back to look for an appropriate pan, Luke pushed the letters down deeper into his pocket. *To keep them safe,* he thought. But really all he wanted was a reason to touch them again because when they were in his hands, he could forget she was gone. Forever.

◆ ◆ ◆

Within minutes they were pumping out stacks of almost Natalie-quality pancakes. When the speckled blue platter was full of golden circles, Annie set the table with some paper plates and plastic utensils.

"May, could you go get Will, please?" Luke asked, but when May tried to stand, she clutched her stomach.

"Sorry, Dad, my tummy hurts. I'm so hungry."

"Sit down. I can get your brother." Poor thing was starving.

"It's okay." Annie helped May climb on the long bench closest to the edge of the tile. "I've got it covered. You get those pancakes onto plates and cut up before the kids pass out." She pushed in May's chair and grabbed her phone off the golden granite countertop. Luke watched her type and pause several times before she replaced it, smiling. "Will says he's on his way."

"Wait, you texted him and he's actually coming?" He flipped May's pancake, the one with the chocolate chip smile. Will never did anything the first time he was asked, not even for his mother. "I'll believe it when I . . ." Footsteps on the stairs echoed through the main floor.

Annie raised her eyebrows with a little smirk. "I can't believe a man who engineers cell phones for a living still uses a flip phone and never learned to text."

"Well, engineers also make airplanes but you wouldn't expect them to own one, would you?" He poked at the pancake, feeling a little guilty he could make jokes at all. Wasn't he supposed to be curled up in the fetal position in his bed right now?

"But look how well it works." Annie pointed at Will as he tromped into the kitchen in baggy jeans and Luke's old Metallica T-shirt.

"So, the food is actually ready? Or am I so hungry I'm hallucinating?"

"You sure are a funny one, aren't you?" Annie ruffled Will's hair after he sat down, and miraculously he let her. She was impressive with teenagers. Her son and only child, Matt, was a freshman at Georgetown University in DC. He'd only come home once since orientation, and it was obvious how much she missed him. Brian once confided that he'd tried to bribe Matt into going to the University of Michigan so he could come home on weekends to do laundry and see his mom. But he wanted to go into political science, so Georgetown was the right place for him.

Laundry. Luke glanced down at his robe and ratty old slippers. If Annie hadn't shown up he probably would've stayed in them all day, but there's something motivating about having a non-family member in your house. And it wasn't just the clothes. His reflection in the microwave revealed what a wild mess his hair was—sticking up in uneven peaks and leaning to one side like the Tower of Pisa. He turned off the flame on the stovetop and added the last few pancakes to the pile.

"Hey, would you mind getting the kids started on these so I can go throw on some real clothes?" He placed a plastic bottle of store-brand syrup on the table.

"No problem at all," she said, arranging plastic utensils next to each paper plate.

"Thank you. I'll be fast." He handed her the full metal tray. "Remember, the smiley one is May's."

"No problem." She shooed him away with a flap of her hands before laying the tray on the table and grabbing Clayton from his spot on the couch in front of the TV. Luke would have to get his act together, or the three-year-old would soon leave a permanent divot.

As he made his way up the stairs, Luke enjoyed the gentle murmur of voices from the kitchen. He'd always loved coming home from work and eavesdropping until someone finally realized he was home. Today he couldn't hear the majority of what was being said, but the tone was so different than when Natalie's mom was there; calm and happy instead of Terry's anxiety-inducing silence and occasional episodes of uncontrolled wailing.

If Natalie's dad had been there, things would've been different. He was always the strong one in that relationship. When he died of a sudden heart attack five years ago, Natalie wasn't sure if Terry would make it on her own. *Why do the strong ones always seem to go first?*

When his feet touched the flat off-color carpet at the top of the stairs, a scream cut through the fraction of peace. It was May, screaming like a monster was chasing her. Adrenaline shot through Luke's veins, and without hesitation, he ran down the stairs, slipping down the last two until he reached the kitchen, winded and worried.

"May!" His slippered feet slid on the slick polished floor. Will sat in his seat, slowly munching on buttered pancakes, dipping each bite in a pool of syrup. Clayton waved and shoved a fistful of cut-up squares in his mouth, but May was gone and so was Annie. The bathroom door slammed.

"She's not in there," May shouted from the hall. "Maybe she's upstairs. Come on, Annie, let's find her."

Luke met the pair at the foot of the stairs. "What was that scream about, May? Are you okay?"

"Yes, Daddy. I was screaming because I'm *so* happy." She wagged her hands at her sides like a girl waiting to see a boy band.

"You almost gave me a heart attack." Luke crouched down to look his daughter straight in her deep blue eyes. "What made you so happy?"

May shifted back and forth on her bare feet, wrapping a damp strand of hair around her finger. She leaned in and whispered, "She's back."

Luke glanced up at Annie, whose face was a flat stone, unreadable. "Who's back, baby?"

"Mommy."

Luke clamped a hand over his mouth, his stubble scratching his palm, tears collecting in his lower lids. "Mommy is dead, baby. She's not coming back." He tucked the wild wet hair behind her ear, tracing the soft curve of her cheek.

"Where did my smiley-face pancake come from?" She took a step back, bumping into Annie's long legs. "Only Mommy makes them like that. I know it was her. I know it."

"It was me, honey. Mommy told me you like them that way. I thought it would make you happy. I'm so sorry." Luke reached out to pull May into his arms, to cuddle her, nuzzle her cheek, and make everything okay like he did when she was learning to walk and bumped her head or when she fell off her bike and skinned her knee. But May wasn't two anymore, and this wasn't a flesh wound. She pushed him away, shaking her head.

"No, no. It has to be her. She wouldn't leave me. She loves me. She said she'd see me again."

"She meant in heaven, May," Will's jaded voice called from the kitchen. "She meant she'd see you in heaven." He walked into the front hall carrying a sticky Clayton, syrup in his curly blond mop. "And Dad doesn't believe in heaven, so you're wasting your time."

"You think she's gone forever?" May glared at her father. "Oh, Daddy, no. How could you?" She looked at her father like she'd found out he was a murderer. Her face crumpled, and she ran up the stairs, leaving Luke stunned, still kneeling on the floor.

"I'll go talk to her." Annie wiped at her face and followed May up the stairs. Maybe she'd know the right thing to say. Luke put his hand in his robe pocket and rubbed the smooth envelopes between his fingers.

"Don't worry." Will stomped past. "I'll get Clayton out of these sticky clothes."

As Will ascended the stairs, Luke thought he should stand and take Clayton himself, give Will a fatherly lecture about family and bucking up and how losing your mother is hard enough without pushing your family away too. Or at least say *something*, but he didn't.

Instead, he shifted on the bottom step, dropping his head into his hands. How did he think he could do this alone? Couldn't they go back one year, start over, find a way to save Natalie, because this wasn't how things were supposed to turn out?

Annie came silently down the stairs and flopped down next to him. "She's going to take a bath. I told her I'd ask if it was okay."

Luke didn't look up, hoping she'd take his silence as permission and return to give May the news. But she didn't leave. Without saying a word, her hand found its way on the broad space between his shoulder blades, where she rubbed large circles on his back and let the companionable silence cover them like a blanket.

Luke's muscles unclenched, and the relief brought the tears he'd been avoiding all day. A deep sob forced its way out and through his fingers, coming out so fast and hard it almost hurt. When he tried to take a breath, it hitched in his throat, making a series of staccato gasps. Why did it have to hurt so badly? He'd had months—months of anticipation. He should've been ready. He should've been bulletproof.

Then he remembered—the letters. If he had those little blue rectangles filled with her words, her voice, he might be able to breathe again. To survive.

The tears stopped, receding to whatever corner of his heart they'd been hiding in. He dropped his hands and used the midnight blue shoulder of the robe to dry his face. Annie, sensing the shift in his mood, dragged her hand across his back, giving one last pat before returning it to her lap.

"Why don't you go shower and change?" she whispered. "I'll take care of May and the kitchen."

He still couldn't look at her, sure his face was swollen and ugly from crying. Staring at an off-color dent in the wood floor, he thought about refusing her offer, showing how strong he was by going into the kitchen and doing all the cleaning on his own. But he wasn't strong. He couldn't even get through one breakfast without his family falling apart, and if he was going to let someone help, it might as well be Annie.

"Sure. Thanks," he muttered. She used her hands to push herself to standing, her footsteps disappearing as she ascended the stairs. Once the door to May's room opened and shut, he forced himself to stand. A shower would help, new clothes, but all he really wanted to do was to sit down and reread the letters and live for a little longer in a world where Natalie was still alive.

CHAPTER 3

It had been ten days since Natalie slipped away in her sleep while Luke dozed on the couch beside her, seven days since the funeral, and three more letters since the first two, all robin's egg blue, with spiral notebook pages neatly folded inside. Luke couldn't seem to make out a pattern to their arrival. Every time the flash of blue was missing from his mail delivery, Luke was sure he'd never get another letter. Then in a day . . . or maybe two . . . an envelope would show up with the same postmark and no return address. He'd given up trying to figure out Natalie's plan. Honestly, he'd never completely figured Natalie out in real life; no way was he going to break that code now that she was reduced to nothing but memories and a few random letters.

At least the next few letters were less dramatic than the first two. Mostly talking about her day, her lingering nausea, the way her hair was falling out slowly enough she couldn't bring herself to shave it like most patients did.

Then there was the letter filled with panic when a clump of hair fell out into her cereal one day and she'd ended up with a mouthful of chemo hair instead of shredded wheat. She said it didn't taste much different, only it got mushy a lot slower. After that, she got a wig.

Luke remembered that—the hair falling out, the wig buying, but it was different reading it again in her own words. It made it seem like they'd had fun using clippers and a razor to shave her head smooth. Like they'd had a blast trying on different wigs and pretending they were secret agents instead of sad people who knew what was growing inside her was more likely to kill her than to be cured.

Yesterday's letter was a little different. It was the first time since the pancake fiasco that Natalie made an actual request in her letter, instead of narration with wishes of kisses and cuddles to the kids at the end.

DAY 6

Luke,

If I actually decided to give you these letters, then I've only been gone for a week or so. I've never been through this losing a parent thing, at least not as a child. You know more about that kind of grief than I do. But remember, our kids have something you didn't—a caring father.

With that said, here's the thing I've been pondering today: I think it's time for you to go back to work. Okay. Take a moment to freak out and be annoyed that I'm telling you to get back to work just days after your wife died. Maybe you won't miss me as much if you remember what a control freak I could be. Take your time. I'll wait.

Long enough?

Listen, work's always been an outlet for you; the numbers and simulators, that's your haven. At work they understand how your mind works in a way I sometimes struggled with. I'm hoping when immersed in your work you can get a respite from all the reminders of me haunting our house. So, when you're done reading this, go pick out your clothes for tomorrow, but don't forget me completely. Here's an idea: you should wear something blue—for me.

And as long as I'm being bossy, let's get those kids back to school. During this whole cancer drama, I've noticed routine is the antidote for this chaos in our lives. Breakfast together, making those lame-ass lunches every day, homework, piano lesson, baseball practice, dinner, bed. Those routines hold our kids up during the week now, and they will for you. It's the quiet times I fear, when those dark thoughts of leaving you creep in and I can't sleep at night. Perhaps keeping busy with work and school can save you from sleepless nights too.

So you know I'm not all talk and no action, I'm starting school today at good old Eastern Michigan University. Since Doc said I couldn't be around my first graders till the chemo is over, I need something to keep my brain working. Only two more classes to complete my MEd. Wouldn't it be awesome if I could kick cancer's butt and graduate school's butt at the same time? This time I'm walking the stage, even if I have to sew a wig into my hat. Remind me not to throw it at the end. Though that might be hilarious.

Have a great day at work tomorrow! I love you.

Love,

Natalie

Luke carefully refolded the letter, following Natalie's lines, picturing her carefully pressing in each crease. He held it in front of him. The last thing he wanted to do was leave his house and talk to people.

Even in his world of computers and numbers, there were people there. Unavoidable, occasionally annoying, people.

◆ ◆ ◆

She's dead. She won't know. She can't. He'd been telling himself the same thing for the past twenty-four hours, but it hadn't worked. Tugging up the knot on his light-blue tie, Luke pushed off his bed, fully dressed. Clayton played quietly in his bedroom, which was refreshing after two weeks of nonstop zombie TV state. Luke poked his head around the doorjamb into Clayton's little-boy room.

"It's time to go to Miss Annie's house. Let's get your shoes on."

"Miss Annie?" He shot up like a missile, a pirate action figure clenched in each fist. "Can I bring my toys?"

"You can bring two," Luke said, spreading two fingers out in front of him to illustrate. Clayton scanned the room looking like Luke had asked whom he'd save first in a house fire.

Ten minutes and four toys later, Luke had successfully packed Clayton and his things up in the car. At least May and Will had grabbed the bus twenty minutes earlier and were probably already at school. They'd gone back the Monday after the funeral. "Luckily" Natalie had passed away over winter break, or at least that's what at least half the out-of-state relatives kept saying. "How nice the kids don't have to miss any school." Luke had to work really hard to bite his tongue.

As he pulled out of the driveway into the street, with his workbag on the seat beside him, he looked back at the house. It was covered in snow, only a few slivers of green showing through the patches of white on the ground. The last time he did this was over a month ago, Natalie still inside watching him leave from her bed in the front room.

He shook his head. It must be surreal for May and Will. They left school three weeks ago with a terminally ill mother, and returned with a dead one. May said the first day back had gone well. The kids were a little distant, the teachers a little too clingy. Will was less helpful with information. When Luke asked how his day was, Will grumbled, "Fine." He'd have to ask Annie to text him later to make sure he was okay.

Luke pulled into Annie's neatly snowblown driveway, Brian's cruiser parked out front. This was all part of the plan. Annie would watch Clayton during the day and do her medical transcriptions in the evening.

They'd always used a day care for Clayton when Natalie was teaching, so Luke was going to reenroll Clayton in Tiny Tots Day Care down the street until Annie had pulled him aside and asked, more like begged, to help. At first it just seemed like too much change for such a young child, but whenever Annie and Clayton spent time together, Luke could almost see their hearts healing each other. When he considered what Natalie would say to Annie's offer, he knew there was no way he could refuse.

But Annie couldn't watch the kids all day. Natalie had been very specific about what should happen with the kids after school. Luke was supposed to contact a college student Natalie had met on campus. Nat was sure she'd be great with the kids, could even tutor Will. A girl named Jessie. But he wasn't ready to have an unknown college kid in his house every day. For now he'd work half days until—he hoped—he'd just know when it was the right time.

"You ready for your fun day at Annie's house?" Luke helped Clayton out of his seat and picked up the overstuffed canvas bag that held four changes of clothes, two bouncy balls, six trains, and a whole set of tracks. There might be a dinosaur or two in there somewhere.

Clayton tiptoed carefully up the well-salted front path, and Luke followed behind him, one hand out, ready to catch his arm if he slipped.

"I'm going to miss you today, buddy." Luke sighed. He'd gotten used to the tiny dramas that filled the days of a three-year-old. He enjoyed a life where getting the wrong color straw or having a sandwich cut the "bad way" was the end of the world.

"Me too, Daddy." Clayton pulled his hood down over his face as far as it would go, flinching away from the wind. "Come home fast, okay?"

"Okay, little Clayton." Luke grabbed the boy's gloved hand and helped him up the front steps. "Love you, kid."

"I know." He shrugged and sighed. "Can I push the button?"

"Sure. Only once though."

Clayton reached up and punched the glowing yellow button like a pro. The bell dinged in a muted double tone. Luke guided Clayton's hand down gently so one ring didn't turn into ten.

"They're here! Are you ready yet?" Brian's voice passed through the door like it wasn't even there.

A feminine voice responded, too far away for Luke to make out.

"Fine, I'll get it. But hurry, okay?" Brian sounded like he was standing on the other side of the door, but Luke still jumped when he yanked it open with a whoosh. Standing a few inches taller than Luke, he was nearly six foot two and bulky with muscles that stood out under his gray T-shirt and sweats. It was easy to imagine what he looked like in his glory days, college football star, dreams dashed by a torn ACL. Now he was a cop in a small town, breaking up domestic disputes and tracking down fake IDs.

"Hey there, how you doing, man?"

How was he doing? Hmm. He hated this question. No one really wanted to know how you were doing. They wanted you to tell them how okay you were so they didn't have to feel weird around you. Luke would rather lie about his mental state than deal with everyone's awkward silence and looks of pity. He always took the easy way out and told them what they wanted to hear. Brian wasn't a close enough friend to cry in front of, so Luke went with his normal response.

"Uh. We're okay. Thanks for asking."

"I'm so sorry for your loss." Brian said the line Luke had heard so often it had almost lost its meaning. "I don't know what Annie will do without her. Appreciate you letting her watch Clayton." He lowered his voice. "She misses Matt, and now with Natalie gone, I'm worried about her."

Luke shifted, sure he was the one who should be saying thank you, not Brian. "She's doing us a favor. You know Clayton—he loves Miss Annie. Right, bud?" Clayton said something muffled by the hood encasing his face. The poor kid was freezing. When Brian didn't seem to notice and the silence bordered on awkward, Luke changed the subject. "I hope your case is going well." Luke stumbled, wondering how Brian didn't seem cold wearing a short-sleeved T-shirt while standing in the front door.

"My case?" His right eye twitched and he stood a little taller, folding his arms across his chest.

"Sorry." Luke rubbed his hands together. "At Natalie's funeral, Annie said you were working an important case."

"Yeah," Brian said, nodding. "Sorry, yeah, the case." He tapped his biceps, his smile back. "You don't even want to know what some people will do to get drugs. It's crazy." Brian rubbed his arms, goose bumps finally developing on his bare skin. "So, you coming in or what?"

Luke took a breath to answer, searching behind Brian for Annie. Leaving Clayton with Brian wasn't within his plans or comfort zone. He was a nice enough person, total guys' guy and easy to talk to, but not exactly babysitter material.

"You know what?" Luke put a hand on Clayton's shoulder. "I'm not really sure today is going to work . . ."

Annie's footsteps on the stairs interrupted his attempt to slink away. She ran toward him, hair still wet.

"Oh my gosh, it's freezing down here. Brian, invite them in; don't let them freeze on the doorstep."

"I was trying to, babe; I'm not stupid." He rolled his eyes at Luke emphatically like he'd get how annoying a wife could be. "Come inside before I get in trouble."

"Brian, get out of the way." Annie ducked under his arm and mouthed, Sorry.

"Good to see you, Luke. You should join us for darts at Willie's one of these nights. I owe you a beer after missing . . . you know." He stepped back and Annie waved them inside. "Sorry to ditch out on you guys, but I'm going back to bed. Got another late night tonight."

"Oh, no problem. It was nice seeing you again," Luke said, attempting to remember the appropriate small talk involved in this particular situation.

"Yeah, don't forget—beer." Brian headed up the stairs.

"How could I?" Luke forced a laugh, relieved when Brian didn't quip back but thankfully disappeared up to the second floor.

"I'm so sorry about that." Annie waved toward the ceiling, where they could hear Brian shuffling around in a bedroom. "He's working nights lately, so he'll sleep all day. But we'll be superquiet, right?" Annie smirked at Clayton like what they'd be doing was going to be nowhere close to quiet. He nodded, his eyebrows waggling.

Annie quickly unzipped Clayton's coat and yanked off his boots like she'd done it a thousand times before. "Hey, buddy, I pulled out a bunch of Matt's old toys. I saved the best ones for when I'll be Granny Annie some day. Why don't you take a look?" She hung his coat on the handle of the closet door and tucked his gloves in the pockets. Clayton smiled and ran off into the office through a pair of French doors.

"We don't have to do this today, Annie." Luke adjusted the bag strap on his shoulder, already exhausted from the effort of acting normal. "My manager practically begged me to stay home and take more bereavement time."

Annie's forehead crinkled. "No. Please, no." She tucked a damp yellow curl behind her ear and leaned in. "Are you worried about Brian? Because he really is going to sleep the whole time."

"No, no." He pressed at his temples. It was refreshing to have someone to talk to. "I don't know if I'm ready to go back yet, that's all."

"Why are you pushing yourself?" She put a hand on his shoulder. He was getting used to people touching him all the time. It must be one of those unspoken social agreements, like patting a pregnant woman's belly. There seems to be a rule when someone is mourning—you can touch him without permission. "You can wait another week. No one would blame you."

"I know." He reached into the outer pocket of his workbag and caressed the envelopes he hardly ever left home without. He could do it—he had to do it for Natalie. "I'll only be gone four hours, back by lunch today. Taking this first week a little slow."

"Sounds like a plan." Annie pulled back, sounding unconvinced. She wrapped one arm around her torso and propped her other arm up on it, nibbling at her neatly trimmed nail. "We're going to hang out here today, but I've already signed Clayton up for story time at the library once a week. We'll think of other fun things to do out of the house. Once things defrost around here, I'm thinking the park, walks, scooter?"

"Those are all things little boys enjoy." Fine, he had to admit it; this was a much better place for Clayton to be than in day care, where he'd be just another kid, or home in bed eating junk food all day. Luke handed over the bag, the collection of toys shifting inside. "You promise you'll tell me if this is too much for you, right? Or at least you'll let me pay you something."

"Nope." Annie shook her head. "There were only two things Natalie asked me to do before she died. The first was to keep an eye on the kids." She hesitated, one shoulder crunching up to her ear. "She may have included you on that list."

"Oh she did, did she?" How could he be surprised? On her death-bed, she'd arranged for letters to be delivered to him with requests from beyond the grave. Of course she had a human backup plan. "Wait, Annie? You don't know anything about these letters, do you?" Luke tugged the bundle of envelopes out of his workbag and spread them out like a hand of cards.

She scanned them with her eyes and ran her finger along the fan, her nail making a soft ticking noise as she passed each one.

"I've never seen them before—well, except that day you showed me the one." She pointed at Luke's name looped across the front. "But that is Natalie's handwriting." She looked up, eyes wide. "You're still getting these?"

"Yeah," he nodded and restacked the blue rectangles into a neat pile and jammed them into his bag. Annie watched him intently.

"Who's mailing them?" she asked so quietly it must've been a question for herself.

"I was hoping you'd know." He shrugged, a wave of frustration churning inside him. "But I guess that's too easy."

It was definitely time to hide away from normal humans again. Pretending was so hard. He'd lived his whole childhood pretending, but twenty-two years later, he'd forgotten what faking it was like. Luke checked his watch, the marbled midnight blue face on a silver band. Natalie gave it to him for their fifth Christmas together. That was the problem with everything he owned: they all carried a memory of her. Unlike the letters, these memories made him feel sad and lonely. "It's getting late; I should go."

"Yeah, no problem." They both glanced over at Clayton, stacking a tower of colored blocks up to his eyeballs. Wouldn't Brian love the sound those made when they fell to the ground? "You want to say good-bye, or would there be tears?"

"I think he'll be okay. He's ready to get out of the house. Plus, he clearly loves you." Clayton talked about missing Annie only slightly less than missing his mom. It really bothered Luke at first, but at three Clayton didn't understand the difference between "gone for now" and "gone forever."

"Well"—she blushed a little—"the feeling is mutual. Now, you'd better get to work. Don't want you being late on your first day back." She put her hands on her slender hips, scolding him playfully. It didn't make him miss Natalie less, but it was still nice to know there was someone else out there who cared about his family. Luke retrieved his keys from his coat pocket.

"Clayton, Daddy is going to work. I love you!" Luke smiled and waved, keeping his farewell light and airy. Clayton glanced up for a fraction of a second and gave a half wave before placing another plastic block on the tower. "See, told you he'd be fine," Luke said, putting his hand on the cold brass doorknob. Reluctantly, he thrust the door open a crack, the frozen January air penetrating the thin fabric of his dress pants. "Have a good day and call me if you have any questions or concerns, okay?"

"Uh-huh," Annie murmured, flinching against the blast of cold air. She took the door from him and leaned against it like a shield, only her head peeking out, shouting behind him, "Have a good day!"

By the time he got to the turn in the path leading to the driveway, Clayton was by her feet, his arms wrapped around her legs. Luke waved one more time.

The big kids were at school, and Clayton was definitely happy about spending the day with Annie. Maybe Natalie was right: it was time for Luke to get back to work. A wave of panic washed over him as he climbed inside his car, still mildly warm from the ride over. This was all happening so fast. Natalie wanted them to pretend life was normal, but life couldn't be normal without her, could it?

Even though things had been hell for the past year, she'd always been there. Even when she was wasting away on a hospital bed in their living room, she'd always open her eyes and smile when he walked by.

Until the one morning she didn't. How could everyone else find it so simple to slip back into life, the world revolving, businesses opening and closing, buying and selling, when the pillow on the right side of his bed was empty every night?

Luke put his forehead against the smooth leather of the steering wheel. Maybe he'd go home and take a nap. No one would ever know. The people at work definitely wouldn't care. In fact, they might be relieved they didn't have to tiptoe around the man whose wife had recently died.

A tap on the window made him jump.

Annie, shivering in her gray yoga pants and long-sleeved cotton tee, stood outside his window holding what looked a lot like one of Natalie's letters. His hand reflexively flew to his pocket to count them. Squinting through the tinted glass, he made out Annie's name on the front of the envelope. Luke fumbled with the button, and his window rolled down with a whir.

"She gave me one too," Annie blurted, wrapping one arm around her waist again while she leaned against the SUV with her other arm. "It was a week before she, well, you know, died. She told me not to tell you, but I guess I'm a rebel."

Luke cringed. So Annie could somehow ignore the ghost of Natalie-past, but he couldn't.

"Did you open it?" He couldn't tell. He could never wait to open his, so he'd used his fingers to tear them open, leaving a jagged edge. Annie's envelope looked brand-new.

"Yeah. She told me I could open it on the day she died." She shook the envelope; it looked puffy, filled with a lot more sheets of paper than his ever had. Luke was curious. What did Natalie have to say to Annie that took so many pages? And why did she give them to her all at once?

"Can I read it?" He put out his hand, expecting Annie would hand the letter over right away, but she shook her head and held on to the envelope.

"Sorry, Luke. She made me promise I'd never let you read it. Like you said before, it's private." Annie repeated his words from the pancake morning.

Luke folded his fingers back and turned his car on with an angry roar. "I don't know why you even bothered to show it to me," he sputtered. He didn't normally let anger get the better of him; he'd made sure to keep that part of him carefully locked away, afraid at how little it would take to turn him into a younger version of his father. That lock had held for over twenty years, and he wasn't going to let it break now. He mashed his lips together, trying to regain control of his emotions. He'd definitely need a few rounds with the punching bag in the basement today.

"I wanted to show you because . . . I don't want you to think I'm the one delivering those letters." She folded both of her arms this time, her breath forming a cloud around her head. She had to be freezing. "There's something funny about those letters, Luke, like someone's playing a game with you. I don't know who it is, but it's not me. If I were you"—she bit her lip, her breath clouding out the corners—"I'd want to know where those letters were coming from before I opened any more."

He nodded but couldn't agree. Of course he'd considered where the letters came from—that was the first question on his long list of questions. But he wasn't going to stop reading them. They weren't fakes; for now that's all he needed to know. He'd take those letters as long as the mysterious someone kept mailing them.

"You'd better go inside; you are going to freeze to death, and Clayton might be turning your living room upside down," he said, placing his hand on the gearshift so she knew he was ready to leave. Her sea-green eyes didn't leave his face.

"Think about it, okay?" She tapped her letter on the side of his door with a heavy clack.

"Okay." He flashed a fake smile and put the car in reverse. Annie stood and folded the hand with the letter back under her arms.

"Well, we'll see you in a few hours." She backed away for two or three steps, maybe waiting for him to say something. There was nothing he could say without losing his cool.

Once Annie reached the front of his car, she jogged inside like she was sprinting to the finish line in a long race. And when she disappeared through the front door, Luke slammed the pedal to the floor and turned the wheel right, hard, toward work.

FEBRUARY

CHAPTER 4

It took two weeks for Luke to get up the courage to actually let the college girl, Jessie, come to his house.

He had been happy enough letting Clayton snuggle in bed with him after a half day of work and letting the older kids live off frozen pizzas and fruit snacks. It wasn't what Natalie wanted, but why shouldn't he be allowed to mourn in his own way, even if that meant eating processed food and fake fruit?

Then, the printed letter came. It was printed on a stiff piece of copy paper, which felt so unfamiliar in his hands. Instead of comfort, it brought panic. Is this when they would end? Would his entryway be empty tomorrow morning? He ran his fingers over the printed words where they'd been smudged by a drop of water. Maybe a tear.

DAY 34

Dear Luke,
This letter is out of order. I don't have energy to write by hand anymore. I know the truth now. I won't be around much longer. You don't want to believe it,

which I find a little funny since you don't believe in miracles.

I can feel it. So now it's time for me to do some things that will make your life easier after I'm gone. I can't talk about them all today—too much work. But there is someone I need to tell you more about— Jessie Fraga. By now I hope you're at least familiar with her name and my wishes where she is concerned. You can't know what it's like to feel like you are unwillingly abandoning your children. The only comfort I've found is knowing that there are people willing to fill in the gaps you leave behind. Jessie is one of those people.

I met her almost a year ago when I went back to school. She's an undergrad elementary education student. We used to study on the same cluster of couches. I never saw her without headphones and some kind of Broadway T-shirt. I thought she was a theater major until one day I noticed her Math Methods textbook and asked if she was studying education too. That's all it took. We became friends right away.

Jessie is a "normal" twenty-one-year-old in a lot of ways, but she's been through a lot in her life. She's a fighter. It's not cancer, thank God, but she knows what it's like for your body to sabotage itself. For Jessie it's her kidneys. She's been living her life with chronic kidney disease ever since she was a very small child. I think she'd be a wonderful example to our children of perseverance despite all odds.

I have more to tell you about Jessie, but for now know she's very important to me. She'll help with homework and dinner. Please, if you listen to only one thing I ask you, hire Jessie. She's special.

I love you. I'm so sorry we had to end like this. It's not fair.

Love,

Natalie

Today the infamous Jessie was coming over, any minute actually. If the "interview" went well, then Clayton would stay with Annie until three in the afternoon, and Jessie would take up the evening hours before he got home from work.

The doorbell rang. Three o'clock already. It was a positive sign that the girl was on time, but Luke wouldn't have minded another ten minutes to make the house presentable. Never mind that he'd had two hours to do it before she arrived, but Natalie's letters had gobbled up all his time, making the hours feel like an instant. He allowed himself to fall into this trap frequently.

Leaping out of bed, Luke carefully added Natalie's printed letter to the growing pile on his nightstand and straightened his crumpled dress shirt. He tiptoed past Clayton's room, hoping the doorbell didn't wake him from a rare afternoon nap. When he stepped off the bottom stair, his foot landed on Clayton's Spiderman pj's, still lying in a sloppy pile on the floor. Luke cursed under his breath, grabbed the pajamas, threw them down the basement stairs, and slammed the door, putting laundry on his list of things to get done.

Going back to work and dealing with the kids was not as easy as Natalie's letters had led him to believe. Maybe Nat was better at it, or maybe she'd tricked herself into believing it wasn't going to be this hard living without her.

Don't ring the bell again, Luke begged silently. Turning the doorknob, he whisked the door open, slightly out of breath. A petite young woman stood on the front porch. Petite was the wrong word. Small. Under five foot, and no way she weighed much more than May. Her long dark hair swept up into a high ponytail looked so grown up on her small frame. Bright-blue eyes sparkled out from under a heavy swath of bangs.

"Hi. Are you Mr. Richardson? We spoke on the phone." Her words ran together as she held out one of Natalie's envelopes in her hand, robin's egg blue. "I knew your wife." Her smile was almost as oversize as her ponytail, but once Luke caught sight of the envelope, he stopped taking account of his new sitter and watched the envelope like a cat with a canary. She tapped it against her palm.

"Uh, come in. Please." He swung the door wide and stepped back, making sure to keep enough space between them so she couldn't see the wrinkles pressed into his shirt from his nap.

"Should I take off my shoes?" Jessie eyed the shoe baskets. Within days of the funeral, Luke had returned the overflowing receptacles to the front hall. They cluttered up the entranceway beautifully.

"We have the kids take off their shoes, but you don't have to if you don't want to." Jessie slipped out of her ballet flats, revealing a pair of thin black socks barely covering her feet. Standing there, sock-footed, in her backpack and coat didn't help make her look more mature. In ten years May would be standing there, full-grown, in the exact spot, but still a child in his mind. Natalie would never see it. He wondered how she could bear to think about all the things she would miss.

Jessie shifted from foot to foot, and Luke realized he was standing silently, staring. If he wasn't careful, she was going to run away from the creepy man who didn't know how to talk to humans anymore.

"Uh," he cleared his throat and turned away, "let's sit and talk for a few minutes." Luke was about to point to the kitchen but remembered the dishes overflowing in the sink. They could easily talk in the formal front room two steps from where they were standing. It had nice furniture and the kids were never allowed to play on the tight shag carpet, but Natalie died there. So, it was kitchen and dishes. "Come this way."

He gestured for Jessie to follow him. She'd see their mess sooner or later, and this way she could make an informed decision.

As they passed through the hall leading to the kitchen, Jessie stopped and scanned the pictures hanging in a pyramid, Luke and Natalie's wedding picture at the top, the three kids lined up underneath.

"Oh my gosh, Natalie was so pretty!" She pushed her bangs out of her eyes and tipped her head back. "You guys look so young."

She was right: they did look young. Well, they *were* young. Nat's dark hair was up in a twist, her shoulders left uncovered by the white satin of her dress. The picture didn't show it, but the bodice had been covered in thousands of tiny pearl beads that kept falling off throughout the day. They laughed through their whole first dance. Every time they shifted, a small shower of beads sloughed off, making tiny pings as they hit the parquet dance floor.

In the picture, Luke stood several inches taller than Natalie, his hair bleached blond at the ends by the summer sun. Lines crinkled happily around his eyes. His smile said he had no idea he'd be burying the woman by his side before they had even celebrated their twentieth wedding anniversary.

"How old were you there?" Jessie asked, still scanning the portrait.

"Um, twenty-one." He sniffed. "We met in junior high, but I moved away before freshman year. Didn't meet again till college. I transferred to the University of Michigan for my senior year." He chuckled, almost talking to himself. "First week of class and I saw her; she was sitting on the quad studying and I knew. Right away, I knew."

"That's the sweetest story." Jessie gasped, one hand over her heart. "I can't believe you found each other when you were so young. I'm twenty-one, and I don't even have a boyfriend! Ha." After staring for a moment longer, she shoved her hands in her coat pockets, the envelope peeking out from one side. She turned to face him. He could feel her eyes on his face as he stared at his stocking feet. "I'm sorry, Mr. Richardson. I'm the worst. My dad always says I don't slow down to think. That was so insensitive talking on and on about Natalie. I'm sure it's not easy . . ."

He shook his head. "I'm fine." He couldn't deal with this girl feeling bad for him. What did she know about losing someone? "Let's go into the kitchen and chat."

"Mkay." Jessie shrugged. She took one last look at the picture of Luke and Natalie before turning away.

Luke rushed ahead, collecting a pile of random mail and May's school papers to clear a spot on the island. Jessie dropped her bag and climbed up on one of the stools. If she noticed the mess, she was good at hiding it. She put Natalie's letter on the counter in front of her, "Jessie" scrawled in Natalie's characteristic script across the front.

"So, tell me about yourself." Luke wasn't sure what he was supposed to ask. Natalie had arranged everything. If Jessie was willing to be their sitter, he was supposed to let her. This was more of a "meet and greet" than an interview.

Jessie ran her fingers through her bangs nervously, a silver medical alert bracelet peeking out from under her sleeve. "Well, not much to tell. I'm an elementary ed student at Eastern. I started my student teaching at Wellbrooke Elementary. First grade. I love it." She shrugged, her small shoulders shifting up and down in her poofy electric-green winter coat.

"Natalie said you guys were close." Luke rested his elbows on the granite, the coolness of the stone leaking through his thin dress shirt. It would probably be rude to bring up the whole medical issue thing. Better to play dumb.

"Yeah, I don't know why, but we really clicked, even with the age difference." Jessie ripped off her coat, hanging it on the back of the stool. She looked even younger without the oversize jacket. She wore a black shirt, which hung off her small frame, with a simple outline of a woman on the front. Underneath, the name "Bette" in white lettering.

"Is that Bette Midler on your shirt?" Luke asked, proud of himself for placing the reference. Foster mom number three had been obsessed with *Beaches*. He had to change the channel any time "Wind Beneath My Wings" came on.

"Yes!" Jessie's eyes lit up and she leaned forward. "Are you a fan?"

His interest in musical theater was almost as great as his interest in abstract art in the twentieth century. "No, sorry. But I'm thinking you are."

"God, yes." She flapped her hand at Luke with so much expression he had to hide his amusement. "I'm, quite literally, her biggest fan. I go to any concert within five hundred miles. That's honestly the radius my dad set for me. Once I get a job, I'm upping it to a thousand."

"Aren't you a little young to be a Bette Midler fan?"

"Bette is ageless. Honestly, have you looked at her lately?" Jessie raised her eyebrows and looked at Luke like he didn't own eyeballs. "But really, it's not just Bette. I love the theater, musicals to be precise. My mom was a beautiful singer. She used to sing all the great show tunes to me when I was sick." She said "sick" like it was a cold. Luke knew better. "Got me hooked, I guess."

"Used to"—Luke knew what that meant. He'd been struggling switching all of his memories of Natalie into that particular verb tense. He didn't want to push her, not knowing how recent her mother's death might have been.

"Are you an actress yourself?" With her overabundance of expression, she'd definitely do well on stage.

"No." Jessie shook her head, some of the brightness from her eyes draining for a moment and then reigniting almost immediately. "Believe me, if I had even a third of the talent Ms. Midler has in her little finger, I'd be on stage day and night. You know, I tried to convert Natalie. She was going to go with me to *Into the Woods* in April. We were going to wait at the stage door for autographs." She shrugged and spun the letter around in a circle on the counter. "I guess I'll just take my dad."

Sounded like Natalie. She made friends so easily. Luke had a hard time making those connections—always had. "Anyway, sorry, back to Nat. It was her passion for teaching that kept me going through finals last year. She loved kids, even the naughty ones. Anytime there was a case study for psych class in which kids were mistreated or had terrible experiences, I swear she'd nearly cry."

"Yeah." Luke bounced his head up and down, knowing exactly what Jessie was referring to. "Nat was almost too empathetic at times. She did this research paper once about a missing girl—uh, what was her name? That Witling girl? By the time she turned it in, she was a bit of a mess. She wouldn't let May go anywhere alone for six months, even out in our backyard."

"I don't know that one," Jessie replied, "but my mom must have. She was kinda paranoid when I was a kid, and she'd trot out news stories of missing children whenever I wanted to do something even halfway daring."

"Ha, that's funny." Luke chuckled. Talking to Jessie was actually easier than he'd imagined, like talking to a long-lost friend he'd never met before. "Are you an only child? I mean, the more kids you have, the harder it is to be neurotic." Luke stopped himself. Sending letters to your husband after you're dead is still pretty neurotic.

"I was a sickly kid, so she was a bit overprotective. I guess I can't really blame her . . ." Jessie trailed off, absentmindedly fiddling with her alert bracelet. Luke knew she was right. There were a lot of things worse than being an overprotective parent.

"Well"—he squinted at the envelope on the counter, sure a detailed dossier for each child was inside—"did Natalie tell you about the kids?"

Before Jessie could answer, Clayton's squeal cut through the ceiling. Naptime was apparently over.

"Now it gets real." Luke put his palms flat on the counter, wiggling his eyebrows. "You want to meet Clayton?"

"Of course. Should I come with?" she asked, tightening her ponytail.

Luke could think of nothing more awkward than leading the college girl up his stairs and into the clutter of his son's bedroom. He shook his head. "No, he's pretty grumpy when he wakes up. I'll be right back."

Clayton was born a poor sleeper, but with Natalie gone, he was horrible. He'd go to sleep all right, but he'd always wake up crying out for Mommy. Sometimes it would take hours to calm him down. The key was to get him as soon as the crying started. Jessie settled back on her stool, and Luke flew up the stairs, crying out, "I'm coming, buddy."

When the door swung open, Clayton was lying facedown on the floor, sobbing, face buried in his arms. He slept in a little toddler bed in the corner. It was easy to get in and out of, and the three-year-old knew how to open the door, as Luke learned from all the times he decided to visit him in the bathroom. But lately Clayton never left his room without someone coming to get him.

"Buddy, I have a new friend for you to meet." Clayton's sobs slowed to sniffles.

"Is it Pete the Pirate?" He looked up, his sweaty blond hair curling at the ends.

"No." Luke sighed. No one can beat an expectation of Pete the Pirate. He sat down beside the sniffling child on the floor. "She is a friend of Mommy's. Mommy asked her to come help me take care of you guys after she . . . went away."

Clayton scratched at the trail of mucus running down his top lip. "She knows my mommy?"

Luke hated the present tense, like she was going to walk in the room any minute now and scoop him up in her arms.

"She knew Mommy. She's very nice. We can be nice to Mommy's friend, right?"

Clayton got up on his knees and used his sleeve to dry his face. "I know—I'll show her my toy." He ran to his tiny bed, rummaged through the ruffled covers, and pulled out a little pirate action figure with a red bandana painted on his head. Clayton's eyes sparkled in a way they rarely did anymore. How long had he been walking around as a little shell of a boy without Luke noticing?

"Yep, buddy, sounds like a great idea." He turned around, still on his knees. "Here, jump on my back; I'll give you a ride down."

Clayton's arms barely met around Luke's neck. When they clasped together under his chin, Luke looped his arms around Clayton's legs and hefted him on his back. Clayton's warm breath was hot against his cheek and a little sour.

Working hard to get a giggle, Luke jogged down the stairs, making sure to bump Clayton up and down with each step. He laughed and clutched his hands tighter, pinching the skin on Luke's neck, which stung, a lot. But hearing his little boy laugh again made the pain easy to bear.

When they reached the kitchen, Luke was out of breath from the run, and Clayton from laughing. He flipped his son on the ground, making sure to help him land on his feet. As soon as Clayton noticed Jessie in the room, he put two fingers in his mouth, all laughter gone from his face. Jessie looked up from her iPhone and smiled. Her eyes seemed to take over half of her face when she smiled.

"This must be Clayton," she chirped and knelt to his level. She held out her hand. "My name is Jessie. It's nice to meet you."

Clayton took his slobbery fingers out of his mouth and wrapped them around Jessie's outstretched hand. Luke cringed, but surprisingly Jessie didn't.

"I brought you a present." She swiveled around on her knees and rummaged through an olive-green L.L.Bean backpack that was stuffed to the brim. When she found what she'd been looking for, Jessie kept

her hand inside the backpack, turning on her knees to face Clayton. Up this close Luke could count the light sprinkle of freckles on her nose and cheeks.

"Your mom told me you love watching Pete the Pirate. Is that right?" She raised one eyebrow with the question like this was a serious interrogation.

"Uh-huh," Clayton mumbled through the fingers in his mouth. "He's da best."

"The best? Well, maybe I should keep this for myself." She flicked a red bandana out from behind her back, a perfect match to the one on the plastic pirate peeking out of Clayton's front pocket. "Do you think it would look good on me?" She went to place it on her head and Clayton gasped.

"Oh!" He bounced up and down like he had springs in his heels. "Is that for me?" The fingers were out of his mouth, and Clayton was smiling right at Jessie. Even though Clayton had a wet face, disheveled hair, and a less-than-welcoming attitude, Jessie wanted to be friends with Luke's boy. She must've really loved Natalie.

"Now that you mention it, I do think this would look better on you." She held out the bandana in front of her, and Clayton snatched it out of her hand. He forced the folded fabric on his head and pushed it down until the folded edge touched his eyebrows. He took a step back as though she might change her mind at any minute.

"I need my ship, Dad. Can I get it?" Clayton squinted up at him, barely able to see through the layer of red material.

"Okay, dude! Go for it." Luke laughed. Clayton started to run off to his room, but Luke called him back. "Wait! What do you say to Jessie?"

"Thank you, Jessie . . ." Clayton shouted as he ran up the stairs. Luke raised his eyebrows, sincerely impressed.

"That went really well," he said, offering his hand to help Jessie off the floor.

"He's adorable." Jessie took his hand briefly, her touch like a feather. She stood with a hop, ponytail bouncing. "I think we're going to be great friends."

"He's a fun kid." Tears burned in his eyes. Luke blinked them away quickly and focused on the random pattern of stone in the polished granite. He ran his hand across it, cringing at the thin film of crumbs and grime that stuck to his skin. "He doesn't really understand what's going on," Luke continued, trying to wipe his hand off on his pant leg discreetly. "I'm afraid the poor kid's going to turn orange from all the goldfish crackers he's been eating."

"Well," she laughed, looking up at the ceiling where the thumps of toys being tossed on the floor echoed above them, "you're clearly doing something right."

It didn't feel that way. In fact, he was pretty sure he was doing almost everything wrong. The only time he felt good about something he did in his post-Natalie life was when it was an "assignment" from one of her letters. Annie still thought it was 100 percent unhealthy, but it was the only way he could keep all the balls in the air and hold himself together at the same time. His father had used alcohol to escape from the pressures of real life; Luke indulged in those ratty notebook pages.

"Anyway . . ." He needed to steer the conversation in a different direction. "Is there anything you want to know?" he asked, trying to remember how interviews are supposed to work.

"Mr. Richardson." Jessie put the letter in her back pocket and slapped her hands on the counter, fingers spread wide. "I want to work here. I want to help Natalie's family and her children." She bit her lip again before continuing, "What you don't know is that I lost my mom when I was twelve. I know how hard it can be for a kid. I promised Natalie I'd be there for them." Real tears sparkled in Jessie's eyes when she looked up at him, almost pleading, "If you'll let me."

Luke blinked twice. "What can I say to that?" He put out his hand. "You're hired."

Jessie took it and shook briefly. Luke yanked a half-sheet paper towel from a dwindling roll and passed it to the girl. She wiped her face and caught most of the running mascara under her eyes. She crumpled it into a ball and searched the room, probably for a garbage can.

"Under the sink." Luke put his hand out. "Here, I'll take it."

"Ew, Mr. Richardson, I wiped my nose with that. I can do it, really." She crossed the room to the sink, unlatched the child safety lock, and tossed the tissue inside. Natalie's letter peeked out of her back pocket.

The front door opened and closed with a slam. May's voice called out, "Dad, I'm home. You upstairs?"

"No, hon, we're in here!" he shouted, interrupting May before she could say anything else embarrassing about his lack of parenting skills. "Come meet Jessie."

May ran into the kitchen, her long, curly, dark hair unbrushed, sprawling across her face. She dropped her backpack by the kitchen table, where they always did homework with Natalie after school and where he'd been making a sad attempt at keeping up with assignments. Now they could do it with Jessie. Now they wouldn't be consigned to a life of forgotten school projects and goldfish crumbs in bed. Once again, Natalie got it right.

CHAPTER 5

Valentine's Day crept up on Luke. He should've seen its billowing pink fluff inching over the horizon and right into his life, but he didn't. Suddenly one day the drugstore aisles and advertising circulars were covered in hearts and cupids. Valentine's Day had never been a big holiday in the Richardson home. The focus was always on getting the kids' valentines signed and addressed, rather than some kind of big romance.

Natalie always claimed the inferiority of the holiday rested in the lameness of the candy. Box of chocolates? *Way* overrated. Luke got Natalie a small box of cream-filled chocolates the first year they were married, thinking he was being romantic. It wasn't romantic. It was gross. Who thought a filling that tasted like orange Creamsicles was a good idea anyway? They took one bite out of each chocolate and tossed the box into the garbage. Every February 14 after that he found a small box of Russell Stover drugstore chocolates on his pillow with one bite taken out of each piece.

When Luke went down to pick up the mail in its normal spot on the loose shag of the doormat, he was surprised to find a bulging

USPS prepaid envelope waiting for him. Inside lay a small heart-shaped box of chocolates with a blue envelope taped to it. The box was small enough to fit in the palm of his hand, a yellow discount sticker half-peeled off on one side. If Nat had bought these, they were more than a year old. In his head, he could hear her laughing, the loud huffing laugh she reserved for moments when she thought she was being hilarious.

It had been a week since Natalie's last letter, and Luke could barely control the urge to tear into the letter right there in the front hall. Instead, he ripped the letter off the red-tinted cellophane. A hand-drawn red heart covered the back of the envelope. What was Natalie up to? He tossed the chocolates on the hall table and went back upstairs to get dressed.

Somehow he made it to his room before opening the letter. It had less to do with self-control and more to do with his new routine. When one of Natalie's letters arrived, first he'd pinch the letter between his fingers and try to guess how many pages were folded inside. He was getting pretty talented at estimating accurately. Today's letter felt like a long one, three or four pages for sure.

Next, he'd take out the long golden letter opener his foster mother had given him for his high school graduation. He'd never needed it before, but after shredding the first few envelopes with his fingers, Luke saw the wisdom in using extra care. Now the quiet whisper of the letter opener made his heart jump with anticipation.

Then, he'd slip out the folded sheets of notebook paper and unfold them slowly, taking in her loopy, semi-sloppy handwriting and the date, count the pages, and smile because he was right at the number. Today there were four pages, but her handwriting was extra loopy, as if she was particularly happy when she wrote it. Oh my, she had dotted every freaking *i* with a heart. Luke laughed out loud. He still loved her so much.

Valentine's Day

Dear Luke,

I'm taking a chance here, trying something new. If I send you these letters, I know your Valentine's Day will land on a different day than mine. So I'll try to put these letters for special occasions aside and make sure you get them on the right days.

It's Valentine's Day, and we're comfortably doing nothing. Well, that's a bit of a lie. I stole some candy from the kids' backpacks, and I'm currently sucking on a handful of red and pink Nerds. Unfortunately, Will didn't bring any candy home. They don't exchange valentines in eighth grade. Annoying. It's getting to the point where, if I'm still around, I might have to start buying myself Valentine's Day candy, even if it is the most subpar of all holiday candy.

But if I'm not hanging out on the couch eating a bagful of candy hearts, you might be missing me today. I know I'll be missing you. So, being the cheeser I am, I decided to write down part of our love story. Bear with me—I might be a little creative in parts, but in general, this is how I remember that day, the day the direction of my life changed forever. The day I met you.

It was three days before my fourteenth birthday when I moved into 815 Winter Lane. It was a really hot day, but we were moving from Mississippi so the muggy heat of Michigan didn't bother me. It did surprise me. Everyone in the coastal town of Gulfport laughed at the idea of lifelong southerners migrating to the frozen north. I think I expected snow when

I got out of the truck, even though it was August. Instead of snow, I saw you: thirteen, with yellow hair so sweaty it clung to your head. Your cheeks were a bright red, and I thought you were about to die from dehydration. As I stretched my legs, you stared at me like I was from outer space.

"Hey, kid, you our new neighbor?" my dad shouted. He didn't mince words, did he? Without answering, you ran away into 813 Winter Lane, right next door. For a moment, when the front door slammed, I didn't mind leaving my friends, the ocean, and eternal summer to live on Winter Lane in freeze-your-butt-off Michigan.

"Natty, come help me in the house." Mom waved me inside, the movers already unloading boxes and pieces of furniture into the mustard-yellow, two-story colonial.

"Mom, can I check out the backyard?" Ben couldn't stop moving. If he'd been cooped up in that van for one more second, he would've exploded.

"Sure, Benny. Dinner at six. Don't get too dirty." Ben got to play, as always, and I got to clean. My mom has always been sexist that way.

God, that house was hot. We didn't have AC— bet my parents thought we didn't need it after all the quips about the cold. I still remember the heat when we opened the door, like taking a cake out of the oven. My job was to open every window in the house, all seventeen. But before I opened each one, my mom wanted me to wash it first. She rummaged through the boxes of cleaning supplies and found me a full bottle of window cleaner and an unbelievably large roll of paper towels.

"There's a breeze coming in from the east, so do the front windows first," my mom ordered. Back then, there was nothing to entertain you during work but your own mind. I thought about starting a new school, wondered if you'd be in my same grade, if we'd take a bus together, if you'd be my first friend. It took an hour to finish all the front windows, and the house had cooled ten degrees from the breeze they let in.

Time was dragging by at an interminably slow rate, and my hair was nearly soaked with sweat. Until I finally got to the windows looking out on the backyard. You were there playing with Ben, popping in and out of the dilapidated shack my mom wanted to tear down. I took my time washing those windows, pushing them open one at a time, trying to decipher the few mumbles and phrases echoing through the backyard.

I spent the next hour and a half spying on you until my mom caught on and gave me a bucket of Lysol and warm water to wash down the inside of the cupboards, which I worked on until dinner.

My brother brought you to our house for dinner that night, both of you dirty from playing in the backyard. I couldn't imagine what you found to do with my ten-year-old brother for three hours in that wasp-infested shed, but I was superbly proud of Ben for remembering his manners and asking you to dinner.

At dinner, I tried not to look at you, but it was hard. You had a bright smile that made me want to smile back and light blotchy freckles on your cheeks that looked like flecks of sand I could brush off with my fingertips. I found out later that you hated them, but I loved them instantly.

Dinner was simple—pizza from Dan's Pizza House and a few bottles of pop. I knew that night must be special because I couldn't remember one meal in my whole life without some sort of green veggie being dumped on my plate. I didn't ask questions; I silently crammed slices into my mouth, trying not to come off as a creepy stalker girl.

You told us about your family, your dad a seasonal fisherman on Lake Michigan, your mom a shopkeeper. You didn't tell us your father's real job was being an alcoholic and your mom's was covering for it. But I could read the sadness in your eyes. I think it was the sadness more than your smile that made me want to know you better. So when Dad asked me to walk home with you to grab our spare key from your mom, my heart almost bounced out of my chest. He couldn't have known what would come of that request.

Our feet whispered through the grass as fireflies flickered in slow circles around us. The night was moist and hot and felt like my home in Mississippi.

"I've never seen fireflies before," I whispered, reaching out to touch one of the lazy bugs flashing in front of my face.

"Never? How is that possible?" The first words you ever spoke directly to me.

"Mosquitos are bad in Mississippi. The city sprays like crazy. Kills the mosquitos, but Dad says it also kills the lightning bugs."

"Hm, well, we have plenty to spare. When I was littler we used to catch them, put them in jars with holes in the lid. I'd put the jar by my bed, you know, like a lantern."

"Oh my gosh, I never thought to do that," I drawled. I never thought I had an accent until I heard my voice next to your plain, halted phrases.

We'd crossed the hedge and were finally at your back door. You kicked up the back mat and retrieved a house key with a metallic scrape. The lights were off inside, and I had this sinking feeling you were going home to an empty house. "So, did it work? The lightning bug lantern?"

"It worked." Twisting the knob and key at the same time, you forced the back door open and disappeared inside, leaving it gaping open. I wondered if you'd forgotten why I followed you home. You showed up with a key in your hand, the moon reflecting off its silver surface. I put out my hand, and you dropped the key into my palm and shrugged. "I stopped catching them though."

"Why? That sounds like a lot of fun." I searched your face, the freckles, the same upturned nose May and Clayton have. I wanted you to ask me to catch fireflies with you.

"I don't know." You shook your head, every part of your face frowning. "They were always dead when I woke up. It seemed like a waste." Then you disappeared into your dark house.

And that was it. I was in love. Sure, we evolved over time, but even when you moved away a year later, I never forgot the boy who stopped catching fireflies.

I love you. Happy V-day and thank you for finding me again.

Love,

Natty (ha-ha)

"Why did she have to have such a good memory?" Luke wondered,
rubbing his eyes as if he could push the tears back in. At some point
during the letter he'd gone to his knees, leaning against the bed like
he was praying. It felt odd. He hadn't prayed since he was a child, and
even then it was under a blanket in his bed while his mom and dad
screamed at each other in the hallway. It didn't work then. It wouldn't
work now.

May burst through the bedroom door fully dressed in a red jumper
with a long-sleeved turtleneck under it. Her tangled hair hung halfway
down her back, the strands surrounding her face chewed short.

"Happy Valentine's Day, Daddy!" She jumped on his back, wrapping her arms around his neck.

"Right back at cha, sweetie." Luke twisted her around into his arms,
gathering her up like a princess needing to be rescued. "You got your
valentines ready?" He kissed her forehead before sitting her back up on
his knee.

"Yeah, Jessie helped me. They're the coolest. She got the instructions off the Internet," she said matter-of-factly.

"Hope you made one for me."

"Of course, Daddy. I'll show you!" She stood ready to run out the
door. "Wait, I forgot." She reached into one of the pockets on the side
of her dress and pulled out a large pink comb with ponytail holders
wrapped around the handle. "Will you braid my hair?"

Luke's mouth went dry. He'd watched Natalie do it countless times;
she even tried to teach him once, but his fingers couldn't seem to figure out the simple pattern of over under. He couldn't bear the idea of
disappointing her.

"I sure can try. Come sit down." He waved her over and sat her down on the floor in front of him. The first attempt at running the comb through May's tangled nest of hair made her squeal and pull away. This would never do. "I'm sorry. Do you want me to try again?"

"Yes! Two braids, one on each side." She paused before adding, "Please," as though it would change the outcome.

"I have an idea. You sit down, and I'll comb your hair and I'll tell you a story."

"A story?" She gasped. "Is it a love story?"

"Yes. A really beautiful one too."

Luke retold the story to May, taking his time to fill in the details and edit out Natalie's commentary. She sat perfectly still on the floor, even when he hit a huge snag halfway through and had to pull harder than he intended to get through it. The first braid took three tries, and the second braid only one. He finished the story as he snapped on the last ponytail holder. May ran to the full-length mirror on the back of his bedroom door and smiled.

"Daddy, it's perfect! Thank you!"

It wasn't perfect, not even close. If he looked too closely, Luke could see where he missed the braid pattern in a few spots and how the top and sides of her hair weren't exactly smooth like when Natalie used to do it. But it wasn't bad either. She turned to face him and curtsied in her red skirt and heart-printed tights. She totally took after her mom with the holiday wardrobe theming. He had a box of holiday socks tucked away in the back of the closet he'd have to give May when her feet grew a little.

"Thank you!" She ran and jumped into his arms and kissed his cheek.

Clayton walked into the room bleary-eyed, holding Natalie's phone. "Mommy's phone is ringing."

The sound of her ringtone gave Luke a bad case of déjà vu, and his stomach dropped. If someone was calling her phone, they didn't know she was dead. That meant he'd have to tell them. He glanced at the screen, but the caller ID displayed a random set of unfamiliar numbers, which was confusing and a relief at the same time. He pressed the talk button after looking each kid in the eye with a finger to his lips.

"Hello?" Luke answered.

A woman's voice responded.

"Hello. I'm looking for Mr. Richardson. This is Ms. Mason from Shepard High School. I'm Will's guidance counselor."

The school was calling Natalie's number? Maybe they tried the home phone first. Luke turned the ringer off a long time ago and never switched it back on. The silence was refreshing.

"This is Luke," he responded. "Can you hold on one second?"

"Of course."

Luke covered the mouthpiece and whispered to May, "Go pop in some waffles from the freezer. I'll be down in a few minutes."

"But Mommy always made pink pancakes on Valentine's Day," May pouted. There was no way he'd have enough time to make Nat's pancakes and get everyone out the door.

"Maybe we can have them for dinner if you can get your little brother his breakfast."

"Yes, yes, yes!" May perked up and nodded her head fast. "Come on, Clayton; time for breakfast." She grabbed the hand that wasn't lodged in his mouth and guided him out of the room.

Luke put the phone back up to his ear. "Sorry about that."

"Totally fine." She paused briefly. "I'm calling to see if you can come in later today for a meeting about Will."

"Is there a problem?" Luke pulled himself off the floor and on the bed, lightheaded.

"I want to touch base with you on how he's doing after losing his mother. He's had a few issues at school in the past few weeks that seem a little out of character for him. I'd love the opportunity to talk to you, maybe get your input. Could you come by around four?"

It sounded like something he definitely didn't want to do, today or ever, but what could he say—no?

"Sure. I'll be there."

"Thank you, Mr. Richardson. Have a nice day. Oh, and happy Valentine's Day!"

"Bye," he mumbled and hung up the phone. Yeah, sounded like it was shaping up to be a great Valentine's Day.

CHAPTER 6

He'd been sitting in the same uncomfortable chair for the past forty-five minutes. After the first ten minutes, Luke brought out a few of the latest letters. He'd stopped carrying the whole pile. Now every morning, he selected a few of his favorites from the shoebox by the side of his bed. Then, he would carefully place the newest one on top. He usually avoided reading them in public—too many questions—but in this case he'd rather read Natalie's thoughts than another college brochure for Michigan State.

DAY 44

Dear Luke,
I'm writing this as I'm getting my third treatment. I remembered to bring a sweater today. Too bad they can't warm the infusion before putting it in your port. Room temperature is definitely not 98.6 degrees. Brr.
I thought I'd write to you now since I'll probably be sick later. This is what I get for wanting to lose ten pounds, isn't it? I'd definitely take fifty extra pounds

over this. Turns out skinny isn't my best look. Maybe it's the baldness, but I think I look like one of those aliens from your sci-fi movies—gray skin, no hair, and bulging eyes. Thank heavens for wigs, fake eyelashes, and drawn-on eyebrows. I think I do a good impression of human on most days.

I hate this. I want to feel better. Will I ever feel better? If you're reading this, I guess the answer is no. I've been thinking about my prognosis lately. Why did I have to get some crazy rare type of soft tissue sarcoma? Why couldn't I have found that lump on my shoulder blade before the cancer got into my lymph nodes? Stage III. Beatable? For sure. Scary? For sure.

Even if we get through the next two rounds of chemo, we still have surgery and radiation and then even more rounds of chemo. This time last year I was floating blissfully along, teaching double-digit subtraction, getting ready for spring break in a couple weeks. And next year or the year after, I could be dead. Gone. Forever, according to you.

I don't know what I believe about death anymore. For a long time, I could see the logic of your beliefs even though I clung to the idea of God like a child with a teddy bear. But I don't know how to face death like that.

So I have a plan. If I die and if there *is* life after death, I'm so coming back to haunt you. I mean, full-on "our house was built on an Indian burial ground" type of haunting. I'll whisper things in your ear like, "I was riiiight. You were wroooong," in an awesome ghost voice.

He laughed out loud as the office door in front of him swung open and people spilled out. Luke folded up the letter and quickly hid it in his pocket, hating that he didn't get the chance to finish.

He recognized Will's guidance counselor immediately. She was at least a head shorter than everyone in the group, even with her six-inch zebra-print heels on. She had long unruly curly hair, with the ends a light copper in contrast to the deep-brown roots.

Ms. Mason had come to the wake and the funeral. When Luke was in high school, all his counselors ever did was make sure he got all the credits he needed for graduation and nagged him about applying for colleges. He'd always thought that was the norm, but maybe they tried harder when you weren't a foster kid who could move to a different school at any time.

The other two adults in the group exiting Ms. Mason's office were clearly a married couple. Their two rings flashed in the light announcing "man and wife." They quickly shook hands with Ms. Mason and made their nose-pierced, hair-dyed son do the same. Ken and Barbie got married and had an Emo child. Once they conducted another insufferable round of good-byes, Ms. Mason turned to face Luke.

"Mr. Richardson, thank you for coming. Sorry for the late notice. Please, come into my office." Her voice was professional, but with her sparkly shirt, dangly earrings, and short stature, she could easily be mistaken for a student.

"Thanks again for coming in." She picked up a silver pen and clutched it in her hand, long manicured nails catching his eye from across the table. "How are . . ." she paused awkwardly. His stomach was churning, already knowing what she was going to ask. "How are you all doing?"

Everyone asked this question. It must've been on a brochure at the funeral with the title "Things to Say after Someone Dies." He was fairly certain no one wanted to know the real answer to that question. Luke always said the same thing.

"Oh, you know, there are good days and bad days."

Ms. Mason's head bobbed up and down. "Yes, I'm sure that's true. Hard times. Hard times." She continued with some extended eye contact that made Luke uncomfortable. When he didn't respond, she took a deep breath and continued, "How about Will? Have you noticed any drastic changes in his behavior lately?"

"He's been fairly withdrawn since losing his mom." There. He'd said "losing his mom" without flinching. It got easier every time. "He doesn't talk to me much, but he has a pretty good relationship with a family friend. She seems to think he's managing as well as can be expected."

Ms. Mason tapped her pen on the table before clutching it under her chin.

"I'm afraid he's not doing well at school," she said, pushing the words out.

"What do you mean? Like his grades?" Luke leaned forward. "He has a tutor."

"I know he does. His grades are going to be fine."

"Going to be? What do you mean?"

"Well, he hasn't been turning in his assignments, but yesterday we went through his locker together and they were all there." She shuffled through a stack of papers on her desk, her reddish brown eyebrows crunching together. "I'm more worried about what he said when we sat down yesterday to talk."

Luke felt like he'd swallowed a stone. "What did he say now?"

"Uh, it's a bit difficult to explain, and I'm hoping you have more information for me . . . I brought Will in for a chat after finding all his missing assignments, and we got to talking." She put her elbows on the table and crossed her arms, picking at the loose knit of her shimmering sweater nervously. "He told me he'd recently discovered he's adopted."

"He said what?" Luke couldn't hold back a loud snort, sitting up straighter in his seat. That was the last thing he'd expected her to say.

"But . . ." she said, clearly relieved, "I'm guessing from your reaction, he made it up."

"Yeah, he's definitely not adopted." Luke ran a hand through his unruly hair. There had to be more to this story. "What exactly did he say?"

"He said he was looking through a box of his mother's things and found some adoption papers. It didn't sound right; that's why I called you." She cleared her throat and reset her facial expression to serious. "Have you considered taking Will to talk to a professional?"

A box of his mother's things. The phrase jumped out at him as her words ran through his mind one more time. He'd seen a box peeking out from under Will's bed when he went in to wake him up for school a week ago, but didn't think much of it. Why didn't he look closer? Why was he always in a foggy tunnel of thought that only seemed to clear out when he was sitting and reading one of Natalie's letters?

"Mr. Richardson? Did you hear me?" She waved her hand, dropping her silver pen on the desk with a loud thump. Luke shook his head to clear it. *Focus. Focus on what Will's counselor is saying.*

"We went to a group for families when Natalie was first diagnosed," he said, staring at one spot on her desk where some kind of graffiti had been buffed out and repainted. "But no, not since."

Ms. Mason selected a single sheet of paper off the top of the pile she'd been fiddling with and held it out to Luke. "Here you go. This is a list of therapists I compiled, ones who specialize in grief counseling. Of course, it's up to you whether you decide to send Will, but I don't have to tell you how worrying this change in Will's behavior is to us."

"No. Of course not." Luke shook his head, wondering who "us" was exactly. His kid was making up stories about being adopted. Even half-blind with grief, he couldn't miss the gravity of the situation. He took the sheet of paper, folded it in half twice, and slid it in his shirt pocket.

After a few more minutes of small talk, Ms. Mason walked him to the door, and they shook hands. To meet his eyes, she had to tilt her head so far back it looked uncomfortable.

"Thank you for your concern for Will. He needs every bit of encouragement he can get," he said.

"Please"—she squeezed his hand for a moment before letting go—"keep me in the loop. I really want to be there for Will. He's a good kid." She sounded like she sincerely cared for Will's well-being.

As soon as Ms. Mason turned her attentions to the teenage girl who was silently pecking at a smartphone, Luke hurried out of the school and into the safety of his car. Flipping out the paper filled with names of therapists, he looked through them, closed his eyes, and pointed.

Perfect—the therapist was five minutes from home. Luke didn't have much confidence in therapy; he'd gone to court-ordered therapy for the year after he was put in foster care. The man's name was Mr. Tragenall, and he did *not* love his job or working with foster kids, and especially foster kids with attitude.

At that point in Luke's life, Mr. Tragenall and all the rest of the adults who cared about him within the confines of their profession only served to highlight that he'd lost the only people in the world who actually cared for him. That's why he hadn't made the kids see someone sooner. Now that the school was involved, maybe he didn't have a choice. Being stubborn and not sending him could lead to far more trouble than just employing some well-placed bribery to get Will into the therapist's office.

Navigating his way home by mere muscle memory, Luke's thoughts turned from therapy to the box. What could Will have found that would make him tell such a ridiculous story? This is one time he wasn't going to look the other way. He had to admit he'd been doing that about Will's sudden outbursts or the hours of time spent alone in his room.

Reaching home in record time, Luke sped past Jessie's burgundy Kia parked in the driveway. When he rushed through the entry, Luke could hear Jessie's voice echoing out to welcome him, and he noticed the air smelled of vanilla and cinnamon again. It was nice coming home to activity. The house felt warm and alive. But today he couldn't enjoy that feeling. He needed to talk to Will.

"Is Will in there with you?" he shouted into the kitchen.

Jessie walked out as Luke was slipping his shoes off.

"Hey, Mr. Richardson, Welcome home." She was wearing one of Natalie's old aprons, the one with the teal and black paisleys and ruffles. A trail of flour streaked through her bangs. "Will finished his homework already, so he's in his room doing . . . who knows what."

"I need to talk to him. I know it's almost five." Luke checked his watch. Okay, it was after five. "Do you mind staying a bit late?" He hung up his wool winter coat in the front closet and turned around.

Jessie had her hands on her hips, biting her lip like she was worried.

"Everything okay?" she asked, and he was sure she really wanted to know.

There was something about this girl that made Luke sad. She had an eagerness to please that reminded him of May when she wanted a new app on her tablet. No doubt she was one of those students who sat in the front row in every class and cried over a B. How could he tell someone so weighted down with her own insecurities about his very real concerns that Will was failing to thrive after Natalie's death, like an infant refusing to nurse? How he worried her death might be the pivotal moment in Will's childhood that would permanently change the course of his life? Or how Luke was sure he was a complete failure as a parent and the only reason the kids were decent human beings was because Natalie had always been there to pick up his slack?

"Yeah." He hung his keys on the small white hook drilled into the wall. They bounced against Natalie's keys with their big jangly key chain. "Just some school stuff. His counselor called me today. Will hasn't been turning in his assignments. She found them all stuffed in his locker. I need to find out what's going on."

"You're kidding me!" Jessie almost squealed, crossing her arms. "He's been working so hard on his homework every day. I don't understand why he wouldn't turn them in. He's such a smart kid. I'm sorry. I should've double-checked. I should've . . ."

"No," Luke cut in, trying to calm her before a full-on panic attack, "this isn't your fault." He placed his shoes on the drying mat next to the shoe baskets. "I don't know what's going on, but I'm going to find out."

"Jessie, I think it's done!" May called from the kitchen, interrupting Jessie before she could speak. "Should I take it out of the oven?"

Her eyes went wide. "No! I'm coming!" She gave a little smile to Luke. "I'd better go check on her. Take as long as you need." She jogged toward the kitchen and shouted, "Good luck!" over her shoulder.

"Thanks," he muttered under his breath before heading for the stairs.

Outside Will's room Luke considered knocking, but that might give him time to hide something. He tested the doorknob. It was unlocked. He pushed the door open wide with one big shove, which was made extra difficult by the large clump of clothes piled behind it.

The room was a disaster. Clothes everywhere. Dirty plates and forks and bowls and spoons sat in piles on various surfaces. So this was why they were always searching for utensils. Luke had bought a bulk box of plastic ones the week before, giving up on the idea of ever finding the whole set again. Apparently the right place to look was Will's room.

Will lay on his bed with his headphones on, phone in hand texting. Luke was a little disappointed his son didn't even notice the dramatic entrance, but he wasn't about to be ignored. With a quick tug he pulled out Will's earbuds, letting a deep bass pump out.

"What the . . . ?" Will sat up on his twin bed, folding his legs into a pretzel. *When did he get so big?* He had his mom's dark hair and Luke's crystal-blue eyes, blotchy brown freckles on the top of his cheeks, but he had Luke's body type. A cross-country runner, his body was lean and muscled, and all his clothes hung off him like hand-me-downs. "Dad, what are you doing?"

No small talk, he had to dive right in.

"I had a nice chat with Ms. Mason today." Luke sat down on the edge of the bed next to Will and started to put an arm around his shoulders. At his father's touch, Will pulled away, leaning back against the wall, with his knees drawn up to his chest. When Will didn't speak, Luke continued.

"I'm sure you are aware of what she called me about. Correct?" He made his voice stern, fatherly.

"Uh, yeah."

Luke thought for sure he could hear remorse in Will's voice. The hint of regret was almost enough to make Luke willing to drop the whole thing. Almost.

"Will." Luke had to pause to take a breath, frustration stacking up inside him like blocks in a tower. "What possessed you to tell her you are adopted?" Will didn't respond; instead, he shrugged and picked at his thumbnail. "No." Luke slapped the unmade bed. "I know I've let you get away with a lot of things lately, but I'm not letting this one go. You answer me. Now."

"Fine." Will hit his crumpled bedding and threw his head back against the old-school Metallica poster on his wall before pushing himself off the bed and on the floor. Digging around under the bed he finally slid a medium-size cardboard box out from under the overhang of his covers. It had the word "Memories" written across the side in Natalie's handwriting.

Luke knew this box. She brought it with her when they got married. At least once a year he'd find her curled up in a corner examining its entrails. Sometimes she shared a scrap of paper or a memento, but most of the time she kept its contents private. He'd never been tempted to look inside, understanding the desire to keep some memories to herself. Natalie had always respected his boundaries, so he'd always tried to return the favor. Knowing Will had broken that trust made Luke angry and jealous at the same time.

"That's your mom's box. You shouldn't be rummaging through it."

Will already had half his arm buried inside the box, shifting objects around, searching.

"She's dead, Dad. Nothing belongs to her anymore, remember? You taught me that a long time ago." He whipped out a business-size envelope with black lines of writing on the back. "Here. This is what got me thinking. *You* tell *me* what this means." He shoved the hair out of his eyes, settling back on his knees.

Luke took the envelope reluctantly. On the one hand, he hated the idea of breaking Natalie's confidence in him by snooping. On the other hand, he was eager to know what Will had found that made him so suspicious. Curiosity and a desire to figure out what his son was going through won out over loyalty.

The back of the envelope was filled with names and phone numbers. Some were first names only, others the names of companies or hospitals in several different colors of ink. Some were crossed out and others underlined. There was no way to know when the names and numbers were written or what they were for. This random list couldn't possibly be the catalyst for Will's lie.

"I don't get it. Is this supposed to explain something?"

"You're holding it wrong." Will took the envelope and flipped it over. The front was addressed to "Mrs. Natalie Richardson," and up in the corner a return address emblem read: "Maranatha Adoptions, Chicago, Illinois." Postmarked the month Will was born. Luke peeked inside the roughly opened envelope, but it was empty.

"What did the letter say?"

"It was empty when I found it," Will mumbled.

"So let me get this right," Luke said, trying to keep his voice steady and his blood pressure from skyrocketing. The large vein in his neck pounded against his collar. "You decided to make up some extravagant story about how your whole life's been a lie off an empty envelope with random names written on the back?" Luke was almost yelling. He took a breath before continuing, remembering how distinctly he and Jessie had heard Clayton through the ceiling during her first visit. "You've seen all the pictures of Mom pregnant with you, of you lying in her arms at the hospital, the videos of you coming home. You really think we staged all those?"

Will went back to picking at his thumb. Luke couldn't see his eyes, but when his son started sniffing, he knew Will was crying. He put the envelope in his shirt pocket behind the folded list of grief counselors. Once his hands were free, he slid an arm around Will's shoulders and touched his forehead to his son's.

They hadn't cried in front of each other since the day Natalie died. Sometimes Luke thought he could hear Will crying in his room as he walked by, but he'd always assumed Will needed his privacy. Now that Will was in his arms, Luke knew he'd been wrong. What he needed was for his dad to tell him everything was going to be okay.

"No," Will sobbed, "I guess I knew it wasn't possible."

"Why did you say all those things to Ms. Mason?" Luke asked calmly, kissing the top of his son's head like he used to do when he was little.

"Because I wanted it to be true," Will choked out.

The admission stabbed Luke in the heart. Will wished he didn't belong to their family.

"You don't feel like you fit in?"

Will sat up and pulled away from Luke's arms. Thick trails of tears traced down his cheeks.

"No, it's not that." Will shook his head. "When I saw the adoption agency and the date, I couldn't stop thinking about it. You weren't there when I was born." He wiped his nose with the back of his hand, catching his breath. "You guys always talked about how you were in China for most of Mom's pregnancy and how hard it was to get pregnant. How I came a month early and you weren't back yet. I thought, maybe, there was a chance."

Luke put a firm hand on Will's shoulder. "But Grandma was here, and I got home the day you came home. Your mom was tired and sore. The nurses had taken those Polaroid pictures for me right after you were born. Plus, no adoption agency would give a baby to someone without the father being there."

Will nodded repeatedly. "I guess I know that, but the more I thought about it, the more I wanted it to be true. I kept thinking: if I was adopted, if that letter was about me, my mom's not dead. She's out there somewhere, waiting for me." When Will choked on the last words, Luke knew why people wanted to believe in heaven so badly. If only he could pretend he believed. He'd say: "Don't worry. Your mom *is* waiting for you. You will see her again." Now he didn't know what to say.

"You still have a mom; she's real, she existed, and you have all your memories of her."

"Lucky me." Will placed the box back under the bed and yanked up his sagging jeans.

Luke ran a hand through his hair, scratching his scalp in thought. "Um, about the adoption, if you are still worried, I can look into that Maranatha place. Maybe find out why they were writing to your mom." Luke told himself it was to placate Will, but he couldn't deny the embers of curiosity stirring in his mind. Will was his child, he didn't doubt that, even with all of Will's convoluted points. But an adoption agency and a list of hospitals—what did it all mean?

"Really?" Will looked at him suspiciously. "You'd do that? Even though you're so sure?"

"Hey, if you tell Ms. Mason that story one more time, she's going to lose it. If this will put your mind at rest, I'm happy to."

Will seemed to consider the idea carefully, like he was trying to balance two sides of a scale. "Yeah, I think that'd help."

"Okay. I'll do some research and make some phone calls. In the meantime, Ms. Mason said we need to take you to a therapist."

"No way." Will rolled his eyes and leaned away from Luke. "I do not want to talk to some stranger about Mom."

Luke wasn't ready for another fight so he settled for a few firm pats on Will's back.

"I know, but when you start making up stories about your life, there are consequences. You go to this doctor for six weeks, you start turning in all your homework, and if your grades are okay and you want to stop, you can. Deal?"

Will grunted but couldn't seem to figure out a rebuttal. Instead, he said, "Deal." They shared a quick hug.

"Oh, and all these dishes need to make their way downstairs and into the dishwasher. No more eating in your room. Meals with us every night. Homework turned in. Got it?"

"Fine. I got it. I got it." Will rolled his eyes and grabbed a plate coated in some kind of dried-on film.

Luke left Will's room feeling like a qualified parent for the first time in a while. He glanced at his watch. He was already half an hour late relieving Jessie. Picking up the pace, he took the stairs two at a time. Jumping off the last step, something fell out of his pocket. He half expected to see one of Natalie's letters, but they were still in his coat pocket. No, this was the mystery envelope from Will's room.

He examined it one more time. Nothing new on the front—adoption agency, Chicago, postmarked near Will's birthday. Knowing Natalie, she was trying to help a friend or a student, right? After a little research and a few phone calls, he'd have a simple explanation to bring to his son and settle the anxious thoughts that kept creeping to the fore.

Luke shook his head. Will was too young to understand—Luke and Natalie were best friends. Over their life together, they'd always told each other everything. Natalie knew his secrets and he knew hers. All of them. Well, except for whatever was in the box . . . and the letters and . . .

He turned the paper over to look at the list of hospitals and names. Something caught his eye. One name in particular stood out to him. He'd seen it before: Dr. Neal. He'd seen that name before on the contact list on Natalie's phone. At the time he'd assumed it was one of Natalie's doctors. Now he wasn't so sure. He ran his finger over the name again.

"Dr. Neal," Luke whispered. "Who are you?"

MARCH

CHAPTER 7

Luke closed the door to Clayton's bedroom with a cautious click. Over the past two months it had become a habit to check on the kids before turning in for the night. A new part of his routine was prying Natalie's iPhone from Clayton's grubby little fingers to charge it.

Every night since Luke had found Natalie's phone tangled in the bedding from her abandoned hospital bed, Clayton had fallen asleep listening to his mom reading one of the six picture books she'd recorded on the phone. She'd also recorded a few songs and favorite memories from when they were little. Luke tried to avoid those videos. Natalie made them when she was in the front room, having hospice visit her, making plans for her funeral. She was a shell of the woman who'd walked into the oncologist's office a year earlier. But the kids didn't seem to mind. Especially Clayton.

Some nights Luke left the phone in Clayton's bed, knowing when he woke in the middle of the night he could tap a button and hear his mother's voice. But tonight, Luke needed the phone more than his son did. Luke tiptoed into the master bedroom, closed the door carefully, and tossed the phone on his rumpled bed.

Right after his discovery of the phone, it was too painful to look through the device. Avoidance had always been Luke's greatest defense against pain. From his brief look through the phone, he found tons of pictures and videos, e-mails with friends and family, and casually noted Dr. Neal's name in her contact list along with about fifty others. That's when he handed the phone over to Clayton's perpetually sticky care.

Then, her two-month death-anniversary came, and along with it, a new letter. Day 60. It was so different than the rest of the notes, less lighthearted, more narrative. There was a man in the letter—the elusive Dr. Neal, the stranger whose name continued to show up. First, as a random contact on her phone, next on the mysterious envelope, and now a real live person in one of her letters. To make matters worse, there was something about the way she talked about him that made Luke bristle.

DAY 60

Dear Luke,

Today was a horrible day. I know it seems like every day of a cancer patient's life during treatment could be described as less than stellar, but that's not entirely true. At least not for me. Most days I only think about cancer for maybe 10 percent of my day. Honestly. Between the kids and you and school and Annie and everything else, I'm usually on an even keel. But not today.

It happened on campus. I like getting to school early to study; we're already paying for childcare so I might as well get some non-kid-interrupted study time in. There's this group of girls, and when I say girls, I mean young female children, who "hang out" in the stairwell by the vestibule where I sit till class starts. They're generally annoying, laughing and swearing like your Uncle Stan. But the other day I smelled something, uh, strange coming from their general direction. Luke, they were smoking pot, right on campus, in the building. I couldn't believe it.

Of course, being a teacher and a bit of a natural-born tattletale, I wanted to report them to someone. But I didn't. They'd be kicked out of school, maybe arrested, and I didn't want to be responsible for all that. Instead, I packed up and poked my head in the smoky stairwell. There were three of them: two average-looking brunettes and one tiny blonde. The short blonde one seemed to be the ringleader. She wore this insanely small pair of shorts over hot pink tights. They were pretty much underwear. It's February. How desperate for attention do you have to be to wear underwear shorts outside in the snow?

I'm getting distracted. So the underwear-shorts girl didn't even try to hide the joint. She gaped at me like I'd walked into her living room after breaking down the front door. She looked me over, eyes lingering on my headscarf. I can't remember exactly what they said, but it went something like this:

The underwear-shorts girl demanded to know what I wanted, the hand holding the joint frozen midpuff.

I gave her the nicest smile I could muster and closed the swinging door behind me.

I got my teacher voice on and said something like, "Uh, ladies, I can smell your pot all the way out in the main hall. You might want to put it out and get to class or wherever you need to be."

The blonde rolled her eyes, took a long drag on the joint, and blew it out in my direction. I'll edit her profanities out because she was proficient in her use of spicy language. "So f-ing what? You might be somebody's mom, but you're not mine."

A door at the top of the stairs opened and closed, and a single set of footsteps echoed through the well. The taller brunette with bleached gold tips shifted uncomfortably and tried to convince "Tiff" to go.

I pulled the door open and stepped aside. "Yeah, Tiff, you should go."

The Tiff girl glared at me as she snuffed out the weed and put it in the pocket of her underwear shorts. But before they made a move to leave, my methods professor, Dr. Neal, came up from behind. He's a tall-ish guy, and on the stairs he stood at least two heads above the crew.

You have to imagine a deep, very authoritative voice here. It echoed in the hallway and almost scared me as much as the girls.

"What's going on here?" He put his hands in the pockets of his tweed sport coat; it even had patches on the sleeves like a perfect professor stereotype. "Do I need to remind you ladies this is a nonsmoking campus, with a zero tolerance policy for illegal drug use?"

One of the blonde's groupies poked her in the back, nearly shoving her toward the door. She hitched her thumb at me. "Look at the scarf; bet she's got cancer. I heard they get pot for free."

I was appalled they tried to use my cancer as cover for their pot smoking. I wanted to tell them off or at least call their mothers and tell them what lovely "flowers" they'd raised, but instead I tried to lighten the mood by flipping the tail of my scarf over my shoulder. And saying, "Shows what you know. Baldness and scarves are hot this spring."

Tiff did not catch on. She rolled her eyes and said something like, "God, lady, the chemo's gone to your brain. That outfit is the ugliest thing I've ever seen."

Dr. Neal shook his head, and I knew Tiff had just said the wrong thing. He asked me to head to class and let them know he'd be a few minutes late. As I backed out the door, I thought I could hear Dr. Neal ask for the girls' IDs.

I hurried to the chair I'd been studying in. My shoulder bag was still there, untouched. It had probably been a dumb idea to leave it out in the open. I took a quick inventory, and everything seemed to be intact. I had pulled the strap onto my shoulder when a hard shove came from behind, knocking me against the back of the armchair. No need for my overactive imagination here. I remember this next part word-for-word.

"Thanks a lot, bitch. I f-ing hope you die." Tiff stood behind me. She wrapped her hand around the loose end of my black-and-gray scarf and yanked. It came off easily, sliding against my smooth scalp and falling to the floor in a pool of satin. For a moment I couldn't breathe. Everyone in the hall stopped and stared. I could feel their stares rubbing over my bald head, hear them whisper, "She must have cancer."

Even Tiff seemed shocked for a moment at the reality of my illness. She backed away into the crowd gathering around us when Dr. Neal broke through.

He took in the scene in front of him—the scarf on the ground, the tears on my face. He grabbed the scarf and my bag, then put his arm around me, leading me through the crowd and to the nearest empty classroom.

By the time we got into the dingy old room, I was sobbing. He put my bag down and held out the scarf and asked if I was okay.

I didn't know what to say. Physically, I was fine. Everyone is always worried about my body, but at that minute, my soul hurt. I knew the scarf wasn't fooling anyone—they all knew why I wore it, but without it I felt naked. I couldn't hide from what was happening inside my body.

I lied and told him I was fine. I wiped my face with the slippery material, hoping my glued-on eyelashes were waterproof.

"Don't worry about that girl. I got her name. I promise, she will face discipline." His face was hard, looking less like a professor and more like a vigilante. He wanted me to press charges, get the girl kicked out of school. He was furious. I told him I didn't want to be involved. For a moment I thought he was going to fight me on it. Then he took a step back, checking the clock above the whiteboard. We were both late for class. He told me I didn't have to go, that he'd e-mail me the notes.

I wiped my nose on my sleeve with a loud sniff and shook my head. If I went home, Tiff would win. I told him that I wanted to stay but that I needed a few minutes to try and get my scarf back on. I tried to smile as I threw the scarf over my shoulder.

Then to my surprise, Dr. Neal yanked the fabric off my shoulder and untwisted the large knot on its side. "My wife used to wear one of these . . ." He trailed off without finishing the sentence and then offered to help.

I hesitated for a moment, but not long. He wanted to help, but didn't look at me like those other people did, like a sick person. He looked at me like a real person who happened to have cancer. I nodded, and he took two steps toward me until we were nearly nose-to-nose. Hands on my shoulders, he whispered, "Turn around."

I spun slowly on one foot, facing the whiteboard at the front of the classroom. When he first touched my shoulders I jumped, still jittery from the confrontation with Tiff. He gave them a kind squeeze, and I let out a sigh I think I'd been holding for a long time. It was nice to be with someone who'd been there before, who had wrapped bare heads and cried useless tears that changed absolutely nothing. He wound the silken fabric around my scalp and tied a simple knot under my right ear. I pulled the tail of the scarf over my shoulder like I used to when I had a ponytail.

I carefully inspected the scarf, dancing fingers over the knot and checking to be sure it fully covered my baldness. It was perfect. I thanked him and he left. A few minutes later I went back to class, and life went on like any other day.

Now I'm home. I can't bring myself to tell you this story. First, I know I'd cry, and you already have to deal with so many of my tears, I don't want to burden you with more. But really it's because I know you.

You'll want to "fix" this for me. You'll want to call Brian so we can press charges, or drive to campus, hunt those girls down, and force them to apologize. So instead, I wrote the story down for you to read later. Let's face it: if I'm dead, then there's nothing to fix. One thing you can do for me though. If you ever meet Dr. Neal, tell him thank you for me.

Hope you and the kids had a better day than I did. Kiss them for me. I love you all!

Love,

Natalie

The first time he'd read the letter a week ago, Luke wanted to jump in his car and hunt down underwear-pants girl and shove a picture of his dead wife in her face.

He'd gotten as far as the highway before realizing Clayton was sitting in the backseat, stuffed into his puffy blue winter coat, ready to be dropped off at Annie's house. Luke made a tight U-turn right before the on-ramp and sped back to Annie's, only a few minutes late.

He reread the letter obsessively for three days, unsure if he was more disturbed by the cruelty of Tiff or the gentleness of Dr. Neal. Dr. Neal. That name—it couldn't be a coincidence. Natalie's grad school professor showing up in three areas of her life made no sense. At least not any kind of sense he liked considering.

He'd already looked up his contact information on the phone, briefly, after seeing Dr. Neal's name on the Maranatha envelope. But upon further investigation, the phone numbers didn't match. Luke took it as a sign he was jumping to conclusions. Now he wasn't so sure.

He stared at the sleeping phone, its screen black and covered in smudges. Avoidance had been the right choice. While the phone was dark, it was as if he could keep a little part of Natalie in suspended animation, like some Disney princess May was always watching on TV. He wanted nothing more than to leave the sleeping princess in peace, but his list of questions was getting longer than his list of excuses.

Luke entered her password. Apps sprawled across her touch screen, never organized in any way he could easily understand. Maybe that's what had kept him from getting a smartphone for so long; they had so many useless applications on them, so many things that consumed time like it was endless. Well, it wasn't endless.

He tapped the green messages button, feeling a little uncomfortable searching through his wife's phone—like a jealous lover. Top and center in black letters was the name Dr. Neal. If his name was on top, Dr. Neal was the last person on earth to send his wife a message. His finger hovered over the name, and he touched it cautiously, as if it could bite him.

The message screen opened instantly, one blue message glowing on the screen. It said: "I'm glad we found each other." Then . . . nothing. Luke tried to scroll down, searching for more messages, for some explanation as to why this guy's moniker was all over his wife's life. But the blue text bubble bounced back into place. "I'm glad we found each other."

What the hell? That was *not* a normal message to get from your college professor no matter how many times he helped you out of a difficult situation. And no way he'd sent her only one text on the day she died. An unnerving thought came to him. If there were no previous texts from Dr. Neal, Natalie must've been deleting them.

Luke switched over to the recent calls. The first four names made him let out the breath he'd been holding, fogging up the screen. This was more normal. Natalie talked to her mom, Annie, Luke, and the hospice nurse Tammy. But he couldn't help swiping his finger up one more time. The fifth name on the recent-calls list was Dr. Neal. They talked for twenty minutes the week before she died. Damn it.

Luke dropped the phone as if it was on fire. He rubbed his eyes with closed fists, and the tears he'd successfully held back for three months burned angrily against his eyelids. No, he wouldn't let an old envelope, Natalie's letters, one text, and a few phone calls make him question the sixteen years they'd had together. Right?

Luke was about to grab the phone again when his bedroom door swung open. Clayton, blurry-eyed and disheveled, squinted against the light.

"Hey, buddy, whatcha doing? It's almost . . ." He glanced at the digital clock on his nightstand, but it blinked 12:00 from a random blackout over a week before. He'd never reset it. What did a three-year-old know about time anyway? "It's really, really late, buddy. Do you need a drink? To go potty?"

Clayton hoisted his tattered baby blanket over his shoulder. "I need Mommy." He stuck the tip of his forefinger into his mouth. He looked so tiny standing across the room, his head barely up to the doorknob of the bedroom door. Luke put out his arms and waved his son toward him.

"I know, buddy." Clayton crawled up on Luke's lap, curling up into a ball like a little lapdog. Luke kissed the crown of his head, surprised he still smelled a little of Annie's perfume. "I miss Mommy too. But we have each other. You can sleep in here tonight if you want."

Clayton gasped and yanked his finger out of his mouth. *"Mommy!"* He lunged across the bed, wrapping his wet fingers around the blue cover of his mom's phone. "I found Mommy." He expertly flipped through the app icons, tapped the video application, and searched through the videos Luke still didn't have the heart to watch.

So, now Clayton's mommy was a phone. When her voice came across the speakers, Luke tried not to look as he crushed the pause button glowing on the screen.

"I'm sorry I took the phone. Do you want to keep it in your bed?"

Clayton nodded. "I want to sleep with Mommy tonight."

"That's fine; you can sleep with the phone." *That phone is not your mom,* Luke wanted to say. He had a real mom, with flesh and blood and a heartbeat he could feel and hear. A heart he grew under for nine months. A body that fed him for another ten. Arms that held him for three years. How did he forget? How could he think this piece of technology could replace his mother?

Luke didn't say anything. He carried Clayton back to bed, tucked him under his pirate sheets, and kissed his forehead before hitting play and running out the door. When he guided the door to a quiet click, he could hear Natalie reading *Goodnight Moon* and Clayton sleepily repeating the words like they used to do when she was alive.

He shook his head; he wasn't angry with Clayton. That child knew who his mother was, and thanks to Natalie's recordings, he'd have some special memories of her even as his real ones started to fade with age. He *was* angry though with Natalie and those letters, for making him doubt her in a way he'd never doubted her when she was alive.

Luke didn't care how late it was; he had to take some time to think. In the corner lay an uneven pile of dirty clothes he'd been putting off washing. Rummaging through the heap, he found a pair of shorts and an old Michigan T-shirt. Within minutes he was in the basement, colder than the rest of the house by at least ten degrees. Almost sick with anticipation, Luke rushed through the ritual of wrapping his hands, forgetting to count how many times he circled his hands with the cotton strips, not caring that he could barely feel his fingers.

Right now he needed two things—to hit the bag hanging in the corner and to think. As soon as he tore the last bit of tape with his teeth, Luke lunged across the room, landing a blow in the center of the heavy maroon punching bag. Jogging back and forth, he hit again, and again, losing himself to the rhythm of the routine. Sweat gathered on his forehead and soaked his hair as if he'd just taken a shower. Each blow he landed sent drops of perspiration flying through the unfinished storage room.

When his lungs burned and he could no longer feel his hands, Luke stepped back from the bag with a little clarity. Wiping his face with the towel hanging from one of the pipes in the ceiling, he knew what he had to do. Even if his fears were irrational, even if he was jumping to conclusions, he needed to know what Natalie was hiding about Dr. Neal. If anyone would know Natalie's secrets, it was Annie.

CHAPTER 8

By the time Luke unwrapped the sweat-drenched bands from his hands, he had a firm, simple plan for the morning. Basically he'd rap on Annie's front door and ask, or demand, anything she knew about Dr. Neal.

But in reality, as soon as Annie appeared from behind her door the next morning, he lost his nerve. There was a part of him ashamed he could be suspicious of Natalie. She'd never given him any reason to doubt her while she was alive. Then there was another part of him, a small but significant part, that worried he'd been made to look the fool.

Not sure how to bring up such a sensitive topic, Luke avoided his plan altogether, walking around in a fog, grouchy and preoccupied.

Yet he had to do something. He considered calling Dr. Neal's number, the one that seemed to mock him every time he opened the phone. Or he could use his advanced tech skills and try to get access to the deleted texts on the phone. Or he could go to dinner with Annie and Brian like Annie had begged him to do for a week. There, he could find an opportunity to ask some of the questions he needed answers to. Dinner seemed like the least insane of the options.

◆　◆　◆

Luke smelled of cologne and was wearing a pair of jeans with a belt. He balanced on a wobbly barstool in a somewhat seedy bar while Jessie was at home with the kids. Will was technically old enough to watch May and Clayton, but Luke never felt comfortable leaving him with them for very long, at least when bedtime was an issue. Clayton and May gave Luke a hard enough time going to bed every night; he wasn't going to make his fourteen-year-old son take over that responsibility. He'd rather pay Jessie to do it. Maybe he should pay her to do it every night?

He took another swig of his beer, wondering if it was the alcohol or the silence helping him relax. He didn't drink often, always afraid he would follow his father down that slippery slope, but tonight he thought it was a good risk to take. Somewhere between the beer and pure desperation, he hoped to finally find the courage to talk to Annie about Natalie's professor.

Luke was there early, waiting for the Gurrellas at the bar. He watched Annie's face as she walked in the door and noticed Jose and Tanner, cops about ten years Brian's junior, hanging out at a table with two pitchers of beer and a plate of wings. She dropped Brian's hand and pulled off her plum-colored winter coat. She was wearing a black skirt and gauzy white top that plunged in the front and was tucked in at the waist. When Brian went over to see his friends before meeting Luke at the bar, she seemed disappointed but not surprised.

"Hey!" Annie called across the bar after hanging up her coat next to Brian's on the coatrack. Luke returned the gesture as she headed toward the stool beside him. In his past life, Luke would be with Brian playing Golden Tee with Jose and Tanner from the station, while Annie and Natalie caught up over a few drinks. But tonight he wasn't there for guy time; he was there to talk to Annie. She sat down beside him, bumping shoulders.

"Hey there." She smiled before dragging a coaster in front of her and signaling to the bartender. "I'm glad you came out with us tonight."

"Yeah, it feels strange. Thanks for letting me tag along."

"I think it's more like we're the tagalongs here." She tipped her head toward Brian, Tanner, and Jose, who were harassing each other over the video game.

The bartender made his way across the bar to Annie. He wore a tight black shirt with his sleeves rolled up unnecessarily high, showing off his biceps. Luke thought he came off as trying a little too hard, but maybe that's how he got good tips. When he rested his eyes on Annie, the man flexed his pecs noticeably. Luke rolled his eyes.

"How can I help you?" the bartender asked, deepening his voice a fraction.

"Just a Diet Coke, please." Annie didn't seem to notice the bartender's attentions. She tapped her fingers on the lacquered wood of the bar.

"You want me to slip a little rum in that Diet Coke?" The bartender wiggled his eyebrows.

"Uh, no, thank you. Designated driver." She reached across Luke and grabbed the dark-brown bottle from the coaster in front of him, put it to her mouth, and took two long swigs before smacking her lips and replacing it. Luke used to watch Natalie and Annie share drinks. But he was not Natalie. Sometimes Luke wondered if Annie remembered that.

The bartender gave a hearty laugh. "I don't think that's how being a designated driver works, but, okay. Diet Coke it is." He placed the drink in front of Annie and dropped a clear straw in her drink. "My name's Mick. Call me if you want something stronger."

"Thanks." Annie took a long sip from her own drink before turning to face Luke, ignoring Mick completely. "So. How're things going? You guys like Jessie?"

Luke nodded. "She's a quirky one. A few days ago I came home to May singing 'It's the Hard Knock Life' while mopping the kitchen floor. Jessie was directing her while singing along. Both were so off-key I'm sure dogs were howling."

"Oh my. I wish I could've seen that."

"Yeah, it was the least effective floor mopping I've ever seen, but May was glowing. Honestly"—Luke took a quick sip of his beer, running through Natalie's description of Jessie in his mind—"she's not exactly what I was expecting; sometimes she seems to live in a Broadway fantasy world. But the kids love her, even Will. Do you know Will does his homework every night now?"

Annie swirled the ice around with her straw. "Really? That's great."

"Yup, and I don't even have to nag him to do it. It's done by the time I get home."

"He seemed almost happy when we texted last week. I was starting to think you'd finally taken him to a therapist or something." She bumped Luke's shoulder again. She'd been bugging Luke to take the kids to a counselor ever since it became apparent that Natalie wasn't going to get better.

"Well, if the therapist's name is Jessie, then yes, you were right." He shifted in his seat again, the uneven legs making a ticking sound as they bounced off the waxed tile floor. "Actually I have an appointment for him next week."

"You do? Good for you. You're a good daddy."

"Well, I wouldn't go that far." He couldn't help but smile a little. It felt strange on his face and reminded him of why he was really there. Luke checked on Brian. He was still playing video games and refilling his second or third mug with beer. "Listen"—Luke lowered his voice— "I need to talk to you about something."

Annie tilted her head and leaned it against her fist, all hints of amusement gone from her face. "What's up?"

The nervousness returned. Why did he think this was a useful idea? He took another sip of his beer, hoping the alcohol would do its job and make him a little less inhibited. But when he put the bottle down and looked up and met Annie's soft green eyes, the words he'd planned out so carefully disappeared. He glanced away, focusing on a long line of flavored syrups with gold pumps sticking out the top. If he didn't look right at her, he might be able to get the words out.

"Did Natalie ever mention a guy named Dr. Neal to you? Her professor or something?" He said it quickly and picked at the corner of the yellow and gold label on his beer instead of meeting her gaze again.

"Hmm. Dr. Neal?" Annie tapped her teeth like she did when she was thinking.

Luke got up the nerve to look at her again. Thankfully she was staring up at the ceiling, like the dingy yellow tiles held the answer to his question. She kept tapping her teeth nervously. "I don't remember a Dr. Neal. I do remember a Pastor Neal though."

"Pastor Neal?" A piece of the label ripped off in Luke's fingertips, sticking under his nail. He shook it on the floor. "Are you sure?"

"Yeah. I'm positive. I swear Nat said he was a pastor." Annie ran a hand through her short blonde bob. "I came over one morning and he was there, sitting by her bed. She introduced us."

"He was in my house?" Luke choked mid-drink and wiped the back of his hand across his mouth before continuing. "You met him?"

"I did." Annie patted his back as he gave one more cough. "Why? What's wrong?"

Luke opened his mouth to answer but didn't know what to say. What was wrong? What could he say that wouldn't sound paranoid and disloyal to his wife and Annie's best friend? This man had been in his house when he wasn't home, a man he'd never met, a man his wife had never mentioned . . . till now. A man who kept turning up everywhere he looked.

Luke dropped his face into his hands, rubbing his eyes with the heels of his hands. Annie's pats turned into large circles on his back.

"Oh, Luke, I'm sorry. This was too soon."

"No. It's not that." He wiped his fingers around the edges of his eyes to catch any escaping moisture. "It's the beer. I think it's making me emotional."

"What has you all worried about this Neal guy?" Annie settled back on her stool, staring at the side of Luke's face.

He finished off the last few drops of beer in his bottle, putting the empty on the coaster in front of him. "His number was in Nat's phone. I'd never heard of him before, but then there was this letter . . ."

Annie shook her head like she was editing herself. "Fine." She held out her hands. "So, what did she say to freak you out like this?"

Luke didn't know how to explain it. There was nothing specific in her letter or even in her phone that made him concerned. It was more the lack of something.

"Nothing really. He helped her out of a bad situation at school. The thing is, Natalie and I didn't keep secrets from each other, and I thought she didn't keep secrets from you. Look, she even lied about who he was when you met him. Why would she do that?"

Annie spun the straw around in her drink—no quick answer or pat on the back this time. The ice clinked against the glass, loud in the silence between them.

"Okay, I don't have an answer for that one. But come on, Luke, don't be an idiot." She placed her hand on his crossed arm, fingers cold from holding the frosty glass. "Natalie loved you. She'd never do anything to hurt you. What? Do you think they were having an"—she paused and looked around to make sure no one was listening before whispering—"*affair?*"

The word made a heavy, nauseous feeling settle in his chest. Did he think Natalie had had a real-life affair with this man? It was almost impossible trying to imagine her sneaking around to sleep with another man. But it didn't matter; their mystery connection made him feel almost as uncomfortable as the idea of an intimate connection.

"I don't really know *what* to think. That's why I wanted to talk to you about it."

Annie put her hand on his forearm. He stared at her long thin fingers, nails painted a delicate shade of pink. They were nothing like Natalie's, but somehow it gave him a similar kind of comfort.

"Think about it this way—when would she even have had time to have an affair? She was too busy with you and the kids and school and, oh, I don't know, maybe . . . *cancer*."

Annie was right. How was he worried that Natalie was having an affair when she was weak, nauseous, bald, and living each day scared of dying? The situation suddenly struck him as ludicrous. "Oh, I'm such an asshole." He shook his head, half laughing. "Okay, I needed to hear that, Annie."

"Well, if you liked it *that* much, next time I can slap you." She smacked his forearm hard enough to sting.

"Ouch!"

"Come on; you deserved it."

"Fine." He laughed. "I deserved it. Now unless you intend to get violent again, I'm going to use the restroom." He stood, letting her hand fall off his arm but caught it in his before it hit her leg. "Thank you for always knowing the right thing to say."

"It's not hard; I just tell the truth." She gave his hand a squeeze and let go. "You want another?" she asked, tipping her head toward his empty beer bottle.

"I'm driving so I'd better not."

"I'm not drinking tonight so others may enjoy themselves more thoroughly," she proclaimed and gave a semibow, laughing. "Don't let me waste all that on Brian. I'll take you home, and we can grab your car in the morning."

Luke bounced the idea around in his mind. He *was* feeling looser.

"All right, one more." Luke held up his index finger, heading to the rear of the bar, where a glowing red sign blinked **RESTROOMS**. Pushing past a swinging door, he flicked on the cold water and threw some on his face. The chill of the water stung his skin and gave him a slight brain freeze but also felt so refreshing. Three handfuls later, he ran his wet fingers through his hair. It was getting longer than he was used to, but a haircut was one of the least important things on his to-do list.

Between his hair and the fluorescent lights, Luke was surprised at how old he looked. His irises were vividly blue, but that was only because the bloodshot whites of his eyes made them stand out. His perma-stubble was so light he wasn't sure if it was blond or white. But it was the circles under his eyes that made him look hollow and old. Natalie wouldn't even recognize him.

He missed her so much it hurt. Two days without reading her letters, and she seemed farther away than ever. Yanking seven or eight paper towels from the dispenser, Luke dried his face, dumped them into the garbage, and then stared at his reflection. Annie was right—he was being an idiot. Forget the beer sitting on the bar waiting for him; he needed to go home, open Natalie's most recent letters, and bring her back to him.

Luke marched out of the restroom, double-checking his pockets for keys. He'd say good-bye and thank you to Annie and go. She'd understand. She always understood.

Approaching the bar, Luke noticed the bartender, Mick, standing in front of Annie. Luke's open beer sat on the counter, and Mick was leaning over it doing that annoying flexing thing, taking obvious glances at Annie's breasts.

Luke searched the room for Brian, hoping to signal him in to rescue Annie. He located him quickly at a table a few feet from the bar, but to Luke's surprise, Brian was casually watching the interaction between Annie and Mick. Next to him sat his severely buzzed buddies. He didn't look concerned at all. In fact, he was laughing.

Annie leaned away from the bar, glancing around the room, arms crossed tightly around her chest, giving obvious signs of disinterest, but Mick didn't seem to notice. When he reached across the bar to tuck a piece of hair behind Annie's ear, Luke had seen enough. He took three long strides across the room and dragged the barstool out loudly, the rubber stoppers scraping the floor.

"Sorry I took so long. You okay?" Luke plopped down, pretending Mick wasn't standing there ogling Natalie's best friend's body parts. Annie met Luke's gaze, and the tension in her shoulders disappeared instantly.

"Sure thing." She flashed a smile that looked like relief. "Glad you found your way back. I was about to send in a rescue team."

Luke laughed as heartily as he could muster, putting on a show for Mick, who was still standing there. When would this guy take a hint?

"Hey, beautiful, my shift's almost over," Mick interjected, his voice deepening in what Luke could only guess was an attempt at sexy. "Can I buy you a drink or something? My place is only a few minutes from here, and my bar is well stocked."

Brian let out a loud "Hah!" behind them. The amount of entertainment he was getting from his wife's distress was starting to irritate Luke. He took Brian for the protective type, not an unfeeling lout.

"Thanks, but like I already told you, I'm married."

"And like I told you, I don't buy it. No ring? At a bar?" He grabbed her bare left hand and lifted it up into the light. She snapped it away, blushing.

"I was doing the dishes and forgot to put it back on," she explained to Luke, like he should care.

"What? Are you married to this guy?" Mick stood tall, like he was trying to show how much more of a man he was than Luke.

"No," Annie and Luke said in unison.

"He's my best friend's hus—" Annie cut herself off. Looking at Luke, her forehead wrinkled. "Actually, he's my friend," she corrected herself.

He'd never thought of Annie as anything other than Natalie's best friend. He had plenty of casual friendships, but the only real, meaningful friendship he'd ever been able to maintain was with Natalie. Growing up isolated by abuse and then again by foster care, he'd never learned how to lean on anyone but himself. Yet if he looked closely at the past three months, she was right. Annie had become his friend. She might be his only real friend.

"Sooooo." Mick broke into Luke's moment of realization. "I got this thing right after all." He stared pointedly at the empty spot on Annie's hand where her solitaire usually sat. "You stand behind a bar long enough, and you get to a point where you can read people pretty well. I pick up on things."

"Yeah, totally FBI material, Mick," Annie joked, flipping her hair before taking a long drink from her diet soda.

Luke had to work hard not to laugh. Mick, as was becoming habit, didn't notice the sarcastic lilt to her voice.

"You think so?" Mick ran a hand over his chest. "I've definitely got the body for it."

Luke was done trying to let Mick down easy. This guy needed a dose of honesty.

"Listen." He snapped his fingers in front of Mick's face. "She's clearly not interested. Leave the poor woman alone."

"Uh, I don't think you know if she's interested or not, so back off."

Annie cleared her throat, catching Mick's attention. "I'm not interested. Sorry. And I *am* married. See that guy back there, the one who's been playing Golden Tee for the past hour? That's my husband, Officer Brian Gurrella, and a few of his work friends."

Luke piled on. "Maybe you'd like to chat with them about your interest in law enforcement. I can call them over if you'd like." He turned as if to wave at Brian and his friends. Mick checked out the group of heavily muscled men hovering around a table covered in half-empty mugs of beer.

"No, no." He backed away from the bar, almost bumping into the bottles of hard liquor behind him, finally finding someone intimidating enough to back off. "I'm good. Uh, looks like you need a refill." Mick pointed at Annie's empty glass, seeming almost professional. "My shift's over, but I'll send Stacey with one for you."

"Sounds great; thanks, Mick," Luke added, finding Mick's reaction to rejection far too entertaining.

When Mick disappeared through the flapping doors, mumbling something under his breath about them being assholes, Annie let out a loud whoop and offered Luke a high-five. He put up his hand, and she slapped it so hard it tingled.

"That was awesome." She was beaming—nothing left of the shy, intimidated woman he'd attempted to "save" a few minutes earlier. "I've never had the guts to do that before. Brian thinks I'm a wimp. I hope he was watching."

When she mentioned his name, Brian poked his head between the two of them, reeking of beer and at least a few shots of whiskey.

"Thanks a bunch, Luke. You lost me fifty bucks. I bet those losers she'd run away and cry before she'd get him to back off." He smacked Luke on the shoulder and gave Annie a brief kiss on the top of her head. "I think the bet should be off since you stuck your nose in there and scared the guy away."

"Hey!" Annie protested. "I think I did pretty great. And not one tear." She shrugged off Brian's arm in mock disgust. Luke was about to join in on the whole strange but playful banter when he caught sight of Annie's reflection in the mirror over the bar. Her face was smooth, eyes hard and unblinking. There wasn't any of the bouncing laughter that filled the words she spoke. In fact, the only thing he could easily identify in her features was desperation. Luke cringed.

Brian didn't see her face, didn't know he was embarrassing his wife. Or that by sitting back and watching Mick hit on her, he'd made Annie feel insignificant.

"I'm giving you a hard time, Luke." Brian stood and slapped both of them on opposite shoulders. "You ladies keep enjoying your girls' night out. The boys are itching to play darts, and I gotta win some of my money back." He eyed Luke like he was checking his credentials. "You can join us if you want to, man. We always like fresh blood."

Luke knew Brian got better at darts when he was drunk, and the other two would soon be throwing like twelve-year-olds. He considered for a moment how easy it would be for him to dominate them all at darts and make a little money. Then he checked on Annie's unchanged reflection.

"No, thanks. You guys have fun." He waved at Tanner and Jose, who were divvying up the darts by color. "You can give me your money another time."

"You wish," Brian said as he walked away.

"You okay?" Luke whispered once Brian was hefting his first dart toward a plastic board. Did Annie and Natalie ever talk about their husbands together? They must have—isn't that what girlfriends do? Now Luke and Annie were friends—it was official—but Luke definitely wasn't ready to dispense relationship advice.

"I'm fine." She took a deep shaky breath before putting on a bright smile. It looked real enough to him. Then Luke had a startling thought: What if he'd never seen Annie's real smile? She turned her barstool around and watched the game of darts from a distance as though she was actually interested. "You can leave if you want; I wouldn't blame you."

Luke hesitated. Before Mick and all his slick moves, he was planning to find an excuse to jump in his car and make it home before *The Late Late Show* came on. The only reason he'd come tonight was to pump Annie for information. She didn't have any more to tell him.

As Luke turned his stool around to match hers, he crossed one foot over his knee and leaned against the bar behind him. Annie wasn't some object he could take out and use every once in a while when it suited him and then put in a closet when he was done.

He wasn't going to use her like Mick wanted to, or ditch her like Brian had.

"Nope. I'm staying," Luke said before taking a long drink of his nearly warm beer. "But since it doesn't look like we are going to get Brian out of here in time for our reservations at Bistro 16, I think we should order some food. Do they even have food at this dive . . . I mean, this incredibly classy facility?"

"Oh, for sure." Annie laughed. "Their specialty is a delicacy from France. I think it's called french fries." She put on a horrible fake French accent. Luke chuckled.

"Sounds very exotic."

"You'll never look at French cuisine the same again. I promise." Annie waved at the young woman dressed in black who had replaced Mick behind the counter. As the girl headed over, Luke watched Annie stare at her hands.

"Um," she said, pausing like she was gathering her thoughts. "Thank you for coming to my rescue. I'm really glad you came out with us tonight." Annie had flawless skin; high, well-defined cheekbones; and a body that was well sculpted by a natural athleticism and hours in the gym. Natalie used to joke that she felt like an Oompa-Loompa beside her fine-boned best friend, which Luke would laugh off with an extra long kiss and smack on the behind. Annie was definitely not his type, but right now, sitting at the bar with her mouth turned up a little at the corners, curving softly—something inside him stirred; he had a sudden urge to reach out and touch the delicate wrinkles settling around her lips.

"Hey, that's what friends are for," he joked, looking away. What the hell was he doing thinking about Annie? He was missing Natalie—that had to be it.

Luke found lots of interesting things to focus on in the bar—flashing lights, Brian's winning streak at darts, the guy in the corner who kept playing "Back in Black" on the jukebox. He looked everywhere but at her. Yet no matter how hard he tried to avoid it, Luke found himself waiting for another view of her subtle smile. When he did catch her once or twice smiling at a joke or story, he'd wonder if this time it was real.

APRIL

CHAPTER 9

"Why do you think she had that envelope? Why keep it?" Will followed behind Luke asking questions. Every morning they went through this routine—Will making lists of evidence trying to prove he wasn't crazy; Luke tamping down his son's concerns while his own grew like an unkempt garden choked with weeds. "She always talked about how she had to take medicine to help her get pregnant. Did you ever *see* her belly? Why aren't there any pictures?" The questions went on and on.

"I don't know why she kept it. *Yes*, I saw her pregnant, and we didn't take a lot of pictures because I was gone and selfies hadn't been invented." Luke reeled off the list of answers like he did every morning. They weren't always the same questions, but the eerily hopeful tone never changed. It was the way Will asked more than what he asked that disturbed Luke the most.

Even without Will's obsession, Luke didn't go more than an hour without thinking about the envelope from Natalie's memory box and the name written on it. It still bothered him . . . a lot . . . but not because he was in any doubt that Will was his son. No matter which way Will spun the story or how many wild assumptions he made, nothing could make Luke question his son's paternity. Why all the secrets?

That was the question that kept racing through Luke's mind during these morning interviews—why all the secrets?

He'd planned to throw away the Maranatha envelope, ready to never think about it again. But then a new letter came, this one all about Dr. Neal giving Natalie a box of his wife's old scarves. That's all it took. The envelope had been staring at him from the top of his dresser ever since.

"I did a little research, if it makes you feel better. The Maranatha Adoption Agency, it's in Chicago, and the folks there won't answer any questions over the phone about something that happened years ago. But that agency has some kind of office in Kalamazoo. It's called Maranatha House."

Will's mouth dropped open. "Are you serious? Isn't that close to where Mom grew up?" He jammed his hands into the front pockets of the sweatshirt, burrowing them in deep. "Dad, what does that mean?"

"Probably nothing," Luke said as he plopped the pile of mail into the back pocket of his workbag. He put up his hand to stop Will before he could argue with him further. "*But* I'm taking the day off work on Thursday to check it out in person. Is that thorough enough for you?"

"I'm coming with you." Will hung his blue backpack over his shoulder. It was covered in all kinds of doodles done in permanent marker. Luke thought they were graffiti, but Natalie always called them art.

"No, you're not. They probably won't talk to me anyway. Do you know how hard it is to adopt a baby, Will?" Luke's voice went up, and he fought back irritation. He took a deep breath and continued toward the front door. Will followed.

"Okay. Okay. Fine. You go alone."

Passing through the hall of family pictures, Luke stared straight ahead, still unable to look at the picture of "wedding day Natalie." Usually it was to avoid the pain inflicted by the happy memories, but lately it was to evade all the doubts clogging his brain.

When they emerged from the hall, Will was behind him, touching his shoulder. "Thank you for doing all this." His arms wrapped around Luke's shoulders in a brief hug, and Luke patted his back, wishing he didn't have to let go.

"I'd do anything for you, Will." Luke leaned back to look him in the eye. "You're my son."

"I know, Dad."

Luke patted his son's cheek and held him an arm's length in front of him. "Now get Clayton, and I'll drop you at school on the way to work."

"Okay." Will nodded and then shouted, *"Clay! Time to go!"*

"Uh, I said *go* and get him. I could've yelled." Luke pointed him toward the stairs.

"Fine." He rolled his eyes and sulked up the stairs, back to his normal teenage-boy self.

◆ ◆ ◆

Luke sped down I-94 past still-bare trees with tiny buds at the tips of each branch. Even though they were already a week into April, there was still a strong possibility it could snow. But the snow wouldn't kill the leaf buds. Somehow they survived the late winter storms and premature springs. If only humans were more like trees.

A large green road sign read **KALAMAZOO, EXIT 72**. He'd been waiting for this moment all week. Flicking on his turn signal, he checked his mirrors, even though no one else had been on the road all morning. It had only taken two hours to get from his house to the western Michigan town, and with everything running through his mind, the time had flown by.

When Luke told Annie about his last-minute "business trip," she offered to watch Clayton at his house so the handoff with Jessie would go smoothly. Despite Clayton's immediate friendship with Jessie,

Annie would always be first in his heart, and lately that meant big fits at three when it was time to go home. Luke was grateful for one less thing to worry about, even if it meant making sure the dishes were in the dishwasher and that Clayton flushed the toilet after his morning potty break.

Annie had been extra supportive since he'd tagged along with her and Brian to the bar. He didn't know if it was because he'd helped her with Mick or because she was worried about his state of mind. Annie was one of the most loyal people he'd ever met; she reminded Luke of his mother a little, which was a good thing and a bad thing at the same time. His mother didn't seem to be able to see the bad in people or even suspect it. This was doubly true of Annie with Natalie. She'd rather assume Luke was going bonkers than question if her deceased best friend had been living a secret life.

Off the highway, Luke focused on slowing down. Pressing gently on the brake, he checked the map on his GPS screen. Two rights, two lefts, one more right, then he'd be there. Maranatha House. He'd been working on his story and his "I need help" face. That morning he'd put on the suit he'd worn at Natalie's funeral. So much for burning it. He needed it today. The sadness that clung to it like cologne would help him appear more convincing.

Luke followed the voice on his GPS to a narrow lane covered in crumbling blacktop. He took the turn cautiously, avoiding a large divot in the middle of the asphalt. Inching down the road he let his foot hover over the gas pedal, never allowing the speedometer to go above ten miles per hour. The driving instructions told him to go 1.2 miles. As he pushed closer to the red and black dot glowing on the navigation screen, Luke felt a growing urge to make a three-point turn and head home.

Unexpectedly the woman on the GPS told him he'd arrived at his destination. Luke slammed on his breaks far more forcefully than necessary, which tossed his body forward, shoulders nearly bumping the steering wheel. Glancing around, Luke was confused. There was nothing but half-bare branches on the trees and the tips of green bulbs peeking out of heavy blankets of half-rotted leaves on the ground. Shoot. He must have put the wrong address in his GPS.

Checking in the rearview mirror once, Luke pulled out the sheet of paper he'd written down the address on and carefully typed it in again. As the GPS recalculated, he took one more glance around. Thirty yards behind him, something stuck out from a hedge of budding bushes. A silver mailbox. Luke clicked the car into reverse and slowly backed up until he was parallel to the large silver mailbox at the end of an over-grown dirt road. The mailbox's red flag was up, and the initials *MFS* were pasted across the side of the box in black letters. *MFS*. Maranatha Family Services.

So, it was real. He'd been so distracted he'd almost missed the entrance. The desire to leave without finding the Maranatha House had disappeared. Someone had put up the flag on that mailbox, which meant there was probably someone on the other end of the dirt road. Maybe that person would have answers. Luke held his breath as he left the road with a giant double bump as his tires settled into the soft dirt. He couldn't turn back. He'd come too far. Will was waiting for answers. Damn it, *he* was waiting for answers.

It took a few accelerations for Luke's tires to finally get enough trac-tion to head down the dusty road; he was thankful he'd gone with an SUV with four-wheel drive. Otherwise, he probably would be walking now, and his funeral suit would be getting dusty. Thankfully he wasn't walking, because the road was much longer than he'd expected.

Luke turned in to an empty spot next to a dark-brown Chrysler that had seen better days. The windows were brazenly rolled down, as if the owner was daring the sky to turn dark and rain. Luke patted his coat pocket to make sure the envelope was still there. Inside was an old picture of Natalie, a picture of Will as a baby, and a copy of Will's birth certificate, just in case. He'd planned out at least a dozen lies he could tell to get information out of the agency, but finally he decided he might as well tell the truth. They probably wouldn't give him any information either way—far too many legal issues with all the confidentiality agreements he was sure they signed on adoptions.

The large white house had a wraparound porch and sat in the middle of a green meadow, an incongruous site given the godforsaken road he'd just driven down. The battered Chrysler was one in a cluster of dusty cars parked by a barn several yards from the house. A wooden sign that said **OFFICE** hung off the white fence, the only hint the house wasn't a private residence. Luke stomped up the steps to the glossy green door at the top. A fluorescent yellow piece of paper, half-bleached from the sun, was taped inside the glass of the storm door. A crude drawing of hands holding a baby was at the top.

"Safe Haven for Babies. Desperate? Need help? You can leave your baby, up to a year old, inside with our staff. No questions asked. Use bell if after hours." A white button glowed beside the door.

Up to a year old. How could someone leave their one-year-old here, all those feedings, sleepless nights, smiles and giggles? Plus, what girl would want to drive down that dilapidated road to get here? He shook his head and walked through the door, a bell dinging to announce his entrance.

Inside was a surprisingly large lobby for what seemed like such a small organization. The chairs, covered in a rough maroon fabric, were placed in a semicircle facing an L-shaped desk. When the door shut, a woman called out from behind a computer screen. The only thing visible was her bright-pink acrylic nails waving him toward the sitting area.

"Be there in one sec. Take a seat."

Luke unbuttoned his suit coat and took the seat closest to the desk in case she forgot he was there.

After a few minutes of clacking, the computer woman stood and put a clipboard on the counter. Only she wasn't a woman; she was a teenager, no older than seventeen or eighteen. She was also very, very pregnant.

"Oh, hey there." She smiled when she saw Luke sitting alone and pointed to a large wooden door with a sign of a man and woman on it. "Your daughter going to the bathroom?" Luke opened his mouth to talk, but the girl interrupted. "Well, my name is Lacey. When your daughter gets out, you can have her fill all this out. I'll call Ms. Stephani so we can get right to orientation."

She put a tan headset to her ear and pressed several buttons, her nails tapping loudly against each one. Luke snagged up the clipboard and scanned the page.

Maranatha Family Services Maternity House Manual (Applicant Edition)

This Crisis Pregnancy Center is a nonprofit organization providing physical, emotional, and spiritual support services to women and families during pregnancy and provides residential services to women ages 12–19, regardless of income, who are pregnant and have chosen adoption.

Replacing the receiver on the phone, the girl called out to him, "Go ahead and read that, and then Ms. Stephani will take you into the office to do the rest of the paperwork. I'm not allowed in there, confidentiality and all." She whispered the last part, cupping her hand around her mouth. She looked at the bathroom door, eyebrows raised. "You sure she's okay in there? Maybe she's carsick?"

"No, I don't think that's the problem . . ."

A tall woman with bleached-blonde spiral curls and dark roots came through the open door. She had a giant smile, a light-blue shirt buttoned to the top, and bigger gums than Luke had ever seen. This must be Ms. Stephani.

"So, you're Dana's dad. So nice to meet you." She thrust out her hand, her excitement so real Luke almost felt bad he didn't have a pregnant daughter hanging out in the restroom for a ridiculous amount of time. Luke shook her hand once.

"Actually, I think there's been some sort of misunderstanding. I'm not here with my daughter."

Ms. Stephani took her hand back and tilted her head side to side like a cockatoo, her friendly demeanor fading fast.

"Oh? Did she change her mind?" Her face looked older when she wasn't smiling. Late fifties maybe.

"No. My daughter is nine and is having fun in the fourth grade learning about tadpoles and long division." He wanted to add "thank God," but thought that could sound judgmental.

"Your daughter is *nine*?" Lacey chimed in, leaning over the counter.

"Hush, Lacey. Go into the house. This is none of your business." Ms. Stephani shooed the girl, flapping her hand toward the open doorway. "Now. Or you lose your front desk shift and have to switch with Daisy in the kitchen."

"Fine," Lacey huffed but stood and waddled toward the door, glancing at the closed bathroom one last time before turning the corner as if she still expected someone to come out of it. Once she was gone, Ms. Stephani turned around to face Luke, her face distorted, suspicious.

"Please, follow me into the office." On the other side of the desk, there was a sliding door with an OFFICE sign printed in bold letters above it. The office within the office. This couldn't be good. Once when Luke was eleven, his fifth-grade teacher sent him to the principal's office when he refused to dissect a frog in science class. Eleven-year-old Luke was only slightly more nervous than thirty-seven-year-old Luke at that moment.

Luke didn't know what to expect inside the Maranatha House office. Judging by Ms. Stephani's appearance, he'd guess piles of dusty books and maybe a cat or two. So what met him inside was a pleasant surprise. First, a large oak desk with a rolling leather chair behind it and two neatly upholstered wing-back chairs covered in a floral print. The room was painted a soft yellow with white trim; pictures hung on the wall with hundreds of anonymous faces staring back at him. He felt like he was in the sitting room of an old country farmhouse, not the office of a mysterious adoption agency. Once they both sat down, Ms. Stephani spoke first.

"I'm going to stop making assumptions about who you are or why you are here. But before you speak, please understand we respect our residents' privacy and cannot release any information about guests past or present or their children. So if you are here to ask questions of a confidential nature, I'm sorry, but I must ask you to leave."

Ignoring her request, Luke reached into his coat pocket, grabbed a slick piece of glossy photograph paper, and slapped it down on the amber wood desktop. "This is my wife."

It was a picture of Natalie two Easters ago, when her mother visited and insisted the children attend church. Before Ewing's sarcoma was a regular part of their vocabulary. Natalie wore a yellow sundress with lace around the shoulders and neckline. The yellow made her skin look like porcelain. May wore a light-pink dress with tiny flowers printed on it. She was seven at the time and looked like a smaller version of her current self. Will had gone through puberty since then. The little boy in that picture, his hair combed back with a perfect part, tie on crooked, was so familiar, yet so different than the son he'd left at home.

Ms. Stephani didn't move to touch the photo, but leaned forward just enough to peek at it. "She seems very nice, but we don't serve adults here, only young women ages twelve to nineteen."

"She's not pregnant." He nudged the picture forward. "Her name was Natalie Richardson, and she's dead." Luke tried to gauge Ms.

Stephani's reaction to hearing Natalie's name, but her face was blank. "While going through some of her belongings, my fourteen-year-old son found an envelope from Maranatha Family Services postmarked a few weeks before his birth. Now the kid has it in his mind he's adopted."

Ms. Stephani kept her arms folded in front of her on the desk, not letting her gaze leave Luke's. "I still don't see how we can help you."

"Listen. I know he's not adopted." He wrestled the folded envelope out of his pocket, a flake of spiral notebook paper fluttering onto his thigh. Luke stared at it for a moment before sliding it off into his palm. As discreetly as possible he dropped it back into his pocket, patting it softly to make sure the scrap of paper was secure. Ms. Stephani cleared her throat, and Luke remembered why he was there. "I mean, I wasn't actually there through the whole pregnancy, but still . . ." Luke unfolded the envelope and held it up for Ms. Stephani to inspect. "I was hoping you'd have some idea where this envelope came from since I can't exactly ask Natalie."

She squinted, her lashes, heavy with mascara, nearly touching. "That is from the legal arm of our organization in Chicago. It facilitates any adoption from a young lady who spent her time at one of the six Maranatha Family Service homes throughout Illinois, Indiana, and Michigan. The adoptions are usually regional. Other than that, there's not much I can tell you." She leaned back in her chair till it squeaked as if the springs were about to break.

This was a dead end.

Swallowing his irritation, Luke snatched the documents and picture off the table and stood quickly. Defeated and disappointed, he needed to get out of the office before he exploded.

"Well, thank you for your help," he spat, twisting the words enough to make it sound like an accusation. He didn't know what he'd expected, but an immovable, compassionless wall was not it. Luke turned to leave, his face hot and teeth clenched, but he heard Ms. Stephani's voice one last time over his shoulder.

"I'm so very sorry for your loss. Natalie was a . . ." Her voice wavered like she was holding back tears. She coughed and tried again. "I'm sure your wife was a wonderful woman."

When her words soaked in, the room began to spin. He caught hold of the door frame and turned around, mouth open. He'd push harder this time, get real answers. But one look at Ms. Stephani's face let him know that all kindness and pity were gone. If he was going to go up against this version of Ms. Stephani, he'd need more information and maybe a lawyer.

"Thank you." Luke cleared his throat and put his hand on the doorknob, ready to leave. Taking a moment at the door he paused, straightened his back, and turned his face to stone before walking into the lobby. In that pause, one of the hundreds of pictures covering the wall caught his eye. It hung right above the door, a group of six smiling couples wearing matching purple T-shirts with Maranatha Family Services across the front. The photo was faded from years of sunlight pouring in from the curtained window on the opposite side of the room, so determining its age was difficult. But looking at the photo he did know one thing—Natalie was one of the faces smiling out at him. Her hair was pulled back in a long dark ponytail, and she was smiling so widely he could almost see her molars. Right next to Natalie was another familiar face: her high school boyfriend, Andy Garner.

CHAPTER 10

Luke stumbled out of the Maranatha House in a fog. With one hard push he opened the front door, the ancient hinges whining back at him. A hand tapped him on his back as he started down the peeling wooden steps, and he slowed only for a second to take the off-white trifold brochure Ms. Stephani silently offered him.

It wasn't until he smashed the unlock button on his car that Luke realized he'd never even told them his name. It was too late; nothing could entice him back inside now. He tossed the brochure onto the passenger seat, slid inside, and slammed the door.

Revving the engine, he forced the car into reverse, creating a cloud of dust. No careful turns and easing over hills this time. Luke needed to get away from this place and the secrets inside it as fast as his three-ton SUV would take him. As soon as his tires hit asphalt, the undercarriage scraping as he left the dirt road, Luke flicked on the radio, punching buttons till he found a song that suited his mood. He needed something confused but angry, with a touch of betrayal.

Once the bass was pumping so loud his eardrums hurt, he pushed the gas pedal to the floor, merging onto the empty highway within minutes. He didn't want to think. Thinking only hurt, only made tears of fury cloud his vision. He didn't know what that picture meant, but it did explain why she had the Maranatha envelope in her box. It's not like he could tell Will that. Damn it. What was he going to tell Will?

Despite the blaring music, Luke's mind raced through various scenarios of why Natalie could possibly be in those pictures and why she was in them with Andy. He'd seen Andy several times since reconnecting with Natalie at Michigan University. Andy'd been to their wedding, and in the early years of their marriage, Andy would sometimes stop by for dinner if he happened to be in town. But Luke hadn't seen him in over ten years.

Instead of going to college, Andy stayed behind in their small, lakeside town of Pentwater to take over his father's real estate business. If Luke remembered correctly, the offices were right off Main Street, only a block away from One More Time, the used bookstore where his mother used to work.

Pentwater was a fishing town turned tourist attraction, and perfectly situated between the resort community of Silver Lake and the small but growing city of Ludington. Between selling vacation homes by the dunes and real homes in town, Andy and his dad were always busy. Especially during the housing boom that accompanied the beginning of the 2000s.

Andy had visited Ann Arbor twice while Luke was dating Natalie and once during their engagement. They'd been kids together, grown up in the same town until high school, but seeing him again in Ann Arbor fifteen years ago was like meeting a stranger.

◆ ◆ ◆

The first time Luke saw Andy at the University of Michigan, he was running through the quad at full speed. As he flew across the yard, the lanky twenty-year-old dropped his shoulder bag halfway between the sidewalk and Natalie. When he reached her, Andy scooped Natalie up in a bear hug more appropriate for a recovered hostage or a returning war hero.

Luke had sized Andy up. Though taller than in junior high, Andy was still a head shorter than Luke and was in his pre-real estate, full-on grunge phase. Back then he still thought he'd get out of Pentwater and make it as a musician. His dark hair brushed the top of his shoulders and fell into his almost black eyes. It looked like he hadn't eaten real food in a month, and the baggy shirt he wore barely covered the boxers showing at the top of his saggy jeans. Andy's appearance had reassured Luke at the time. Natalie liked clean-cut guys, or at least that's what she'd always said.

After spinning Natalie until she yelped, Andy put her down gently, holding her at arm's length for a second longer. When he let go, she wobbled on her feet, grabbing Luke's arm for balance. Her cheeks flushed pink in the way they did when she was truly happy.

"I've missed your pretty face, Nats!" He pushed the long clump of hair out of his eyes. "Why don't you come home anymore?"

Natalie looked at her shoes, drawing circles in the dirt. "Life is busy, I guess. Plus, my parents don't even live there anymore—kind of lost my excuse for visiting."

Andy clutched at his chest like his heart was going to explode; one of his fingernails on each hand was painted black. "Oh, you know how to wound a man's pride! Lost your reason to visit? I'm not reason enough?"

"Stop it." She swatted at him playfully. "Of course you are. Maybe Luke and I can take a visit out there for spring break. I know it's a bit early for the seasonal stuff, but we could get a room for next to nothing."

When Natalie mentioned Luke, Andy seemed to notice him for the first time since the dramatic reunion. Andy ran his eyes over Luke, looking warily at his tucked-in polo and belted jeans.

"Hey there, Luke. Been a while." They'd been in school together from kindergarten to eighth grade. Andy had been a chubby kid with a huge bug collection he'd bring to school every year for show-and-tell, which did nothing to help him make friends. Then again, Luke was the son of the town drunk, so neither of them was exactly "cool." Andy gave two strong shakes and let his hand drop. "Nats used to talk about you all the time back in the old days. You know, when you left and broke her heart." He chuckled like it was a joke and not a dig.

"Well, I'm okay now. I mean, when you're fourteen you don't have a whole lot of choice in where you live . . ." Natalie broke in, probably sensing the hostile undercurrent between her current boyfriend and her past boyfriend. "I forgave him a long time ago." She put another hand on Luke's arm and stood on her toes to place a soft kiss on his cheek. Yeah. That's all it took. He never worried about Andy and Natalie again.

◆ ◆ ◆

Luke was never a jealous guy, and though he found Natalie and Andy's relationship immature and slightly annoying, it had never concerned him. Now Luke wished he'd been the suspicious type. How on earth did he go from never questioning his wife's loyalty when she was alive to questioning it constantly now that she was gone?

The next two hundred miles went by in a blur of bare trees and small towns. When Luke finally pulled into his driveway, passing Jessie's car on his way into the garage, it was 5:15 p.m. Perfect timing. He took a second to gather the papers he'd thrown on the front seat, including the brochure he'd rather burn than look at ever again. Carelessly, he tried to shove them into the back pocket of his workbag.

It wasn't until he walked through the door and was hit by the scent of tomatoes simmering with garlic and butter that he remembered he hadn't eaten all day. His stomach growled, but he still took the time to place his workbag out of sight. He needed to ensure no prying hands could uncover the secrets stowed inside. Reentering the hall, Luke removed his still-dusty dress shoes. When the second shoe fell out of the overflowing shoe basket, a rush of footsteps stomped out of the kitchen.

"Daddy!" May ran toward him, her long hair streaming behind her except for the frayed damp chunk hanging next to her face. She jumped into his arms and pressed her moist cheek against his. "How was work?" she chirped like Natalie used to.

"Just fine, sweetie." He kissed her forehead.

"Dad!" Luke couldn't remember the last time Will came out to greet him after work. Even worse, he couldn't recall a day Will seemed excited to see him. After a long day, Will's happy face reminded him why he had so many covert errands. "How was your trip?"

"Trip?" May tugged at the arms of her oversize blue-and-green sweater, her fingers making giant holes. Luke was almost certain it belonged to her mother. "I want to go. Is it business? I can be very perfessional," she said proudly, although struggling with her new word. "I help at the school store, Daddy, and Jessie says I can have a garage sale this summer if it's okay with you."

Jessie stood in the hall leading out from the kitchen dressed in her usual uniform of jeans, an oversize T-shirt—this one filled with rainbow letters—and ballet slippers. She really wasn't much taller than May, and her features were small, nymphlike almost. Her dark hair was pulled back, as always, in a high ponytail that touched her shoulders. Today the darkness under her eyes made him wonder if she was working too hard—or maybe if the medical problems Natalie mentioned in her letter were acting up. He really didn't know how to bring that up though. Better not to.

Jessie leaned against the picture wall, in between a picture of Will from eighth-grade graduation and another one of Luke and Natalie, all in white, sitting in the tall grass together during a professional photo shoot they had done when Clayton was three months old.

"Sorry," she said, giving a short wave before folding her arms and clearing her throat. "I thought I'd have plenty of time to pass that plan by you."

"You definitely have plenty of time to pass it by me. I know it's April, but that doesn't mean the snow is over."

"I'm ready for sketti now, Jessie!" Clayton shouted from the kitchen. "I'm waaaaaaaiting!"

"I sure taught that kid some awesome manners, didn't I?" Luke chuckled, shrugging out of his suit coat. As soon as it was off, May pulled it out of his hands and ran toward the stairs with it.

"I got this one," she shouted. Her overattentiveness should have been adorable, but it made him worry she was trying to fill her mother's shoes with her nine-year-old feet. Will sat down on the bottom step, apparently willing to sit through all the boring adult small talk in order to get the lowdown on what happened at Maranatha. Luke stalled, heading to the kitchen, still unsure of how much to tell his son.

"Did the handoff with Annie go all right? Any temper tantrums today?" Luke asked Jessie, rustling Clayton's hair. The eager boy was already seated at the table with a fork clutched in one hand and a butter knife in the other. Luke expertly whisked the knife away and replaced it with one of the strips of garlic bread cooling on the counter.

"It was actually really great. I don't know if it was the early nap or being home all day, but he was a happy boy today."

"That's great." Luke took a quick sweeping glance around the spotless room. A pot of sauce bubbled on the stove, bread sat on the cutting board, a colorful tossed salad looked appealing on the table with a small dish of homemade dressing—not the bottled Paul Newman stuff—nearby. No wonder she looked so tired. "Dinner looks great. You really didn't have to—"

She cut him off, holding up both her hands. "Oh, no! Can't take credit for any of this. It was Annie. She had everything ready when I got here; all I had to do was set it on the stove at five to warm up."

So it was Annie. "Hey, you remembered to warm it up, so I'm giving you some credit." Luke counted out four plates from his fresh stack of paper products and laid them on the table. He paused and looked Jessie over again. "You should stay for dinner. Looks like we've got plenty, and after all, you did *so* much work . . ."

"Ha-ha. Hilarious." Jessie flapped a hand at him and twisted her lips up to one side. Natalie used to do something very similar when he teased her. "I actually have a date tonight, so I'll have to pass."

"You have a date?" May ran in, breathless from her errand. She almost bumped into Will, who was leaning against the wall, still waiting and listening. "Who is he? Where are you going?" She folded her arms, looking over Jessie with a sour pout on her face. "Are you wearing *that*?"

The questions poured out of her mouth without stopping. She was so excited you'd think she was the one invited to meet a boy for dinner. May raised both of her arms above her head to free her hands from the giant sweater's engulfing sleeves and clasped them in front of her. Jessie shook her head, bangs tickling the top of her eyebrows.

"Yes, I am wearing this," she answered, smirking defiantly and pulling the bottom of her oversize T-shirt taut so they could better see the logo of *Joseph and the Amazing Technicolor Dreamcoat*. May rushed across the kitchen to stand beside her beloved Jessie, who ran her fingers through May's tangled hair, each nail painted a different color of the rainbow. "And I'm sorry to disappoint you, but it's only a date with my dad."

"Oh," May huffed, obviously disappointed Jessie wasn't meeting her Prince Charming. "You need a boyfriend."

Jessie's smile stiffened, and she pulled her fingers out from a knot in May's hair. "It's not really that easy, honey."

May shrugged. "I guess, but Jessie, who wouldn't like *you*?" She gazed up at her babysitter and newly acquired role model. What May couldn't see was the way Jessie's eyes were moist, lips pressed together like she was holding back a story.

"You'd be surprised, sweetie." This time Jessie laughed. "Anyway, Dad is waiting."

"Don't go yet!" May yanked at Jessie's arm. "Can you stay for pizza next week, then? Please? It's for my birthday."

"I'm sure Jessie has something more important to do with her Friday nights than spend it eating pizza with us." Luke placed the steaming pot of drained noodles in the middle of the table and pressed a clawed serving spoon in the center. Will put out paper plates and plastic forks. He was never this helpful. Poor kid must be dying for information.

"Next Friday? Actually, I'm totally free. I could bring ice cream to go with the cake."

"Oh *yes*! Thank you, Jessie. We'll have so much fun." May yanked at Jessie's arm for the fifth time. Jessie pulled it away gently, letting the tiniest ripple of irritation wrinkle her forehead.

"It's fine with me," Luke said, and added, "if you really want to come."

"I do," she reassured them.

Luke watched them together, hiding behind the refrigerator door as he fished out the green container of Parmesan cheese. May flitted around Jessie making detailed plans for the night of her party as Jessie collected her things and pulled out her keys to leave. May didn't know how to read the "I need to leave now" social cue.

"May, let Jessie go. She's had a long day," Luke called out, waving his hand toward the table. "Anyway, it's time to eat."

May stomped her foot but then complied after giving Jessie one more quick hug.

"Thanks again, Jessie," Luke said.

"No problem, Mr. Richardson. You have a nice weekend," Jessie called over her shoulder as she disappeared into the front hall. She seemed sincere, like she really wanted to spend her free time with his children, like she didn't mind working to the point of exhaustion. Yet there was still an uncomfortable gnawing in his gut telling him it wasn't compassion or even the money motivating her, but her obligation to Natalie. What would they do when the obligation wore out and she left them?

CHAPTER 11

After Jessie left, everyone stuffed themselves full of Annie's special spaghetti sauce. Then Clayton settled on the couch for a show before bedtime, while May took a much needed bath after getting more sauce on her face and clothes than in her stomach.

Still in his dress shirt, somehow spotless even after the messy dinner, Luke rolled up his sleeves to do the few dishes in the sink. He ran the water until steam rolled off the faucet, wanting the water as hot as the heater in the basement could get it. He wanted to focus on the sting of the water, the way his skin screamed and begged him to stop. Pain was better than remembering everything else that happened that day. As he was about to plunge his hands into the bubbly water, Will called to him from the front room.

"Dad! Where did you put the brochure you said you got? Is it in your workbag?" He'd given Will a brief rundown of his Maranatha visit as they cleared the table together. It was a highly edited version of the story, of course, but Luke hoped it'd keep Will's curiosity at bay for a little while at least. As he heard Will messing with the zipper on his bag, he remembered the new Natalie letter behind the brochure. That would only bring up more questions for the already confused teenager.

"Wait! I'll get it for you," Luke shouted, pushing away from the sink. He reached Will barely in time, as the boy was peering into the black laptop bag.

"I'll find it."

Luke stuck out his hand.

"Ooooo-kay." Will held out the bag and Luke grabbed it. Sitting down on the second step, it only took him a few seconds to find the brochure he'd tucked behind the unsorted mail, and right behind that, an unread Natalie letter that had come in the mail the day before.

Luke took the unopened letter out of the bag and nearly bumped into Will when he stood up. Before he could think better of it, he held out the sepia-toned brochure to his son.

"This is all I've got. Sorry."

Will didn't seem to mind. He grabbed it eagerly and stared at the words on the front page as if they held the secret to eternal life.

"No, this is perfect. Thanks for going, Dad."

For a second Luke thought Will was going to hug him again. Two hugs in a month would be a record. Instead, he gave Luke a crooked smile and settled into a chair in the front room.

Luke returned to his spot on the stairs with Natalie's letter. After everything that had happened, he didn't want to read it. It'd feel better to put it away unopened, or even better, shove it through the shredder at work, where it would end up chopped into tiny, unreadable confetti squares. But the blue envelope was already in his hands, his expert fingers estimating two pages folded inside.

He ripped open the letter and two pages of notebook paper slid out—right again. But seeing her handwriting never got easier. The first line caught his eye: "Dear Luke, I'm going to make you so mad at me today." Luke quickly folded the paper in half, afraid of what he might read next. His hands shook so badly; it all felt like too much in one day—the long trip to Kalamazoo, the picture of Andy and Natalie smiling back at him like they shared a secret he wasn't supposed to know, Will's anxious questions. Now, this letter. Luke traced the lines of Natalie's handwriting through the back of the thin notebook paper.

What could make any of this worse? Luke wondered. Even if she confirmed one of the million scenarios rolling around in his head, answers, any answers, would be better than not knowing. He needed answers.

DAY 103

Dear Luke,

I'm going to make you so mad at me today. First, let me remind you I've been a nice girl lately and haven't been bossing you around nearly enough in the past few weeks. If you think about it, you really, really miss my nagging. I know you do.

So here it is. We had one of our deep conversations last night, the ones you hate where we talk about what happens if I don't make it through this thing. I only have two rounds of chemo left, and then we get to find out how I did, how my body did fighting off those cancer cells that could right now be burrowing into my body like seeds in the dirt, ready to burst to life after a dormant season.

As usual, you didn't want to talk about the very real possibility that those post-chemo and radiation scans at the end of June might not bring good news. I guess I don't totally blame you. I'd probably be the same way if things were the other way around. That's why I'm writing these letters, right? So I can say things to you I couldn't in real life . . . even if I know it will make you mad. It may be a cowardly way to handle things, but I think it's better than leaving those things unsaid, don't you?

I've been watching you sleep. It's not as creepy as it sounds; I do it when the worry keeps me awake. Usually I run through scenes in my head, potential endings to this nightmare. Last night was a little different though. The insomnia was brought on by something you said before you dozed off.

I was curled up against you, careful to keep the side of my chest with the chemo port tilted away. You kissed my forehead and said, "You can't leave me; I love you too much."

"I know; me too," I said. I nuzzled in closer, pressing my lips against your stubbly neck, enjoying the familiar smell of Zest soap on your skin. "Unfortunately, cancer isn't scared off by love."

"Mmmm, I guess not." Your eyes were closed, and I wasn't sure if you even remembered what we were talking about. "But our love is different. It's a once-in-a-lifetime kind of love. I could never love someone else like I love you."

I raised my head up. Tried to look into your eyes. You didn't notice, half-asleep. "No, you're wrong. You could and you will. You have to." I waited for you to argue back, tell me why you could never remarry, why I was wrong, but you didn't. You slept, and I cried because I don't want you to be alone.

You're a good man but a quiet man, and I'm afraid of how you'll cope being alone. Except for those few years in high school and college, we've been together for most of our adult lives. You have no living family besides the kids and me; your social group is made up of Brian, a few engineers who, combined, have all the personality of a protractor, and we all know my mom isn't so happy to spend time with you (sorry about that).

It's probably only been a few months since you buried me, and I understand if that's a little fast for you to feel open to a new relationship. You don't have to start right now. I'm asking you to keep your mind open to the idea of someone new.

You deserve to be happy. I know a relationship wouldn't mean instant happiness—I'm not that naive—*but* I'd feel better knowing you'll at least give it a try. Here is a heads-up: you have two months to arrange a date on your own, and then I have a few plans on how to help you, even if I'm not there in person.

I hope you're not too mad at me. At least I'm not there to see your face; you know I could never resist your grouchy look. Kiss the kids and tell them I love them. Keep your eyes open. You never know when you could meet someone new.

Love,

Natalie

Luke barely got to the end of the letter before crumpling it in his palm. Four months into treatment—what did Natalie know back then? She was almost done with chemo. She still had surgery on her shoulder blade and five weeks of radiation before those damn scans that said she was cancer-free. She had no idea back then that the letters she was writing really did predict the future, that she was going to die and leave them behind. Reading letters where she blithely blathered on about dating and remarriage made Luke want to throw the ball of paper across the room.

He crunched the papers as hard as he could until the crumpled edges pressed into his palm. Then he had an unsettling thought—perhaps she could talk about "finding someone new" because she had someone new. Maybe she knew from experience that it's possible to love your family but love another person too—another person like Andy.

Luke put the compressed ball of paper into his pants pocket so he could dispose of it later when the kids were sleeping. He knew it should make him feel strange to throw away one of Natalie's letters, but this time it felt good. There was too much to think about with his visit to Maranatha House and the picture he'd discovered there. He shook his head, finally remembering the sink full of dishes and steaming water waiting for him in the kitchen. With a yank at his rolled-up sleeves, he headed for the kitchen. Will intercepted him as he was about to put his hands in the sudsy water.

"Dad! Wait!" Will shook the glossy brochure in Luke's face. "I found something."

Luke glanced at the water and back at his son. He took the trifold brochure out of Will's hands.

"What did you find?" Flipping it open, Luke wished he had looked through the booklet before letting his fourteen-year-old have a go at it.

Will pushed his hair out of his eyes and placed his index finger at a small thumbnail photo in the corner of the Maranatha House brochure. It was a close-up black-and-white photo of a smiling young man. Looked like a stock photo until Luke squinted. He knew that face.

"Isn't that Uncle Andy?" Will took a step back and studied his father, crossing his arms across his chest.

"Uh, I'm not sure. Kinda looks like him though, doesn't it?" Luke couldn't let on what he already knew—the picture of Andy and Natalie wearing matching T-shirts, arms around each other, smiling like they belonged together.

"Yeah, it does, but he looks really skinny there. Is that what he looked like when you and Mom met?"

Luke nodded and slowly folded the brochure. He held it out to Will, who grabbed it and opened to the same photo again, studying it carefully.

"It looks a little like him, but I told you, that place wouldn't give me any information."

"You should call him. This is a good clue. Maybe Uncle Andy and Mom knew someone there, or maybe it was for their high school community service hours, or maybe Andy is my . . ." Will's voice trailed off, and a lump filled Luke's throat. That wasn't the thought he'd been avoiding all day, but it was close. He coughed.

"Okay, I'll call him in a few days," Luke said in an attempt to end the conversation even though calling Andy Garner was the last thing in the world he wanted to do. Luke rolled up his sleeve one more time until it hugged his bicep. "First, I need to do the dishes."

Will hesitated, his shoulders slumping inside his grungy hoodie. "Or we could wait until we know more."

Luke nodded and plunged his hands into the water. Will tucked the brochure into the front pocket of his hoodie and pulled out a pair of white earbuds. He put one in his right ear and then paused. "Yeah, we should wait. We don't even know if the guy in that picture is Uncle Andy." Without waiting for a response, Will put in the other earbud and stomped up the stairs to his room.

Luke yanked the plug in the sink, angry. Angry that the water had turned cold, that his son was peppering him with questions, and most of all, angry that he knew the man in the picture *was* Andy Garner.

The picture had been cropped so only Andy's face and shoulders were showing, but he hadn't been the only one in the picture when it was taken. Over his left shoulder a hand hung down, and on that hand was a ring. Natalie's engagement ring.

The sink emptied quickly, and Luke turned on the water and let it run until it steamed. When the sink was full, Luke submerged his hands into the water and savored the scalding. This time it couldn't distract him, not enough anyway. He could stop all Will's questions permanently with one simple paternity test. Then, when the results came in, Luke would show them to Will and say, "See? I am your dad!" The test would stop Will's questions, but it couldn't stop the questions percolating in Luke's mind. It definitely wouldn't quiet the one thought that had stopped him from enjoying the spaghetti or laughing at Clay's sauce-covered face. Maybe Uncle Andy was someone else's dad and that child's mother was Natalie.

MAY

CHAPTER 12

Luke slathered the last bit of chocolate frosting from the can onto the angel food cake. May's birthday request. Luke hated canned frosting, but he wasn't up for an attempt at homemade. Once all the crumbs were concealed under another layer of frosting, Luke checked in the family room to see who wanted to give the chocolate-covered spatula a lick.

"Hey, is that up for grabs?" Natalie peeked around the corner and snatched the spatula out of his hand. She was wearing her favorite pair of jeans, the ones with a hole in the knee that hugged her hips and rear in precisely the right way. A clingy blue V-neck T-shirt set off the deep blue of her eyes.

"Hey! I usually charge a kiss." He laughed, pretending to reach for the utensil.

Natalie swiped a finger full of frosting into her mouth. "Mmmmm," she mumbled. "Totally worth it."

"Pay up, hot stuff." He took a step closer. She smelled like her favorite shampoo and body lotion. A smudge of frosting clung to the corner of her mouth. Luke wiped it away with his thumb, tipping her chin up at the same time. He'd loved that face almost as long as he could remember, and it only grew more beautiful with age. The fine lines on her forehead, between her eyes, and around her mouth were subtle, a delicate record in flesh of the life they'd lived together.

"I love you, Nat," he whispered, watching her lips, wanting to kiss her as much as the first time he'd gotten up the nerve as an eighth-grade boy. He ran his tongue over his lips and met hers gently. They fit perfectly, her head tipped to the right, his to the left.

"I love you too," she said, the words flowing out over his lips in a warm wave. Luke put his hand around her waist and pulled her in close, her body pressing against his. Her lips parted, and Luke's fingers threaded through the loops on her jeans. She tasted like chocolate.

The doorbell rang in the background. Luke groaned as Natalie pulled away, placing one last kiss lightly on his tingling lips.

"You'd better get that," she whispered and took another step back. Somehow Luke knew she wasn't heading for the door.

"They can wait. Don't go," he begged, but her hand slipped out of his, their fingertips brushing as she backed away. The doorbell rang again. Luke ignored it. He wanted to go after her, but his feet wouldn't budge. Natalie took another step backward and another, the darkness from the dining room swallowing her whole. "Natalie! No!"

A swirling blackness flooded in around him, touching his skin, filling his mouth with each breath until he couldn't take in any more air. The room turned dark, and terror wrapped hands around his throat so he couldn't scream.

A hand on his shoulder shook him, and Luke started awake. It took a moment to understand his surroundings. The family room, kitchen, door to the dining room, cake on the counter only half-frosted, Natalie's latest letter across his chest.

"Daddy, everybody's here." May knelt beside him on the couch dressed in a blue tulle skirt and matching shirt with sequins. It was a present from Grandma Terry. Not something Luke would pick for a nine, almost ten-year-old girl, but May couldn't resist the sparkles. Her

144

hair hung over her shoulders in two semirespectable braids. It had taken months of practice, but he was getting close to proficient.

"Sorry; I dozed off." He tugged on one of her braids affectionately. "You can get the door."

"Will got it," she chirped before kissing his cheek. The noise from the hall moved toward the back of the house. Annie stuck her head through the doorway.

"Hey there. Heard you fell asleep on the job." She hugged a thin cardigan around her torso, far more dressed up than he was used to seeing her in his house. Her straight-legged jeans brushed the floor with each step, short hair pinned back from her face with bobby pins. Her eyes lingered on the letter pressed to Luke's chest, and a little frown tugged at the corner of her mouth.

"Yeah, sorry. I think I taste tested a little too much of the frosting and it put me in a sugar coma." Luke laughed it off, trying to forget the very real dream he'd been sucked out of.

"That cake looks like it could use a little help." This time her frown was playful. He glanced over at the white cake, half-covered in chocolate frosting with little bits of cake mixed in it.

"I never turn down free help," Luke said, folding Natalie's letter quickly and putting it in his front pocket.

"Free? Who said it'd be free?" Annie laughed. "Hey, do you have an apron?" She gestured to her fancy getup.

"I'm sure I still have some in one of the pantry closets. Let me look." Luke crossed from the couch to the white bifold doors against the back wall of the kitchen, opened them, and rummaged through a box of fabric, pot holders, and bibs till he grabbed a long thin string of fabric that appeared to be an apron ribbon. "Here you go!"

Luke tossed the apron across the room and Annie caught it. She shook out the wrinkles from the oversize white apron and froze.

"Do you have another one?" Her voice quavered like she was about to cry. She turned the apron around. It was Natalie's Mother's Day apron, with all the kids' hand- and footprints on it. They'd made it with Natalie's mom before Clayton could walk. Luke turned away before he could remember the last Mother's Day together before the diagnosis.

He cleared his throat and searched more carefully this time, selecting the apron he used when grilling. It said something stupid like "Kiss the Cook," but it was better. May's birthday was the first big family celebration since Natalie's death, and though they were all putting on a convincing impression of having fun, the fewer reminders of what was missing, the better.

For Luke, remembering was hard in a different way. On days like today, Luke missed the old Natalie—his wife, mother of his children, the woman he thought he knew. But in order to miss her like that, he had to push all of his questions aside.

As for Andy Garner, Luke had gone as far as finding him on Facebook, but the guy's account was set to private. He hadn't come to the funeral, but Natalie used to take the kids to visit him. On Facebook, all Luke found was a picture of a man, who must be Andy, in a hat and sunglasses holding up a large silver fish. Dr. Neal, in contrast, remained a mysterious figure, and all efforts at digging up information had come to a halt as Luke focused on planning May's party.

Suddenly Annie was beside him, a hand on his back between the shoulder blades. That was her normal spot now. Her liberally displayed affection used to bother him, but he was starting to remember how nice it was to be comforted by another living human. There's only so much comfort that notebook paper could provide.

"I'll put this back in here. It's special. I wouldn't want to get it dirty." She placed the folded apron into the bin and slipped the new one over her head. "Besides, this is more my style, don't you think?" She modeled the red-checkered apron with hands on her hips.

Luke chuckled. "Oh yes. Very chic."

"Will you tighten this for me?" She'd already wrapped the strings around her waist three or four times and tied them in the front, but the neckline sagged low, providing little protection for her top half. Annie turned around and stared at her feet, exposing the metal buckle at the base of her neck. Luke took a step closer, suddenly overly aware of how she smelled like flowers. He wiped his hands on his pant leg and reached for the aluminum clip. As he grabbed it, Brian's deep voice interrupted.

"Where do you want me to put this salad, babe?" Brian didn't wait for a response and instead tossed a green plastic bowl on the kitchen island, where it bumped against the already pathetic cake. "Nice apron." Brian laughed, making his way across the kitchen. He ran his index finger along the words printed on the fabric sagging across her chest. Kiss the Cook. Grabbing her chin roughly with his thumb and forefinger, Brian whispered, "Don't mind if I do," and planted one right on Annie's mouth.

Annie's head jerked back at first, but Brian didn't seem to notice. He wrapped one hand around her waist, pulling her into him just like Luke had dreamed about doing with Natalie. It took Luke a moment to realize he was still holding the clip on Annie's apron.

He dropped it and backed away, staring at the ground, wishing he didn't feel a swell of jealousy in his chest. He told himself that he wasn't jealous because Brian was kissing Annie. He was jealous because he could never kiss Natalie ever again.

Annie pushed Brian away, out of breath.

"Brian!" She slapped his shoulder. "There are children present!"

"Who, Luke?" Brian nuzzled Annie's cheek with his nose. "I'm sure he's figured out the birds and the bees by now."

Annie glanced over her shoulder, cheeks flushed and worry lines around her eyes. Luke had become far too familiar with that look on her face. He was getting good at reading Annie. The more time they spent together, the less she felt like this image he had of Natalie's best friend and the more she seemed like her own, three-dimensional person, a complicated puzzle for which he didn't have all the pieces.

"There's beer in the fridge if you need to cool down, loverboy," Luke joked in an attempt to make Annie feel better. He'd never figured out the whole dude-bro thing, but he'd been around long enough to know how to fake it. "Annie promised to help me finish this cake."

Brian spun Annie out like a professional ballroom dancer, and her laugh echoed through the kitchen. Clayton must've heard it from his bedroom because seconds later there was a chorus of stomping feet on the stairs.

"Annie!" A little blond head bobbed up and down in a blur through the kitchen, leaping into Annie's arms. "I missed you."

"I missed you too, bud." Annie kissed the top of his head and gave Clayton a hug that could crunch bones.

"It's been less than a day. I don't think that counts as long enough to miss someone," Brian said under his breath.

"I missed you too, Mr. Brian," Clayton said before shoving his pruned fingers in his mouth.

Brian cocked his head to the side like a dog hearing a sound for the first time.

"Huh?" He chuckled and ruffled Clayton's hair. "I missed you too, kid."

Annie smiled up at her husband in a way Luke had never seen. He'd seen embarrassed, entertained, happy, and annoyed, but at this moment she looked proud. Snuggling Clayton in tighter, Annie headed for the cake.

"You want to help me decorate May's cake?" she asked. "I'll let you lick the spoon." Propped on Annie's hip, Clayton nodded emphatically.

Brian stood in front of Luke, suddenly dropping his jokester demeanor.

"So, Luke, I have a huge *favor* to ask of you." He'd found a beer from the fridge and opened it already. The way Brian emphasized "favor" made the muscles in Luke's shoulders tighten.

"Sure. What's up?"

"I don't know if Annie told you or not, but I'm interviewing for a new job right now."

"A new job? Like a promotion within the police department?"

"No." Brian took a swig. "Not with the police department at all. It's with this private security company." He smoothed out his button-up shirt—always put together, tidy, efficient.

"Oh, that sounds . . . great." Luke raised his eyebrows and pretended he knew what a job in "private security" entailed.

"I'm trying not to get my hopes too high, but I'm pretty excited about the opportunity. More flexibility, more perks, more money." He said the last part quietly.

Luke shuffled his feet and tried to figure out where the whole conversation was heading. "Sounds exciting," was the best he could muster.

"It's cool stuff, like Secret Service for rich people." He finished off his beer in one long drink. "So, anyway, I needed some personal references, and it couldn't be anyone from the station. I wondered if I could, maybe, put your name down? They might call you, ask some questions. You up for that?"

Brian placed a heavy hand on Luke's shoulder, and Luke could see why the police officer was good at his job. If you'd committed a crime, Brian standing over you with his dark eyes, thick muscles, and knowing smirk would make you want to pee your pants. He wasn't a man you said no to easily; besides, it sounded like the position would be good for Annie. No more late nights, less danger, better salary.

"Yeah. Sure. Put me down. I'd be glad to help out."

"Great." Brian slapped his hand down on Luke's shoulder one more time. "They might not even call you, but if they do, let me know. Okay?"

Luke nodded as Annie walked up.

"Jessie's here. Should we order the pizza?" she asked.

"I already did. I need to pick it up from Sammy's. I've got a coupon somewhere." Luke searched through the countless pieces of paper held to his fridge by various-size magnets. Natalie had a requirement for students who took a trip during the school year; they had to bring back a magnet for Mrs. Richardson. Over twelve years of teaching, she had quite a collection. She could tell the story behind each and every one. "You guys okay staying with the kids?"

"Uh, how about you give me the coupon, and I'll pick up the pizza?" Brian yanked the slick square of paper out of Luke's hand and pulled a large key chain out of his pocket. "I'm not much of a babysitter."

"Sure." Luke grabbed a couple of twenties out of his wallet and handed them to Brian. "That should cover it."

"K. Shouldn't take long." Brian retucked his shirt into his belted jeans. He took one step and then turned, like he'd forgotten something. Grabbing Annie's arm, he flipped her around and dramatically threw her toward the ground, his arm stopping her right before she hit the floor. Then he kissed her.

Will and May watched from the table with a chorus of "ewwwww," which only seemed to encourage Brian to dip Annie down farther, like they were in a movie. When they finally parted, Annie was gasping, and the kids were laughing harder than they had in weeks. Luke wasn't sure if he was imagining things, but he could've sworn Brian gave him a little look after letting Annie go—a look that said, "I can do this because she's mine."

"That was so gross," May said, still laughing. She was having fun on her birthday, and for a moment she wasn't missing her mom. As Luke watched May, she caught his eye, and her smile fell. The room was filled with laughter and celebration, all for her, but her eyes were asking him a question—is it really all right to be this happy without Mom?

"It's okay. Be happy," Luke mouthed. Little pools of tears gathered on her lower eyelashes, and when she smiled, one tear fell down her cheek. She wiped it away quickly and laughed again when Will made exaggerated kissing sounds.

Jessie rapped her knuckles on the table. "Hey, guys! I have some party hats I brought for us to decorate. Let's get started while we wait for the food?"

"Yay!" May shouted. Will rolled his eyes but was a good sport, putting Clayton in his booster seat before sitting next to Jessie, whom May was hugging while saying over and over, "Jessie, you're the best. *The best.*"

"Do you think Jessie is 'the best'?" Annie asked, turning her back to the table and straightening her smudged lip gloss with her index finger. Luke turned to face Annie. This close he could make out the color of her eye shadow, a light shimmering blue, and see the mole on her right cheek that she always tried to cover up with makeup. Today she was covering more than the mole. Luke could make out a dark spot on Annie's cheek, covered by a heavy dose of concealer. He leaned closer; something about the coloring was familiar to him.

"Well, probably not the way I'd put it, but yeah," he answered, distracted. "She's been great."

"So, you know she's pretty sick, right?" Annie rolled a piece of paper towel between her palms. "Will said she can't eat certain foods, takes all kinds of medicines, and I hate to say it, but sometimes she comes off as a little immature. Do you really think she's up for taking care of these guys?" She folded her arms, waiting for Luke's reply.

Luke cocked his head, trying to get a better look at what he was now sure was a bruise. It wasn't just the mark on her face that startled him. Annie usually saw the best in people; her concerns about Jessie seemed very out of the blue.

He answered in slow, fragmented sentences. "She looks tired sometimes, but she's good with the kids. Maybe a little immature, but she's an only child and her mom died when she was twelve. She's a grown woman. I'm not going to start telling her what she can and cannot handle."

"Hmm, okay. I mean, nothing against the girl. She seems like a very genuine person, but I just want what's best for the kids." Annie turned to watch the kids at the table again. Jessie, wearing a *Wicked* T-shirt today, had five bottles of glitter, two bottles of glue, and a stack of multicolored paper. The kids were all in various stages of hat making, and Jessie was busy covering her fingernails in glue and glitter.

"Well, maybe she's a little spacey and childish," Luke agreed, "but . . . what happened to your face?" Luke reached out and brushed the discolored spot on Annie's cheek. She flinched back.

"Nothing; I just slipped in the shower. I hadn't put the rubber mat down . . ." She covered the side of her face with her hand. "Is it bruising badly?"

"No." Luke shuffled closer, inspecting the injury with his experienced eye. As he searched for swelling, all those memories he continually tried to push away rose to the surface. His father's booming voice shaking his bedroom door, his mom crying and begging him to stop, the garnet and gold class ring his dad wore on his left hand that left welts on his mom's arms and legs and occasionally her face.

He dropped his hand. He didn't like to let himself think about his father or how he had destroyed their family in that little house on Winter Lane. "Does it hurt? What about your head—any headaches or blurred vision?"

Annie shook her head. "Nope, I'm fine, really." She swooshed her hands in front of her body like she was wiping the concerns away and then turned around, ending Luke's inspection. "Here, can you tighten this?" She pointed to the buckle behind her neck that had never been adjusted. This time, Luke didn't let himself think; he yanked the tail of fabric through the clip with a snap. Annie spun around. "By the way, don't think I didn't notice the letter you were clutching when I came in." Annie raised her eyebrows, and Luke read the accusation in her pursed lips. She was deflecting any more scrutiny of the bruise on her face.

"I could tell you noticed." Luke picked up the spatula Annie used to frost the cake and tossed it into the sink with a thud before turning on the water and grabbing a damp sponge. "I'm not trying to hide it from you. They help me, and I don't think I should be ashamed of that."

"I'm not trying to shame you," Annie said as she appeared beside him at the sink. "But shouldn't you at least *try* to find out where they are coming from?"

Luke breathed out slowly. These conversations with Annie were his least favorite. No matter how many times she said she wasn't judging him, it still felt like she was.

"I visited the post office, talked to the manager. There's no way to trace them. What else can I do? I'm not going to stop reading them, and I don't know why you'd want me to." Annie had come to the party with plenty on her mind and wasn't holding back.

"I'm not trying to be cruel, Luke. I just don't want you to get hurt or delude yourself into thinking Natalie is somehow still here." She grabbed a neon-green sponge and scrubbed the spatula, rinsed it, and placed it into the drying rack before starting on the bowl, encrusted with cake batter.

"Well, maybe Natalie knew that someone as logical as me could use a little illusion or delusion or whatever you mean. The letters aren't hurting me," Luke said with finality. "And if we're going to talk about someone getting hurt, let's talk about—"

Annie wouldn't let him finish. "Okay. I get it," she said, passing him a bowl to dry. "I won't bring it up again." She blew at a bit of hair that had slipped out of her bobby pins, and pulled her shoulders back as she washed. "So, what were you and Brian chatting about over there?"

"He was asking me to be a reference for the new job." When she didn't say anything, Luke checked her face, wondering if the job was what had her acting out. "What? You're not excited about it? I know, you're worried you'll miss getting out of tickets once your husband isn't a police officer anymore, aren't you?" Luke elbowed her side, trying to bring back playful Annie.

"I'll have you know I'm an excellent driver." She laughed halfheartedly and flicked a few soap bubbles at his face.

"Hey!" Luke held up a glass. "I'm working here."

"I . . ." Annie cleared her throat, growing serious again. "I'm surprised he talked to you without me."

"It's not a big deal, Annie. We only talked for two minutes, tops. He seems really excited about this job."

"Oh, *he* is." She dried her hands with the dish towel and then threaded it through the drawer handle. When she looked up Luke tried to recall the meaning of her expression from his ever-growing dossier of Annie's emotions but drew a blank. "I'm not. Moving away would be breaking my promise to Natalie. Those promises are very real to me. I can't turn my back on them because he suddenly decides he wants a new career."

The hair on Luke's forearm stood on end. Move? Brian never mentioned anything about moving.

"Wait. What are you talking about? Where is this new job?"

"He didn't tell you? Ugh. That man." She started to push her fingers through her hair until she realized it was pinned back and ended up patting the swollen spot on her face instead. "DC," she whispered. "The job is in Washington, DC."

Luke felt his knees start to buckle. So this is what had Annie on edge, why she was worried about Jessie's competence, his overreliance on Natalie's letters. She was preparing to leave them.

Luke steadied himself as nonchalantly as possible, one hand on the counter, the other in his pocket. Washington, DC. Annie was right; this was definitely not in Natalie's plans. He shook his head and took a deep breath. Why had he let himself become so dependent on her? Because Annie begged him to let her help? Because he needed someone in his life to help him and to talk to, who could share the day-to-day challenge of parenting grieving children?

God, now Clayton, who barely slept when he was home, had no problem sleeping when Annie put him down for a nap. And Will, who hardly showed his face outside of his room, much less made actual speaking sounds in Luke's direction, texted with Annie daily and lit up when she walked in the room. And poor May would lose her only remaining mother figure. Who would she talk to about boys and puberty and . . . all those other things Luke had no idea about?

She could do all those things when she lived five minutes away, but not if she lived in DC. He couldn't say any of that. This shouldn't matter to him. Annie could move to Mongolia, and he should be happy for her.

"Don't you worry about us." Luke took a step back and put on his "I'm okay" face. He'd had lots of practice with this one and hoped it was convincing by now. "Natalie would want you to be happy." Luke reached out and lightly patted Annie's upper arm.

She shook her head. "Really? You're fine with it too? I knew Brian wouldn't get it, but I thought for sure you would." She pressed her lips together till they blanched white. "I promised her, Luke. I'm not following some instructions in a letter." She gave him a cutting look, and the words hurt like she'd scratched him with a knife. "I sat at her deathbed. I looked into her eyes, and I swore I'd be there for you guys."

"Natalie is gone." Luke sliced at the air. Annie was right; he played games with his own grief by indulging in the mysterious letters, but he didn't want to condemn Annie to that prison. He looked around to make sure all the kids were involved with Jessie's art project and then lowered his voice. "She is *dead*. She doesn't *care* about us anymore because she doesn't exist anymore."

The words came out more bitter than he'd intended, and Annie recoiled. Damn it. Luke crunched his eyes closed and rubbed the bridge of his nose, almost hoping when he opened them she'd be gone. But she was still there, staring at him like she was trying to figure out what was going on inside his head.

She leaned toward him, whispering, her voice clogged with tears. "I don't believe that. She's watching over us; I know she is." His arm was warm where she pressed against him, her biceps softer than he'd expected. He opened his mouth to tell her belief doesn't change fact, but the front door slammed, making May squeal and Luke jump.

"Pizza!" May yelled, and a flurry of activity broke out across the room around the table; markers, glitter, and stickers were tossed into boxes and dropped on the floor to be picked up later. Brian stomped into the kitchen and tossed the stack of pizza boxes on the table.

"I don't know about you, but I'm starving," Luke said, turning away from Annie to grab a spatula to serve the pizza. He could feel her watching him. He'd hurt her feelings; she wanted him to care that she might be leaving, might be breaking her promise to Natalie. He did care, but he couldn't show it.

Instead, he busied himself by counting out seven paper plates from the dwindling stack on the counter and placing them on the table. Remnants of glitter were stuck to the wooden surface, and he didn't bother to wipe them off. May would think they were festive.

As the room filled with the warm scent of garlic and melted cheese, each person settled into his or her own spot at the table. Annie was the last person to join them, dragging out the chair closest to Brian. Clayton climbed on her lap, reminding Luke of a needy little dog. Annie casually wrapped one of her arms around his midsection. Clayton put his head on her shoulder and gently patted Brian's arm. Luke had to look away.

May smiled through the rest of the party, and Luke tried to find comfort in that. He'd told her she was allowed to be happy; he had to pretend to be happy too, but he was far from happy.

Part of the heaviness holding him down came from all the reminders of Natalie. Yet that ache wasn't as profound as he'd feared it would be, almost as though he was adjusting to the pain, like when your eyes adapt in a darkened room. Underneath this understandable sadness was a simmering anger.

It had been five months—five. He was finally starting to get the hang of life, or at least parts of it, and Annie was a big reason behind the transition. Natalie knew Annie was integral to their survival. That's why she'd acquired promises, sent Luke letters, made plans. How dare Brian go and mess that up? Luke was also mad at himself. Why did he tell her it was okay to go?

And then of course there was that last worry, the one he'd been telling himself was nothing, the one that had to do with the mark on Annie's face that he couldn't stop looking at. Was Annie's reluctance connected with the reason for her injury?

Out of the corner of his eye, Luke watched Annie as she shoveled a giant bite of cake into Clay's mouth, frosting smudging on his chin. She erased it with the quick swipe of a napkin. He chewed slowly, his cheeks puffed out like a squirrel gathering nuts. Once his face was clean, Annie gave him a little peck on the top of the head, and he snuggled on her shoulder, swallowing loudly. Brian's arm draped around the back of Annie's chair, absently stroking her arm as he read through his phone.

Annie caught his eye and gave him a morose smile, and Luke knew—she was going to leave. Even if he asked her to stay, it wouldn't make a difference because no matter how much Annie loved Natalie and the kids, she'd never go against Brian. Never.

CHAPTER 13

Luke carefully slipped the pile of mail into his over-the-shoulder work-bag, the Velcro scratching as he ripped the front flap open. On top of the pile of outgoing mail, he placed Natalie's most recent letter. They'd become more sporadic, but he still pored over every one, searching for clues for his ongoing investigation into the Maranatha House, Andy Garner, and the elusive Dr. Neal.

The past two weeks had been strained between Luke and Annie. Annie kept a wall up whenever he brought Clayton over in the mornings, had turned down an invitation to join the Richardsons for dinner after May's spring concert, and avoided coming inside when she dropped off Will after taking him on a shopping trip to the mall.

Luke knew what Annie wanted. She wanted Luke to tell her to stay. She wanted him to refuse to give the recommendation Brian had requested at May's party. She wanted him to acknowledge the necessity of her presence in their lives. But how could he do those things? Brian was her husband, this was her life, and if she didn't want to move, she'd have to stand up and say so. But she wouldn't. So the stony silence continued.

When he dropped Clayton off at her house Monday morning, they ran through the same script they'd been stuck in since the party.

Annie opened the door. "Hi, Clayton!" She went automatically to her knees. Luke gently guided him across the threshold and tossed the heavy black duffel on the floor beside him. Clayton wrapped his arms around her neck as she picked him up.

"I missed you, Annie." He'd dropped the "Miss" in front of her name months ago, and Luke decided not to care.

She pressed her nose against Clayton's. "I missed you more," she whispered and gave him an Eskimo kiss, pretending to drop him a few inches before setting him on the floor. When she looked up, Luke's gaze flew to his shoes.

"Well, thanks." He flipped his keys around on his pointer finger. "You two have a fun day."

"We will," she said in the same overly chipper voice as always, flicking the door closed with her fingertips. Luke stomped to the car, looking back to see if they were watching from the front window. It was empty, like it had been for the past two weeks. He shook his head once and headed down the tulip-lined brick path to his car.

So far no one had called him for a reference, and he couldn't help but be relieved. He had all his selfish reasons to keep Annie here, but there were an increasing number of more pressing ones that he was having a hard time ignoring and they all had to do with Brian. How had he missed the warning signs for so long? Brian had always been controlling and condescending with Annie, but in the past few weeks Luke couldn't help but notice a fading bruise on Annie's hip when her shirt flipped up as she leaned over to get Clay's shoes and another on her upper arm just a day ago when she wore short sleeves for the first time in a week. He'd been telling himself that they could be from a stray weight at the gym or a fall while running.

Had there been signs all this time and he'd never seen them? Did Natalie know? Probably not. Whenever they had a double date with the

Gurrellas, Luke always knew the first words out of Natalie's mouth at the end of the night: "Brian's such an ass." Luke agreed—Brian was an ass. But was he a physically abusive ass?

Luke flopped his head back against the headrest. Maybe he was being paranoid. Brian was their family friend and a police officer. If anyone should know better, it would be Brian.

But what if I'm wrong? How many people had been wrong about his father? How many could've done something sooner and saved his mom? Luke didn't hesitate. He made a sharp U-turn at the next green light. Clayton couldn't spend another moment in that house until he knew for certain.

Luke pulled into Annie's driveway minutes later. Mid-May the grass was finally turning green, and Brian's lawn was neat and orderly as always. A row of yellow and red tulips traced the curved brick path, glowing against the freshly turned black soil. It always amazed him how something that is broken on the inside can look so perfect on the outside. Nearly running now, Luke leaped up onto the front porch and pounded on the door with the side of his fist. Annie opened it, eyes wide, Clayton hiding behind her legs.

"Oh, Luke, it's just you!" She tossed the dish towel she was holding over her right shoulder, hand covering her heart, giving him a clear look at the bruises on her upper arm. "You nearly gave me a heart attack!"

"Hey, guys. Sorry to come back so soon. I . . . uh . . ." He should've thought this through a little more clearly before rushing back. What was he supposed to say now? "Can we talk for a second?"

Annie stepped back. "Come on in."

"It's okay; I don't want to stay long. I realized Clayton has a doctor's appointment today." He leaned against the doorjamb, trying to act casually so he didn't frighten her off like an injured animal. Annie's nose wrinkled, folding several freckles in half.

"Oh," she breathed out, even her fake smile fading fast. "I'll go get his stuff." A trail of toys led from the door to the family room, where

Annie and Clayton spent most of their time. His plan for a fast escape seemed unlikely. Luke stepped inside and closed the door behind him.

"Let me help." He picked up a mini-teddy bear with blue fur and an unopened box of markers and tossed them in the open duffel bag. Annie dumped another armful in right after him, and some electronic toy started talking in a whiny British accent.

"A says ah, A says ah . . ." the voice sang.

"God, I hate that toy," Luke grumbled as he searched through the bag for the white ABC tablet, opened a hidden panel on the side, and flicked the power switch off.

"I have been trying to turn it off for the past six weeks. I don't know what kind of batteries you put in there, but they never die." Annie laughed, crouched down beside him.

"Only happens on the annoying educational toys." Luke smiled back, meeting Annie's eyes for the first time in two weeks. "Batteries on the fun toys run out after two days, I swear."

"I'm calling conspiracy on that one."

"I'm thinking lawsuit. We'll be millionaires." Luke threw the toy back in the bag along with a few others and then zipped it up. He stood, the bag clanking with all the random toys flopping around inside. He was enjoying the friendly banter with Annie that had been missing in their recent interactions.

Once he reached his full height, he offered his hand to Annie. She hooked a chunk of short blonde hair behind her ear before placing her hand in his. Her fingers were long and cool, so thin he was worried he could crack them if he pressed too hard. Luke couldn't imagine anyone wanting to hurt Annie.

"Annie. I'm sorry . . . about May's party . . ." He fumbled as he searched for the right words to say. "I know I hurt your feelings."

"It's okay." She pulled her hand away and glanced around his shoulder at Clay. "You were right. Just because Natalie thought you guys needed me, it doesn't mean you do."

"Is that what you thought I meant?" he asked, then readjusted the bag on his shoulder. He'd been trying to protect Annie, but he was hurting her instead.

"Mm-hm." She nodded.

Luke shook his head and stepped closer, reaching out to touch her but stopping halfway.

"We need you, Annie. A lot." He swallowed a few times. How much was too much to tell her? "I didn't want to make you feel guilty for leaving. That'd be selfish. You deserve to be happy."

She wrapped her arms around her torso. The flecks of brown in her eyes darkened like they could reflect her mood.

"Yeah. Happy." She said the word like it was from a foreign language.

Luke took a step closer, seeing his opening. "*Are* you happy?"

She squeezed her body even tighter, biting at a spot on her lip. An old scar. Wondering where it came from made it hard for Luke to be patient. "Are you safe?"

She looked up, squinting. "Wait—why did you really come back today?" Even though they were inches apart, there was suddenly a wall a mile thick between them. "Clayton doesn't have a doctor's appointment, does he?"

"I don't know what you're talking about . . ." Luke replied, glancing around for Clay. He'd made a tactical error, said a little too much. Once, soon after moving in next door, Terry had come over to have a talk with Luke's mom. In her matter-of-fact way, Terry told Luke's mom that they'd heard his dad's outbursts and were worried about her bruises. His mom smiled, thanked Terry for her concern, and then walked her out without so much as a cup of tea or doughnut.

"It was one of those letters, wasn't it? What did it say, Luke? Tell me." He'd never seen her this aggressive. She leaned in till they were almost touching.

"It wasn't a letter." He slapped at his thigh, wanting to back away but feeling like it would make him look weak. "I'm worried, that's all. I want to help you."

"Help me with what?" She eyed him suspiciously.

"Brian. I'm worried that he's . . ."

Before Luke could finish his sentence, a door opened to one of the upstairs bedrooms. Brian came around the corner, groggy. Annie let out a little *"eep"* and jumped back.

"Hey, Luke. Thought I heard you down here." He leaned over the banister, shirtless in police department sweatpants, crossing his arms casually, obviously unaware of the tension. His right bicep bulged, highlighting a tattoo of barbed wire. Another tattoo scrawled across one of his pecs, one word, but Luke couldn't make it out from so far away.

"Hey, Brian. I was about to leave." Luke shifted the strap on his shoulder and waved to Clayton, who'd been curled up on the stairs stacking and restacking a bucket of Lincoln Logs.

"I don't want to go to the doctor. I hate shots." Clayton cowered against the carpeted step he was resting on.

Luke took Clayton's little hand. "Don't worry; no shots. Just ice cream when we're done." He might have to actually go to the doctor after all this buildup.

"See you tomorrow?" Annie asked, leaning against the wall, as far away from Luke and Clayton as she could possibly be.

"Uh"—Luke hesitated—"I'll call you later."

She tipped her head to one side like she didn't completely understand what he was trying to say.

"Sounds good," she answered in an incredibly normal voice.

When Luke turned to leave after waving his good-byes, Brian called to him.

"You get any calls yet? They said they'd be done with the background check in the next week or two."

Luke didn't turn around. The idea that he was leaving Annie in the house with a man who might also be her abuser killed him. Now that man was asking him for favors.

"Nope, nothing yet. I'll let you know if I hear from them though."

"Hey," Brian called after him as he stepped out the door, "maybe they won't call you at all!"

When the door slammed behind him, all Luke could think was, *Let's hope.*

JUNE

CHAPTER 14

Luke clicked the button on the top of the camera, Will and May framed in the display screen. The digital software made a soft click, reminding him of the days when a shutter actually opened and closed inside a camera.

When they were kids in Pentwater, Luke and Natalie used to pool their spare change to buy those disposable cameras. They'd have a photo shoot in the backyard fort, taking turns making the funniest faces they could imagine. They never had enough money to actually develop the film.

Clicking another picture, Luke wondered if those cameras were packed in an old box somewhere. He'd have to ask Will to check with Terry while he was at her house.

"Dad, are we done yet? You're going to make us late," May said through clenched teeth as she held her smile, posing with her hands on her hips. Will rolled his eyes.

"It's the last day. I don't think anyone cares if we're late." Will flipped his hood up. It was the first week of June and seventy-eight degrees outside, but he was still wearing the hoodie. Maybe it would dissolve one day due to overuse. "But, seriously, can we go now? Last day I get to see my friends for the whole summer."

Luke flicked the power switch off and placed the camera on the side table in the hall. The pictures weren't his idea. Natalie reminded him a few days ago in a letter. Every year she'd take pictures on the first and last day of each school year and then put them side by side in a set of frames on the mantel in the family room. The first and last day of school was always treated as a holiday in the Richardsons' house. It probably came from Natalie's career as a teacher.

There was one part of the "last day of school" letter Luke loved. He read it again this morning before waking up Will and May. She'd said: "I don't understand why parents cry on the first day of school. For me, that's the best day. The anticipation and excitement for what lies ahead always gives me goose bumps. It's the last day that makes me tear up. The year is over, and my students walk out of the room first graders and into their parents' arms second graders. It's the end that marks a beginning, not the first day." Every time he read it, he couldn't help thinking she'd been talking about more than school.

"Don't be so dramatic, Will. We aren't leaving for another two weeks." May hefted her faded purple backpack on her shoulders. Why it was so heavy on the last day of school, Luke didn't dare ask. The rocks he'd seen May and Jessie decorating a few days ago were probably the culprits. "Plus," May continued, "Grandma Terry said she's going to take us to Disney World and the beach and to see alligators and—"

"I don't care about all that. I just want to stay here and chill with friends." Will yanked on the drawstring on his hood, closing it around his face. "Clay! We're leaving."

"Hey, be nice to your sister," Luke said, grabbing his keys off the holder by the door. "And stop yelling. Annie's going to think we live like a bunch of wild people."

Clayton's feet stomped on the hardwood floor as he ran in from the kitchen. Annie walked behind him in measured steps like she was sure he was about to trip and fall. Annie was a new addition to their morning routine. She'd called him a few hours after he picked up Clayton for his nonexistent doctor's appointment. With no reference to Luke's insinuations, Annie offered to care for Clayton at the Richardsons' house. She also explained that she'd changed her mind and was ready to move to Washington, DC with Brian, asking, halfheartedly, if Luke would still be willing to give the promised recommendation. He agreed, not wanting to push her away again, but still not sure what he'd say if the call ever came.

Soon he wouldn't be seeing her much anyway. When Terry asked if she could have the kids visit her in Orlando for six weeks over the summer, Luke couldn't find a reason to say no. The shift to being a single dad had been exhausting. He'd be working on a new project, and as grateful as he was for Annie's help, he didn't feel right about making her watch all the kids through the whole summer.

"Don't worry; I was already aware of the wild people in this house. You're not as shocking as you think." Annie tugged at May's high ponytail and stood in front of Will. "Though after spending a few minutes in your room, I think *National Geographic Explorer* could do a whole series on the things growing in there."

She gently yanked at the gathered fabric around Will's face and pushed back the hood. With Will already a head taller than her and still growing, Annie had to stand on her toes a little. She patted down a few flyaway hairs and smiled.

"That's better," she said, stepping back to stand by Luke. "You took the pictures without the hood, right?"

Luke nodded, glancing at his watch. Seven forty-five, time to go.

"Okay, everyone, say bye to Clayton and Annie." Luke clapped his hands together. "We're going to be late."

"You mean *you* are going to be late for your meeting with Ms. Mason," Will said, raising his eyebrows. "What is this, the third or fourth time in the past six weeks?"

"Hey, we are talking about you in those meetings, so I wouldn't be counting so closely," Luke said, trying to push the conversation away from Will's insinuations. Will insisted the only reason Ms. Mason kept asking for meetings was because of some underlying romantic intentions. "You're stalling. Let's go." Luke leaned down and gave Clayton a kiss on his sticky cheek. "Be good for Annie."

"I'm always good, Daddy. Annie says so." Clayton put his hands on his hips and pouted as though he was really offended.

"This is true. Always good, I swear," Annie said, giving Will a side hug and pulling May in on her other side. "You guys have a great last day and don't be so hard on your dad. He's going to miss you guys."

"Yeah, right . . ." Will said, shrugging. Annie wiggled her fingers against his rib cage, and he flinched away, trying not to giggle. "Hey!"

"What?" She looked at him with wide innocent eyes.

"Out the door now." Luke glared at Will, pointing to the garage door. Taking May's hand, he turned to face Annie. "And you are *not* helping!"

"Hey! Remember when we were happy to see him smile?"

"I know. I know." He paused. He wanted to tell Annie she had a lot to do with Will's progress, but they hadn't had a real conversation in weeks. Instead he said, "Well, have a fun day, you two."

"We will." Annie's lips pressed together like she too had something to say she couldn't get out.

Luke dropped May off at her elementary school, waiting through a slow line of cars. By the time he parked and stealthily said good-bye to Will, Luke had four minutes to spare before his eight-thirty appointment.

Fine. He was looking forward to seeing Ms. Mason again, and their past two meetings could've easily been done over the phone. He enjoyed her company, and if Natalie was going to pressure him into dating again, he'd rather spend time with someone he already knew and kind of liked than whatever Natalie had in store. These were not exactly dates, but they were as close as he could manage now.

Usually he had to wait in the uncomfortable chairs lining the hall outside of Ms. Mason's office until she came out of whatever meeting she'd been wrapped up in. But today, she stood outside her office, leaning on the door frame of the open door. She was wearing heels, as always. This pair was a scaly red, with at least an inch of platform under the sole. Her black skirt and flowy gray top were bland in comparison, but the contrast was enough to make the shoes almost appropriate.

She was wearing her hair down, and the tight, natural spirals hung down her back, nearly reaching her waist, the ends four shades lighter than the dark amber at the top of her head. Luke didn't know if it was from an old dye job or a new fashion trend. Natalie never followed trends but always had her own sense of style. Every once in a while she'd get really dressed up for school, as though there was some special event going on. After a few years he'd stopped asking when she threw on a dress and a pair of dangly earrings because every time he asked, she always answered, "It felt like a dress day today."

You've got to stop, Luke told himself. He couldn't think about her nonstop anymore. If she were only dead, he'd never want to stop thinking about her, but since she was dead and had left him with questions about two different men in her life, thinking about Natalie was doubly painful.

Yes, he read her letters when they showed up, and sometimes he even enjoyed them when he allowed himself to forget. But he also read the letters in case she slipped up and let a secret spill and to count mentions of Dr. Neal (twenty-four) or a casual drop of Andy's name (only once). But Ms. Mason was right in front of him, waving him over to her office. She was a nice, professional, intelligent woman, and Luke hated to admit it, but Will was right—she liked him.

"Mr. Richardson, good morning." Ms. Mason shot him a wide smile, uncrossing her arms nervously. "Thanks for meeting me early." She gestured for him to enter the office. On the desk were two cinnamon rolls as big as fists and a pair of sweating glasses of iced coffee.

"I hope you don't mind iced coffee. It's finally getting hot out, and I can't stand drinking hot coffee on a warm morning."

"Iced sounds great." Luke smiled and sat down, pulling his chair up to the desk. He picked up the see-through plastic cup, wiping the pool of condensation off the tabletop. He took a quick sip and tried not to cough. The drink didn't taste anything like coffee, more like milk with sugar and caramel mixed into it. Ms. Mason settled into her seat and crossed her legs to the side.

"Can you believe it's the end of the year already?" she asked, pinching off a small piece of pastry and popping it in her mouth.

"Yeah." Luke nodded, working hard to make small talk. Why was he suddenly so nervous? Perspiration beaded up on his forehead. "It really snuck up on us this year."

"So true," Ms. Mason said, nodding slowly like he'd meant more by his comment than intended. Like he was talking about Natalie. An awkward silence passed between them. Luke shifted in his seat, a bead of sweat trickling down his back. He coughed and instinctively reached for another sip, only to fight back his gag reflex when he tried to swallow it.

"Uh, so . . ." He put the drink down, determined to not mistakenly drink it again. "Was there something you wanted to discuss? About Will?"

"Mmm, yeah," she mumbled, mouth full of cinnamon roll. She took a drink and coughed. "Whoa, that's way too sweet, right?"

"Maybe a little."

"I'm so sorry." She held up the cup like she was searching for the mistake. "It's a new place. Starbucks had a line, so I tried Java Joe's. Lesson learned. They're on my bad list now."

"You have a list? Are you searching out coffee shops to blacklist?"

"Oh yeah, I'm undercover in Michigan to find all the subpar coffee shops. It's my main mission."

"Wow, that sounds dangerous. Anyone try to assault you with their grinder yet?"

"Not yet, but no worries; caffeine triggers my training, so I'll be a ninja in no time." She laughed. Luke liked her laugh; it was careless and a little loud, like she'd fit in with a group of kids on a playground.

Luke laughed; he could see why she was so effective with the teenagers. Her humor was captivating.

"I'm officially scared." Luke held up his hands like he was fending off an attack.

"No, I only use my powers to fight evil. You're safe."

"Whew." He wiped at his forehead and was surprised at how wet his hand came back. He was almost tempted to try the iced coffee again to help him cool down. A loud bell rang in the background. Luke tried not to check his watch. School must be starting.

"Well, I don't want to keep you. Should we get down to work?" Ms. Mason flipped open the manila folder lying on the desk. He braced himself, like he did every time he walked in her office. "I wanted your approval on some of these honors courses I mentioned last time you were in here. With his test scores and final grades, he's qualified for honors English, Chemistry, and American History. I need a parent's signature to enroll him. I wanted to make sure you think Will could handle the pressure and the workload."

"I looked at those syllabi you gave me, and I think he can manage it. I know he had a rough patch, but he's come a long way in the past few months." He squinted at Ms. Mason. "What do you think?"

"He has. I give you both a lot of credit . . . and I agree. I think he's ready."

"You definitely get credit too, and I'm glad we agree. I'll sign the papers now if that's easier."

"Sure," she said, smiling so her dimples showed. Okay, she's cute and definitely has an original personality, not to mention she's dedicated to her job. He could acknowledge all those things, but Luke still wasn't sure he was ready. "So, how's the therapist working for Will? He seems to like Mr. Cotton."

She nudged the page his way, and it swooshed across the desk.

"Yeah, it's been good," Luke said, distracted by the page full of words in front of him. "I thought for sure he'd bail as soon as his six weeks of forced therapy were up, but he seems to like it. May's gone a few times too . . ." Luke's words came to a halt as he searched for empty lines to sign. He could feel Ms. Mason watching.

"Well, that's good. A little therapy never hurt anyone."

"I guess not," Luke said as he finished the *n* at the end of his name. He passed her both the pen and the paper and stood to leave.

"Oh." The smile on her face fell, and Luke felt a twinge of guilt. It had never been this hard with Natalie. But then again, they were mere kids when they met.

"I'm sorry; this was so nice of you." Luke gestured to the drinks and snacks. "But I'm late for work." The second bell rang in the background, and a voice droned over the loudspeaker in the hallway.

"No, I'm sorry. I didn't mean to keep you. You . . . we . . . I don't get many involved fathers. I guess I wanted to say thank you." She crossed to the door and put her hand on the silver hooked door handle.

"I think you give me more credit than I deserve," Luke said.

He wasn't a "good" dad. Natalie had planned it all. Between Annie, Jessie, and now Will, who occasionally decided to be helpful, most days he felt like little more than a figurehead and paycheck.

"No, you're wrong. Will told me how you did all kinds of research on the letter he found. I think that's amazing." Her yellowish-green eyes looked right into Luke's, and his heart beat a little faster. He opened his mouth to respond with some kind of self-deprecation but closed it again, not wanting to come off as unappreciative.

"Thank you, Ms. Mason. We're lucky to have you," Luke said, grabbing his coffee more from guilt than an actual desire to drink it. "I'll take this with me if you don't mind?"

"Of course. And you are welcome to the roll too. I put a whole box of them in the teacher's lounge, so I definitely don't need any more."

"Thanks." Luke rolled it up in the napkin, his hands awkwardly full. "Well, you'll let me know if you need anything else?"

"Of course." Ms. Mason opened the door and leaned against it to keep it open.

Luke lifted his drink in her direction. "I'm sure I'll see you next year."

"Um, Mr. Richardson." Ms. Mason tapped the toe of her shoe nervously as she dug around in the wide pockets flaring out at the hip on her black skirt. "I . . . I wanted to give you my card. I won't be checking my work messages very often over the summer, so I wrote my cell number on the back." The card rested between two of her fingers, the red nail polish matching her shoes almost perfectly.

This was it, the moment where he had a choice to make. He had to take the card, but what would he do with it? Stuff it in the glove compartment in his car, or put it in his wallet, wait a few days or weeks, and then, when he was finally ready, give her a call?

"Oh, your hands are full. Here." She placed the card on top of the wrapped-up cinnamon roll. "And please, call me Felicity." The name Felicity Mason flashed up at him from the off-white card stock.

"Thanks for breakfast, Felicity. I'm glad we have you and your ninja skills on our side," Luke joked, which made Felicity Mason give another one of her hearty laughs. "And I can't get my business card out right now, but you can call me Luke."

"Well, Luke"—Felicity balanced on her heels without wobbling— "I hope you have a wonderful summer, and I look forward to hearing from you."

"Yeah, you too." As he walked out of the guidance office, he refused to look back in case Ms. Mason . . . Felicity . . . was still watching him. By the time Luke got to the parking lot, his shirtsleeve was soaked in sweat. On the corner of the sidewalk stood a garbage can, filled with papers, food wrappers, and insulated cups. Luke tossed his drink in the can without stopping. As he headed for the car, a wind gust made the business card flutter. Luke grabbed it before it blew away. On the back, a handwritten message caught his eye.

"Call or text anytime," with a phone number scrawled underneath. Luke tucked the card away in his back pocket, shaking his head.

God, Natalie, what have you gotten me into this time?

CHAPTER 15

"Hey, we're home!" May shouted, running into the house at full speed. She clutched a new doll in her arms. With its long brown hair and blue eyes, the doll looked like a little mini-May. "I got a doll; her name is Sally!"

Luke stepped over the threshold and closed the garage door. The smell of bleach tickled his nose. Usually when he came home to relieve Annie, the house was filled with the smell of dinner cooking or a bag of microwave popcorn for a movie. Bleach was unexpected. Wandering through the front rooms of the house, Luke was surprised and a little horrified at how clean they all were.

"Annie!" he scolded, shaking his head. "You didn't have to clean my house."

In the kitchen, the cleanliness continued. The family room was tidy, the TV stand shockingly clear of dust, and Annie stood at the sink, wearing yellow rubber gloves up to her elbows.

"Annie." He sighed. "You didn't spend your whole day cleaning, did you? Please don't feel like you have to clean up after us. It makes me feel really guilty."

She waved a gloved hand at him. "Don't worry. I didn't do it alone. Will is impressively talented at getting mildew out of bathroom tile."

"Daddy, I did the feathers." Clayton jumped up and hugged his leg, smiling like he'd built the house himself.

"Feathers?" Luke asked.

Annie peeled off her gloves with a snap. "Dusting," she whispered.

"Oh, dusting." Luke took three steps toward the island, Clayton hanging on for dear life. "You, sir, are one amazing duster."

"I know." Clayton giggled.

"So, how was the American Girl store? May seems happy." They both looked at May, who was sitting with her doll at the table, explaining that she needed to eat all her green beans if she wanted any dessert. "You feel extra girly today?"

"Yeah, we had tea." Luke held up his pinky finger like he was holding a teacup. "Did I mention I'm a good dad?"

"You didn't need to." She yanked off the KISS THE COOK apron she'd taken to wearing and hung it on a hook by the fridge. "I already knew."

"Make sure to tell Terry that when she gets here."

Annie put one hand on her hip. "You know I would, but I don't think I'll get the chance to see her. Brian and I are going out to DC next week to look at . . . places." She lowered her voice when she mentioned the semi-taboo subject.

"Ah, yeah, I forgot." Luke was trying very hard to be supportive. "So, any official news?"

She shook her head. "Not yet. He's on the 'top of the list,' whatever that means."

They stood there in silence for a second. Whenever they spoke about the impending move, Luke always had an intense yearning to ask her to stay. So, supportive or not, he had to force himself not to speak, afraid of what might come out.

"Well, thanks for watching Clayton so I could have my special date with May." Luke had taken off the past week to spend the kids' last week at home without Terry. She'd spend the next week with them in Michigan and then take the kids back to Florida with her for six whole weeks.

After spending just one week at home with the kids, Luke was more certain than ever that summer at Grandma Terry's would be better for everyone. In the past week they'd gone to the pool, taken a trip to the zoo, and played an epic game of hide-and-seek on one particularly rainy afternoon. But summer was Natalie's forte, and now it felt like they were all trying a little too hard.

"You never have to thank me for the time I spend with your kids. I adore them." Clayton, who'd unsuctioned himself from Luke's leg, was now hanging from Annie's yoga pants. She didn't seem to mind, patting his blond hair affectionately. "What you *do* have to thank me for is cleaning out that fridge. Jeez, Luke, please don't tell me this is the first time it's been cleaned out since Natalie did it."

"No, you didn't." Luke breezed past Annie and Clayton, yanking open the refrigerator door. The shelves glistened and were nearly empty. The faint scent of bleach was almost refreshing when mixed with the clean cold air of the refrigerator. "Annie." Luke lowered his voice. "You've got to let me pay you. You work too hard."

"No way; I won't take your money." She wrapped her hand around the refrigerator door handle under Luke's and pushed it shut. "I only did it because of Terry visiting this week. I didn't want to give her any added ammunition to be mean to you."

"Oh"—he hesitated—"Natalie told you?"

"It wasn't very hard to pick up on." She let go of the handle first. "I was here every day at the end. She is not an easy mother-in-law, that's for sure." Annie leaned her head against the fridge and crossed her arms across her loose electric-blue athletic shirt.

Luke rested against the freezer door. "Yeah, I'm used to ignoring her disapproval at this point. I did do something sneaky though."

"Oh! What?"

"I got a smartphone."

"What the? For real?" She smacked his shoulder. "So you can text now?" She smiled mischievously, tapping her fingers together in front of her like she was developing an evil plan. "Oh, you might regret this."

"Yes, I can text." Luke rolled his eyes. "I can also video chat with Will now or even send videos to the phone Clayton uses at bedtime. Then I won't have to bother Terry—or well, interact with her."

"Wait, so you still pay for service on Natalie's phone?"

"Yeah," he admitted.

"Aren't you worried Clayton will start making calls?" She ran her fingers through Clayton's hair again, but he didn't seem to like it this time. Detaching himself from Annie, he ran off into the front room without a word.

"I put it in airplane mode when he has it. I just . . ." Embarrassed, his cheeks flushed. He'd always told himself he'd never tell anyone about his phone calls, but telling Annie secrets about himself was becoming easier and easier every day. "Sometimes when I'm feeling lonely, I like to call her."

He stopped himself before he told her that on the really bad days, he'd leave messages and talk about the kids or how much he missed her. Lately his messages were filled with questions and anger. He always felt better after those desperate messages. Maybe that's what prayer felt like to other people.

"God, Luke . . ." Annie reached out and squeezed his hand. "That's the sweetest thing I've ever heard. Can I call too? I never could bring myself to delete her contact information."

Luke casually pulled his hand away and tucked it into his pants pocket.

"Sure. I turned her ringer off a long time ago. Though you might want to do it before they go to Terry's. I have no idea what she'll do with the phone once she gets her hands on it."

"I wish they weren't leaving." Annie pushed off the fridge to the counter, where her glistening white smartphone sat. "I'm going to miss them so much. You know you'll have to fill that void with a generous amount of texts, right?" She put out her hand. "Here, give me your fancy new phone."

Luke slipped the phone out of his front pocket with two fingers. He still wasn't used to its size and weight after living with a palm-size flip phone for years. When Annie held it in her palm, she started flipping through the apps, typing with her fingertips.

"There. I put my info in and called myself so you can get in touch with me whenever you want." She handed the phone back to Luke when the doorbell rang. Her eyebrows shot up. "You expecting a package or something?"

Luke cursed silently. Annie was supposed to be gone by now.

"Uh, it's Jessie." Luke cleared his throat and projected his voice. "Will! Could you get that?" A distant grunt and stomping feet followed. No way Will would emerge from his teen cave for anyone other than Jessie or Annie.

"Jessie?" Annie's forehead wrinkled. "If you needed a sitter, why not ask me? I'm already here."

Luke returned his phone to his shirt pocket and sighed. "I was going to be out late, and you've already been here all day. I didn't want to take advantage."

"Late? What are you up to?"

Jessie sauntered in, barefoot, with shorts and a BroadwayCares .org T-shirt, eager for the few months of summer like every other Michigander. She slid a pair of thick-framed white sunglasses on the top of her head and joined them at the counter.

"He's going on a date," she whispered. Her bubbling anticipation reminded Luke of the moment a few weeks earlier when May had thought Jessie was going on a date.

Annie stood and put her hands on her hips, head cocked to one side. Luke couldn't decide if she looked confused or annoyed.

"A date? With who?"

Dang it. He had to tell her now. "Ms. Mason, from school."

"The guidance counselor? I thought Will was joking."

"It was a joke, but she gave me her number and . . ." *And Natalie told me to do it.* No, he couldn't tell her that.

"I think it's great, Mr. Richardson. After my mom died it took my dad forever to date again."

Jessie was trying to be sweet, but she was also just socially awkward enough to not catch on how her comment could make Luke feel like an ass. He wanted to explain—this wasn't his idea. Sure, he liked Felicity Mason, but if it weren't for Natalie's letter and her nagging reminders, he never would've thought of her as more than Will's guidance counselor. Jessie might not be wondering how he'd moved on so fast, but one look at Annie told him she wasn't impressed with his date.

"I better get going," Annie said, collecting her drawstring bag and flinging it over her shoulders. "You need to change for your date, and I need to get home to make dinner for Brian. Have a nice summer break, Jessie. Don't get into too much trouble."

"You too!" Jessie called after Annie as she walked briskly toward the front door.

"Hey, stop." Luke followed her, hoping for a chance to explain. "I'm sorry I didn't tell you about Ms. Mason. I didn't want to upset May. I'm not sure she's ready for any of this."

Annie shoved her feet into her brightly colored athletic shoes, using her fingers to slide them over her heels. "No, she's not." She stood and flipped her hair out of her face, cheeks flushed with blood from being upside down. "Are you ready for this? You still read those letters like they are your own personal bible, and I see the way your face twists whenever the kids bring up Natalie. I'm a little surprised you'd rush into a new relationship."

"Relationship?" Luke's knees wobbled at the word. "This is not a relationship; it's one date. And I don't understand where you get off thinking you can judge me on this." He slapped his leg, frustrated. "This whole damn thing was Natalie's idea, not mine."

Annie stopped breathing for a second and then took a step back. "That is so strange, Luke. How can you not see how dysfunctional it is that you've fallen sway to this whole Natalie letter-writing campaign?"

"*My* relationship is dysfunctional?" Words bubbled up inside him, angry words. His ears rang, and he couldn't hold back. "How about you and Brian? You can't tell me he's never laid a . . ."

Annie's mouth hung open. "I have to go."

"No, Annie. I'm so sorry. Please don't go." Luke reached out and grabbed her hand, but she ripped it away and opened the front door in a giant swing, the golden mail-slot cover flapping with the sudden movement.

"Have fun on your date." She slammed the door in Luke's face.

CHAPTER 16

It had been eighteen years since Luke's last first date. Even that wasn't really a first date since it was with Natalie and they'd technically had their first date six years earlier. Back then they had eaten pizza and watched a movie on the threadbare couch in his apartment—not gone to a gallery opening followed by dinner at a fancy restaurant.

Felicity had called him the day after she'd handed over her number with an offer—if he would be her plus one to her brother's art show, then she'd treat him to dinner. Luke, like Felicity, enjoyed their conversations during his office visits, but this was a huge step. Not only their first date but also his first date since becoming a widower. He told her he'd think about it. Then he got the first e-mail.

It was a nice note from a woman with the screen name JerseyPrincess, a thumbprint photo of a smiling woman with dark, curly hair in the corner. She explained Natalie had contacted her several months earlier during what must've been her last months of life. JerseyPrincess apologized because she'd recently entered an exclusive relationship, so she wouldn't be able to fulfill her promise to Natalie to help him transition into online dating. This was getting crazy.

Later that day, another e-mail came through. This time it wasn't an apology—it was an offer. StaceysMom sent Luke a long message detailing her e-mails with Natalie, a very thorough family history, and several semisuggestive pictures.

That decided it. He'd rather date Felicity than the total strangers Natalie had picked. Returning Felicity's phone call and accepting the date was more uncomfortable than answering May's questions on impending puberty after one particularly explicit day in health class.

So far, he couldn't say he regretted going out with Felicity. What he regretted was the fight he'd had with Annie and the way he made her face crumple with mortification. The art gallery was fine, a little odd maybe. All the pieces in the gallery were made with "found objects," which seemed to translate to garbage in his linear engineering mind. Every piece of art in the gallery made him think of Annie and how easily their friendship had turned into a heap of trash. He couldn't stop himself from checking his new phone to see if she'd texted.

No, he told himself, forcing the phone back into his pocket. He focused in on Felicity's voice explaining the pieces.

He'd always laughed at "art," but there was this one figure, a sculpture crafted out of discarded bottle caps, some nailed flat, some twisted or cut. They came together to form a sculpture of a man crying. Even though the bust wasn't behind any kind of velvet rope, Luke resisted the urge to reach out and touch it. In many ways he felt like that metal man, pieced together out of old, once useful objects, cold and sharp and empty on the inside. No way he'd buy the statue, but it did speak to him. It was beauty out of chaos, art out of refuse. Maybe art wasn't always lame.

It took about an hour to walk, a little slower than Luke would have liked, through all three floors of the small art gallery. Felicity's silver stilettos clacked on the polished oak flooring, the black tulle of her skirt nearly touched her knees and swished with every step. She wore a sparkling top that tied around the back of her neck where her hair was twisted in a low knot.

Luke tried not to notice the little curls struggling against the elastic band holding them in place. He didn't want to notice the little mole by the corner of her right eye that bounced up and down whenever she smiled. As they walked he made sure to remain at least two steps behind her, hands behind his back at all times.

"Let me say good-bye to my brother, and then we can go to dinner. I have a seven o'clock reservation around the corner." Felicity patted Luke's shoulder, and he had to hide a flinch. It wasn't her fault he was broken.

"A reservation? Sounds fancy."

"I owe you, remember? You come with me; I treat you to dinner." She took each stair gingerly, grasping the railing tightly.

"When you said you'd buy me dinner, I wasn't expecting more than getting a number two at the drive-through."

"Wow. Those are some spectacularly low expectations." Felicity flashed him a smile over her shoulder and jumped down the last step. As she wobbled on her heels, Luke reached out and grabbed her hand to keep her from falling.

"Whoa! Careful."

They stood toe to toe, her left hand in his right. She threaded her fingers through his, sending a jolt up his arm and into his midsection.

"You keep saving me. I think you just earned dessert." She tugged on his hand, tilting her head toward the tall, scrawny brunette man with glasses and beard that made him look homeless. "Let's say bye to Cole."

She held tight, her fingers pressing gently into the back of his hand. Her palm was tiny against his. Holding her hand felt strange, foreign. He followed Felicity across the gallery's ancient wood floor. Cole didn't seem very interested in talking to his older sister, and Luke couldn't help but feel appreciative.

It was exciting to be pursued by an attractive woman and he liked the way her fingernails played with the back of his hand, but the part of his brain he'd turned off long ago, the one that told him it was okay to hold hands with women who were not his wife, hadn't gotten the memo that Natalie was dead.

His hand felt cold and empty when Felicity dropped it to put a loosely knit crocheted shrug over her shoulders. But with his hand empty, the uncomfortable weight of guilt lifted off his chest almost instantly. Luke held the glass door to the gallery open for his date and hid his hands in his pockets when the slight chill of early evening greeted him.

"Do you mind walking? The restaurant is only a few blocks away," Felicity said.

"If you can walk it in heels, I can walk it in loafers." Luke scanned the storefronts around him; bass thrummed out through the walls of the club beside the gallery, and a crowded hot dog bar was filled to the brim with college kids, laughing and flirting behind the glass window. Everything was vaguely familiar in the twilight of the early evening. The trees lining the streets were taller than the last time he'd dined near campus; a few students milled around the sidewalks, the summer remnants of the once-overwhelming student body. After one more turn, Luke knew where they must be headed.

"Ashley Street? No way." He gaped at Felicity. "The Earle? You really got us reservations?"

Felicity giggled and pumped a fist. "Yes! I knew you'd be into jazz."

"I wouldn't say 'into,' but the Earle is a classic. Natalie and I always said we'd go for our twentieth anniversary . . ." The words caught in his throat. "I'm sorry. I didn't mean to . . ."

The clicking of Felicity's heels went silent, and Luke ended up three full steps ahead before he noticed she'd stopped walking. Now he'd done it—brought up his dead wife on a first date.

"Don't do that," Felicity said to his back. Her footsteps tapped closer until she was by his side and slipped an arm through his bent elbow. "Please don't ever feel like you can't talk about Natalie. She will always be a part of you."

He pressed his lips together, unsure what to say, but Felicity didn't try to force him to talk. Instead, being the ever-patient counselor she was, she tugged on his arm and looked both ways before crossing the street toward a maroon awning with white lettering on it. Felicity glanced at a small silver watch wrapped around her forearm.

"We're a few minutes early, but my brother's girlfriend is the hostess. I bet she can get us moved up on the list."

So Felicity was familiar with the "ignore it" method of dealing with personal issues. Her arm might feel heavy wrapped through his, but the weight of it also made him feel safe, like the pressure of a seat belt.

"Don't worry about me. I'm in no rush," Luke said, and he almost meant it.

◆　◆　◆

"And then the dad slid an envelope across the table and said, 'This should cover it.' I was tempted to point out that I have no power to change any grades, much less whole GPAs, and even if I did, twenty-five bucks wouldn't even come close to covering it."

Felicity laughed, and her curls bounced along with her shoulders. Luke chuckled. The food had been delicious, the music even better than rumored, and Felicity's company was extremely enjoyable.

"So, what would be the going price for changing a D to an A? Assuming, of course, that grade changing was within your purview."

"I can't recall off the top of my head, but if you let me ask around, I'm sure I can give you a competitive price." She took another sip of her wine, nearly emptying her glass. Luke decided to refrain from his own glass, not sure it was wise to rid himself of too many inhibitions when he was a proud owner of so many. Plus, he was driving, and even one glass made him nervous when he was going to have to drive on the highway to get home.

"I doubt I could afford you." His cheeks hurt from smiling so much, or maybe his facial muscles were out of practice. She put her glass down on the table with a clink and sighed, staring at the half inch of red liquid inside.

"Do you want dessert?" she asked, flicking her greenish-gold eyes up at him.

His heart jumped in his chest, a tightness spreading through his throat and lungs. If only she wasn't so pretty, this would be much easier. Or if it wasn't so obvious she liked him or how badly she wanted Luke to like her back. *Not ready,* a voice said inside his mind, and he knew it was right. He wasn't ready for a relationship. He was still irrevocably in love with Natalie, even if he wasn't sure she had truly loved him back.

"No, but thanks for the offer." He shook his head and put the maroon napkin from his lap on the table. "I'd better get home and let Jessie go before it gets too late." He glanced at his watch. Only 8:30 p.m.

Felicity's face fell, and for a moment Luke wondered if he should reconsider. But then the phone in his pocket rang. Too new for a personalized ringtone, it was the factory-setting ring on full volume, accompanied by a violent buzzing. A few of the couples at neighboring tables sent glares over to Luke, especially one bald guy with light hair and dark-framed glasses who looked like a professor type. Dr. Neal? The phone rang again, and the professor shook his head. What a ridiculous and borderline paranoid thought. Could he not go one night without thinking about that man?

"I'm sorry; I should probably get this. Only Jessie has this number . . ." Jessie and one other person—Annie. Ugh, Annie. The guilt was back.

"Go ahead; grab it! I'll pay the check and meet you in the lobby."

The phone rang and buzzed again, and Luke pulled it out of his pocket.

"You really don't have to treat me, you know."

"I know, but I want to. Now, answer that phone before the guy at table four knifes us."

Luke raised his eyebrows and tilted his head at the professor guy. Felicity rewarded him with another laugh, and Luke touched the green talk button before pressing the phone to his ear.

"Hello?" Luke answered, pressing his way through the cluster of tables toward the lobby.

"Hello, can I speak with Luke Richardson, please?" a masculine voice replied on the other end of the line, making Luke glance at the phone's screen to check the number. He'd been so sure it was Annie or Jessie he hadn't checked before answering.

"Uh, yes, this is Luke. Can I ask who's calling?" Luke's mind raced through possibilities but landed on solicitor.

"This is Dennis Bormet. I work for Tanglewood Securities in Washington, DC. We are a private security provider. You've been listed as a reference for a candidate for head of private security. His name is Officer Brian Gurrella. I came by your house this evening, but the young woman there said you were out and gave me your cell number. Do you have a moment to answer a few questions?"

Luke cringed. Why did he have to call now? He still hadn't decided what he was going to say to whoever called about Brian. Time had run out.

"This is pretty bad timing. I'm out to dinner right now. Is there a way we could discuss this at another time?"

"Yes, sir, I understand; your time is valuable to us. This will only take a few minutes. I can come by tomorrow to meet with you if that's a better time?"

Tomorrow. No, Terry would be there tomorrow. He didn't want her nose in this business.

"Well, if it will only take a few minutes, I can do it now," Luke answered, resigned. He'd much rather answer questions about Brian over the phone. Less likely this Dennis guy would pick up on the disdain Luke tried to keep hidden if he couldn't see his body language.

"All right. First, this background check is for security clearance within Tanglewood Securities. If approved, Officer Gurrella will be privy to classified information. We are interested in anything that could be used against him in the case of ransom or blackmail. So, some of these questions will seem odd or personal, but Officer Gurrella is aware of the intensity of this investigation. He wants you to be honest. If it's all right, I'll jump right in." Papers rustled in the background, and Luke thought he could hear the faint clacking of keys on a keyboard. "How long have you known Brian Gurrella?"

Luke counted back to the first time Brian and Annie came over for dinner. Will had been five, Natalie pregnant with May. Brian and Annie's son, Matt, was nine or ten. He'd spent the whole night curled up next to his mother, picking at his food, saying less than three words. It took another three or four visits for the boy to warm up, but Natalie was always good with pulling kids out of their shells.

"Around ten years, I think. They've lived in Farmington Hills for longer, but that's when I met Brian." There was silence and clicking on the other end. The silence made him uncomfortable, like he was supposed to say something else. Maybe that was the intention.

"How well would you say you know the Gurrellas? What is your relationship with them?"

"I know them fairly well, Annie better than Brian though. Annie was my wife's best friend and now is a caregiver in my home. Brian I see less, but I guess you could say we are friends." The answer sounded a little like a question when it came out, but at least it was honest.

"Does he gamble or have any debts you are aware of?"

"Uh, besides the normal things like a car and his house, no, I'm not aware of any debts." This was very different than Luke had expected.

He'd thought there would be two or three general questions; maybe he'd have to make a statement about Brian as a friend or vouch for him. This was far more intensive.

"Have you or your wife spent any time in the Gurrella home? Would you say there is any evidence of drug or alcohol abuse? Any relationship problems that could be used against Officer Gurrella in any way to gain leverage?"

Luke swallowed and turned toward the wall. "My wife passed away a few months ago." He took a breath and let the words settle in before continuing. "She spent a lot of time at Annie's in the past. I've only been there recently. She used to care for my son in her home so I was there nearly every workday. Brian was usually there too. He works the night shift, so he'd sleep during the day." Luke was aware he was babbling, but was too nervous to slow down. The investigator sat silent on the other end again, and Luke's mind raced for more information. "Uh, in the past few weeks she's been watching the kids at my house so Brian can get more sleep." He lied for the first time in the interview.

"And the other part, about the drug and alcohol abuse and Mr. and Mrs. Gurrella's relationship?"

This was the moment he'd been dreading. Should he tell the truth, explain that it was possible Brian abused both his wife and alcohol? Or should he do what Annie had asked, tell Dennis everything was sunny at the Gurrellas' house and Brian was Ward freaking Cleaver?

"Brian drinks socially, but I'm unaware of any problem. As for Brian and Annie . . ." Luke picked at the seam in the wallpaper in the corner where he stood, trying to walk the line between a lie and the difficult reality. "They seem like a normal couple."

Behind him, Felicity cleared her throat. He spun around, the phone still pressed against his ear. With her purse slung over her shoulder and doggie bag in her hand, she looked ready to leave. Dennis was droning on with his next question. This one inquiring if he'd ever witnessed any suspicious activity or visitors at the Gurrellas' house. Luke held up a finger to Felicity, asking for one minute. If the conversation went on any longer, he felt like he was going to throw up.

"Mr. Bormet, I haven't seen anything suspicious about Brian or his family. I wish I had more information for you, but I don't. I'm sorry; like I said, I'm out to dinner right now, and I really need to go. Do you have any more questions?"

Dennis Bormet went silent on the other end of the phone. Luke didn't know if it was a good sign or not. He shrugged at Felicity.

"Take your time," she mouthed. But he didn't want to take his time. He wanted to be done.

"I understand. Your time is valuable to us." Dennis Bormet repeated the same line he'd used at the beginning of the interview, which made Luke wonder if he was following some sort of script. "I have one last question."

"Almost done," Luke whispered to Felicity and rolled his eyes. She smiled at him, that stunning, broad smile, and pointed through the glass door at the dark street, lit only by tall, black streetlights crowned with glowing golden lamps. "I'll wait outside."

He nodded at her and answered the investigator, "I can take one more question." Luke watched Felicity push open the tinted glass door and pull her shawl a little tighter over her shoulders, even though there was no way it could be cooler than seventy out there.

"Mr. Richardson, as a personal reference, would you recommend Officer Brian Gurrella for high-level security clearance with access to sensitive information?"

The question caught him off guard, and he flinched away from the front window, suddenly finding it impossible to think about frivolous things like dating or jazz or wine. It was a question that brought Annie's face into focus as clearly as if it was reflected in the glass he'd been staring through. Now that he thought about it, she'd been there all night in the back of his mind, his most recent memory of her tainted with a look of betrayal. Luke was friendly with Brian but didn't know him, not really. Second only to the letters, Annie was the reason he was still able to stand and breathe and get out of bed in the morning. He'd do almost anything to help her, including lying to Dennis Bormet.

"Yes," he answered into the phone firmly, "I would."

CHAPTER 17

Luke stumbled down the stairs behind Clayton's bobbing bed-head hair. How did he have the uncanny ability to wake up an extra hour early on weekends? Did he have a printed schedule? A hidden calendar or alarm set on Natalie's phone? Whatever quirk was responsible for the early waking, Luke planned on blaming Natalie's genes because, let's be honest, she couldn't exactly fight him on this one.

The sun was already beaming in from the half circle of windows on the front door and the tall, thin windows flanking each side of it. Summer's sun made up for the seemingly eternal darkness of the Michigan winter, but today he had a slight headache. Not a great day to have a headache, not when Terry was coming over. If ever there was a headache producer, Terry was one.

"Daddy, you left your letters downstairs yesterday." Clayton held a pile of mail in his hands. "Annie picked them up." Luke had been so distracted by his trip with May, fight with Annie, and the date with Felicity that he'd forgotten to check the mail.

"Thanks, bud." Luke snagged the pile of bills stacked on top of a Natalie letter from his little hand. "Why don't you go snuggle up on the couch and I'll make some pancakes? Can you watch your shows, though, until I'm ready?" He measured the envelope between his fingers, counting silently in his mind. Five pages. For sure.

"Can I have a granola bar now?" Clayton was already a skilled bargainer. He knew his dad wanted some peace and quiet, so if it would cost a granola bar, so be it.

"Sure." Luke grabbed the golden letter opener he kept on the rectangular entry table and ran it under the sealed flap, hesitating for a second before calling after him. "Just one!"

"Okay!" Clayton shouted back, the crinkling of wrappers almost drowning him out.

Luke sat on the bottom stair, his favorite letter-reading spot. The letter unfolded neatly. Every time Luke opened one of her letters for the first time, he couldn't help but imagine Natalie sitting in her hospital bed in the front room, carefully folding the pages and slipping them into the robin's-egg-blue envelopes, licking the seal or maybe using a wet towel. He might not always like what was written inside the letter, but knowing she made such an effort to get it to him gave him more comfort than any condolences he'd received.

When Luke saw the date on this letter and calculated the gap between this letter and the one he'd received a week ago, he shuddered. Oh no.

DAY 270

Monday, September 9

Dear Luke,

My doctors are liars. They said I was in remission. They said I could move on with my life, that my hair would grow back, that I'd look back on this whole cancer thing as a little smudge on my book of life . . . well, they're freaking liars.

Why did I stop writing in this journal when I got those clear scans three months ago? Stupid optimism. Why did I go to that appointment alone? Stupid naiveté. I have cancer on my brain, Luke. *On. My. Brain.* Unlike the Scarecrow, I do need a brain to live.

I knew something was up when I walked into the office. Usually Dr. Saunders is very chatty, asking about the kids and work, even you. Today he looked at me with these sad eyes, like he was about to tell a kid he had to put down his beloved dog. After a brief greeting he sat in his rolling chair, elbows on his knees.

"Natalie." Then he sighed. That was a dead give-away. "So, last week we discussed some abnormal labs and how it was important to do a follow-up scan to be careful."

I nodded like a good little girl in school. Last week he'd told me it was probably nothing. He'd said I'd be fine. He told me not to worry. So I fasted, drank the disgusting orange-flavored contrast, lay in the PET machine for nearly forty-five minutes. Annie took me out to lunch after for pizza and I scarfed down three slices without any effort, trying to fill the ever-growing pit in my stomach. Maybe it was a premonition, though I'm not sure because when the words "metastasized" and "brain and lungs" and "stage IV" came out of his mouth, all the air sucked out of my lungs and my head spun.

I'm still not sure what Dr. Saunders actually said to me in those next few minutes, something about treatment options and prognosis. It is hard to believe my death sentence started as a microscopic lump of cells inside my body. I've let myself blame the chemo and the radiation for how horrible I've felt, losing the hair, becoming so unbearably weak. But it was cancer. Hiding. Waiting. Why? What did I ever do to make my body turn on me? Doesn't cancer know I have children? That killing me so ruthlessly will leave a permanent scar on their lives much deeper than the one on my body?

I tried to call you after the appointment, but you weren't at your desk or answering your cell. I was relieved because telling you that kind of news over the phone was probably not the best idea. I needed to think before breaking the news to you or even Annie, so I drove to EMU and started walking. I didn't get far before sitting down on an abandoned bench in the quad. It was packed with freshmen, some flanked by parents, walking through campus wide-eyed and ready for a new phase in their life. That's when I lost it. I was entering a new phase in my life too, the end of it. That's not supposed to happen at thirty-six or thirty-seven. It's not fair. *Not fair. Not fair. Not fair!*

As I tried to hide my tears behind my hand, the bench shifted beside me. Great, I thought, some oblivious teenager won't even let me have my "I'm dying of cancer" pity party. But then I felt a warm arm around my shoulders.

"Natalie, what's wrong?" Dr. Neal whispered in my ear. I yanked my hand off my face, not caring how horrible I must look after the crying jag. He had a gentle smile on his face. "It's not Tiff and her gang again, is it?"

I laughed, which felt so weird at the moment. "No, I think I got her kicked out and doomed her to a life of 'Welcome to McDonalds. May I take your order?' No wonder my karma sucks."

He told me she probably deserved it, but then his face grew serious, and he asked, "So, are you going to tell me why you are crying on the quad and scaring all the freshmen?"

I shook my head, knowing if I spoke, the tears would start again. He must've been able to read it all over my face because he knew, Luke. He just knew.

"It's back, isn't it?" he asked, and I nodded. "How bad?" I shook my head, and he asked again.

I said "stage IV," out loud for the first time. Told him that I'm a goner. Then, how Dr. Saunders said I have a few months, maybe a year if I'm lucky.

I closed my eyes against the flood of tears. His arm tightened around me, and I was suddenly grateful to have the comfort of a friend, especially someone who'd been the recipient of equally terrible news in his own life.

Dr. Neal sat with me for a while and told me it was okay to be scared, but that I didn't have to spend the last few months of my life terrified. He told me about how his wife, Maria, wasn't scared to die and how she got all Zen at the end. He kept saying, "She was a good, strong woman."

That made me mad. Why shouldn't I be scared? Since I was scared, did that mean I was weak? Did it mean I wasn't "good" enough? I'm not sure how Maria wasn't scared, but maybe she had less she was leaving behind. How dare he compare me to his saintly dead wife on the worst day of my life?

But then he asked me a question that I somehow heard through my terror and anger. He asked: "Are you afraid of death, or are you afraid of leaving your family?"

I considered his question carefully. Yes, the promise of pain was frightening, not knowing what would happen . . . after. But the thought that crushed my throat like hands around my neck was the thought of leaving you to suffer alone. Almost worse was the jealousy I felt at you living out the life we'd planned together without me. Leaving. I was definitely more afraid of leaving.

Dr. Neal said that Maria felt the same way, so she wrote letters, made videos, and set aside meaningful keepsakes to leave behind. He said that those plans made it easier to "let go." "Let go"—the phrase sounded so ridiculous to me. I'd never let go of my family, not willingly. Death will have to peel my fingers off the life I'm living to get me to leave you and our kids. I shook my head, crying harder than I ever had in front of someone that wasn't family. I asked Dr. Neal how I could "let go" when there were no guarantees?

He responded: "Sometimes you have to be your own guarantee."

That's when I realized that I already had my own plan. I'd been writing to you for months. I had two spiral notebooks full of thoughts, stories, and instructions. They'd been a safety net at first, a way to keep my fear of the cancer at bay. But now they are my final opus. I need you to take them seriously. I have so many things I need to tell you before I go. Things I've wanted to say for a long time. The only positive thing about dying is knowing I won't have to see your face when you find out all the reasons you should hate me. Maybe that's my final gift—when you find out all my secrets, you'll be glad I'm gone.

I'm in the north lot, car parked, writing. I'm still not sure what I'm going to say to you tonight in real life. I'm half tempted to keep Dr. Saunders's news a secret instead of making you all go through this again.

Love,

Natalie

Luke read the last paragraph three or four times, reading each word carefully, as though he could figure out her secrets in the spaces between her words. As he flipped back to the first page and started again, the flap on the mail slot clanked, and a single sheet of folded paper fluttered to the floor.

The paper wasn't framed on one side in spiral notebook fringe. It wasn't even in an envelope, not to mention that it was far too early for the postman to come. But after reading about Dr. Neal's and Natalie's ominous plans for some big reveal, he refused to sit back and wait.

Luke threw Natalie's letter on the stairs, the pages exploding against the steps, and took two long lunges toward the front door. He yanked at the handle, forgetting it was locked. Flustered, he fumbled with the dead bolt and tried again. This time the door flew open, letting in a damp gush of summer air turning warm in the sunrise.

Without his contacts in, he couldn't focus on the figure walking down the asphalt driveway, but he could make out a tall, slender woman in a formfitting yellow tank top and black shorts, wearing headphones connected to an armband wrapped around her bicep. She stopped at the street to fiddle with the device inside the band.

Luke rushed out of the house, his bare feet collecting dew as he ran through the grass. He grabbed the woman's elbow and spun her around. Annie's wide eyes and muffled scream made Luke drop his hand.

"What are you doing here?"

Annie yanked the earbuds out of her ears by the wires and placed a hand over her heart, her face flushed and framed with sweat. "Oh my God, Luke! You almost gave me a heart attack!"

"I'm so sorry. I saw the letter come through the mail slot and thought I might . . ."

"Oh," Annie interrupted, "you thought it was one of your Natalie letters."

Luke shrugged, suddenly aware he must be a disheveled mess barefoot, wearing only his boxers and fitted undershirt. He ran a hand through his wild hair, self-conscious.

"I guess. I was being stupid. Wrong time, wrong color, wrong method of delivery. I overreacted."

"Uh, so you didn't read it then?" she asked, fumbling with the rubber earpiece on the end of her earbuds.

"No. I didn't get a chance before running you down like a crazy person. Did I mention I was sorry?"

"Don't apologize; that was my fault. That's what the note was for," Annie said, blushing. Luke started to disagree, but a pointed look kept him silent. "Maybe that was cowardly."

"Cowardly?" Luke asked, a tightness hitting him between the shoulder blades. What could she tell him in a note she wouldn't want to say face-to-face? "Listen, I'm sorry about last night. It was such an asshole thing to say. I can't believe that came out of my mouth." Luke scratched the stubble on his cheek, wishing Annie would look at him so he could decide if she was still mad or just embarrassed.

"It's okay. I shouldn't expect you to understand me and Brian." She shook her head; a chunk of her clipped-back bangs fell into her eyes. "But we're working on it. That's all I have to say about that." She swept a flat hand in a semicircle in front of her, like she was washing the memory away. Luke gritted his teeth and took a step closer to Annie, touching her on the elbow, gently this time.

"Hey, I won't make you talk about it, but please"—he paused, trying not to get angry—"if you need me, you can call me, day or night. You don't have to let someone hurt you."

"That hasn't happened in a long time. I swear. We are doing great." Luke raised his eyebrows. He knew better; he'd seen the finger-shaped bruises on her arm just a few days ago. Annie ignored him. "I know you can't understand. You and Natalie had the perfect marriage. Not everyone has that, Luke."

"Don't do that. Don't assume my marriage was perfect. No one is perfect." *Not even Natalie.*

"Well, not perfect, but still, you guys were happy and in love. It was so obvious. Last night, when I left here, I was mad. Really mad. I didn't want to talk to you ever again, honestly. But then when I thought about how my life with Brian must look to someone used to such a happy life, I understood."

Luke ground his teeth, trying to keep himself from reliving all the moments in his early life he thought of when he imagined Brian and Annie. It wasn't his happy marriage that made him afraid for Natalie's best friend; it was his unhappy childhood. But Annie didn't know about any of that.

"Yeah, I thought Natalie and I were happy too." He ran his hands through his hair, forgetting to care what it looked like. "I don't even know if any of it was real anymore."

"You don't mean that." Annie finally looked him in the eye, dropping her earbuds.

"It's true. You can't assume everything's okay inside the house just because the paint isn't peeling and the yard is neatly mowed."

"What the *hell* are you talking about?" Annie asked, stomping her foot.

"I'm saying that I think . . . I think Natalie had a child with someone else and didn't tell me about it." He punctuated each word, lingering on "someone else." It hurt to think it, but to say it out loud? It was cathartic. The anger he'd been hiding and holding inside rose to the surface, seeping through his skin like sweat.

"Luke." Annie grabbed his bare arm, her cold hands shocking him. "What haven't you told me?"

"It's possible"—he shook his head—"no, it's probable that Natalie had a baby with Andy Garner and put it up for adoption."

"Wait, her high school boyfriend? From Pentwater?" Annie's nails dug into his skin. "Why would you think that?"

"Will found this envelope in some of her old stuff. It was from an adoption agency in Chicago and postmarked fourteen years ago. Will was having a hard time at school one day and told Ms. Mason . . . Felicity . . . that the envelope was proof he was adopted. So, to calm Will down, I went to visit one of the agency's maternity houses in Kalamazoo."

"And they actually told you about Andy and Natalie? I thought that was illegal."

"They didn't tell me anything," Luke confirmed, wondering why he was telling her so much, "but there was a picture of Andy and Natalie there. Another one in the brochure they gave me."

Annie stood in silence for a moment, playing with the cord to her headphones. "First, I think you should take a paternity test. That should take care of Will's concerns."

"We already took a test," Luke interjected, "after that trip. Will's imagination was coming up with some wild scenarios. I thought it was the simplest way to get proof."

"Perfect. So, what did it say?" Annie asked, tossing her headphones over her shoulder. Luke thought she answered with more curiosity than someone so sure of Natalie's fidelity should.

"Still waiting on results, but I'm not worried about who Will's dad is. I'm more worried about . . ." Luke shrugged, hoping Annie would pick up on the hint so he wouldn't have to explain his suspicions again.

"And that brings me to my second thought." Annie slid her hands down Luke's forearms, sending goose bumps across his skin. Holding both of his hands in hers, she looked him square in the eyes. "*We* are going to Pentwater—to figure out this so-called love child Natalie had with Andy Garner."

"No, I couldn't," he sputtered. "I've already taken off so much work, and besides, I'm not very good at confrontations."

"We can't leave today. We need time to plan," she said, swinging his arms back and forth. "Brian and I go to DC the twenty-eighth for some house hunting, but I come home before his final interview. That means I'll be here alone for the Fourth of July weekend. Is Andy still a realtor?"

"Yeah, took over his dad's business."

"Okay, I'll make an appointment to look at houses with him in Pentwater. We'll drive out there, and when he shows up for our appointment, we'll get the whole story, together."

Luke considered the plan, staring past Annie at the pinkish-yellow sunbeams filling the sky, the sun rising slowly from behind the house across the street. Her plan could work, but there was only one flaw.

"I might not want to know." He wanted to know, and he also didn't want to know. Imagining Andy confirming that he and Natalie had a child together out there somewhere made Luke want to go back to bed and hide under his covers.

"Take a few days to consider it. I think talking to Andy is what you need. There has to be a less complicated explanation for *all* of this."

Luke sighed and nodded, not sure being in the same town—much less the same room—as Andy would be good for anyone. "I'll be able to think a lot clearer when Terry is gone." He let go of Annie and checked his pockets for his phone before remembering he was still in his boxers. Desperate, he tapped the screen on the phone strapped to Annie's arm. Six thirty already. "She's going to be here in two hours. I need to get breakfast made, cleaned up, and maybe some clothes on Clayton before she gets here. I better go."

"Sounds terrifying." Annie readjusted her rogue bangs in a large tan clip and tightened her stubby ponytail. "And I better get back to my run."

"Okay," Luke said, folding his arms again, this time from a sudden chill. "I'm sorry, again, for interrupting. I'll call you later this week about Pentwater."

"Or you can always text me," Annie added, raising her eyebrows and pushing her sporty pink earbuds back in. Luke nodded—texting would be a far easier way to turn down Annie's offer. Turning back for one quick wave, she launched off the driveway and headed down the nearly sunny street. She bounced from one foot to the other in one fluid motion, like it came to her as naturally as walking. He'd never been interested in running before—he'd rather spend his workouts with some dumbbells or a punching bag—but watching Annie run made it look almost enjoyable.

When Annie turned at the end of the street, Luke headed back into the house through the open front door. Sheets of notebook paper littered the entry, crinkling under the ball of his foot. Luke shut the door with his elbow and then leaned over to pick up the pages off the floor, the squeaky voices of cartoon characters echoing through the entry. He tried not to read any of the words scrawled across the papers. Lifting his foot, he grabbed the last remaining page, this one folded in half. Definitely not Natalie's.

Luke unfolded the page. The stiff, fancy card stock felt strange after spending so much time reading off cheap lined paper. On the top of the page was Annie's name, written neatly in black lettering, and below it, one sentence:

You were right.

CHAPTER 18

"Who are you texting? Is it Natalie's friend again? What's her name?" Terry asked for the fourth time since Luke parked the car in the airport parking lot. The week with his mother-in-law was mercifully over, and the only reason he felt any sort of sadness was because the kids would be leaving with her.

"Annie. Her name is Annie," Luke reminded Terry for the tenth time since they had dinner with Annie two nights ago. Terry knew Annie's name—she'd seen her every day for weeks before Natalie died— but for some reason she'd been "forgetting" it recently. Undoubtedly some form of passive aggression aimed directly at Luke.

"Ah, yes, Annie." She said her name like she was holding out a stinky sock. "Why doesn't that lovely Jessie girl take care of Clayton full-time? I really think he needs more consistency, and that Jessie is impressive. Have you ever heard her sing? She was playing that karaoke video game with the kids in the basement. She can't carry a tune, but if talent was measured by spirit, she'd be starring on Broadway." Terry stopped in front of the sliding doors as if she doubted they'd open. When they slid apart, she waved the children through so she was standing next to his side when they entered the busy terminal. "If it's about money, I'm willing to pitch in."

Pitch in? The last time Terry had to pay a sitter, the price would've been in cents per hour rather than dollars. She'd probably send him a crisp ten-dollar bill every month and feel like a saint.

"Jessie was in college, and she's looking for a teaching job. We're lucky to get as much of her as we do." Luke searched for the correct airline counter.

"That girl in a classroom full of children? No, she's far too frail for that. She'd probably catch every cold. I saw her bracelet." Terry raised her eyebrows like that explained everything. "Think about it," she said and then entered the line for the ticket counter.

Standing in line at the ticket counter, Luke took every opportunity to squeeze May's shoulder or bump Will's side or wrap an arm around little Clay. Six weeks with no kids—it felt like an eternity, and he didn't know if he should be excited or reticent. Part of him craved a few extra minutes of sleep, eating a meal while it was still hot, or using the bathroom without small fingers waving at him from under the locked door. But another part of him knew that as soon as they went through the point of no return and headed toward security, he'd miss them. The house would be too big and far too quiet.

"You guys be good for your grandma." He tried to put on a stern voice with limited success. "And don't forget, you can call me anytime you want. *Anytime.*"

"We know, Daddy," May said like she was annoyed, but she gazed up at him with wide eyes, filled with admiration. Luke gave her cheek a quick peck.

"Yeah, you told us like six times on the way here." Will wrapped his hand around the tall handle of his suitcase and wheeled toward the security area, stopping a few feet away expectantly. "You need help, Grandma?"

Terry wrestled with three bags, all plainly too big to be carry-ons. One of them was so heavy she had to pay a fifty-dollar fee to get it on the plane. But letting Will bring his guitar was "too much of a hassle." Luke would never get Terry and her priorities.

"Aren't you a dear?" She beamed at Will. He'd always been Terry's obvious favorite, though she'd never admit it. At five foot two, with her bobbed silver-streaked reddish-brown hair and faded gray eyes, Terry usually looked nothing like her daughter. But when she smiled, Luke could see some of Natalie in her, and it made him remember why he was happy the kids were going to spend the summer with her.

Terry handed over her shoulder bag and second roller suitcase. Everyone, including Clayton, was pulling some kind of carry-on at this point. "Thank you, Willie; you get an extra scoop of ice cream tonight. Don't let me forget."

"I could never forget ice cream," Will said, without even flinching when she called him Willie. Only Grandma Terry could get away with that name.

"May, get Clayton's hand, please, and take him to the couches over there." She pointed to a cluster of upholstered chairs kitty-corner to the security lines. "I need to speak to your father for just one more moment. You too, Will. You can look through those bags and make sure we got out all the fluids."

Will shrugged and adjusted the bag on his shoulder before following May and Clayton. Luke turned to face Terry. Her muted gray eyes stared back at him in that critical way he was well used to. Instead of waiting for whatever she was going to say, Luke took the silence as an opportunity.

"All right, don't forget May needs Benadryl if she's going to be around any animals. She can't take the pills though, only the liquid. And Will has to have his EpiPen nearby during all outdoor activities where there might be bees. And it's not just bee stings, also wasps and hornets and yellow jackets. Basically anything that flies and has a stinger is dangerous . . ."

Terry held up a hand, interrupting and unapologetic. "Luke, I already know all this. That's not why I wanted to talk to you alone."

"Oh, okay," Luke said weakly. He worked on pulling down the edge of his shirt, bunched up under the duffel hanging by his side.

"Before I go, I want to know one more thing." Terry crossed her arms and took a long breath through her nose before finishing her thought. "How long have you and that Annie woman been lovers?"

"What?" Luke ejected, not sure if he should yell or laugh hysterically. "Lovers? Is that why you want Jessie to watch the kids? My God, Terry. What the hell?"

"I didn't expect you to be honest, but don't treat me like an idiot. If you want to make a fool of yourself with a married woman, that's your choice. But I need to know when this started. Did you at least keep it in your pants long enough for my daughter to die?" Terry's cheeks burned crimson, and her voice was getting loud enough that the security guards chatting about twenty feet away were starting to take notice.

Luke stared at her incredulously, trying to figure out why in the world Terry would think something sordid was going on between him and Annie. After Annie's trip with Brian had been delayed a few days, she'd come over for dinner to see the kids and say hi to Terry.

Nothing seemed off back then. Terry and Annie spent a few hours after dinner reminiscing about Natalie and some of the better times they'd had together. When she left, Annie hugged Terry tightly, like they'd finally bonded. Annie came back two days later to say one last good-bye before she left for her trip to DC with Brian. She'd given Luke a hug too, maybe an extra squeeze of his shoulders than normal, but that was only because she knew how much he was struggling. And the texting . . . okay, there had been a lot of texting.

"Terry, I'm only going to say this once—Annie and I are not now, nor have we ever been, lovers." Luke cringed at that word. Somehow he managed to keep his voice steady, not letting on as to how hurtful her accusations were.

Terry wheezed a quick breath in and out. If she kept breathing like that, she'd pass out, which would solve Luke's annoyance issue but ruin the kids' trip.

Luke continued before Terry could open her mouth and make him say things he'd regret. "Annie and I are definitely close friends, but Natalie wanted that. I'd never cheat on Natalie, and I'd never encourage Annie to be unfaithful to her husband." Luke had more reasons to question Natalie than Terry had to question him. Then again, if Natalie had had a baby with Andy Garner, then Terry probably knew about it. She was such a hypocrite. "Now, if you don't mind, I think you should be going. You don't want to miss your plane."

Terry's face went from red to stark white. Luke had turned to join the kids and escape the accusations when he heard Terry mutter something so low he was sure she didn't mean for him to hear it.

"I always knew you'd end up like your father."

Luke's foot froze midair. Like his father? Like the abusive drunk who destroyed everything beautiful and innocent in his childhood? Who robbed him of his mother, his sister, and his home? Before he could think better of it, Luke whipped around. Terry crashed into him, her bronze-rimmed glasses smashing up against the bridge of her nose.

"If I find out you are telling my children anything about Walter Samuel Richardson, you will never be allowed to see your grandchildren again. Understood?" Luke was trembling and about five seconds from pulling the plug on the Florida trip altogether. Clayton ran up and tugged on the handle of one of Terry's suitcases. She didn't seem to notice, still staring Luke down, her glare saying more than any words could.

"Gramma. Hurry. Will says we're gonna be late."

Luke looked down at his son's eager face, the dimple on his right cheek showing like it always did when he was ecstatic about something. The fury immediately drained out of him as if someone had pulled out the stopper in a tub.

"We're coming, bud. No one is going to miss his or her plane today. Right, Grandma?" Luke gave Terry a pointed look, eyebrows raised.

"No, no, dear, we have plenty of time. Go get your brother and sister, and we'll be on our way."

"Okay!" Clayton dragged the dark-blue carry-on behind him, even though it probably weighed as much as he did.

"Good-bye, Luke," Terry said coldly, not making any effort to look at Luke as she walked past him. The wheels of her suitcase rolled over his toes. Every part of him wanted to tell Terry where she could shove it, throw the kids in the car, and never see that woman again. He could do it, and he would do it, if it weren't for the kids and Natalie.

So, he went through the motions and said his farewells to the children. Clayton and Will were unfazed, while May cried like she was going off to war. Once he got May settled, Luke managed a polite wave to Terry and then stood back so they could go through security together.

Unfortunately, the line was short, so much sooner than he wished, they'd all passed through the metal detector and were gathering their belongings on the other side of the X-ray machine. He tried not to watch as they disappeared down the hall leading to their gate. He briefly contemplated purchasing a ticket and rushing through security for one more hug, and then his phone buzzed. A text.

He slipped the phone out of his pocket. He'd finally put it in a black case and tempered-glass screen protector after dropping it three times in the first week. When he glanced at the screen, he couldn't help but smile. A text from Annie.

Hope airport goodbyes went okay.

Luke used the tip of his index finger to answer, still finding texting awkward and slow.

Luke: Goodbyes okay. A few tears.

Annie: You or May? Haha.

Luke: Both.

Annie: Aw. Terry is gone! Focus on that. Don't forget—I come home tomorrow which means: ROAD TRIP!

Luke had been trying to figure out the best way to tell Annie he'd changed his mind, that facing Andy and finding out the truth was not his idea of a fun way to spend his holiday weekend. Felicity had asked him to go to the fireworks on the fourth. They'd been exchanging e-mails since their last date, but Luke hadn't had the gumption to take her out again while Terry was there.

But this could be his best chance to finally discover the truth. And if Terry was going to stand over him all preachy and morally superior while lying to him about his wife's past, Luke needed to know. How could he find a future with someone if he couldn't stop obsessing about what happened in the past? Fine. He needed to know what really happened between Natalie and Andy Garner, and he needed to know now.

Luke: I'm in.

JULY

CHAPTER 19

"Hey, you want a Twizzler?" Annie had her elbow deep in a paper grocery bag filled with snacks. They were twenty minutes away from Pentwater, and in the past three hours, Luke had eaten half a bag of pretzels, a whole can of Pringles, two sticks of jerky, and a sixteen-ounce bottle of Coke. He kept thinking he couldn't eat any more, and then Annie would pull another treat out of her magic bag and somehow make it sound amazing.

"Do you have the whole candy section of the grocery store in there or something?" Luke tried to peek inside the bag but was distracted by the two twisted strands of licorice in Annie's hand.

"Here, open your mouth." She waved the ropelike treat in front of his face, and Luke dropped his jaw. Annie flung the candy into his mouth, and he bit off the tip, taking his hand off the wheel long enough to grab the rope before it fell into his lap.

The sugary-sweet treat tasted like strawberries and flashed him back to Sunday afternoons in Natalie's backyard fort, chomping on a pack of Twizzlers they'd snuck from Terry's "hands-off, kids" cupboard.

"Natalie and I used to bite off both ends and stick them in a can of pop as a straw. It usually made the pop taste disgusting, but we didn't care."

"Mmmm . . . gross." Annie snorted. "I love that you guys met when you were kids. Will you show me around the town a little if we have time?"

Luke didn't have a lot of love for Pentwater. He'd lived there with his parents for fourteen years. He could close his eyes and recall all the best bike paths and the days of the week you could pass through Mrs. Sterling's yard without getting a call to your mom. But when he let those memories in, the others came too, like the fear that heavy footsteps and clinking bottles could bring to a little boy or how small his baby sister looked lying dead, blood-soaked, in his mother's arms. Luke shook his head as if by doing so, he could rid himself of these haunting memories.

"You're lucky we're going to be there during the summer, when all the tourists are in town and the fishing boats are running. We should be getting there early enough to see the fishermen bring in the catch of the day." When Luke's dad was sober, he was one of those men heading out before sunrise, returning smelling of fish guts, beer, and sweat.

When he was younger, Luke would go down to the harbor and watch his dad gut and fillet the fish he brought in. His hands were so nimble, and Luke was sure his fingers would never be able to work so efficiently. Turns out it wasn't a skill he needed to learn. He still avoided the seafood section at the grocery store, the smell bringing back memories he liked to pretend he didn't have.

"First things first though. We are meeting Andy at 813 Winter Lane in about fifteen minutes. Think we'll make it?" Annie asked.

They'd exited the highway a few miles back, and the sun was playing with the thick greenery that acted as a canopy over the two-lane highway. A green sign with an arrow said PENTWATER 5 MI. Luke's hands tensed on the wheel. They were almost there; this was really happening. He still hadn't worked through what he was going to say. One of his biggest worries was that Andy wouldn't remember him at all and he'd have to go through some explanation instead of skipping right into the questions and accusations.

"Oh yeah, we're very close. Look, there is the old MacTarlton house." He pointed to a blur of old cars and garbage stacked into non-descript piles of brown. "They were hoarders before being a hoarder was something that could get you on TV."

"Wow, you have a very accurate memory."

"Not that hard. Fourteen years is a long time to live somewhere."

"But you were only a kid. I don't think I remember half of what happened to me before the age of twelve. Then again, we moved around a lot, so I guess I wouldn't know what living in a small town would be like."

"Why'd you move so much?" He took a quick glance at Annie, preferring to hear stories about her life than think about ones from his own.

"Army brat." She pulled her knees up to her chest, the seat belt straining against her shoulder. "I was used to it. It was a lot harder to learn how to stay in one place once I met Brian."

"Funny, I was the opposite. I moved around a lot from fourteen until I turned eighteen. It was hard to go from being a small-town boy to living from a suitcase." The trees suddenly opened up to Pentwater Lake on the left and Pentwater River on the right. Luke's fingers started to twitch and he grasped the wheel tighter, hoping Annie hadn't noticed. It was time to turn on the road to his childhood home. He took the turn cautiously, checking left and right several times before pressing forward, trying to act casual.

"Oh, and here is the Hexagon House. It's still a B&B." Luke took another bite of his Twizzler and bit down until it split open. He was overcome with an urge to take a quick right into the long paved drive-way of the yellow, two-story, hexagonal house. He and Annie could have lemonade on the wraparound porch and walk into town for dinner, watch the sunset at the Pierhead Lighthouse, and have ice cream at the Pentwater House of Flavors.

"It's changed hands at least twenty times since I was a kid, but it was gorgeous sixteen years ago when Nat and I visited."

"You haven't been here for sixteen years?"

"Never had a reason to visit. Nat's parents moved after she went off to school, and I have no reason to come back here. The only reason we came last time was to see . . ." Oh, yeah. Luke stared at the dotted yellow line flashing down the middle of the road. "It was to see Andy." His name was hard to say, and Luke bit the tip of his tongue to keep from saying more.

Part of Luke wanted to hide inside that bed and breakfast and behind the buoying effect of Annie's friendship. But when he thought of Andy, the way he used to watch Natalie's face when she wasn't looking or how his fingers sometimes lingered on her hand when they touched, an unfamiliar jealousy stirred inside him. Luke forced his foot down on the gas pedal, speeding past the yellow house and the temptation to hide inside.

"Ugh. Sorry, Luke, I didn't mean to bring him up." She took a bite of the licorice she'd been wrapping absentmindedly around her finger. "Whoa—look at all those fish." Annie gasped.

The speed limit slowed to twenty-five when they rolled on the main street of Pentwater. On the left were two docked fishing boats, both glistening white and one taller than his house, far more high-tech and luxurious than when his father had been a fisherman.

A group of men were clustered around the muck trough, expertly gutting and filleting their morning catch while their clients and a cluster of tourists gathered around to observe their flashing knives and expert fingers. Long, long ago, before he'd learned to hate his father, he'd come down to that very shelter and watch his father work from behind one of the painted burgundy pillars.

"Is that where your dad used to work?" Annie asked. She had no idea that it was ten times harder to talk about Walter Richardson than Andy Garner.

"Yup. He was a fisherman but also worked on a charter boat for a little while." They pushed forward, the rows of hanging silver fish blurring in his periphery.

"Did you ever do that?" She hooked her thumb over her shoulder back toward the marina.

It wasn't until Luke turned ten that his father even acknowledged his presence there. He'd ask him to pass a tool or turn the water on when it was time to rinse out his station. The whole pavilion stunk of fish guts and his dad's breath reeked of beer, but it was one of the few happy memories Luke had with his father.

As the summer came to a close, Luke had become proficient at assisting his father and the other men that used the pavilion. They'd often give him a couple of coins or, if he was really lucky, a bill or two. His father would pat his head, and even though his fingers smelled like fish and stuck to Luke's hair, he never pulled away.

"Only once," he muttered, feeling the memories pulling him down. "When I was ten."

◆　◆　◆

One morning after bringing in a significant haul, Walter Richardson called his son over to the trough. Luke grabbed the last beer out of the cooler and ran to his dad, holding the offering out to him. His father took the beer in one hand and opened it with the end of his filthy paring knife, foam racing down his arms.

"Hey there, bud. You wanna try?" He held up the knife and pointed to one of the fish hanging on the hooks beside him and then took a long drink out of his can. "It's time you learned."

Luke had never heard his father talk to him that way, with pride and confidence. He wanted nothing more than to please him, to stab the knife into the belly of the fish, perform the precise cuts, remove the still warm fish guts without flinching. Luke took the knife; it was sticky and heavier than he'd expected.

"First things first; gotta pick a good fish. I think one of these smaller salmon will do." Walter unhooked a silvery gray fish from the post and tossed it down in front of Luke on the cleaning station. The fish's blank black eye stared back at him accusingly. He swallowed back a flood of bile that burned the back of this throat. His father took another loud sip of his beer and then dug his index finger up under the fish's gills. Luke had never liked the way gills looked, like fleshy sandpaper with tentacles, and he was certain he wouldn't like the way they felt even more.

"Damn it!" His father slammed his hand down on the metal frame of the sink, and Luke's arms instinctively went up to protect his face, but his father was too distracted by the fish lying in front of them to notice. "Glenn didn't bleed this one out. Damn. Way to ruin a perfectly good fish." Luke saw the gills give a slight ripple, as though the fish was still gasping for breath. It was suffocating, drowning in the air, right in front of his eyes. Apparently a slow death made the meat taste bad. If the animal hadn't been 90 percent dead already, Luke may have been tempted to toss it back in the lake and worry about his father's reaction later.

His father shrugged. "Guess we'll take this one with us. Your mom won't care if it tastes a little off. And if you do a hack job of the cleaning, it won't matter. Your mom thinks you shit rainbows. Take the knife and cut right here." He drew an invisible line with his dirty fingernail down from the gills to the fish's jaw. "A quick slice will do it."

Luke tightened his grip on the hilt, sweat on his palm making it slippery. He took a step forward, really intending to cut the fish, to bleed it out, as his father said, but once he pressed the sharp tip of the knife against the fish's pliable skin, a wave of nausea hit him and he had to brace himself against the cool metal of the sink.

"Come on; we're wasting time." His father glanced at the two remaining fish on the hook and the half-empty marina. Most of the other fishermen had finished cleaning their haul half an hour ago, and if they didn't get the fish in the cooler soon, they'd be spoiled for sure. "You're embarrassing me. Stop being such a little girl. Stab the fish, Luke," his father growled.

It really wasn't very hard. All he had to do was press down a little, and it'd be over. The fish would be out of its misery, his father would be proud, and Luke would be able to run and hide, but even though he knew all that, his hand still wouldn't move.

His father slammed down his can of beer, and it sloshed out and on the trough, gathering into a golden pool of liquid.

"Damn you." He yanked the knife from Luke's hand, stabbed the fish in the neck, and raked the knife down from the gills and along the jaw. The gills gave one last flick and the fish went still, blood pouring out from the cut. His father turned with the knife clenched in his hand and pointed it at Luke.

"How hard was that?" he yelled, and the small group of tourists that had been on the charter his father worked on turned their heads toward his voice. He didn't notice and moved in closer to Luke, knife still raised. "Slice the gills and cut down, fast, like this." He pressed the blade against Luke's jaw as if to illustrate. Luke gasped when the sharp edge nicked his cheek, a hot trail of blood racing down his neck. Tears of fear and pain filled his eyes involuntarily. When his father saw them, he shoved Luke's shoulder, hard, knocking him to the ground. "Your damn mother turned you into a sissy. Go home; I can't stand looking at you right now."

"Walt!" A deep, familiar voice echoed through the marina's pavilion. Alex Kerks, the owner of Kerks Charters, stood above Luke. "What the hell do you think you're doing?" he half whispered, half yelled at Walt as he dipped down to kneel next to Luke. "Are you hurt?" He ran his eyes over Luke like searchlights.

"I'm fine," Luke whispered, covering the cut on his cheek, hoping Alex wouldn't ask about the blood. "I tripped on the bucket." He pointed to a black waste bucket several feet away, not nearly close enough to be in his way. Luke couldn't look at his father, so he pulled himself to standing and wiped his face with the inside of his collar. Alex's dark eyes bore into Luke's, and he could see the questions in them: Did Luke really need help but couldn't say it? Why was he covering for his father? What should happen now?

"You run home and get a Band-Aid for that cut." Alex patted him firmly on the shoulder, and Luke swallowed a lump in his throat, sure that the last place he should go was home because his father could find him at home, and after today, the cut on his face would be nothing compared to the hard whooping he would get. "I'll help your dad finish the fish."

Luke stared at the ground and mumbled, "Yes, sir." Then he ran, up Route 31, past the Chamber of Commerce, past Andy's dad's real estate office and the toy shop, past the House of Flavors and the post office. As he turned left on Lowell Street, he could feel a warm trail of blood pulsing out of the cut on his face, down his neck, and pooling around his collarbone.

He didn't slow down until the grass turned to sand and he could make out the concrete barricades that surrounded the Pentwater River. He slowed to a walk, ignoring the sand that filled his tennis shoes, making them feel like weights on his feet. A few families were sprawled out on the beach under umbrellas; one toddler in a swollen diaper poured buckets of sand over his father's feet, burying them only for a second before his father wiggled his toes and undid the little boy's work. Luke picked up his pace a little, trying to escape the happy giggles of the child as much as the expected wrath of his father.

There was an abandoned house about half a mile off the public beach that had a set of stairs nearly two hundred yards long. Luke liked to climb to the top and look out over the curve of the beach, watching the birds hunt for their dinner and the boats bounce in the waves. He'd watched the sun set countless times while sitting on those steps, hiding from his drunk father or crying mother, but always leaving before it got too dark for him to find his way home. But that night he didn't leave. When the sunset and the world turned black and cold, Luke curled up on the knobby wooden step, turning into himself, wondering if he could ever go home.

He did finally go home, but not until Officer Granson woke him with his flashlight and announced, "Found the kid," into his walkie-talkie. Apparently the whole town had been out looking for him after Alex fired his father and called the police to report the incident at the marina. The officer took him to the hospital twenty miles north in Ludington. Two stitches later, he was released into his mother's arms. A social worker was assigned to his family and visited monthly for the next two years. His father never laid a hand on him again.

◆ ◆ ◆

"Is this it?" Annie asked, breaking the silence while pointing to a gray one-story house on the left side of Winter Lane. Twenty-two years ago he'd walked out that door and swore he'd never ever walk back in, and he hadn't. He barely let himself think about what happened inside those walls, much less revisit them in person. Back then it was a white ranch, with red shutters and a peeling roof. It was a symbol of all he'd lost when he was forced to move away that hot July day.

Today, the house looked completely innocuous. The previous own-ers had the house re-sided in gray. By now it had probably been re-sided several times. The roof was new as well, white shutters framed the front windows, and a small addition jutted out to the right side of the house, where the ash tree used to be. That tree used to drop massive amounts of leaves on the house each fall, so Luke could see why they'd nixed it. The biggest difference was the green lawn and the large white and green **FOR SALE** sign in the front yard, with **GARNER REALTY** written in bold white letters.

To the right of Luke's childhood home, where Natalie's house used to sit, there was now a giant McMansion. Tearing down the old cottage-style homes and replacing them with modern palaces was a popular practice when the area's tourist traffic increased in the early 2000s.

Annie glanced between the two houses, resting her eyes on Luke's old home.

"This is a pretty little house. I wonder if people live here year-round or if this is a summer place."

"I don't know about now." Luke shook his head, putting the car in park across the street from his house. "This was a family neighborhood when I lived here."

"Why did you pick it?" Annie had made the call to Garner Realty to set up the appointment, but only after Luke sent her the listing for the house on Winter Lane. He was surprised to find it mixed in with all the vacation homes and empty land. It was the perfect location for this conversation to happen.

"I knew the people who used to live here." Luke couldn't stop staring at the house, noting all the changes. Maybe he was like that house, so changed that all those bad things from years ago didn't matter anymore. Though he was fairly certain he was more like Natalie's old house, a teardown that needed to be built again. "I don't know; I thought it might be nice to be somewhere a little familiar."

Annie ran a hand through her hair and slipped back on the black flats she'd taken off a few minutes into their trip. She was dressed up in a black pantsuit with a dark-blue silk blouse that matched the water in Lake Michigan. Twisting, she grabbed her purse from the backseat, slipped it over her shoulder, and pulled out a tube of lip gloss.

"So, do you think that's his car?" she asked, brushing the tip of the applicator across her bottom lip, squinting at the silver Mercedes parked in the driveway.

"I think so." Andy's grunge days were clearly over. "Our appointment was for ten minutes ago. I'm sure he's wondering where we are."

Annie mashed her lips together, tossed the lip gloss back in her bag, and stared at the side of Luke's face. "You never answered me earlier. Are you ready for this?"

Ready? No. He was not ready for any of this. But the more he'd considered Annie's crazy plan, the more he knew it had to happen.

"Yup." With a flick of his wrist Luke turned off the car and pulled the keys out of the ignition. He turned to face Annie. Her eyebrows were bunched up, cheeks flushed with nervous excitement. Luke let himself give one last smile before giving the go. "Thank you. I would never have done this without you."

"Don't thank me yet." She squeezed his shoulder. "Meet me inside in five minutes, okay?"

"Okay." He nodded. This was the plan. She'd go inside and get Andy comfortable, and then Luke would come in a few minutes later to take him off guard. "Good luck."

She readjusted her purse strap and rubbed her glossy lips together one more time. "Good luck," she said in return before jumping out the door and rushing across the street. He watched her knock on the door, the realtor lockbox hanging from the knob. A shadowy figure opened the door, and once Annie slipped inside, Luke let out a breath. No turning back now.

CHAPTER 20

Luke watched the glowing green numbers on his dashboard clock tick by. He attempted to distract himself with his phone, flicking through the videos and messages Will had sent during the past two weeks. Only two weeks, and Luke already missed the kids so badly he was tempted daily to catch the next plane to Florida so he could kiss them good night. Eventually he always remembered that visiting the kids meant visiting Terry too. After their exchange at the airport, he definitely wasn't ready for that.

The numbers finally clicked over to ten fifteen. He swung open the car door without even checking to see if any cars were coming up from behind him. The front path was still made of cement; a crack or two had been patched with darker cement than the original. He hopped over the cracks in between the slabs of cement, remembering the game he used to play as a kid. It was an unexpected happy memory from this house, a welcome change.

When he finally reached the glossy navy-blue door, Luke raised his hand to knock. Then he noticed the knocker. It was golden but covered with dark-bronze splotches where the gilding had peeled off. He knew that knocker. He knew that door. Nobody had taken the time to change either fixture. This was his house, and he'd be damned if he was going to knock. Turning the knob slowly, he pushed his body through the smallest crack he could fit in and shut the door behind him noiselessly.

The front room was dark, but he could make out the curve of carpet where it met the tile entryway. The house smelled of onions and potpourri, not at all familiar, and the carpet was a fluffy shag instead of the tight Berber of his childhood. But the ceiling fan was the same, the lights covered in those frosted-glass cuplike fixtures. Annie's feminine laugh floated out from the kitchen, and the deep rumble of a male voice followed it. Luke pulled his eyes away from the fan and followed the voices, his feet sinking into the unfamiliar carpet, his pulse beating in his ears.

The kitchen was on the other side of the living room. To get there, Luke had to pass the hallway leading to the bedrooms. The last time he was in that hall, it was covered with blood. Logically he knew it wasn't still there, but he still averted his eyes as he passed by. His feet were heavy, as though they were trying to tell Luke to turn around and go back. Then he heard Andy's voice, and the world turned still around him.

"This house is great for a family. It's been totally redone, inside and out. New plumbing five years ago, new carpet very recently, and the appliances are all still under warranty."

"Wow, did you know the previous owners?" Annie asked, sounding distracted, probably wondering what was taking Luke so long.

"It's a small town, so we all know each other pretty well, but lately we've had a lot of out-of-towners redoing houses and renting them out during the summer. I grew up in this town, so I did know the family who lived in this house before it became a rental cottage. Went to school with their kid."

"You did?" Annie sounded actually interested, even though she didn't know this used to be Luke's house.

"Oh, yeah." His voice deepened like he was going to share a secret. "It's a very sad story. The father was an alcoholic, used to beat the mom and the kid. One day, when the mom was pregnant, the dad came home blasted and . . ."

No. Luke refused to listen to Andy Garner tell this story. His feet woke up again and let him walk the last three steps into the kitchen. As he rounded the corner, Annie was leaning back against the white laminate counter. Andy Garner stood in the middle of the gray-tile floor, tan dress slacks with a belt, tailored blue shirt tucked in neatly. He definitely hadn't grown since their last meeting, still a head shorter than Luke. Every other thing about him had changed: his hair, what was left of it, was neatly trimmed, his clothes actually fit, and his midsection was thick, with twenty extra pounds.

"Hey, honey," Annie said in a singsong voice, "you made it." She stood straight and waved Luke over. That's when Andy Garner turned around with his hand extended, ready for a shake. It only took two steps before he stopped in his tracks.

"Luke? Luke Richardson? Hey there! What the heck are you doing here?" He seemed happy to see him. "You want to buy your old house? I thought you hated this place!"

"Maybe I want to buy it so I can tear it down," Luke quipped, an unexpected flash of anger escaping from deep within. Annie pushed off the counter, standing at attention.

"This is your house?" she asked quietly, like she was confused that he hadn't told her this information earlier. Andy glanced back at Annie and back at Luke.

"Wait, you got married again?" he asked. It sounded more like an accusation than a question. He could hear the word Andy had left out of that sentence. "You got married again . . . *already*?"

"No." Forget the plan. There was no way Luke was going to let Andy Garner act as the morality police. "She's just a friend." Andy snuck a quick look at Annie, who was standing erect, arms crossed tightly, face completely white.

"When she called," he tipped his head in Annie's direction, "she said she was your wife. Said your name was Charlie Fairbanks. What the hell is going on here, Luke?"

Andy's voice surged, all friendly curiosity gone. Luke instinctively took his hands out of his pockets, ready for a fight. He'd never hit a man before, but he wasn't about to let Andy Garner get one in without any warning, especially not in this house. No one was going to hit him in this house ever again.

"I needed to talk to you," Luke said simply.

"And calling my office didn't seem like an option?" Andy's signature sarcasm leaked through his professional exterior. For a moment Luke could see him like he had on the quad—oily hair, baggy clothes, steely brown eyes.

"This conversation needed to happen in person." Luke paused to gauge his response, but Andy's face was hard and mocking. No sign he knew what was coming. "Tell me about Maranatha House, Andy."

After the words left his mouth, it took a few seconds for them to register with Andy. But when they did, Luke could see the impact. Andy let out a deep sigh and shrunk at least three inches, like one of those Thanksgiving parade balloons deflating.

"Natalie promised me she'd never tell," Andy said, using up his last bit of oxygen. He took another breath; this one stuttered as it went in. He placed a hand over his eyes. "My wife doesn't even know." His voice was thick with emotion now. He looked up, panic in his eyes. "You aren't going to tell her, are you?"

Luke's mouth was completely dry. So, it was true. How could it be true? Every time his mind took him to this moment, the moment when he found out Will was not Natalie's first child and that his wife had been lying to him his whole marriage, he'd talk himself out of it.

He'd remind himself that Natalie hated dishonesty. Once, when they were kids, she'd gotten two gumballs out of the vending machine at the IGA, so she went to the counter and gave them an extra quarter. The owner was so impressed he'd put a picture of her behind the help desk with the words "Most Honest Customer" underneath. She'd never had a speeding ticket, cheated on a test, or snuck candy into a movie theater. How the hell did she keep this a secret?

Annie cleared her throat, still standing by the sink. Forming words became difficult through the red haze of anger creeping in around Luke's vision.

"Luke," she whispered, "you okay?"

He ignored Annie, narrowing in on Andy, who was standing in the middle of the room with his hands still over his mouth. He took a deliberate step toward the ever-shrinking man.

"Maybe we should tell her," Luke growled through gritted teeth.

"Luke"—Annie's voice was full of caution—"you never said anything about talking to his wife."

Luke curled his hands into fists, over and over, wanting to hit something, someone. He'd spent so much of his life forcing himself to be gentle, kind, to never let anyone flip the switch inside him that might turn him into his father. Now he was close, closer than he'd ever been, to surrendering to the force of a man who still haunted the memories of his childhood, even though he was long in the grave.

"I think she has a right to know."

Andy begged him, "Please, you can't." Luke felt no sympathy.

"Did you hold the baby when it was born? Did you kiss his head? What about my wife? Did you kiss her too?"

"Wait." Andy yanked at his collar. "I'm lost. This is about Natalie?" Andy began to inflate again, his nose nearly close enough to touch Luke's shoulder. "Listen, if you're not interested in the house, I need to ask you to leave or I'll call the cops." In a flash Andy had his phone out.

"You've got to be kidding me." Luke pushed back a sudden urge to slap the phone out of Andy's hand. "What were you two hiding, Andy?"

Andy jutted his chin out and shook his head slowly. "I can't believe Natalie married *you*," he said softly, like he was talking to himself. "I tried to warn her. You're a total psycho, like your dad."

Before he was aware of it, a growl started in Luke's lungs and crawled into his throat. His feet shuffled toward Andy, closing the gap between them. His hands curled into themselves, like he was getting ready for a workout on the bag at home. It'd only take a swift upper-cut with his right, jab in the stomach with his left, and if that wasn't enough, an elbow to Andy's back as he fell to the ground.

Suddenly Annie was wedged between the two men, one hand on Luke's chest and the other on Andy's shoulder. Her touch was gentle but firm, and it brought him back to reality. Luke's hands fell limp at his side, aching from how hard he'd been squeezing them. He'd almost hit someone. When that thought sunk in, it was heavy, like the sins of his father were suddenly his as well.

"Stop," Annie said, giving Andy's shoulder a sharp thrust. "Luke, tell him about the picture. Tell him."

"What picture? Who *are* you?" he asked, glaring at Annie before taking a large step back, making Annie's hand fall.

"Like he said, I'm a friend." She yanked out the brochure peeking out of Luke's shirt pocket and flipped it open. A polished fingernail pointed at the younger version of Andy, more hair, gigantic smile, and Natalie's arm hanging around his neck. "Tell us about this, Andy. Tell us about Maranatha House—why you were there with Natalie and why there are pictures of you all over that place." Annie held the trifold, cream-colored brochure up to Andy's face, other hand on her hip.

"How did you get that?" Andy asked, flustered.

"Luke's son found an envelope from Maranatha Adoptions. It was postmarked from around the time he was born. It had Natalie's name on it." She listed the facts like accusations. "That led Luke to Maranatha House. Okay. Your turn."

Andy reached up and took the dangling brochure from her hand and took a step back, staring at the open booklet. He touched the sepia-toned picture, and the corner of his mouth turned up like he was remembering something happy.

"I never had a child with Natalie," Andy said, still lost in the picture, "but I do have a daughter. Her name is Jill, and she lives in South Carolina with her adoptive parents, Carol and Jim Fletcher. She attends Davidson University. She has black, curly hair like me and light eyes like her mom."

"What?" Luke blurted, the paralyzing haze of anger lifting a little. Annie seemed to sense it and moved out of his path. "A daughter?"

"Yeah. I met her last year. Natalie helped me find her before she . . ." Andy's words caught in his throat. "Luke, you know Jill's birth mom, Nancy Gillingham." Andy's bravado was gone. "She sat between us in Mrs. Tillman's fourth-grade class. I had a huge crush on her. Junior year when she was a cheerleader and I was suddenly cool because I'd learned guitar, we went out for a few months.

"Then she got pregnant, and it felt like the end of my world. But Natalie, she knew what to do. She told me about this place her pastor worked at, this home for unwed mothers, or at least that's what they used to call it. Nancy lived there till she had the baby. No one knew but me and her parents and Natalie. The other kids thought she was living with her aunt in Indiana. Natalie drove with me to visit her at Maranatha. Every year they have a reunion and fundraiser in June. This year was the first time I've ever gone without Nat."

Andy looked right into Luke's eyes. "I didn't know she was lying to you. I'm sorry. Nothing ever, ever happened between us. I mean, I was in love with her, but she never could get over you." He chuckled like there was something funny about it. "I never really thought you two would make it, but after a while I stopped hoping she'd leave you, and I got on with my life—a pretty damn good one too."

He refolded the brochure and handed it to Luke, then retrieved a worn black wallet out of his back pocket. Slipping his pointer finger behind a stack of credit cards, Andy pulled out a wallet-size photograph and held it up for Annie and Luke.

"This was her senior picture. Jill sent it to me after she turned eighteen, after Natalie helped me track her down. Nat said she looks a little like a younger version of Minnie Driver."

Luke took the picture and flipped it over. In feminine handwriting, the name "Jill Fletcher" was written across the back with a phone number. Luke tried to memorize it, still not sure if he should believe Andy, but finding fewer reasons to question his story. The girl looked nothing like Natalie, and until that moment Luke hadn't realized that fear was lurking in the back of his mind. Luke passed the picture to Annie.

"She's beautiful. I can definitely tell she's your daughter." She handed the picture back to Andy and grabbed her purse, the metal clasp scratching against the countertop.

"We should go." She sighed, and hooked the strap over her shoulder as she turned to face Andy. "Thanks for your time, Mr. Garner. We'll get out of your hair now."

Annie brushed past Andy, who had his hands back in his pockets. Luke stared at the short, balding, thirty-something man he'd wanted to punch in the face only a few minutes earlier. Did he really believe Andy's story? The part about Natalie helping him was definitely convincing. He could even reason why she'd keep it secret, never one to break promises to friends.

"Sorry about the misunderstanding." Luke put out his hand, and Andy shook it briefly.

"I'm sorry for the stuff I said about your dad," he mumbled back. Luke was more sorry that, at the moment, Andy had been right.

"Yeah, well, we both were saying things we didn't really mean." Andy nodded and followed Annie out the door.

Alone in the front room, Luke took one last look around. The house was only a shadow of the home he'd grown up in, but paint and wallpaper wasn't strong enough to disguise the film of evil still clinging to the hallway where his sister died. Luke shook off the memory. It was just a house.

As Annie and Andy filled the awkward exit with small talk on the front porch, Luke counted the steps from the kitchen to the door. Twelve. When he'd walked out of the house with the CPS agent twenty-two years earlier, it had been nearly double, twenty-three. Back then he cried as he was escorted into the waiting car. Today he felt relief.

"I can't believe that just happened," Annie said, staring at the ground as she walked across the lawn while Andy locked up. "I've never seen that side of you."

"I . . . I didn't plan it," Luke said, coming up beside her. "And I think I could say the same thing of you, stepping between me and Andy. That was . . . bold." Not a word he'd usually use to describe Annie. A few months ago she couldn't get a word out when that bartender was coming on to her. Today, she was strong and stood up to both Luke and Andy.

"I know." Annie stopped at the curb to look both ways. Luke wanted to laugh because the road was visibly empty, plus the speed Nazi, Mr. Slattery, strictly enforced the ten-miles-per-hour speed limit. If he still lived there, he'd call the police if anyone edged above twelve. But Luke wasn't ready to make jokes, so he paused and pretended to look up and down Winter Lane. "Once you two started arguing, it was obvious Andy knew more than he was telling us. Something snapped. I didn't expect his story, though, did you? About Natalie's pastor help-ing Andy and his girlfriend? Then the picture of the girl who looked creepily like Andy."

"I still don't know what to believe." Luke's foot hit asphalt as Andy's car beeped open in the background. There was something about his story that struck a nerve. It wasn't Nancy hiding away at Maranatha or

Andy keeping the whole thing a secret from his wife or even Natalie helping them in a difficult situation. Luke pulled the keys out of his pocket and handed them to Annie. "I'll be right back," he said and took off across the street without looking before she could respond.

Andy was already buckled in his seat, window up. He'd barely clicked the gearshift into reverse when Luke reached his door. Luke beat against the glass with an open palm. The music was loud inside the car, so it took three attempts to get Andy's attention. Noticing Luke on the other side of the window, Andy rolled the window down with a whir, letting out a gush of cool, conditioned air.

"Uh, did you forget something?" Andy asked, holding the wheel tightly, the gold band on his left hand catching the light.

"I had one more question." Luke took a few deep breaths, still worn out from running. Andy didn't look eager to wait, so Luke blew out his last breath and leaned into the car window. "The pastor you mentioned, the one Natalie referred you to . . ." Andy nodded. "What was his name?"

"Uh, that was a long time ago. Natalie contacted him when we were looking for Jill. His name was"—Andy scratched the top of his bare head—"Townsend, I think."

Luke let out a breath and cracked a very brief smile. He was being silly, thinking Andy and Natalie had some big adoption scheme going on. Stupid.

"Yeah, that was it," Andy added, rolling up the window. "Pastor Neal Townsend, but Natalie always called him Pastor Neal."

CHAPTER 21

Luke pushed the power button on the side of his phone and put it back in the front pocket of his jeans. He wouldn't check the profile again. There were only so many times he could look at the few snippets of information he had tracked down on the Internet. He'd searched Pastor Neal Townsend, Dr. Neal Townsend, Dr. Townsend, and the all-too-familiar: Dr. Neal. All searches brought him back to the same man—the man in Natalie's contacts list.

Unfortunately there wasn't a whole lot of online info about the former pastor turned college professor. A grainy photo on the Eastern Michigan University website, a brief and seemingly outdated bio of Dr. Neal Townsend, and the words "associate professor" underneath. Luke had even pushed the boundaries on crazy and paid for a background check, but the guy was a saint. Not even a traffic ticket.

The mystery of Maranatha House was all but over. This Neal still bothered Luke though. He couldn't put his finger on *why*, but it did.

Luke scanned the sandwich shop for Felicity. They were meeting for dinner and a movie, and he was so nervous he'd ended up getting there early. This was their third official date, not counting the cinnamon rolls in her office. It wasn't until halfway through their second date that

Luke felt comfortable being alone with Felicity. Sure, he spent plenty of time with Annie, but that was . . . different.

Luke and Annie had already been through the "getting to know you" phase and the "seeing you at your worst" phase of friendship. He could be in the same room with Annie for an hour without feeling the need to say a word. At the same time, there were a few nights when they spent the entire evening texting about almost nothing. She was his main accomplice in the hunt for Neal's digital footprint, which was nearly nonexistent; his association with Maranatha House must have been in the pre-Internet days. They'd been in touch constantly, even though there hadn't been a reason to see one another since the visit to Pentwater, which was probably for the best. The new job at Tanglewood was nearly a sure thing. A dream house had been selected in Virginia and a realtor hired in Michigan. Luke hoped the move would wait until after the kids got back in a few weeks.

Even while ignoring the impending move, Luke was thankful for the distraction of Annie's friendship. The few letters of Natalie's he'd received recently were shorter than ever. Her handwriting was sloppy and light, as if she didn't have enough energy to press the pen down on the page. Those letters used to be the highlight of his week. Now they were only a reminder of how she slowly faded away from him and turned into a shell of her former self. Exactly the fear she'd written about on her first day of chemo.

Today's letter was dated from the end of October. She'd caught a cold from one of the kids, and it nearly killed her. She came home to the hospital bed in the front room, knowing they'd set the stage for her death. That day she wrote six sentences.

DAY 294

Dear Luke,
I'm finally home from the hospital. Thought I might never see these walls again. It feels right that I'll leave

this world surrounded by those I love. You are doing such a good job taking care of us all. I know now I should've told you the truth a long time ago. Now it might be too late.

Love,

Natalie

She mentioned her secret more and more the closer she got to her death. If it wasn't about Will and Andy, Luke was certain the mysterious Dr. Neal was involved in this big secret somehow. Annie almost had him convinced that no matter what Natalie had been hiding, it didn't matter anymore.

Felicity yanked open the heavy glass door into the sandwich shop, stunning as always. Today her unruly curls were somehow tamed and flowed out in curly rivulets from under a paisley scarf. The blue in the scarf headband matched her eyelet sundress.

"Hey there!" She waved. Luke pushed his chair out and stood. Felicity crossed the room and put her arm around his shoulders, went to her toes, and kissed his cheek.

"You look nice." Luke tried to remember all the right things to say to your date.

"You too." She pulled back and looked him over, smiling broadly. He wasn't sure how jeans and a polo could constitute "looking nice." He had put on some cologne, so maybe her olfactory senses were overriding her sense of sight. "You ready to order?" she asked. "The movie starts at eight, so we only have an hour."

"Yeah, I'm ready. Actually, I'm starving. What's good here?" Luke asked, glancing up at the counter, where a sign suspended from the ceiling read **ORDER HERE**. As he squinted to get a better view of the menu, Felicity slipped her petite hand into his, interlacing their fingers. His pulse raced, and he still wasn't sure if it was from excitement or dread.

A group of teenagers poured in through the door, and Felicity tugged him forward, into line just ahead of the horde. Like it or not, he had to make some choices soon. Kisses on the cheek and playful handholding wouldn't suffice forever. Soon Felicity would want a real relationship, and Luke needed to decide if he was ready to put the letters and his suspicions down and pick up a new phase in his life.

Half an hour later they were sitting across from each other, both with half-empty cups of pop and empty sandwich wrappers. Luke found it easy to banter back and forth with Felicity. As Luke sucked up his last bit of Diet Coke, the real questions started.

"So, the paternity test. Is it back yet?" She asked it so simply, Luke wished he had a simple answer as well. She didn't know about Andy or Maranatha or Pentwater.

"I have the test."

"What?" She leaned over her cup, mouth hanging open a little. "Did I know this and I have the worst memory? Or did it just come?"

"Got it a few days ago. Sorry, I wanted Will to know first. We opened it together on FaceTime." The phone in his pocket buzzed against his thigh. He put his hand over it, hoping to muffle the sound.

Felicity didn't notice. She took a sip of her drink and placed the cup down gently. She held the liquid in her mouth for a second before swallowing.

"Sooooo." She twisted her lips up to one side in a half smile. "Can I know the results?"

The phone buzzed again. The irregular notifications must mean texts. If it was an emergency, Terry would definitely call. Luke tried to refocus.

"Oh, yeah, it's what we thought. He's my kid, 99.999 percent sure." The phone buzzed again, and Luke swore mentally.

"Well, that's wonderful. Do you think he's ready to accept the results?"

"Definitely. I think he always knew it, deep down. I guess I'll be able to gauge things better when he comes home next month—" Another buzz cut him off midsentence, and Felicity leaned on her elbows like she always did at her desk during their meetings. Usually she was about to suggest something he might find uncomfortable.

"Luke, you want to check that? I really don't mind. It could be your mother-in-law." She swatted at a stiff strand of hair that had wrestled loose from the scarf and was flapping against her eyebrow.

"It's okay. Terry doesn't know how to text and Will's phone is on the fritz, so the only person who texts me is . . ." Annie. He finished the sentence in his head. It had to be Annie texting him. He yanked the phone out of his pocket, his shoulders tightening with anxiety. Usually he would assume the text was a smart comment about finally getting out of the dark ages of technology or a picture of a cat sleeping in a cup, but she knew he was on a date. If it was Annie, then there had to be a reason she was texting so frantically.

The screen was so full of message notifications he had to scroll down to see them all. The first one said: Call me.

He traced his finger down the screen to read the next one: I need your help. ASAP.

What did that mean? Annie almost never asked for help, even when it meant using a stepladder to reach stuff on the top shelf in the pantry rather than asking him or Will to grab it for her. The next message made the hairs on his neck stand on end: I'm scared.

That simple sentence made so many memories come flooding back to him. Blood on the carpet, his mother crying and holding her stomach, his father throwing an empty bottle on the kitchen floor and walking out the front door without bothering to close it.

◆ ◆ ◆

"I'm scared," his mother said, reaching out her hand to fourteen-year-old Luke. Her blonde hair was streaked with bloody highlights where she'd run her fingers through it. It was bad. Worse than he'd ever seen. Where was all the blood coming from? He searched her body for a gaping wound but didn't find any. She grabbed her stomach as another pain hit her. "The baby is coming."

"What?" Luke knelt beside her, counting the bruises. "But it's too early."

"She's coming." His mother moaned, a tear falling down her cheek, washing away a streak of blood. Horror settled on Luke's shoulders. The baby wasn't due for another two and a half months. If she came now . . . what should he do? He lunged for the keys in the bowl on the counter.

"I can drive you to the hospital; I know I can."

"No, no." She shook her head. "Too dangerous."

"Tell no one" had always been the family motto when it came to his father's drunken fits, but the first name that came to his mind now was Natalie. Her parents were sane enough. They'd know what to do to help.

"I'll get Mrs. Egart. She can help. She's had babies. I can't do this; I can't . . ."

His mother's face hardened, eyes like steel. "No. Not her." Pain broke through her mask, and she let out a gasp. "No one can help now."

◆ ◆ ◆

"Luke. Luke? Everything okay?" Felicity pulled him back to reality. Luke read through the messages again.

A busboy walked past their table. "You finished? I can take your garbage."

"Thank you," Felicity replied without taking her eyes off Luke or the phone.

"Can I get you anything else?"

Luke blinked up at him. "No. We're fine. Thank you." Which must have been the magic words because the busboy finally backed away.

"What's going on?" Felicity asked, staring at his phone as if she could make out the words on his screen if she looked hard enough.

He didn't know how to answer her. The scared protector inside him wanted to leave the table, run to his car, speed to Annie's house, and pound on the door until someone answered. If there was blood or bruises or anything short of a completely healthy Annie standing behind that door, he didn't know what he'd do. Probably something he'd regret in the morning.

"I . . . I'm sorry, but I think I need to go." Luke put his phone in his pocket and checked to make sure his keys were easily accessible.

"Oh no, are the kids okay?" Felicity grabbed her purse and put it over her shoulder like she was planning on joining him.

He shook his head. "It's not the kids. It's a friend. She's . . . she needs help."

Felicity stilled and cocked her head. "A friend?"

Already standing, Luke realized his mistake seconds too late. "Yes, sorry, Natalie's best friend. She said it's an emergency. She wouldn't ask if it wasn't something serious."

"Okay." Felicity put her purse back up on her shoulder, sounding a little suspicious, but Luke didn't have time to worry about perceptions. He took a step away from the table, feeling guilty.

"Thank you for meeting me here." He gestured to the restaurant and her chair. "I've had a wonderful time. I'm sorry, but I swear this is life or death. Rain check on the movie?"

Felicity nodded, another clump of hair breaking free, by her ear this time. "It's okay; it'll be in theaters for a long time," she said in a way that made Luke think she might never cash in that rain check.

"My treat next time, no arguments."

"Oh, you mean a number three off the value menu?"

"Well, maybe not quite that fancy." Luke tried to smile back, but his hand was already in his pocket, grasping at the phone.

"Drive safe."

"You too." Luke gave a little wave and headed out the door.

CHAPTER 22

Driving through the darkness, Luke had to fight back memories of the night his sister was born. Something about the way the headlights cut through the mist and the bite of the evening air blowing against his face as he drove with the windows down reminded him of that summer night.

◆ ◆ ◆

One hour after begging her teenage son not to call for help, Abigail Richardson gave birth to a tiny baby girl. The baby was stillborn, blue, and so small she could fit easily in the dish towel Luke retrieved from the kitchen. Even as tiny and discolored as she was, Luke thought she looked like a miniature doll.

His mother asked Luke to hold the baby as she cleaned up the mess in the hallway, refusing his help. With the still baby in his arms, Luke imagined her alive, with chubby cheeks and all the smiles he'd never see. Then he closed his eyes and prayed. Prayed harder than he'd ever prayed.

"Please, God, let this be a bad dream; please let Violet live," he begged. He squeezed his eyes shut and continued to pray that God could turn back the past four hours and he could do something to stop his father from hurting them, for good.

But Luke's mother changed out of her blood-drenched clothes and crawled into bed, cradling baby Violet beside her. Luke begged her to go to the hospital. They'd had enough of these conversations for him to know she'd never give in.

He didn't think to ask what was going to happen when the sun came up, how his mom was going to explain that she suddenly wasn't pregnant anymore. In fact, he couldn't think at all anymore. As soon as he turned off the light and closed the door to his mother's room, Luke sprinted out the back door, his bare feet slapping on the cold concrete of the porch.

Twisted weeds filled his unkempt yard and poked at the soles of his feet, but he didn't stop. He wanted to be away from the house and the horrors he'd witnessed. His baby sister was dead, and it was his fault. He couldn't stop his father or convince his mother to let him get help. He was useless.

Luke reached the gate to Natalie's backyard in three seconds flat. Squirming his finger through the crack between the gate and the fence post, he lifted the latch on the other side, impatient to be away from anything his father had ever touched. The only place he felt safe anymore was Natalie's shed, old and metal, with a hole in the roof. Natalie's dad had built a new shed when they moved in, but never took the time to pull apart the old one. When the kids took it over, Mr. Egart nailed a board on the roof and kept pretending he didn't have time to get rid of the shed.

Painted white aluminum sheeting acted as a door and was kept shut by a piece of wire hooked over an old nail. It was hard to maneuver it in the dark and with his hands shaking so violently. Once the door opened, a gust of stale warm air hit him in the face, taking the chill out of the night breeze. It was the smell of safety, a place he'd go often to get away from the screaming in his house and his inability to do anything about it.

Natalie wasn't there. He knew she wouldn't be. She was asleep inside her house like any other sane person. Part of him had hoped she'd somehow be there. They could have some Twizzlers; she'd curl up against him and pat his chest, kiss the underside of his jaw, her breath smelling slightly of strawberry, and everything else would melt away.

◆　◆　◆

After breaking the speed limit the whole way home, Luke pulled into Annie's driveway, flicked off his headlights, and checked his phone for the umpteenth time. Annie hadn't answered any of his phone calls or texts or sent a new one in forty minutes. There were two from Felicity: one thanking him for the night, and a second checking in to make sure everyone was okay. He'd have to answer those later. He couldn't think beyond the dark windows of Annie's house.

Should he be scared or angry? Both emotions were coursing through his veins, and which one would win out was still to be determined. To be safe he carefully typed 9-1-1 into his phone and slipped it back into his pocket. This time no one was going to die because he was afraid to call for help.

Turning the corner, he could tell the front door wasn't closed all the way. The same way Mr. Egart found the Richardsons' front door the morning after Violet's birth, or at least that's what Natalie told him.

Luke knocked lightly on the door, hoping Annie would pop out of the darkness and explain this was all a misunderstanding. He listened for footsteps or voices or anything. There was nothing but silence.

"Annie," Luke whispered as he pushed open the door with an index finger. Crossing the threshold, something glittery crunched under his dress shoes. Squinting down, he tried to make out what was sparkling up at him. Glass. Long silver fragments littered the floor, like someone dropped a mirror from the second-floor hall. "Annie?" he called again. She'd never leave the house like this, sharp glass on the floor, front door open. Not voluntarily.

Luke took out his phone, cleared the 9-1-1 message, typed in Annie's cell number, and then put the phone up to his ear. It trilled once, and then in the darkness, a mellow blue light flicked on behind the railing at the top of the stairs. Luke let the hand holding the phone drop to his side and followed the light. The shattered glass crunched under his rubber soles, but once he reached the carpeted stairs, each step became a whisper.

The phone continued to ring against his thigh. When Annie's happy voice-mail greeting picked up, the glowing light ahead of him clicked off. He pressed redial. The light flicked on again, and as he stepped on the landing, he saw the phone. It sat on the floor next to a slumped figure. Annie.

Luke landed on his knees in front of her, close enough to hear her breathing. She was alive, but her eyes were closed. She didn't seem to be aware of his presence. Reaching out slowly, he touched her shoulder.

"Annie. It's me. Are you okay?" He shook her lightly, and Annie's blonde eyelashes, tinted blue by the light of her still ringing phone, fluttered open.

"Luke. You came." She started to smile but faltered halfway through.

"Of course I came. I told you I would come when you needed me." She nodded. Her voice mail picked up again, but he pressed her phone against his leg to interrupt it. "What happened here?" Luke tried to check her for any visible injuries but didn't find any in the darkness. "Where is Brian? His car's outside."

Annie shifted her weight and cleared her throat. "He's in there." She pointed at a closed bedroom door at the end of a short hall.

Luke had to ask the question that might make her hate him. "Did he hurt you, Annie?" He held her by the shoulder.

"I didn't call you for me, Luke." Her voice was gravelly, and even in the black hallway he could tell her eyes were bloodshot. "I called you for Brian."

"What?" Luke released Annie and fell back. He didn't leave a date, rush across town, and break into Annie's house to help Brian.

"There's something wrong with him. He's been drinking a lot lately. Then tonight, he was waiting at the garage door when I got home from the store, ranting like a lunatic, completely delusional, screaming that I need to clean the house better because we have bedbugs." Annie cringed as she repeated the accusations. So far Luke couldn't see any reason why he should give a damn about Brian, even if he was supposed to be his friend.

Annie pressed the back of her hand to her cheek, breathing heavily. "He yelled at me, and I knew what was coming so I ran away, but he started throwing things. The mirror missed me by a few inches. So I locked myself in the bathroom," she said quickly, as if illustrating her escape. "He pounded so hard, he ripped a hole in the door." She shuddered. What would've happened if Brian had gotten that door open?

Annie ran her wrist under her nose and sniffed. "Then it was all quiet. I came back out, and the house was trashed, front door open. I thought he'd left to cool down. So I came up to shower and grab some things so I wouldn't have to disturb him when he got home, but the door was locked. I used a hanger and picked it, but our dresser is in front of the door. I can only get it open a crack. He's passed out on the bed, and I can't tell if he's alive or dead."

"We should call 9-1-1."

"No!" She scrambled upright, pushing down the hand holding his phone. "We can't call anyone. He's a cop. They know him. He'll get fired."

"But he could be dead! Which is more important?" Luke pushed the home button on the front of his phone and started to type in his password. He should've called 9-1-1 as soon as he crossed the threshold and noticed the glass.

Annie wrapped both of her hands around the phone, her fingernails digging into the back of his hand.

"If you call the police, he will kill me." Tears poured down her cheeks in thick streams. With her face so close, he could see delicate crimson scratches across her face where the glass had flown past her. Her lips trembled as she spoke, spittle gathering at the corners of her mouth. "He will do it; I know he will."

Every instinct told him to get help, reminded him of what happened the last time he didn't. But the fear from years of abuse was more obvious than any scars, and he wanted to make her feel safe.

"Fine." He released the phone and wiggled his hands out of her iron grasp. "I'll check on him, but I want you to stay here." He tilted his head to the side so he could look her in the eyes. "If there's any trouble, you have to make that call."

She held the phone in her clasped hands like she was praying. "I will. I promise."

He checked her over one more time. "You sure you're okay?"

"Yes," she said, raising her eyebrows impatiently. "Go."

Luke stood quickly, gravity pulling blood from his brain, making him stumble. Annie was in her own world: arms wrapped around her legs and head down on her knees. She didn't seem to notice his stumble or really much of anything. He'd have to make sure she was really unharmed once he could turn on some lights.

To think he started this night worried about avoiding a goodnight kiss. Now he was heading into a barricaded room to face a man with a history of violence who carried a gun for a living. Luke stepped boldly toward the master bedroom door. A bent hanger hung out of the bronzed doorknob. He yanked it out, the metal scratching loud enough to make Luke cringe.

Quickly this time, he rammed the door. It opened a crack, immediately slamming into something hard. *There goes the element of surprise.* Might as well get it over with. Luke peeled off his jacket and tossed it on the floor behind him. With his right shoulder, he slammed against the door. It gave a little. Luke took a breath and tried again. One, two, three more times until there was a large enough opening to squeeze through. Sucking in his stomach, he squeezed himself through the opening. His buttons scratched against the doorjamb, one catching for a moment on the latch.

He scanned the scene in front of him. He'd never been in Brian and Annie's room, but he was certain this wasn't what it normally looked like. The lamp by the bed had lost its lampshade, casting a harsh glow against the back wall. To the left was the bathroom, door gaping open, with a trail of clothes and towels pouring out of it like it was vomiting laundry. On the right was a walk-in closet, or at least Luke thought it was. He couldn't tell because everything once on the shelves or hangers was now piled in the doorway, with a wall of fabric and shoes. It looked like robbers had tossed the room. What could've enticed Brian to do this? It wasn't time to figure out that mystery. First, he had to check on Brian.

He was alive, that was clear enough. As he lay on the bed in only a pair of black boxer-briefs, Luke could make out the rise and fall of his back. After two more steps, Luke was close enough to hear Brian snoring softly, a dark pool of drool slowly soaking into the pillow his face was smashed against. Sprawled out across the king-size mattress, Brian was definitely asleep, not dead. But the closer Luke got to the unconscious man, the more he realized that this wasn't a nap.

On the bedside table the naked lightbulb cast a crescent glow against the wall. Beneath it was a collection of several other small objects. At first, Luke couldn't make out what cluttered the painted black surface of the side table. There was a small empty prescription bottle with no pharmacy label. Squinting in the strange light, he leaned forward. A few stray, multicolored pills were scattered across the nightstand and at least half a dozen empty beer bottles.

Pills and alcohol? No wonder the guy was passed out. He had to get Annie out of here. They'd deal with the disaster of a room later.

"Luke," Annie whispered through the crack in the door, "is he okay?"

After all this, how could she still be concerned about Brian?

"Yeah, he's sleeping." Luke grabbed the wastebasket wedged between the bed and nightstand. It had a few used Kleenex but was mostly untouched. With one sweep he tossed the contents of the tabletop into the shiny black bin. The bottles clanked together in the bottom of the bin liner. Luke yanked the bag out by the edges and tied it at the top. He wasn't going to help Brian, but he wouldn't leave him to accidentally overdose either.

Luke took one more look around the room. Annie couldn't clean this up alone. She'd need help, maybe even professional help. There wasn't any time to make those plans tonight. He needed to get Annie somewhere safe. He was going to take her home with him.

CHAPTER 23

"Let me get you some clean clothes. Do you want some pajamas?" Luke flicked on the cylindrical hanging light in the front hall. Annie flinched against the brightness of the hundred-watt bulb after the darkness on the car trip over. Luke had to hold back a gasp when he saw her in full light.

Her usually tidy hair was disheveled. Along her collarbone and right cheek, thin lines of blood had dried where fractured glass must have sliced her when Brian sent it exploding behind her. Across her right forearm was a reddish bruise that looked like she'd fallen against something straight and hard. And her eyes, her eyes were the worst. Swollen from crying, red-rimmed and bloodshot, they told of the pain she was feeling even more than the blood or bruises.

"Yeah, maybe I should." She fingered a slash in the thin fabric around her ribs.

"Why don't you go lay down on the couch? I'll grab some clothes, then make you something to eat."

She nodded and popped the tennis shoes off her feet, the only thing she'd grabbed during their mad rush out of the house. When

Luke pressed his body through the crack in the bedroom door, leaving half-naked and totally zoned-out Brian behind him, his only thought was to get Annie out of that house. Reluctant but dazed, it only took a little encouragement to get her out the door. He told himself they could talk about the drugs and the violence when there were miles, not feet, between Annie and Brian.

Luke headed toward the stairs, and Annie's head shot up like she thought of something. "Nothing of Natalie's, okay?" she yelped. "A pair of your old sweats or something is fine."

"Okay," Luke said, unsure if it was stranger having Annie wear his wife's pajamas or his. For a moment he considered searching through May's drawers to see if there was anything in there that could work, but quickly reconsidered.

In his room, Luke pulled out his nicest pair of plaid flannel pants and a soft gray cotton T-shirt that had shrunk in one of his first solo laundry attempts. He stacked them on top of his dresser and quickly changed out of his date-night clothes and tossed them in his laundry pile. Normally during the summer he'd sleep in his boxers, but tonight he decided to go for something more conservative—cotton pants and a larger version of the shirt he'd picked for Annie.

"I hope these fit," Luke called out as he rounded the corner. Sitting on the couch with her back to him, Annie didn't seem to notice his entrance. He placed the pile of clothes on the kitchen counter and approached Annie from behind. Face down on her hands, her shoulders shook with silent sobs. He slowly placed his hand on her back, sliding it across the ribbed fabric of her shirt.

"Hey," he whispered. "It's okay. You're safe now."

Annie lifted her head out of her hands. The rivers of tears on her face joined together into an ocean, her cheeks shimmering when the light hit her skin. Using her shaking hands, she swiped at her face as she sat up. Luke grabbed a tissue out of the box on the coffee table with one hand while leaving the other in the space between Annie's shoulder blades. They regularly ran out of every other paper product, but Luke made sure to always keep enough Kleenex in stock.

"Thank you." She took the tissue and wiped under her eyes and nose. Her breaths came in short puffs, and Luke was sure he'd interrupted a much-deserved breakdown. The last thing she probably wanted was Luke in her face as a reminder of her secret world being exposed.

"If you want to be alone, I understand," Luke muttered. "Your pajamas are on the counter." He leaned back and let his hand fall off her back. They could talk in the morning, or next week, or whenever she wasn't feeling so broken that any of his words would inflict more pain. "Let me know if you need *anything*." Luke stood to leave, but Annie grabbed his hand in both of hers.

"Wait." She tugged him down and moved over to her left, leaving an empty spot. "Please stay." He hesitated. She'd been there for him countless times over the past eight months. He wanted to help her, to save her, but all the things he needed to say would do nothing but hurt her. Annie squeezed, and Luke lost his interest in altruism. He settled into the empty space beside her and was surprised when she didn't let go, even after he was settled into his spot. Instead, she hugged his hand against her side.

Holding Annie's hand was very different than holding Felicity's. Felicity's hand was small, soft, and gave him a sense of comfort and companionship he'd missed since Natalie. But Annie . . . her long, cold fingers somehow burned his skin, making him want to let go and hold on forever at the same time. Her touch scared him more than comforted him. His heart pounded, and with each beat he thought: *Run away!*

"Thank you for coming for me. You're the only person I can trust." Her voice hitched, and she paused to clear her throat. "I heard what Andy said about your dad. You know what it's like to have someone who loves you hurt you." She said it like he was going to agree, but his hand closed around hers, squeezing firmly.

"My father didn't love me," he said flatly. "Annie, what happened tonight, that's not love."

Annie stiffened beside him. Luke was prepared for her to get defensive and shut down.

"No," she answered, letting out her breath in one big quavering sigh. Luke braced himself for the rest of her sentence. "I guess it's not." She rested against him and put her head on his shoulder. Luke was too relieved to be uncomfortable. "Will you tell me what happened with your dad?"

Luke licked his lips. Tell her? He'd never told the story to anyone but Natalie, and that was more than twenty years ago, in their hideout. Every time he was sent to a new foster home, the foster parents would try to get the story out of him. They already knew what happened—it was in his permanent file—but for some reason people thought he needed to say it out loud. It was different with Annie. He knew her secret; it was only fair to share his.

"You heard what Andy said; he was a drunk. My whole life. My mom used to say he loved too much and that's why he'd get mad. I believed it until I was about ten. I started to notice I was the only kid sitting out at recess because my back still hurt from where my dad whupped me with his belt buckle." Annie flinched. He wondered if she knew what that felt like or if Brian had ever tried to harm their son. Maybe that's why he hadn't been home since the start of the school year.

"What he did to me was nothing like what he did to my mom. He'd come home late, calling her vulgar names I'd never heard before. If she was lucky, he'd stop with the slurs; if she was unlucky, or left something out of place, or said the wrong thing at the wrong moment, he'd beat her. I prayed every night someone would save us, that God would strike my father dead. Unfortunately my father went on breathing." Luke shook his head, still angry that he'd once believed in a God who would care about one child out of billions.

"What's worse," he continued, absentmindedly placing his head on top of Annie's, "everyone in town knew he hit her. Terry knew; she's told me that before. It was like this big extended family of enablers. No one called the cops, least of all my mom. I think she was far more scared of my father getting arrested than any physical harm he could do to her. When I was fourteen, she got pregnant. She'd had a tough delivery with me that ended with a midline cesarean. The doctors told her because of the damage from the emergency surgery, she might never have another child.

"Violet was a miracle from the day we found out about her in more ways than one. My dad stopped hitting my mom, he drank less, stayed home more, and by the time my mom was six months pregnant, he was interviewing for a new job. It seemed like baby Violet put our lives back on track. For a little while I let myself believe we were going to be a real family."

"I didn't know you had a sister," Annie whispered.

"I don't."

"I thought you said Violet was your sister?" Annie pulled their intertwined hands on her lap, drawing in closer to Luke's side.

"She was," he answered, dreading what he had to say next. "But she's dead now."

"Oh," Annie said softly. "I'm sorry I made you tell me this. You can stop."

"I don't want to stop. I want you to know why I worry . . . about you." When she didn't respond, he continued with his story. "My father didn't get the job. He went to the bar to drown his sorrows. That's when he saw Alex Kerks, one of the supervisors over at his old job. Alex made the mistake of asking how things were going and mentioned he'd heard my mom was expecting. I still don't know what happened, but my dad left convinced my mom was sleeping around and the baby wasn't his.

"I'll never forget the slam of that door; it shook the whole house. I knew, I just knew, everything was going to go back to the way it had always been. It didn't take long, a few shouts, several well-placed hits, and one last swift kick before he ran out the front door. It was enough. My sister was born that night in the hallway by the kitchen. She was already dead." A lump rose in Luke's throat. Until now, he'd been able to maintain a monotone delivery, telling the story as though he was recounting a movie plot. Annie was still beside him, the warmth of her body seeping through his T-shirt.

"Were you there?" she asked, shuddering. He could feel her eyes on his, but he tried not to look at her because he didn't want to cry.

"Uh-huh," he grunted, barely able to hold back the burning in his eyes. He had to keep going. She had to know the risks of staying when you should run. "I left after Violet was born; I went and hid in the shed in Natalie's backyard. In the morning she came and found me there. The whole town was out searching for me and my dad."

"Your mom called the police?"

Luke shook his head slowly and turned to meet Annie's gaze. The swelling was going down, and the whites of her eyes now looked like porcelain. Several crimson scratches lined her face, as if they'd been drawn on carefully with a colored pencil. A sliver of glass was entwined in the tangles of her hair. He reached out and gently worked the shard out of its resting place.

"She didn't call the police," he said, sweeping his gaze over her face as she stared at the glass he had removed from her hair. "Natalie's father did. He noticed our front door gaping open the next morning. When he went inside to check on us, he saw the blood, followed the trail into my mom's room, and found her and baby Violet in her bed."

"So he called the authorities." Annie took the glass from his hand and held it in her own. "Was your mom scared?"

"No, Annie, she wasn't scared."

"Oh?" She looked up in surprise.

"She was dead."

"What?" It took a few seconds for the shock to register on her face.

"She bled out while she was sleeping."

"Oh my God." Annie gasped and dropped the glass on the carpet as though it had cut her.

"They all thought I was dead too. But Natalie figured out where I was hiding. The way she kissed me when she came through the make-shift door told me more than words. We hid in the shed together for hours. CPS came for me a few hours later, and I never spent another night in that house."

"So, you think *that* could happen to me?" There were tears in her eyes, but they were different than the torrent when he'd found her just a little while earlier. These tears collected slowly on the rims of her eyelids, still, like a pool or a lake.

"I'm not afraid Brian's going to kill you." Even as he said the words, he wasn't sure he believed them. "That's not true. After what I saw tonight, I'm scared as hell I could lose you. But what scares me almost as much as you dying like my mom is you living like her."

It seemed like Annie hadn't taken a breath in over a minute. When she blinked, twin tears fell down her cheeks, one running over her top lip. Luke wiped it away with his fingertips. Annie closed her eyes and leaned in, her breath coming a little faster. He'd never noticed how soft her lips looked; he'd never considered what it would be like to press his mouth against hers, to put his arms around her waist, pull her against his body and never let go.

Oh no, no, no. He couldn't have these thoughts about Annie. Not only was she still in a very committed, though abusive, marriage, she was also his wife's best friend. *His* only real friend. Luke yanked his hand back and stood suddenly. Annie slipped to one side, her head nearly hitting the armrest. She brushed the wet trails off her face and looked up at him, startled.

"You okay?"

"It's getting late, and I'm sure you're tired. We can talk more in the morning." His bare feet smacked at the cold tile in the kitchen.

He patted the pile of clothes as he spoke. "Um, so, here are your pajamas, and you are welcome to sleep in May's room if you like. Probably safer than Will's habitat." He waited for her to laugh but realized too late that laughter was out of the picture tonight. "I'll put a toothbrush in the kids' bathroom and a towel. Anything else I can get for you?"

Annie sat upright and ran a hand through her hair. It had a little curl to it tonight, flipping up at the ends instead of hanging evenly above her shoulders.

"That's fine," she answered. "But I think I'll sleep down here if it's all the same to you." She rolled her head back and forth, stretching her neck. Luke couldn't help but notice the slope of her shoulders, the curve of her neck. How could he turn this new voice off inside his head? The only plan was distance. Putting a whole floor of house between them should help. It had to help. He was tired, overwhelmed from the events of the night. He'd be back to normal in the morning. They'd have a nice quiet Sunday morning and then figure out what could possibly come next.

"Yeah, of course." He took another step back, eager to be within the confines of his safe, welcoming bed. "Make yourself at home."

"Don't I always?" A trace of a smile tickled the edge of her mouth. Wobbling as she stood, she braced herself on the back of the couch. "Guess I'm more tired than I realized."

She rounded the couch. Luke waved as he backed down the hall toward the front door and said, "I'll see you in the morning."

"Okay." She gathered the pile of clothes into her arms. They looked very masculine next to her pink and black pajama pants and the frill around the neckline of her shirt. "Hey, Luke?"

"Yeah?"

"Thank you for telling me your story."

Luke closed his eyes, a new emotion pushing against his mind. Maybe it was regret. Or was it relief?

"You're welcome," he said simply. Without waiting to hear her response, he checked the door to make sure it was closed all the way before turning the dead bolt. When the lock clicked into place, he did the same with the lock on the knob and then on the door to the garage. He may not have been able to keep his mother safe from his father or Natalie safe from cancer, but he was sure as hell going to keep Annie safe under his own roof. Rechecking the lock one last time, Luke continued on his way upstairs.

Quickly closing his bedroom door, he rushed over to the tall dresser at the foot of his bed. Sliding the top drawer open, he shuffled through the piles of shirts and underwear until he found a stack of old receipts and business cards. On the top was the plain white card he'd gotten in the mail a few weeks ago:

Dennis Bormet, Tanglewood Securities.

CHAPTER 24

Luke woke with a start. The sun was already shining high enough through his bedroom window to make him check the time. Ten thirty a.m. Great. The events of the past twenty-four hours flooded back to him, and he shot up in bed. Annie was probably awake downstairs, wondering where he was. He threw back the thin blue blanket and searched the room for his robe. It had been a long time since he'd made the effort to put it on, but this seemed like a robe moment. Just as he spotted the fuzzy blue fabric peeking out from behind a pile of clean folded towels he'd been meaning to put away for the past two weeks, the doorbell rang.

The first name that came to his mind was Brian. How did he know Annie was here? Maybe he didn't. Maybe he was searching for her. If that was the case, then Luke should be the one to open the door, avoid any kind of contact between Annie and Brian. He freed the robe with one hard yank, toppling the tower of clean towels in the process, and forced his arms in the sleeves. When he opened his bedroom door, a familiar voice echoed up toward him. Not Brian—Felicity.

"Hi, I'm looking for Luke Richardson. I'm sorry; maybe I have the wrong house." Felicity's voice was unmistakable.

"No, you're in the right place," Annie chirped back as Luke rounded the corner. Through the oak banister he could see Annie, drowning in the gray T-shirt and green plaid pants he'd given to her last night. She held the front door open wide, welcoming Felicity in.

"Uh, thank you." Felicity's voice turned up at the end, full of questions. "I'm sorry, I missed your name."

"I'm Annie," she responded.

"Oh. Annie . . ." Felicity said, slowly like she had finally remembered the answer to a difficult exam question.

Luke cleared his throat as his bare feet landed on the floor, the wood planks warmed by the sun shining in through the front door.

"Hey there, sleepyhead." Annie laughed. Even after surviving the terror of last night and sleeping on his couch, she looked brighter this morning. He'd never seen her without makeup, but her skin had a creamy texture that made him wonder why she ever took the time to put on makeup. Even the scratches on her face looked like they'd been applied by a paintbrush. "He honestly just got up," Annie was explaining.

Felicity didn't seem to find the situation funny. She held her phone in one hand and played with the broken corner of the cover nervously, hair up in a tight ponytail, wearing a pair of khaki shorts and a white transparent shirt flowing over a long tank top of the same color. Luke knew what this looked like. Damn it.

"Sorry, I guess I was tired."

"Long night?" Felicity asked pointedly, glancing between Annie and Luke and their unintentionally matching shirts. "I'm sorry I woke you. I was worried when you didn't respond to any of my texts, so I thought I'd come over and make sure the *emergency*"—she stressed the word, shifting her gaze to Annie—"went all right. You both seem fine, so I think I'll go."

"Oh . . . *Oh!* You are Felicity. Will's guidance counselor." Annie raised her eyebrows at Luke.

"Yes, she is. Felicity, this is Annie. She watches Clayton while the kids are at school."

"Natalie's best friend," Annie said, extending a hand. Felicity shook it briefly. "This is not what it looks like."

"No, not at all," Luke reinforced, glad Annie finally caught on. Felicity crossed her right leg behind her. For the first time since Luke had met her, she wasn't wearing heels. Seeing her in a pair of drugstore flip-flops seemed so foreign and made her look more vulnerable.

"A pipe burst in my house, and everything flooded. My husband"—Annie lingered on the word—"is a police officer and couldn't get home to help me, so I called Luke. I'm so sorry if I interrupted something." Annie slapped Luke's arm. "Hey, next time tell me you are out on a date."

He wasn't sure the playful touching was the best choice at the moment. At least the tone of the conversation changed dramatically. Felicity took another long look at Annie as though she was using her finely honed tools for uncovering deception in teenagers on the two of them.

"Hey, it's none of my business." She pressed her phone back into the purse resting on her hip and took out a set of keys, not buying it. "I'd better get going. Enjoy your breakfast; the bacon smells delicious." Luke had been too distracted by the confrontation to notice the mouth-watering scent hanging in the air. Felicity turned and headed down the front path toward the green Nissan in the driveway.

"Go after her," Annie urged, gesturing with her eyes. "Go."

Luke pulled back his shoulders, unsure if he wanted to follow. He didn't want to hurt Felicity, and he definitely didn't want things to be awkward between them during the next school year. At the same time, he still wasn't sure he wanted to define a relationship with her. Annie poked his shoulder and pointed her head out the door.

"Fine." Luke rushed out of the house, calling after Felicity. She stopped but didn't turn around.

"Let me go, okay? I have no right to be upset. We've been on two and a half dates, held hands a few times, and had one semiawkward good-night hug. I'm about twenty thousand miles away from being your girlfriend. I have no right to judge you." She adjusted the leather purse strap on her shoulder. She was using her best counselor voice. Her calm justifications made him feel worse.

"She really is just a friend, I promise."

"Uh-huh." She turned around and looked up at Luke, her green eyes flashing. "But when she called, you answered. I was worried about you, Luke. You didn't respond to a single one of my texts last night or this morning. Did you even *think* about calling me?"

Luke opened his mouth but couldn't put a sentence together that made sense. He had checked his phone and seen Felicity's texts before he drove Annie home, but he hadn't even picked his phone up since he walked in his own door. Felicity was right. Since Annie's first desperate text, every thought in his brain was for her.

"Yeah, that's what I thought." She lifted the thick trail of hair cascading down from her ponytail off her neck like she was searching for a breeze. She dropped it and readjusted her purse again. "I really don't think you're ready for something outside of Natalie's shadow. For now, that's Annie."

"I do like you, Felicity. I admire how much you care about the kids you work with, and you make me laugh when we are together." He blushed, feeling like the words were tripping out of his mouth into a mound of embarrassing mush.

"But . . . ," she added before he had the chance to say the word himself, "you aren't ready."

As hard as it was to do, he shook his head. "No, I'm not."

"Yeah, I know." She reached out and gave his hand one quick squeeze. "Give me a call when you are; maybe we can try this again."

"I will." He squeezed back and let go. He watched her walk away without any urge to stop her.

Luke waited until Felicity drove away to return to the house. The sun warmed his shoulders through the robe, the thin shirt underneath clinging to his chest and torso. Annie's matching shirt was two sizes smaller and still hung off her as if she was a little girl wearing her father's clothes.

Annie. It was embarrassing how easily his thoughts turned to her. It was like his world was swirling around one spot lately, and he wasn't sure if it was the gentle tug of gravity or the dangerous currents of a whirlpool. The only thing he was sure of was who was at the center of that spiral.

When he crossed the threshold of the front door, the coolness of the AC and lingering scent of bacon made him smile. His house felt like home with Annie inside it. He couldn't decide if she was part of Natalie's "shadow," as Felicity suggested, or if he was feeling something new and real. Today wasn't the right time to delve into those questions. Today it was time to help her start a life free from abuse, and he was relieved she finally was going to let him.

"You ready for breakfast?" Annie called from the kitchen. When he entered the kitchen, Annie approached him with two plates in her hands, both completely full of bacon, toast, and scrambled eggs. She placed them on the counter in front of the stools on the opposite side.

"I didn't know I had bacon," Luke said, slipping into one of the seats. Annie slid a full glass of orange juice in front of him. "Or juice. Did you go shopping?"

"Yeah, wearing this superstylish outfit." She gestured to the baggy loungewear. "No. You had all this stuff in your fridge. All the dates check out. The juice is concentrate from the freezer. Remember, I cleaned out your fridge a few weeks ago; I know where stuff is."

Luke stabbed a few egg chunks and shoveled them into his mouth. When he swallowed the first bite, his stomach growled. He hadn't eaten for almost sixteen hours, and the taste of food woke up his taste buds and made him more hungry rather than less. By the time Annie climbed on the stool beside him, Luke's plate was half-empty.

"So, you clear things up with Ms. Mason?"

"I think Felicity believed me when I told her you and I aren't having a torrid love affair." Luke tried to make it a joke. "But we decided to take a break from the dating thing."

Annie's eyebrows shot up, the one with a scratch through it wrinkling unevenly. "What? Why?"

Luke put down his fork. "She thinks it's too soon, that I'm not ready." He stared at his plate full of food and remembered the last time Annie had been in his house for a midday breakfast was the day after Natalie's funeral. "Maybe she's right."

"Hmm." Annie's mouth was full of toast, but it seemed like a convenient excuse to keep mum about what she was really thinking.

Luke took another bite of eggs, and a silence settled between them. They had so many things they needed to talk about, but he didn't know how to start.

He wanted to ask, "What now?" Did they go over to Annie's house and pack up all her belongings? Should he take her to a women's shelter, or should she stay in a hotel or spend another night on his couch? How could he face Brian now, knowing . . . everything?

Annie's cell phone rang, cutting through the silence and through Luke's thoughts. The vibrations were muffled by one of the couch cushions. Annie jumped off her stool, the fork clattering on the counter, spraying egg residue on the granite surface. Once her phone was in her hand, she stared at it.

"Is it him?"

She nodded. Of course it was Brian. Who else would make her turn white as the phone in her hand? Annie mashed the power button on the top of her phone, silencing it, and dropped it on the couch. She covered her face with shaking hands, her shoulders heaving up and down.

Luke shoved away from the counter. His bare feet were silent on the tile floor, and Annie jumped a little when he put his arm around her. At his touch she turned in to him, pressing her face against his shoulder and encircling his midsection with her arms. Working on their own volition, Luke's arms enfolded her protectively, pulling her in tightly against him.

It was a strange feeling holding someone this close to him again. Physical closeness with anyone but Natalie had always made Luke uncomfortable, nervous, but with Annie in his arms, it felt right. Her tears gathered in the fabric of his shirt, soaking in like rain into spring soil. With a light touch he ran a hand over her back, wanting to comfort her, wishing he could take away her pain.

"I can answer next time." He kissed the top of her head. "You never have to talk to him again."

Annie's arms went limp, releasing from behind his back. An embarrassed heat crawled up Luke's neck and made his ears ring. He'd gone too far too fast. Touched her too easily, comforted her too aggressively. Luke cleared his throat and backed away, staring at his big toe instead of daring to see the look on Annie's face.

"I'm going home," Annie said. "That call was to tell me he's on his way."

"What?" Luke blinked rapidly.

She put the phone in the pocket of her flannel pants. "I threw away my clothes. They were beyond saving. Can I wear these home?" she asked, gesturing to the borrowed clothing she was wearing.

"You're going *back*?" Luke asked, ignoring Annie's question. She folded her arms across her chest and pulled at the hem of her shirt.

"It was a stupid fight. He . . . he wasn't feeling well. He . . ."

"He was on pills, Annie. I saw them. Pills and booze. Stop covering for him."

"It's the alcohol. I know it is. It changes him. And he takes the pills to calm down. He's going to get treatment. He promised." Annie twisted a gray string around her finger from the hem of her shirt. "He never laid a hand on me until Matt left."

Luke could barely breathe. No one goes from "wonderful husband" to "heinous abuser" in one fell swoop. But he wasn't going to argue about her honesty because if she was anything like his mother, hiding was easier than truth. Pacifying the monster inside her husband was easier than slaying it.

"Annie," he said softly, biting back any kind of judgmental tone, "how will he get treatment when he doesn't want anyone to know about his problem?"

"I don't know; I . . . I don't see any other options." She looked up at him with half-squinted eyes. "Where would I go?"

"A shelter," Luke interjected. "Or I could take you somewhere far away. You could hide. You could . . ."

"No," Annie said, slashing her hand through the air. "He'd find me. You know he would."

"Since when is that a reason to stay with someone who is hurting you?" Luke lost his nonchalant air, tapping his head like he couldn't figure out a math problem.

"You don't understand," she bit back. "You can't. What you had with Natalie, I don't have that, okay? I don't get to have someone who loves me, cherishes me. I've come to accept it. If I leave with you, he won't stop at hurting me; he'd hurt you and your family. I can't accept that."

Luke shook his head, unable to believe what he was hearing. A panic-filled fury filled him. He forgot restraint and lunged forward, grabbing Annie's arms, firm but gentle. She looked up into his face, eyebrows raised in surprise but not fear.

"You can't go back. I won't let you." His voice caught in his throat. "You shouldn't have to live this way."

Annie avoided eye contact, and Luke knew he was watching her defenses go up like homeowners boarding up their windows before a hurricane. She shook her head, hair bouncing off her cheekbones.

"Let me help you," he begged, letting go of her arms with one hand, brushing a tangled clump of damp hair off her face. A few strands stuck to the corner of her eye, glued there by the silent tears trailing down her cheek. "Let me help you like I couldn't help my mom."

"I am not your mother," Annie said bitterly, lips curled back. Luke snapped his hand away. It was over. She was going to leave, and there was nothing he could say to change her mind.

The doorbell rang. Annie whipped her head around, eyebrows raised in terror, as if she'd just heard a bomb explode instead of the doorbell's one-note ping. As Annie brushed past him toward the front door, Luke grabbed her hand by her fingertips.

"You can call me if you are ready to leave him." He stared at her slender fingers, nails painted a soft peach, and took a staccato breath. He couldn't ignore the ache he'd been hiding from since his childhood. He'd ignored too many pains in his life. No more pretending. "But until then, please don't contact us."

"Fine. If that's the way you want it." Annie yanked her hand away, glaring at him. She was too far into her protection mode, far beyond his reach. "Good-bye, Luke."

"Good-bye, Annie," Luke whispered. She turned the corner into the foyer without looking back. Collapsing onto the couch, he covered his ears, trying to block out the sound of the front door opening and the echo of Brian's tentative "hello."

CHAPTER 25

Lying in bed, Luke wondered how he'd gotten here. In an empty house, empty bed, alone on his seventeenth anniversary. Natalie—gone. Kids—gone. Felicity—gone. Annie—gone.

He'd replayed Annie's farewell over and over in his head for the past week. It followed him to work, to every meeting. It followed him and echoed off the walls of his strangely empty home. What did he do wrong? What should he have done differently? Every single scenario ended the same way, with Annie never talking to him again. At least this way, it was his choice.

A few hours after Annie left, Luke finally got up the courage to use the business card he'd dug out the night before. Dennis Bormet, the investigator from Brian's new job. Nervous but determined, he dialed the number on the card. The phone rang, one, two, three times. Just when Luke was coming up with what he'd say in a voice-mail message, a man answered.

"Hello?"

"Hello," Luke responded automatically. "Uh . . ." He cleared his throat, trying to remember the story he'd planned out before the call.

"I already know who you are if that makes this any easier," Dennis Bormet groused, like Luke was interrupting him in the middle of something important. Luke realized, belatedly, he was calling on a Sunday afternoon.

"This is Luke Richardson. I spoke with you a few weeks ago about Officer Brian Gurrella . . . you called me about a security clearance check?"

"Mm-hm, yeah, so?" Eating, it definitely sounded like he was eating something. Luke made himself continue, focusing on the cuts on Annie's feet and face, the thought of Brian losing control, going too far.

"I need to retract my earlier recommendation. Some new information has come to light, and I . . ." Luke faltered, sure his script sounded juvenile rather than sophisticated. Playing nice wasn't going to get him anywhere. He took a deep breath and blurted, "Brian Gurrella is an alcoholic. I don't know if you test for that or if it's relevant, but I felt like you should know."

When Dennis Bormet didn't answer immediately, Luke wondered if he'd hung up the phone. Listening closely, he heard two long gulps and a muffled burp.

"What evidence do you have of Officer Gurrella's alleged alcohol abuse?" Papers rustled in the background, and unless it was a bunch of very stiff napkins, Luke was sure he'd finally gotten the investigator's attention.

"I saw him when he was passed out. I . . . I saw some unlabeled pills and . . ." He hesitated to mention witnessing Annie's injuries. "Also there was evidence of violence in his home. Broken furniture, glass, everything."

Dennis Bormet paused for a minute, letting an uncomfortable silence sit between the two men. Luke recognized the interrogation tactic from when he'd been questioned about his mother's death. Pauses were very tempting to fill with more information.

"Mr. Richardson, I'd like to talk about this with you in greater detail. Can I call you Monday morning and get this all on record?"

"By 'on record' do you mean you'll record our conversation?"

"Yes, sir. But it's all confidential. No one will ever know you spoke with us."

A thrill of danger and revenge sent a shiver through Luke. If he told them the truth, maybe they wouldn't hire Brian. Annie would remain safely a few blocks away. If Brian tried to hurt her again, she could call Luke for help, and this time he'd call the police.

"I'd be glad to speak with you tomorrow. Sorry I bothered you on your day off." When he touched the red end button, Luke dropped the phone on his bed triumphantly. In the middle of his self-congratulations, an uncomfortable thought came to him—he wasn't really doing this just because it helped Annie. He was doing it to make her stay.

Luke shrugged off the guilt. Calling Bormet might not be an entirely altruistic move, but that didn't make it the wrong one. In the morning Luke had a long discussion with Dennis Bormet as he drove into work. The next morning he spoke with Bormet's supervisor. Then Luke waited, keeping his phone in his hand as he slept, sure Annie would make her desperate phone call sooner rather than later.

Today he was avoiding sleep and avoiding leaving his bed all at the same time. Soon he'd have to get up and log in to make it at least look like he was working from home. He didn't want to go far from home today. There would be a Natalie letter with the mail today, he knew it. And it would be all about their wedding day. Knowing Natalie, she'd write about every detail, how they wrote their vows together the night before, and then up past midnight before realizing he'd officially seen the bride on their wedding day. There was a time in his grieving process that letter would've been refreshing, could get him through another few days without her. But now the idea of reading a letter about the happiest day of his life only made his current situation stand out as even more depressing in comparison.

Eventually it was his bladder, not his stomach, that got him out of bed. Then the shower called to him, asking him to return to the world of fresh-smelling humans. After scrubbing himself till his skin tingled, Luke stood in front of a steamy mirror, wondering if he should shave or leave the day-old stubble Natalie always begged him to grow out. Closing the stopper in the sink, Luke grabbed a new razor from the clear plastic bathroom organizer. It rattled around inside the tub, half-empty without Natalie's overflowing beauty supplies.

The sink reached its capacity, and Luke turned off the scalding water. Then a faint ding sounded from the main floor, followed by loud pounding.

"Damn it." Seeing people was definitely not on his approved activities list for the day. When all the noise downstairs stopped, Luke leaned over the still-steaming sink, dipped his hands in, savored the stab of the superheated water, and splashed it onto his face.

The doorbell rang again. Luke sighed, yanked up the stopper, placed the canister on the counter, and pulled out a half-wet towel from the laundry basket to dry off. He snatched a thinning cotton T-shirt off his bed, grabbed his phone out of habit, and rushed down the stairs, barely getting the T-shirt over his head before the pounding started. With his free hand, Luke swung the door open. A tall, thin college kid with thick black hipster glasses frames stood on the other side, a blue ceramic vase packed with at least two dozen tulips cradled in the crook of his arm.

"Oh, hey, you Luke Richardson?" The guy read his name off a folded yellow invoice.

"Yes." Luke opened the door a little wider, squinting against the late-morning sun.

"These are for you. Here." He passed the tulips to Luke and shook the invoice open, offering the pen resting on his ear. "Sign here, at the bottom."

"Um, sure." Luke juggled the glass container of flowers and his phone. "Hold on, let me put these down."

The delivery boy shrugged; his drooping name tag read **KAL**. Using his elbow Luke moved the collection of mail to one side, making a spot where he could put down the vase. The thick glass hit the wood with a thunk, and a blue envelope fell out from its resting place inside the flowers.

Whoever sent the flowers had been delivering the letters. Without stopping to check the thickness of the letter or estimate a number of pages, Luke rushed around his front door and on his front porch.

"I'll take that paper now." The kid fumbled with the invoice, and Luke resisted the urge to yank the paper out of his hand. When Kal finally passed it over, Luke ran his gaze across the crinkly yellow page, not sure what he was looking for.

Deliver to: 9317 Orland Dr.

Flowers required: 2 doz. Tulips.

Payment: Cash.

Then he saw it, bottom of the page, a name, smudged by the carbon on the old-fashioned order slip.

From: N. Townsend.

The name was crossed out with a simple *X* and next to it was written:

Anonymous.

The flowers. The letters. Everything—they'd all been sent by the infamous "Dr. Neal." Somewhere deep inside he'd known it ever since he saw Neal's name on Natalie's phone. But to see the proof in his hand, scribbled down by a careless florist, made his fist clutch the pen he'd

taken along with the invoice. Why? Why was this man such an important part of Natalie's life? Why did he keep showing up in every corner
of her existence? Who the *hell* was he? That anger he'd been running
from his whole life boiled deep in his gut, crawled up his arms and neck,
and made him want to hit something.

"Uh, you sign there." Kal pointed vaguely at the bottom of the
page. Luke lifted the pen to sign but then had a thought.

"Is there any way I can get a copy of this?" Luke held the pen off the
paper. If he signed it, Kal wouldn't have a reason to help him anymore.

"I only get paid if I turn in the yellow sheet . . . with your signature." Kal waited with his hands in his pockets, his grungy brown hair
hanging into his eyes. "But you can take a pic of it if you want," he
added.

Yes. His phone. Holding out the paper, Luke centered it in the
frame and enjoyed the sharp click of the phone's internal camera.
Finally some proof. After checking to make sure the quality of the picture was clear enough, Luke scribbled his name across the bottom and
handed it back to Kal.

"Thanks," he said, heading back inside, closing the door behind
him. The picture on his phone was clear enough to read every line. Luke
glared at the flowers. There was a small rectangular card from the florist
shop with a handwritten note in unfamiliar handwriting.

July 30

*Luke, Happy Anniversary. My love for you goes on
forever.*

Love, Natalie

"Liar," Luke whispered. Yes. That's what she was. Whatever she was
hiding with Dr. Neal as her accomplice, it was something she'd been

lying to him about for years, decades even. "Liar," he said again, louder, his voice reverberating through the nearby stairwell. The room turned a hazy shade of red, his breathing coming fast, like he'd been running. He picked up the vase full of tulips, each happy blossom another reminder of all the beautiful lies she told him. *"Liar!"* Luke yelled.

The cool vase suddenly burned in his hand. He couldn't stand looking at it anymore. Listening to the monster inside him, he hefted the vase, bouquet and all, across the room. The ceramic bounced off the wall with a thunk and then crashed into a million turquoise pieces when it hit the floor. Water, flowers, and glass spread out across the floor like blood.

"Damn it!" Luke slammed his hand on the side table. His knees buckled, and he fell to floor. Who was he anymore? Where was that life he—and everyone else—thought was so perfect? Broken. Just like the vase. And the parts of that man, his father, who he'd worked so hard to keep repressed, they were taking over.

The water spread across the floor, and one edge crept slowly toward the letter he'd accidentally dropped earlier. He watched it eagerly, both wanting it to stop short of the envelope and wanting to watch the letter consumed at the same time. When the water's edge touched Natalie's sealed letter, Luke stretched out one hand, ready to save it, read it, add it to the pile in the box on his end table. No. He curled his fingers back into his palm, pushed off the floor, and turned his back to the destruction behind him. He'd let her words drown.

AUGUST

CHAPTER 26

Luke grabbed another handful of dresses from the closet, including the floral one from their Easter pictures and the silky green one Natalie wore when they went on that cruise. He yanked on them till they flew off the hanger with a crack. Another one broken. Luke didn't care, and he had a whole rack full of broken hangers to prove it. Beside him was a large black bag, like the ones he used when doing yard work.

He took in another deep breath through his mouth, trying to avoid inhaling her scent, forcing himself to live without it. Two more dresses, and then he'd be on to shoes. Each bag, once full, went to the attic. At first he'd planned on donating all the clothes to Goodwill, but as he stared to write down the items for his taxes, Luke knew he wasn't ready to give away her things. Not because he thought she was coming back or even because he was sentimental, but because May would kill him. So, the attic it was until May was old enough to go through the belongings herself.

The attic was stifling. And after working six large bags through a human-size hole, Luke's shirt was starting to stick to his back. Time to take a break, and also time to do what he'd been avoiding all day, for two days actually. Guiding the pull-down ladder back up into its resting spot, he wiped his face with the bottom of his shirt. Then Luke made his way downstairs to the thermostat, going the long way into the kitchen so he didn't have to look at the shattered vase and wilted flowers on the floor in the entry.

Rummaging under the sink, Luke collected a garbage bag, a pair of yellow gloves, and rags from underneath the kitchen sink. Armed with these weapons of redemption, he forced himself into the entry, where the wreckage of his temper tantrum lay undisturbed. Slivers of thick blue ceramic dotted the floor. Starting at the door to the basement, Luke went to his knees, his joints creaking as he lowered himself to the floor. The yellow gloves were stiff and made his palms sweat as he picked up each piece of fragmented ceramic and dropped them into the empty garbage bag. As each piece clinked into the bag, Luke turned the fragments into a puzzle in his mind, trying to figure out which piece went where in the ruined vase.

When the last few chunks of ceramic tumbled into the sagging bag, all the pieces came together into a mental mosaic. Only one piece was missing. Luke scanned the room, searching for the rogue blue splinter. The floor, the stairs, the front door—nothing. Then he saw it, a little piece of turquoise and white sticking out from under the dried-out, crinkled envelope of Natalie's ruined letter.

Luke rushed over to the rectangle and tried to push it out of the way, but it clung to the floorboard greedily. He went down to one knee and reached out again, pulling at one of the corners until it came up with a rip. A patch of blue stuck to the floor, adhesive from the envelope trapping the last piece of his puzzle underneath. Pinching the shard between his gloved fingertips, Luke held it up to the light. It was the right one. He dropped it into the bag with a satisfying clink. As he was about to dump the damaged letter into the bag along with the vase, something caught his eye. A few words peeked out from the gash in the envelope.

"It was our little secret . . ."

Luke put down the bag of broken pieces on the counter and snatched the envelope out of the garbage. Without the usual time he took to anticipate the letter or estimate its length, he ripped it open, the fragile envelope dissolving wherever he touched it.

As soon as it was free, he unfolded the smudged pages. He'd been wrong; the letter wasn't about their wedding anniversary. It was about a day he'd rather forget. Rushing through her niceties and anniversary wishes, Luke zoned in on the first mention of their other anniversary.

I'm having a good day today, so I thought it was time to write this letter. I've been dreading this one, but before I die I want you to know what that day was like for me. I want there to be a record of what I saw so maybe you can understand the choices I've made.

My father found your mother and sister in your parents' bed at 10:00 a.m. Two officers drove up to your home within five minutes, an ambulance twenty, and a coroner forty-five minutes later. The police thought you were dead, and for about an hour, I believed them.

They were in our house, talking to my father about what he'd seen. They didn't know I could hear them, but I could. Your mom and your baby sister, both dead. You and your dad, missing. They ran through so many possible scenarios my head started to swim. When they found your dad's car up by the lighthouse, I almost believed their murder/suicide setup.

I knew about your spot on the stairs down by the Ganisters' abandoned beach house. If you were alive you'd more than likely be there. I slipped quietly down the last three stairs and out the back door.

It was barely past noon, and between the sun and the humidity, nearly a hundred degrees outside. Feeling certain I was safe, I sprinted across the yard and headed to the shed. My emergency pack was there, with candy snuck from my mom's supply, crackers, half a jar of peanut butter, and two or three juice boxes. I jumped inside before anyone could spy me from the house.

The shed was hot, like the kiln at school. I ran my hands along the wall of the shed, trying to remember where I'd left my pack. But I didn't find my pack—I found you, huddled in the corner by a split in the boards. A glaring white slash of light fell across your lap and hands.

Your hands, arms, and chest were covered in dried blood, and you were lying so still that for a moment I thought you might be dead. When I reached out to touch you, I didn't know if you'd be stiff and cold or warm and alive. I laid a trembling hand on your chest, relieved to find it was warm and I could feel your heartbeat through your shirt. At my touch, your eyelids fluttered. "Natalie?"

"Luke! You're alive." I ran a hand across your forehead, checking for any injuries.

You looked over your hands, stomach, legs, and feet as though you were almost surprised to be there still.

"Yeah," you said, sounding disappointed, "I am."

"I thought you were dead." I couldn't think about what I'd believed for the past hour. Instead, I leaned in and pressed my lips against yours. We'd kissed before, had quite a few make-out sessions in our little shed, but that day it was different. I know you felt it too.

The first kiss was soft and gentle, like a thank you for the fact that you were still alive. But the next kiss was stronger, like you were afraid I was going to run away and this was the only way to keep me there. I didn't want to leave.

"I love you," I whispered as you slipped my shirt over my head.

"I will never stop loving you," you said, kissing my neck and shoulder as I worked to take off your bloody shirt, to get closer to you, comfort you.

As we fumbled in the darkness, I had no thoughts beyond those four walls. When you laid me down on the floor, I didn't care that clumps of dried dirt were clinging to my hair or the air smelled like grass clippings and sweat. All I wanted was to stay with you forever, to make you forget whatever happened to you that night, to become one.

I'll never regret losing our virginity together on that day. Our passion didn't last long. When it was over, I curled up into your side, your skin stained red. I've gone back to that moment hundreds of times in my life, especially lately. In the middle of the ruins of your life, we found one beautiful moment together, and in that shed we performed a magic no sorcerer or magician could ever achieve—we froze time. But like any great magic, it couldn't last forever.

"I can't believe my mom finally called the police," you said dreamily.

I sat up, your arms still looped behind me. You didn't know.

"Luke." I kissed you again. My lips had worked once; maybe they could help again. "My dad called the police." I looked into your eyes, praying you'd see the truth there so I wouldn't have to say it.

"Shit. Why did he do that? My mom is gonna be so pissed." You sat up and pulled your shirt over your head, searching for your shoes, then realizing you didn't have any. I sat back, replaced my blouse, and adjusted my shorts.

I told you to slow down. I reached out to touch your arm, but you pulled it away. I put my arm around your shoulder, trying to stop you from frantically gathering your belongings. You shrugged me off with a growl and took a step toward the door. I stood and blocked your way.

"Natalie, get out of the way. I have to go. If he finds out, if he comes back, he's gonna hurt her." You spoke to me, but you didn't look at me.

I told you to stop. I pushed you back, trying to make you listen, but instead of calming you or shaking you out of whatever frantic haze you were in, the gentle pressure of my hands on your skin triggered something. You reared back, your face twisted with anger. I didn't know that face, the person who lived behind that face. You used to be the boy who wouldn't hurt a lightning bug, but in that moment you turned into a new person—a man who would hit a woman. When your hand made contact with my cheek, I was already in far more pain from knowing that I'd been wrong about you.

My eyes filled with tears of pain and betrayal. I covered my cheek where it burned from your slap and stepped back. I wasn't going to try to stop you again, but you didn't leave. Your face softened, your blue eyes catching one of the rays of light peeking in from the ceiling like a prism. It was your real face, your real eyes, but I still flinched when you reached out toward me. You apologized and then looked at your hand like you wished you could cut it off. I didn't feel sorry for you. I wasn't going to end up like your mom.

"Your mom is dead," I spat, inching backward toward the only exit. You looked at me like I'd slapped you back. I didn't care. I wanted it to hurt. "Yup. Dead." I cracked the door open, the heat of the midday suddenly feeling like a cool breeze.

You tried to argue with me but then trailed off. I took the opportunity to escape. You begged me not to leave, reaching out, grabbing me by the forearm. Your touch didn't thrill me anymore—it scared me. I yanked my arm away.

"Don't you touch me," I rumbled, tripping backward, nearly falling on my back.

You called my name and rushed forward to help, but I dodged away, putting more distance between us.

Somehow I got out the words, "Go home, Luke. Go home," before running into my house. I covered my face with my hands and escaped to my room.

A few hours later my mom came up and told me the whole story: your mom died from a hemorrhage, your father had been arrested, and you had been taken away by child protective services. She asked if I wanted to see you one more time before you were shipped off to live with some distant relatives out of state. I rubbed the tender spot on my cheek and said, "No."

I never told anyone about our little secret—our intimate moment in the shed and the violent one right after. I was so angry at first that I was glad you were gone. But the longer I lived without you, the more I realized how special we'd been together. There were other boys, not many, but some. I could never really love them while you were still lodged in my heart. I couldn't get you out even though I desperately wanted to.

When we met six years later, I wanted to love you again, trust you again, but was terrified you were going to transform into the monster I met in that shed. I told myself that if I saw even a glimpse of him, I'd turn around and leave. But he never returned.

That's when I realized you are a far better man than your father, and knowing the demons you conquered only made me love you more. Before I go, I need you to know—I forgive you. I love you, and I'm lucky to be able to call you the father of my children.

But, Luke, even though you are not your dad, I do worry about the anger you keep bottled inside, the punching bag in the basement, how you'll handle your grief and the demands of being a single dad . . .

There was a whole other page of writing, but Luke put the letter down. He wouldn't read any further. Was she really so cruel that she could possibly want to force him to relive the worst moment of his life? He'd changed his life because of what happened between them that day. He'd learned how to lock away the beast, and until recently, it had stayed subdued.

Wasn't a lifetime of happiness enough for Natalie, or was she still try-ing to pay him back? Is that what all this was—one last shot at revenge? Luke crumpled the letter in one hand, compressing it into a ball inside his fist. He took aim and tossed it into the open garbage can, knocking the lid down with an open palm. No more letters. No more.

CHAPTER 27

Luke returned to the half-empty closet. He'd thought it would be a more rewarding sight, but now it only made him remember his regrets. In his mind he lined them up, one behind the other, filling the empty hangers on the rod.

No, he couldn't keep going this way. Counting regrets would only lead to new ones. He had to fill the newly emptied space. Lacing his finger through several filled hangers, Luke whisked three work shirts, two pairs of khakis, and one somewhat dusty sweater across the space and put them on the empty rod with a clank. *There, that looks better,* he thought, feeling a little satisfied.

In the corner of the closet, part of the baseboard looked askew. Maybe he'd kicked it during his packing frenzy. Great, another thing to put on his to-do list. With Natalie's clothes gone, it was easy to examine the damage.

Luke crawled toward the crooked piece of wood. Up close it was easier to see several black scuff marks and slight dents in the drywall above. Holding the baseboard with his fingertips, Luke tried to adjust its position enough to cover the marred wall. It fell off into his hands. He held it, frozen. A long, rectangular opening stared back at him.

What the? Luke leaned the piece of baseboard against the wall and ran his hand along the jagged edge of the drywall. Immediately his fingers brushed a solid object. Unable to actually see the item, he hoped it was something inorganic he was touching and not the remnants of a mouse nest or something else equally disgusting. Whatever it was, it was defiantly stuck. He pulled down one of his shirts, hanger and all. Ripping open the top button of the faded blue-and-white work shirt, he forced the plastic hanger out through the neckhole. Perfect.

He got down a little lower, now on his stomach, inserting the flat side of the hanger into the opening and swiping it across the edge of the carpet, not letting up when he met resistance. Then, with a swish and thunk, a maroon rectangle about the size of a child's picture book flew out from the hole in the wall.

Luke picked up the fabric-covered book. *What in the world?* Plastic pages stuck out around the edges, and the binding was cracked on the top and bottom. Flipping the book over to what he thought was the front, Luke stared at the empty cover, and, fingers trembling, he opened the book.

There was no title page, no description of what he was looking at, just a newspaper clipping from the Mallory Witling investigation. Mallory Witling. The name was familiar. Luke searched his memory, trying to figure out where he'd heard that name before. Oh yes, it was when Natalie took a continuing ed class. Maybe a psych class? That's right—she wrote a paper about this girl. Maybe the scrapbook was part of Natalie's project.

The date on the article was from nearly twenty years ago, just after senior year of high school. It was cut out of an actual newspaper, not printed off a computer. Strange. Mallory Witling disappeared at three years old without a trace from her home in Lansing. Her parents, Mark and Eva Witling, were begging for any news regarding her disappearance and offering a reward.

The clipping didn't mean much to him. All Luke knew about the story he learned from an episode of *Dateline* Natalie had forced him to watch as part of her research. Beyond that, Luke could barely remember much about the Witling case, just a few hazy details.

Luke turned the page; another newspaper article. This one was from a week later when the case was upgraded to "missing, presumed dead." The police found blood all over Mallory's pillow and bedding, and cadaver dogs detected her scent in Eva Witling's car. The next page had an article about Eva Witling's lie detector test. She'd failed it miserably and soon after hired a lawyer. Another article when she was arrested. Page after page of articles followed: when she posted bail, when the husband came to police with evidence pointing to his wife, when they divorced, when the police exhumed the body of the oldest Witling child—Diane, when they performed an autopsy, when the results reported Diane had died of ethylene glycol poisoning. After the first three or four pages, Luke flipped through the rest of the pasted-on clippings just reading the headlines, the pages making a thump with each new turn.

Finally, he reached the last article. The headline read: "LIFE." Luke, now fully invested in the story of poor little Mallory Witling, read every detail eagerly.

After being confronted with Diane's autopsy, Eva Witling was offered a plea deal. She took the deal and pleaded guilty to both Mallory's and Diane's murders. Her attorneys pushed for placement in a mental health facility rather than prison, claiming Eva suffered from Munchausen syndrome by proxy. They claimed that Eva didn't mean to kill the girls, just make them sick enough to need to go to the hospital. It was the attention she craved, not the illness. Eva testified that both deaths were accidental overdoses rather than premeditated murder.

In the end the judge showed no mercy, stating that repeatedly poisoning her daughters with antifreeze was not an accident. Eva ended up in the state penitentiary serving twenty-to-life, the death penalty off the table only because of her plea deal.

It was a heavy read. Luke flipped through the pages one more time, hoping there would be some kind of hint as to why this one event stuck with his wife and why she hid the scrapbook. Lansing. Not close to Pentwater, but not exactly far away either. Maybe she knew the family. Or maybe she knew the kids that died. He slapped the book closed.

A folded piece of paper fluttered out of one of the pages. It must've been hidden behind an article, inside one of the plastic pockets. The paper was folded in thirds, stiff and felt textured between his fingers. Far more expensive than the notebook paper Natalie used for her letters to him. Unsure what to expect, he unfolded the paper, a typed letter, one page long.

> Dear Natalie,
> It is with heavy heart that I contact you. I'm breaking with agency protocol, but seeing that we've never had anything like this happen before, maybe there isn't protocol for this kind of thing. After your years of service for our organization and the support you've given other birth parents during your time with us, I feel like I have no other choice. I have to tell you the truth about what happened to your daughter.

Luke reread the line again. "Your daughter." The date on the letter was from a month before Will's birth, the same as the one he'd memorized from the Maranatha envelope, so the daughter wasn't May. Then he thought of Andy's daughter, who was supposedly his with Nancy. Or was that child really Natalie's? Luke kept reading.

> When you gave up your daughter eight years ago, you trusted Pastor Neal, Maria, and me to find a safe and

loving home for your baby girl. We thought we had. I swear we did everything by the book, followed every step in the process. This family, they'd lost a child to a hereditary illness and, afraid they'd pass that disease on to another biological child, decided to adopt. They passed all the tests and visits and had been on our list for over eighteen months. I felt so right about that family, but I've never been so wrong. I feel the weight of that decision every day of my life.

You may have heard of little Mallory Witling, missing, presumed dead. I'm sorry to tell you, Natalie, Mallory was your daughter. I've kept a detailed scrapbook of all the significant events in her investigation and court case if you want to know more. The one comfort I can send you is that Eva Witling is in prison. I couldn't make myself write this letter until I knew that I could give you that small bit of consolation.

I can never speak with you about the contents of this letter. I'm already risking my job by reaching out, and after losing Mallory the way we did, I now see even clearer how important my job is here. I don't want this to ever happen again. I won't let it.

I hope to see you and Andy at the convention again this summer, but I'd appreciate it if you kept this information private. I wouldn't want Andy to worry about his own daughter's placement. After this unfortunate loss, we've made an effort to check in with all our adoptive parents and changed some of our procedures when it comes to child placement.

Wishing you the best,
Christina Stephani

Doing some mental math, Luke counted back years and months. Mallory went missing when she was three years old. The letter was dated a month before Will's birth. That meant Natalie was only fourteen when her daughter was born. Her first child was born sometime after her freshman year of high school.

Luke dropped the fancy paper; sweat was running down his back. The closet suddenly felt too small, like the walls were pressing in on him, ready to crush him. Leaving everything he'd been working on, Luke scrambled out of the enclosed space, suffocated by the weight of his new knowledge—*this* was Natalie's secret.

That time in the shed, where they fumbled through the steps of lovemaking while Luke tried to forget his losses in their passion and Natalie tried to comfort him with it—not only was it their first time together but it was also his first time ever. Did they make a baby in that moment of desperation? It was hard to fathom but explained a lot—Andy, Maranatha House, those pictures, her secrets, and definitely why Terry still hated him for knocking up her fourteen-year-old daughter. And Ms. Stephani from Maranatha House, she'd kept a detailed scrapbook about his secret daughter's disappearance, death investigation, and the court case surrounding it. He'd *known* that woman had more information than she'd let on.

Luke tried to remember the dark-haired girl from the fuzzy newspaper picture. Did she look like May? He hadn't taken a second glance at the smiling girl in the picture, hadn't looked to see what his first child even looked like. He might not know what it felt like when Mallory kicked inside Natalie's stomach or what color her eyes were when she was born, but he could at least try to make out the shape of her smile, the texture of her hair. Luke dashed across the worn patch of carpet flattened by the door and retrieved the scrapbook.

Settling back down into his spot by the bed, he flipped through the pages again. This time slowly, deliberately. When he got to the first picture of Mallory, he held it out at arm's length. She looked a lot like Will when he was little, darker features, with Natalie's bright eyes. Why did he have to add this beautiful little girl to the list of people he'd lost in his life? Why hadn't Natalie let him mourn *with* her instead of leaving him to learn of their daughter on his own? And one question this discovery didn't answer was who Neal, professor or pastor, really was.

CHAPTER 28

"Daddy," Clayton whispered, pulling at Luke's eyelid. "Daaaaddy," he sang. "Daddy. It's my birthday! Wake up! Wake *up*!"

Luke squinted up at the face of a smiling four-year-old. Well, almost four-year-old.

"Sorry, bud, not today. Your birthday is Friday." Luke tugged up two of Clayton's fingers, wondering how they were already sticky. "Two. That's two more days."

"Oh man!" Clayton flopped on the bed. If he were a cartoon character, "Oh man!" would be his new catchphrase. "It will never get here."

"Two more sleeps, that's it. Don't worry; it will be here before you know it." Luke rubbed the top of Clayton's spiky hair. He wrapped his arms around his back and slung him over in a tackle/bear hug combo. When he held his kids in his arms, Luke could feel how much they'd grown in the past six weeks. It was bittersweet to see their faces; he'd missed them more than he could even realize, but every change he noticed reminded him that he never got to see Mallory grow up.

He thought back to getting that first glimpse of his kids at the airport. Terry had taken it upon herself to cut both May's and Clayton's hair while they were in Florida. Clayton's was buzzed so short that his white-blond stubble made him look bald. May's hair was bobbed above her bronzed shoulders; the long strand of hair she usually nibbled on was gone. Occasionally she'd grab for it when she got nervous, like when they first stepped into the family greeting area after landing. Luke watched as May passed the security guard, tugged at the hair near her ear like she was urging it to grow.

Terry had dressed the kids in nice clothes for the airplane, as though they were flying in the 1950s, when dressing up on a plane had been the norm. The boys, tan and handsome, looked a little silly in their button-up shirts and dress slacks, surrounded by casual passengers wearing yoga pants and jeans.

But not May. She looked like a flower in the middle of a garden choked with weeds. Her hair was smooth for once, even after a long flight, the blue flowers on her dress flapping with each step. His eyes burned when she glanced up and caught him staring at her. A bright smile spilled across her face. She dropped the worn Disney princess duffel she'd had slung over one shoulder and went into a full sprint before jumping into his arms.

He never should've let them go for so long. The house needed children.

◆　◆　◆

"Show me how big you are," Luke said, encouraging Clayton. "You go get yourself dressed, and then we can see what Terry is making that smells so yummy." Luke sniffed the air. He hadn't planned on Terry's extended visit, not sure if he was ready to confront her about the secret she'd shared with Natalie. Then again, maybe she didn't know that Natalie's baby was Mallory Witling. If she didn't know her first grandchild was dead, Luke did not want to be the one to tell her. He was starting to understand why Natalie found secrets easier than the truth.

Funny thing, Terry never asked if she could stay. She proclaimed her new departure date, went to the ticket counter, and made her new reservations, all without consulting Luke. He wondered if the real reason she stayed was because she couldn't bear to let the kids go. Or maybe she couldn't bear to let them go to him.

"I know! I'll wear my pirate shirt!" Clayton wiggled across the half-slept-on bed.

"That's fine," Luke shouted after him, even though this would be the third day in a row for that shirt. He'd let Terry deal with it. "Make sure to put on new undies." Clayton slammed the bedroom door behind him, muffling Luke's last request.

He listened to the staccato of Clayton's footsteps fading into the other room. When Clayton's door clicked shut, Luke let out a breath, the smile melting from his face. It was easier when he was alone—no one to pretend for. At least there was one reason to be happy Terry stayed—he couldn't let himself go when she was around. So now it was only in his bedroom and occasionally in the car when Luke could indulge his craziness. Like how he drove past Annie's house every day, looking for lights, watching for signs of movement, estimating the amount of time since the grass had been cut.

Today, while he was at work, Terry was going to take Clayton in for a doctor's appointment, giving May the opportunity she'd been waiting for—Jessie time. They hadn't seen Jessie since the day before the kids left. Six weeks was a long time to not see someone after seeing them daily for six months.

Luke hefted himself out of bed. His shins yelled at him, still angry from the run he'd forced on himself the day before. He'd never been much of a runner, just the mile at school and the bases when he played on the softball team at work. He'd always kept in shape with the punching bag in the basement and a set of weights, but he'd felt jittery lately, uncomfortable in his own skin. Though hitting something had always been enough of a release, now it seemed to compound his anger rather than release it. Then one night while he was working out, hitting the bag rhythmically, Luke remembered how free Annie looked when she ran. He wanted to feel free. Apparently a precursor to feeling free was feeling sore for a few weeks first.

Luke tugged at his boxers, loose from the running or maybe because he hadn't eaten well or much when the kids were away. His clothes were starting to sag on his body. Limping across the room, he headed for his closet before remembering it was empty. It still felt wrong to go into that place, so he'd made a pile of clothes in the corner by a window. Most were clean despite being creased with wrinkles. On the top of the pile was the pair of slacks he'd worn to work the day before, belt still threaded through the loops, only wrinkled down one leg. They would have to do.

◆ ◆ ◆

A hesitant knock came from the front door before Jessie walked through it like she belonged there. It had taken her a few months to be willing to barge into their house unannounced, but Luke had insisted she do away with the formality of knocking. He'd been trying to get her to call him Luke instead of Mr. Richardson for the same amount of time, but with fewer results.

"Hey, Jessie, come on in." Luke was bent over his workbag, making sure he had all the proposals he'd brought home to review. May must not have heard the door, or else she would've been up in Jessie's face before she got two feet past the threshold. "It is so good to see you again. I hope you had a nice summer." He stood up and got a good look at her.

She was wearing a dark-blue *Mama Mia!* T-shirt cinched at the waist, with a navy skirt covered in white polka dots and a pair of white flats. In all her time babysitting, Luke had never seen the same shirt twice. It almost made him tempted to go to a show.

She'd left her backpack at home today, and it was strange to see her without it. Instead, she wore a purse about the size of a note card slung over one shoulder. She looked tired and her face was a little puffy, and compared to his suntanned children, her skin was as pale as if it was the middle of winter, not the end of summer. Her clothes looked the same, but there was *something* off. Luke stood, hands full of proposals in plastic covers, but too preoccupied with this new version of Jessie to keep reviewing them.

"Summer was boring, as always." She laughed weakly.

"Did you take in any good shows? I heard *The Lion King* was in Chicago last month. Did you go?"

Jessie removed her shoes, using her toes to slip them off. "Nope, not this time."

"What? I thought you never missed a chance to see the hottest shows from Broadway." Luke loved to tease Jessie about her obsession with pretty much anything Broadway. "Do you need a raise? I'd gladly donate to any travel fund."

"Ha, no, I was busy . . . interviewing. I couldn't take the time."

"You're already working too hard, and you haven't even started your job yet." Luke shook his head in mock disappointment. "I don't know if I can support this."

Jessie forced a smile. Her lips, blanched white; the thin red cracks at the corners of her mouth; and the dark circles under her eyes made him worry.

"Uh, so . . ." He didn't want to be nosy, but she didn't look well. "When do you start your job, Miss Fraga?" Luke used her "teacher name." She'd used Luke as a reference when she was job hunting. About a month ago she called with good news—she'd landed a job at a local elementary school. She promised she'd still be available for the kids, but Luke knew there was no way she could keep up with that kind of sched-ule, not as a first-year teacher. He'd already started to make other plans. Once Terry left, Clayton would be in the preschool's extended-day program, May in the afterschool program, and Will, well, Will was old enough to fly solo when he wasn't going to cross-country.

"Actually, I didn't end up taking that job," she said, letting her purse drop to the floor like the phone-size bag was too heavy to bear. "And my last name's not actually Fraga. That was just the name I used at school. I thought Natalie would've . . . told you." Jessie wavered, breaths coming faster. She was going to vomit or pass out; Luke wasn't sure which. "Whoa, dizzy." She covered her eyes, like that would make the room stop spinning.

"Jessie." Luke took a half step forward. "I think you need to sit down."

"My name . . ." she continued, her words slurring, her body tilting from side to side.

Luke dropped the reports he'd been sorting through and caught her by the forearms before she fell headfirst into the banister.

"Jessie?" May called from upstairs. She must've heard Luke's feet hit the floor as he jumped the six feet to catch her.

"May, get my phone!" Luke shouted. Jessie's eyes rolled around, and she muttered under her breath. He couldn't make it out. "Jessie." He patted her face, not sure if this was something like low blood sugar, which Will sometimes suffered from, or if this was something more serious—something that had to do with the medical alert bracelet on her arm. "Jessie," he called again.

"Call my dad," Jessie mumbled, half-conscious. She held up her wrist before her eyes rolled back in her head, unresponsive. Phone in hand at the top of the stairs, May screamed.

"Jessie!" May stumbled down the stairs, sounding like a herd of elephants instead of one child.

"What is going on?" Terry shouted from the kitchen. But when she reached the foyer and took in Jessie passed out across Luke's lap, she covered her mouth, her own scream nearly as shrill as May's.

"May, give me the phone." He held out his hand, anxious to get someone on the line that could tell him what to do, how to help Jessie, who was unconscious and breathing in a frighteningly labored manner. May passed him the phone, and Luke dialed the digits. As almost an afterthought, he turned over her arm and read her bracelet to be ready for the 9-1-1 operator's questions. Her arm was limp like a sleeping baby, but nothing about Jessie was peaceful at that moment. Luke scanned her alert bracelet as the phone rang against his ear.

JESSIE TOWNSEND
CHRONIC KIDNEY DISEASE
ALLERGY: PENICILLIN
ICE: NEAL TOWNSEND 734-555-4673

Townsend? Luke read through the bracelet again. It couldn't be . . . right?

"Farmington Hills 9-1-1, what's the emergency?" a female voice asked through the phone.

Jessie is Neal's daughter. The thought pounded in his mind like a battering ram. He opened his mouth to talk to the operator, but no sound came out. He swallowed and tried again. Nothing. He couldn't get his brain to focus on anything else. *Jessie is Dr. Neal's daughter.*

"Dad!" May squealed, now kneeling next to Jessie's lifeless form. "Help her. She can't die, Daddy. She can't."

"Hello?" The voice called out again. "Did you have an emergency?"

Jessie's back arched and she began to shake, the convulsions slamming her against his knee and the floor over and over. This was Jessie. He had to *do* something.

"Yes, my babysitter passed out. Uh, she has some kind of kidney disease. She's shaking; I think it's a seizure." Luke had to almost shout over May's pleading and Terry's sobs. Will stood back by the hall to the kitchen, trying to hide Clayton behind his legs, his face mute with shock. "Send an ambulance, please," Luke begged, not caring in that moment whose daughter she was.

CHAPTER 29

Inside his car, Luke tried to figure out what had just happened. He started the car with a hard turn on the ignition. Blasting the air conditioner, Luke set his sweaty face in front of one of the vents. The air pouring out was hotter than the August air outside, somehow superheated by the engine and summer sun. When the burning air finally succumbed to the cooling process, he closed his eyes, letting the crisp mechanically chilled air clear his crowded mind.

The ambulance had just left for the hospital, and Terry had hung up with Jessie's dad, Neal Townsend. He was going to meet Luke at the hospital. May wanted to go, but Luke knew she was too young to manage all the stress of the ER. Plus, at this point, it wasn't clear if Jessie would even survive the trip. When the paramedics looked at Jessie's medical bracelet, one of them asked if she was on dialysis, if she was taking any medications, what site was used for her treatments. All Luke could do was shake his head and say, "I have no idea."

When Terry finally got Neal on the phone, she passed him over to the medic and then herded hysterical May and confused Clayton into the kitchen so they couldn't see as the paramedics put a tube down Jessie's throat and pumped air directly into her lungs.

The thought of losing Jessie was nearly enough to keep the fact that she was Neal's daughter out of his mind. He pushed the gas pedal harder, not wanting Jessie to be alone in the hospital before her father got there. He'd spent enough hours in Botsford Hospital that he used to say it felt like a second home.

Passing the school where Natalie used to work, Garden Grove Elementary, Luke checked the window to her old classroom. She'd always drive past with the kids and tell them about the projects in the window, talking endearingly about the students who did each one. Luke frowned; with the school year not quite begun, the window was empty now, covered by some brown butcher paper so no one could look inside. Distracted by the pang of sorrow the empty window shot through him, Luke didn't notice a set of red and blue lights were flashing behind him.

Damn it. A ticket was not what he needed today. He needed to get to the hospital. Luke twisted the wheel to the right, pulled over to the curb, and watched the driver's side mirror as he fished his wallet out of his back pocket. A uniformed police officer exited his squad car and walked briskly toward his door. Luke slid the stiff license out, tapping it against the steering wheel as he waited.

The window. He pulled at the switch and made sure the window was rolled all the way down before letting go, hoping to shave a couple of seconds off the police stop. The officer stopped a little ways back from his window, hand resting on the hilt of his gun. Luke had only had two tickets before, both for speeding. In both cases he'd openly admitted to being over the speed limit. Those stops took fifteen minutes altogether and even though at the end he was down a hundred dollars, gained points on his license, and had a hike in his insurance bill, cooperation seemed to be the way to go.

"I'm sorry if I was speeding, officer. My friend is in an ambulance on the way to the hospital. I . . . I was trying to get there. I didn't mean to . . ." He'd been distracted, so going too fast in a school zone was definitely a possibility.

"You have a taillight out back here; looks smashed." The officer talked over Luke's explanation. "You been in an accident lately?"

"Not that I was aware of. Maybe someone backed into me at work and didn't report it." Luke used the side rearview mirror to try and get a look at the damage but couldn't see anything. "I'm serious about that friend in the ambulance. I really need to get there. You can give me any ticket you want."

"We will get you to your friend as soon as possible. License and proof of insurance, please," the officer said, not a hint of compassion in his voice. Luke passed his license up to the officer, whose name tag read **J. RABOLD**. Officer Rabold stared down at him over the top of his sunglasses.

"I'm sorry I didn't notice the light. I'll get it fixed immediately." The officer's face remained still. "Uh, the insurance card is in the glove compartment. I'll grab it." He made sure to keep his hands visible and explain his movements to Officer Rabold. Luke looped his finger under the latch for the glove compartment and pulled. It wasn't always the most compliant latch, so he yanked extra hard. The latch hitched but didn't open.

Luke smiled over his shoulder at the officer and then tried again, this time harder. The latch made a loud pop, and the door fell open, papers rushing out behind it in an avalanche. Luke shifted back, stunned. The usually neatly organized glove compartment now stood empty, its contents scattered all over the passenger seat and floor. On the seat was the blue, white, and gray service manual, a pair of headphones, and a small folder with his insurance card peeking out. What he didn't recognize were four or five prescription bottles.

"What the hell?" Luke swore, forgetting about the officer for a moment. He leaned over to pick up one of the bottles; he looked at the colored pills inside. It reminded him of something . . . it reminded him of . . .

"Sir, I'm going to need to ask you to drop that and exit the vehicle immediately." The officer's voice cut through Luke's rambling memories; he took a step back from the car and slipped Luke's ID in his vest pocket.

"Sure; no problem." Luke dropped the container and sat up, stunned at the sudden change in the officer's demeanor. Luke pushed open the door slowly to avoid startling the officer, hand on his gun, badge bouncing slightly as he stepped back toward his squad car. Once Luke had closed the car door behind him, the officer gestured for him to stop his progress.

"Put your hands on the hood of the car, please." He pointed to the car, his face still, lips set in a hard line.

"What? Why?" Luke asked, running through all the possible infractions he could possibly be guilty of. Surely a broken taillight was not grounds for this. Luke followed orders, flinching as he pressed his palms against the superheated hood. The officer came up behind him and pushed his legs apart, shoes making a scratching sound as they dragged through the dirt. Then he ran his hands up and down Luke's arms, legs, chest, and torso. Apparently satisfied with his search, the officer reached over Luke's left shoulder and clapped a cold metal cuff around his wrist.

"What the? I need to go to the hospital. Jessie is sick. I need . . ." Luke tried to look back at the officer. "Wait—am I under arrest?"

"Look forward." He yanked the other arm around Luke's back and tightened the other half of the handcuffs around his wrist, so tight they dug into his skin. Guiding him by his elbow, the officer turned the shackled Luke around and leaned him against the car again. "Sir, you want to tell me more about those bottles in your glove box? You have a valid prescription for those pills? If I get a dog out here to look through your car, what am I going to find?"

Luke's heart was pounding, and his mouth was so dry he didn't know how to form words. "I swear I've never seen those bottles before.

I . . . I have no idea what they are doing in there." Luke spewed out the answer.

"Uh-huh. Then you don't mind if we take a look through your car, right?" He didn't sound like he was seeking permission, but Luke gave it anyway. He wasn't hiding anything and definitely not drugs.

"Yeah, of course." What would he get for saying no—an even more aggressive body search? A cavity search? Luke cringed at the thought. Whatever was in those bottles, they were a mistake. Something left over from Natalie's days filled with endless prescriptions, no doubt. They'd search the car, find out it was a big misunderstanding, and have a laugh.

"Sit down." The officer led Luke to the curb, speaking into the radio on his shoulder. "Cross your legs," he ordered, and Luke complied, glad he was partially sheltered from onlookers by the tail end of his car.

Three more squad cars later, Luke's SUV was being towed to the station for a more intensive search, and Luke was under arrest. Through the back window of the squad car, he watched as they passed the green-and-white street sign that usually signaled home. Terry was there; the kids were there; they all expected him to call from the ER, to have an update on Jessie, and to eventually come home. But he wasn't going to the hospital, and he definitely wasn't going home—he was going to a police station.

CHAPTER 30

More people should spend a day in jail, Luke thought, his wrists still sting-
ing from the handcuffs. It was scary and humbling. If he'd ever been
tempted to break the law, this would definitely have scared him off.
He'd only been there a few hours, as far as he could tell. They'd taken
him in, processed him, taken fingerprints and a mug shot, performed a
humiliating strip search, and given him a drug test and health screening.
After four hours of increasingly invasive procedures, Luke was finally
put in a holding cell. He'd be arraigned in the morning for . . . well, he
wasn't sure, but he could guess that it'd at least be drug possession and
intent to distribute.

After trying to deny any knowledge of the pills found in his car,
Luke finally wised up and shut his mouth. No one believed him. He
needed a lawyer, and he wanted to know Jessie's status and let everyone
know he was okay. That meant calling Terry.

It was painful to have to ask Terry for help. He tried to explain the
few details he understood and asked her to find a lawyer, no matter the
cost. They could use Natalie's life insurance for a defense, might even
have enough for bail. He hadn't spent a penny of it yet, but getting out
of jail had to be his first priority. Terry definitely didn't believe Luke's

side of the story, but she was literally the only person he could call for help. He hoped she'd find someone—fast.

The only good news was that Jessie had made it to the hospital and had been stabilized. Terry only had two minutes to give him information before they were cut off on the ancient precinct pay phone. What he did get out of that two minutes was that Jessie had been in total renal failure like the paramedics had predicted. She'd been going for dialysis three times a week for the past month and had been going downhill fast. May was supposed to go and visit her at the hospital tomorrow. The last thing the kids needed to deal with was worrying about Luke being in jail, so the plan was to keep his arrest a secret for as long as possible. Hopefully forever. For now the fairly weak excuse was an emergency work trip, but Will wouldn't buy that story for long.

When the phone cut out, a uniformed officer escorted Luke to a holding cell at the back of the station. At least it was empty, a row of benches bolted to the wall and a urinal in the corner. There were bars, though, cold, metal, and painted off-white. He wasn't sure why they painted them since it seemed like there were at least twenty coats in spots where the paint continued to peel. He was sore and exhausted.

The small, rectangular windows on the other side of the room gave him the only hint to the time. It was black outside, yellow lights from the parking lot filling the room with eerie shadows. It was hard to keep track of time without a watch or a phone, but it must be near midnight by now. He should sleep, but the cell was undoubtedly not made for relaxing, the painted-green benches his only option for stretching out besides the floor. He briefly contemplated taking off his shoes to help him unwind, but then the idea of what might be on the floor made his toes curl.

Luke threw himself on the bench that lined the back wall. The shadows from the bars of the cell made patterns on the ceiling, and soon his mind was turning them into images like when he'd watch the clouds with Will and May. However, these weren't happy bunnies or silly Santas; these images were much darker. In the corner, the shadows clustered together over a watermark in the ceiling, making it look like the face of an old woman was looking back at him. Over by the door to the cell was a splash of black shadow that reminded him of a pool of blood.

He tossed his arm over his eyes, pressing down hard, trying to keep the panic from taking over. What was he going to do? There had to be some way of proving he hadn't done this. He could lose his job, his house, and his kids—everything he had left.

As far as he could tell, being arrested was good for one thing— bringing into focus the most important parts of your life. On a day when he thought discovering Dr. Neal and Jessie's connection was the worst moment he could imagine, sitting in a cell, rubbing his chafed wrists and dreaming up horrors on the wall, made him feel like a fool for ever being obsessed with Neal and those letters.

If Neal had helped cover up the adoption and the death of Luke and Natalie's child, if they had a deep connection because of it, or even if they had planted Neal's daughter into his home as a spy, Luke didn't care. Natalie was dead and he was alive. One more reason he should be living for his kids, not for some dead woman, even if that woman was the one person he'd ever felt loved him unconditionally. The kids were worth more than his pain.

◆ ◆ ◆

On the last night of Natalie's life, Luke pushed the fancy white couch in the living room up right next to her hospital bed. He had spent large portions of the past several nights sleeping in a chair, but it made Natalie feel so guilty. When he let his body settle into the stiff cushions of the pristine fabric, Natalie put out her hand.

"Will you hold my hand tonight?" she asked. Luke took her frail hand in his, counting the bones on the back of her hand through her skin. "Ah, that's nice." She sighed and one tear slipped out of the corner of her lashless eyes. It followed one of her new wrinkles, the ones that came once she lost the protective layers of fat under her skin. He loved kissing those wrinkles and pretending they'd grown old together.

"You're too far away; get up here." She tugged at his arm, and Luke cautiously crawled up into her bed. Weakly, she tried to shift over to the other side of the bed but stopped, out of breath after her first attempt.

"I've got you," Luke whispered in her ear, letting his lips brush her cheek as he moved her over the last few inches.

"Thank you," she whispered, always grateful for anything Luke did. You don't have to thank me, he wanted to shout, but he wasn't mad at Natalie. He was mad she was in pain and that soon she'd be gone.

"I love you, Nat," Luke said, nuzzling his nose into her neck and wrapping an arm over her torso.

"I know, I know." She patted his back, like she was comforting one of their kids. He cried a lot back then, even though he tried not to. It was his intention to make those last moments with Natalie happy ones, to leave the kids with thoughts of a cheerful farewell. But that night, he didn't want to pretend to be happy. Sometimes Luke wondered if some ancient instinct told him his wife was that close to death.

"This reminds me of what it was like when we were kids. All we're missing is pop and Twizzlers." She took a labored breath, and Luke picked up his arm.

"Am I hurting you?"

"No." She grabbed his arm and pressed it back down on her stomach. "I like feeling you. I miss your touch, I miss kissing you, I miss . . . everything." She kissed his forehead again. "I want to go back and do it all over again. Can we start over? Is that a thing?"

Luke tried to turn a sob into a laugh, but it came out sounding like he was choking. "You want a do-over? If this was a video game, I could erase the memory, and we could start at the beginning." He curled his body around hers, trying to touch her in as many places at the same time as possible. "But we'd lose everything, all the levels we'd beat and coins we'd won. I'd do it; would you?"

She was silent for a moment, and Luke wondered if maybe she'd fallen asleep. Every night she took a sleeping pill to help her sleep through the pain, and it was probably kicking in.

"No," she answered suddenly. "I wouldn't start over, not if it meant giving up our memories." Her breath hitched in her chest, and he watched her collarbone go up and down with each cry. "That's all you'll have left of me, memories."

Luke couldn't talk. If it hurt to think about losing her while she still lay in his arms, he didn't know how he could even breathe once she was buried under six feet of dirt. "We won't forget," he finally forced out. "I could never forget . . ."

"I hope you're wrong"—her tone turned suddenly hard—"about death. I want you to tell me I'll see you again, that our years together weren't a waste." She pushed Luke's head back with her chin, and he looked up at her eyes. Still deep and blue, they were the only thing unchanged by chemo and cancer and impending death. He didn't believe, he hadn't for a long, long time, but when he saw those sparkling eyes, the ones he'd first noticed as a boy and saw every day when May asked for pancakes or Clayton giggled at a television show, he couldn't tell her that. He loved her enough to lie.

"I'll see you again. I promise . . ." He pulled her limp hand up to his lips and kissed her fingertips. "I promise."

"Mmmm, thank you, Luke." She closed her eyes, her body falling asleep part by part. "I'll see you soon . . ." She breathed out before succumbing to her medication and exhaustion. He waited until he was certain she was asleep and then rolled off the hospital bed, pulled her favorite fleece blanket up to her shoulders, and then settled back into the couch, where he got his first full night's sleep in weeks. When he woke up in the morning to the sun shining in from behind the front window curtains, Natalie was dead. He'd slept through her last breaths.

◆ ◆ ◆

"*Hey!* You have a visitor; get up!" A loud voice shattered Luke's memory. He wiped at his eyes, not wanting anyone in this place to think he'd been crying. Squinting through the poorly lit room, Luke tried to make out who could possibly be visiting him in a holding cell in the middle of the night. An officer, dressed in his street uniform, stood at the door to the cell. Luke rubbed his eyes, and the man came into focus. It was Brian Gurrella.

"Luke, you okay?" Brian held a tray of food, a sandwich wrapped in a paper towel, an apple, and something that looked like a juice box lying on its side. "I have your dinner. Made it myself."

Luke wasn't hungry even though he hadn't eaten since breakfast. Still, he crossed the cell and took the steel tray from Brian's hands.

"Thanks." He placed the tray on a bench without inspecting it further, only caring about how to get out of that cell and back home to his family. He returned to the door and Brian, who was watching him carefully.

"You want to tell me what happened?" Brian asked, his thumbs looped through the belt loops on his pants. There was none of the usual humor in his face. No, he looked like a cop ready to interrogate a "perp."

"I have no idea. Really. I guess I had a busted taillight and got pulled over, but after that . . . I don't know what happened." Luke approached the door, wrapping his hands around the bars. "What did they tell you?"

Brian stepped back, like Luke was too close or potentially dangerous. "I'm not really supposed to discuss charges with you. I heard you have a lawyer coming. This isn't official. I just wanted to talk to you, man-to-man."

"No, no, it's okay. I have nothing to hide." Luke pressed his face between the bars. "Please, what did they say?"

"Fine," he said, brushing out a wrinkle on the front of his uniform. "They said you had drugs in your car, pills. That you had them in bottles, ready for distribution."

"I've never seen those before, damn it," Luke growled, squeezing the metal bars until he was sure he could break them.

"I have to tell you, Luke, that's what they all say." Brian shook his head like he didn't know what to think. "No one sits in that cell, looks back at me, and says, 'Yeah, I did it. I sold drugs.' So you can see why it's hard to believe you."

"Hard to believe me? You've got to be kidding. We've been friends for ten years. I barely even drink, much less use illegal drugs. Please tell me you can do something." Being accused by a stranger was one thing, but to be accused by Brian, wife-beating, drug-abusing Brian, was nauseating.

"Wait, let me get this right." Brian took a large step toward the bars, making them face-to-face, minus the metal barrier. "You want someone who knows you, who you've been friends with for a long time, to put in a good word for you? Is that what you'd like to happen here?"

A dark hole formed inside Luke, sucking out any hope he'd been holding on to. Brian knew he'd called Bormet. He released the bars and took a step back. Is this what Annie was talking about when she said that if Luke helped her, Brian would come after him too? Those pills weren't Natalie's after all. Brian put them there.

"It wasn't really that hard to figure out. I find Annie at your house; she's gone and told you all kinds of stories, and you believed her." Brian put his arms through the bars this time and clasped them on the other side. "Then, a week later, I fly to DC, only to find out my orientation has been canceled and they gave the job to someone else. I might not be an engineer, but I can put those pieces together—you screwed my wife, and then you screwed me."

"I can't believe you'd do this to me. I tried to help you. I gave you a recommendation, but . . ." Luke grabbed handfuls of hair in his fists, unable to look at Brian. "You'd been hitting her."

"No, no, no, that's ridiculous." He kicked at the gate. "She's not stable; you've got to know that by now."

"Not stable? *You* are the least stable person I know."

"That's not what my twenty years of service shows," Brain explained, still infuriatingly calm. "No one here would believe your story. Why do you think Annie told you instead of someone who could actually help her, like the police?"

"I know you did this." Luke squinted at Brian through the darkness. There was a smug confidence about the way he leaned against the bars, how much he seemed to enjoy Luke's outburst instead of being incensed by it. "You broke my taillight, put drugs in my car, called in an anonymous tip, and got me arrested."

Luke grabbed the tray next to him, rushed to the horizontal opening in the cell door, and crammed it through, almost hitting Brian in the gut. "I'm not hungry." Brian stepped aside, and the metal tray clattered to the ground. Silent, he watched the apple roll until it came to a stop short of hitting the cement wall.

The briefest of smiles rippled across his lips before he stood and sniffed loudly. "That's an unfounded and bold-faced lie. You sound desperate."

"How could you?" Luke shook with half-restrained anger. "I could lose . . . everything."

"Maybe you should've thought of that earlier," Brian scolded, sounding like a "scared straight" officer from a TV show. Bending one knee, he collected the tray and other items off the floor. Standing, he unwrapped a corner of the plastic around the mangled sandwich and took a bite. "Mmmm," he mumbled, mouth full, "not bad."

"You son of a bitch," Luke growled, lunging at Brian, arms straining through the bars until the metal cut into his armpits. Brian sucked his teeth and shook his head.

"Now, now. If you wanted some, why didn't you say so?" He rewrapped the sandwich and tossed it into the cell like he was playing catch with a dog. "You do seem to like my messy leftovers." Dusting a few crumbs off the otherwise immaculate uniform, he wiped the corners of his mouth with his thumb and index finger, still holding the tray in his other hand. "Hope you enjoy your stay."

"No!" Luke shouted. "Come back! You can't do this. You can't!" The sound of Brian's quiet chuckle and slam of the holding cell's outer door reverberated through his bones. He collapsed on his knees and fell backward. This was it. Tomorrow he was going to die, or at least what was left of his life would end and he'd lose everything he still cared about. With Natalie, he could blame cancer, but this . . . this death was his own fault.

Luke slapped the cold cement floor. Once, then again, then over and over until pain sliced through his palm, fingers, wrist. There was no way out of this trap. Even though he'd spent his whole life trying to not turn out like his father, Luke still ended up in the same place—jail. He slapped the floor again, expecting another dose of pain, but instead . . . nothing. No more pain, just numb.

Good, Luke thought. If he was going to get through tomorrow and whatever domino effect his arrest caused, he had to be numb. Laying his numb hand across his chest, Luke let the chill from the floor soak through the skin on his other hand. Lying there in the silent blackness, he let the feelings of hopelessness and fury build up inside him again. Images of his mom, his sister, Natalie flashed in vivid detail. When the turmoil rolled inside him, growing uncontrollable, painful even, he slapped at the floor. Once, then again and again, waiting for the pain to turn to nothingness.

CHAPTER 31

Sleep didn't come easily that night, but when it finally overcame him, it was deep and consuming. When the morning sun was high enough to peek through the elevated windows and its warm, end-of-summer rays landed on Luke's face, he stirred. Blinking against the beams of light, it took him a moment to remember where he was and why. Then, the pain from his hands. They were swollen and stiff. He turned on his side to avoid the invading sunlight, his joints groaning.

Going back to sleep seemed like the best plan to avoid reality, but his mind was awake, on fire with possible scenarios. Hopefully Terry would have a lawyer for him soon, and then . . . okay, he didn't know what would happen then. Whatever happened at the arraignment, it had to be better than sitting in this tomblike cell, waiting, suspended in time.

The main door to the holding area clanked loudly, like the lock was being turned. Luke, in a zombielike state, jumped at the sound. Some flight instinct triggered inside him and he scrambled backward, wanting to be far away from the gate in case Brian was back to taunt him more. He couldn't lose his temper again. It wouldn't take much to turn this already horrible situation into a disaster, and certainly attacking an officer would do it.

Luke stared at his hands, tracing the crimson handcuff lines still visible around his wrists. He forced a look of submissiveness and remorse, trying to get some points for good behavior until he could tell his lawyer about the conversation he'd had with Brian last night.

Keys clanked, and the hinges of the seemingly ancient door creaked as it opened. Luke peered up over his clasped hands. Not Brian this time, thank God. Instead, a short older officer with a thickening waistline crossed the cell toward him. He was wearing white, and there were parallel gold bars pinned to his collar. A younger officer with a shaved head and ill-fitting uniform followed him closely. Luke sat back slowly, sure any sudden movements would be a bad idea.

"Mr. Richardson, you are free to go." The older officer, a police chief maybe, held an opaque bag out toward him that looked a lot like the bags they offered Natalie at the end of her hospital stays. "All charges have been dropped."

"I'm sorry, what?" Luke coughed, not sure if he should believe the officer or if this was another one of Brian's dirty tricks.

"We're going to process you out. Charges have been dropped," he said matter-of-factly, as though that statement didn't create twenty questions in its wake. "Follow Officer Miller here, and he'll take care of you." He shook the bag at Luke, without taking his eyes off his well-polished shoes. Even with his lack of legal experience, Luke knew something strange was going on. But he was being offered a chance at freedom, and he'd be ridiculous not to take it. Still in cautious mode, Luke grabbed the offered bag and slipped it over his shoulder.

"Miller, take Mr. Richardson to processing." The chief turned on one foot, the heel of his shoe screeching against the wax on the floor.

"Yes, sir," Officer Miller responded succinctly. Luke eyed the young officer, the way he watched every step the chief took as he walked out of the cell and through the main door, and how he silently tugged on the cuff of his sleeve like he was trying to make it longer. "Come on now, Mr. Richardson. Time for you to go home."

Home. Last night he'd forced himself to believe that he might never be allowed to return home. Now they were opening the gate and setting him free. Luke moved toward the exit, each step echoing through the empty cell. He had to force himself to keep his steps slow and measured, still half-convinced this was some sort of a trap.

But it wasn't a trap. Luke followed Officer Miller through Booking, where they'd taken his mug shot, searched his clothes, and yelled orders. When Miller offered him a doughnut and some orange juice, Luke started to believe everyone was going to jump out and admit to being part of some elaborate reality TV show.

"Thank you." Luke took a cruller with chocolate frosting from the mauve box, far too hungry to resist. The police station was busy, despite the holding cell now standing empty. Uniformed officers milled about the hallways; another two in police-issued sweats crossed the hall holding half-full water bottles. One of the interview rooms had its door closed, occupied light on above it. To all these people it was another Friday morning at work.

"Why don't you go talk to Janice?" Officer Miller pointed toward a window in the wall down by the waiting room. "I'll grab you some coffee. How do you like it?"

Luke swallowed the mouthful of cruller, disappointed he couldn't savor it longer. "Uh, black is fine. Thanks."

Luke followed the hallway to Janice's window. He'd been expecting an older woman with cropped hair and a surly attitude. Instead, he was greeted by a smiling woman in her midtwenties, hair pulled back in a French braid that even May would envy.

"Mr. Richardson?" Janice asked as though she was calling out his name at a Starbucks because his latte was ready.

"Yes." Luke sighed, ready to be out of the police station and back at home with his family. "Do I need to sign something?"

"Yup. I need you to sign here saying you received all your belongings. So, could you take a look real fast?"

Luke wiggled his fingers into the top of the drawstring bag and forced it open. Inside were his phone, his wallet, an old Natalie letter, and a few random pens. He should probably check his credit cards and cash, but he didn't want to waste any more time in case they suddenly decided to change their minds and put him back in a cell.

"Looks good," he answered, picking up a pen. She pointed to a line at the bottom of a page. Luke scanned through the document to make sure he wasn't admitting to anything. Satisfied, he scribbled out his signature.

Janice took the clipboard and checked it over. "Looks like everything's in order. Now, it might take a day or two to get your car from impound, but Officer Miller has arranged a ride home for you. I'll give you a call when it's ready."

Luke felt like he'd fallen through the looking glass and into some kind of upside-down world. Miller was getting him coffee and arranging rides; Janice was helping him get his car out of police custody. Last night he'd walked into the station frightened. Every person he met, intimidating. Something must've changed in the past twelve hours, but what?

"Uh, thank you," Luke replied, giving Janice a half wave.

"Here's your coffee." Miller showed up beside him with a steaming disposable cup. Luke grabbed it, still holding on to the half-eaten pastry. "If you'll follow me."

The glass double doors leading to the front of the police station were only a few feet away now. His feet itched to sprint through them to freedom, but there was something he still needed to know.

He cleared his throat, which was clogged with cruller crumbs. "So, all charges have been dropped? Nothing will be on my record? I don't need a lawyer or anything like that?"

"That's right. It was a bit of a . . ." Miller stretched his neck to one side, then the other. "We are calling it a 'misunderstanding.'" He straightened his shoulders, and his voice turned very official. "I'm afraid I can't comment on an open investigation."

"Okay, that's fine." Luke took a sip of his coffee. It was very hot and very strong. He held back a cough. Maybe he'd hire that lawyer after all, try to get some answers.

Miller didn't wait for any further questions. "Follow me," he ordered, turning his body to hide the code he typed into the pad beside the doors. After a beep, the doors unlocked, and Officer Miller held one open. "Your ride is waiting outside."

"Uh, thank you," Luke answered. Without making eye contact, he hurried past the officer, trying not to notice the rows of worn black chairs lining the walls or the receptionist in the corner who seemed to be waving at him—or maybe she was waving at Officer Miller; he didn't care to find out which. As he burst through the front doors, the summer heat hit him immediately. He forgot to check the time inside, but it must be close to noon.

Taking the last two bites of his cruller, Luke heaved the empty napkin and full cup of coffee into the tall blue garbage can outside the station door. Still chewing, he glanced around the parking lot, expecting to see a squad car or maybe even Terry with the minivan. There were two police cruisers—one a beater that looked like it couldn't start even if someone showed up with keys, and the other a blue Accord. A slender woman stood beside the Accord wearing a flowing blue blouse and fitted jeans, head down looking at her phone. Luke let out a disappointed sigh. No one was here for him. His phone was probably dead, which meant going back inside to make a phone call. Great.

He heard his name. The blonde woman by the car glanced up from her phone and waved. Luke's stomach did a little flip. It was Annie.

"Luke! Over here," she shouted across the parking lot. He wanted to run to her, pick her up in his arms and tell her how much he'd missed her, but they were at the police station where her husband worked, her husband who'd tried to frame him. He wouldn't run or pick her up, but he couldn't stop himself from responding.

"Annie?" he called out. "What are you doing here?" He glanced around one more time. "Are you my ride?"

She didn't wait for him to reach the car. Using all her speed and agility, she ran across the blacktop and wrapped her arms around his waist. It happened so fast it took a moment for Luke's arms to catch up with his mind. He lightly placed his arms around her shoulders, keeping his eyes open in case Brian came out from some hiding place. But once he could feel her warmth and liveliness against his aching body and feel her hair brush his cheek, he forgot to hold back, to be on guard. His muscles tensed, and he pulled her in hard, engulfing Annie in his arms.

"I've missed you," she said. He was relieved she said it first.

"You have no idea how much I've missed you," he said, barely resisting the urge to kiss her on the top of the head. Brian's jail-cell accusations came back to him in a rush, and Luke forced his arms to drop. "Um, so, Brian?" He took a step back and folded his arms across his chest.

"I'm sorry I got you pulled into my drama. I didn't think he'd do . . . this." She gestured at the police station and cars.

"Wait, you knew he set me up?"

"It wasn't hard to figure out. He's been furious with you since he picked me up from your house. And then when he didn't get the job . . ." She trailed off. Luke was afraid to know how she was going to finish that sentence. "Let's just say it was bad." She rubbed a spot on her wrist. Luke noticed the brace on it for the first time.

"Damn it," Luke cursed to himself. "He hurt you, didn't he?" Forgetting to keep his distance, he took her braced hand carefully. "I thought I was helping. I'm so sorry."

"Hey, you didn't break it; he did."

"No, I knew it was a risk." Luke ran his thumb over the palm of her hand. "I was being selfish. I didn't want you to leave."

"Well, it worked." She pulled her hand away and gestured to the car. "I told Terry I'd take you over to the hospital. She's there with May. They filled me in on what happened."

"Yes, please. I was on my way over there when all this happened. But wait." He touched Annie's elbow, stopping her from turning away. "Brian won't mind?" he asked, trying to keep his bitterness toward Brian from leaking into his feelings for Annie. Though it *was* strange getting picked up from a night in jail by the wife of the man who put him there.

Annie stopped, keys in hand. "Luke, Brian is under arrest."

"What?"

"He's going to jail for a very long time," she said with a confidence she rarely displayed. "Get in the car; I'll explain on the way." She kept walking, unlocking the car with a beep. The wind caught in her shirt, blowing the sleeves back, away from her body. For a second she looked like she was flying.

CHAPTER 32

Luke tossed the plastic bag into the backseat of the car and ducked into the passenger seat. Annie already had the car running and backed out of her parking spot as soon as he closed the door, her unbraced hand crossing over her damaged one as she turned the wheel. Could Brian really be in jail?

"Are you going to tell me what's going on?" Luke asked, turning his body to face Annie until the seat belt pressed against his neck. He felt impatient; he wanted to get answers quickly, but sitting in the car together reminded Luke of their road trip and how close he felt to her on that drive home.

"I turned Brian in," she said calmly, as if it wasn't the bravest thing she'd ever done. "I've been compiling evidence against him for weeks now. I was going to use it if he ever hurt me again"—she held up her wrist—"but then Terry called and asked Brian about finding an experienced lawyer. I knew he was behind your arrest as soon as I saw his face. So, I put it all together, got my own lawyer, and went down to the police station first thing this morning."

"And they believed you?" Luke asked. It seemed pretty far-fetched after twenty years on the force.

"It wasn't that simple." She shook her head, eyes fixed on the road. "They brought Brian in for questioning, and I gave them permission to search the house. Once they found the pills, I mean, the evidence tags were still on some of them, *then* they started to take me seriously. In the end, it was Brian who got you off."

"He seemed pretty set on sending me away for a long time when he came to see me last night."

"Oh God. He came to gloat? Did he hurt you?" She shot him a quick glance, checking him over with her eyes.

"No. I'm fine." Luke pushed his hands farther under the hem of his untucked shirt. Self-inflicted wounds were far more embarrassing to explain. "He didn't admit to anything openly, just implied it."

"Well, he screwed up on the denial game during the interrogation. My lawyer was listening in, and he said that once they presented him with the evidence, Brian didn't try to avoid the possession claim. His excuse was that the drugs weren't for him. He'd borrowed them to set you up because"—she hesitated, embarrassed—"because you were sleeping with his wife." Annie flicked on the turn signal and glanced an extra three times down the road to make sure it was empty. Luke chuckled despite Annie's discomfort.

"Hmm. I'm guessing his fellow officers didn't seem to find this a good excuse for stealing evidence." Brian had been so sure that his time on the force would save him. Luke was relieved to see that his coworkers despised crime from any perpetrator.

"Nope. And this is serious stuff. He's in big trouble." She shook her head as she spoke, almost as though she were delivering bad news. "There's so much evidence against him, no way he'll be getting out anytime soon." Her words turned up a little at the end, sounding almost boastful, but her eyes were moist. "At least I hope not."

"You are so brave." Luke looked at her with new eyes. Annie saved him. She was the reason for his freedom and why Brian was behind bars. After all these years of abuse, it took having to save someone else to motivate her to leave. Why was saving herself never enough? She was stronger than he'd ever been—she stood up to her abuser, freed herself. She was his hero. "I'll help you. You'll never have to face him alone. I promise."

A blush crawled up the side of her face he could see, her lips twisted to the side hiding a smile. It felt so right having her back in his life.

"You know that letter Natalie sent me?"

"The one you told me I could never read right after you waved it in front of my face?"

"Yup," she chirped.

"Nope, never heard of it," Luke teased, feeling lighter than he had in nine months. It was gone, his obsessive desire to read any and all of Natalie's letters. If he never saw another flash of blue when he collected the daily mail, he'd be okay.

"Do you want to know what it said? 'Cause there's a lot about you in there." She took another right turn onto the street with the shopping center with Kroger and a semidecent Chinese place he used to sneak Natalie egg rolls from. They were getting close to the hospital.

"Only if you want to tell me."

"I want to tell you." She looked at him out of the corner of her eye as they pulled into the hospital parking lot.

"Then I want to hear it."

The parking lot was nearly empty. Annie found a spot on the right side of the large, boxy structure, shut off the engine, and then turned to face him.

"She told me lots of things about the kids, about life, stuff that was only meaningful to the two of us. But at the end she told me two things." She held up one finger on her braced hand. "One—that I deserved more than the life I was living." Her gaze lingered on her brace, and she dropped her hand. "And, two"—another finger went up—"that I should be your friend. Not just a casual friend either. Close friends. Best friends."

Luke covered Annie's hand, and her fingers tightened around his. He dared to look her in the eyes. They were nearly transparent, like the sea glass Alex Kerks kept in his office when Luke's dad still worked for him. Alex's glass was cloudy, but Annie's eyes were crystal, shining with tears.

"Soooo," he dragged out the word playfully, "you're saying Natalie forced you to be my friend?"

"No." She smacked his arm, and he faked a flinch. "At first I thought she wanted me to look after you. Then, after our trip to Pentwater, I realized she wanted us to be friends because"—she paused and bit her lip—"I needed you too."

The admission hung in the air, and Luke inhaled it like oxygen. All this time he'd been feeling guilty, selfish even, for feeling like he needed Annie. To know their relationship was symbiotic, that Natalie had recognized that fact long before either of them knew it was a possibility, almost made him forgive her for all the secrets she'd hoarded.

Luke sniffed. "I should really get in there." He pointed to the five-story brick structure. "You want to come in?"

"I can't actually." She fiddled with the key chain dangling from the ignition. "Will is watching Clayton, and I promised I'd relieve him so he could get to cross-country practice."

"Oh, that works," Luke said, wanting to tell Annie about Jessie being Neal's daughter and how he wanted her by his side the first time he met the man, but Annie jumped back in before he could say anything more.

"So, here's the thing." She turned her body toward Luke. "I care about you . . . a lot. And if you feel even a little bit of the same in return, then us, together"—she gestured back and forth between them—"could be *great*." She bit the inside of her cheek, turning her hopeful smile into a smirk. Luke knew she was right. He could definitely fall in love with Annie.

"But?" he added, knowing it was coming.

"But"—her smile faltered—"I'm not ready to be with someone right now. I don't think you are either."

"I'm not looking to rush into anything." Luke licked his lips, hoping what he said next wouldn't scare her away. "But I don't think you should stay away either. Haven't we spent enough time apart?"

Annie picked at the leather stitching on her steering wheel. "Oh, you're not getting rid of me anytime soon." She pointed a long finger at him. "Now don't be getting cocky. It's the kids I find irresistible, not you."

"You forget—I can tell when you're lying."

Annie tried to hold back a snicker, but failed. Luke promised himself he'd give her more reasons to snicker, giggle, or outright laugh. Then he saw his opening. "Tomorrow is Clayton's birthday party. I'm not sure if everyone still feels up to it—it depends upon what happens with Jessie—but we will at least have cake. Would you want to come?"

"Actually, Terry already invited me before this mess." She gestured at the air, frowning. She was trying to cover up her sadness, but Luke could still see it. "I told her no."

He nodded, working very hard to be understanding. She was in mourning. It was different than his, but valid nonetheless. "Okay. Just text me if you change your mind."

"I'll let you know. Matt is flying in from DC for the weekend."

"He is? That's great news. He hasn't been home for . . ."

"Over a year," she said, finishing his sentence. "When he left for college, he told me he'd wouldn't come back if Brian still lived there. I never told you." Her eyes grew damp, nose quivered, about to break down. She threw a hand over her mouth like she was trying not to throw up. "I was too ashamed. I chose Brian over my own son. That's messed up."

"Hey." Luke forgot the invisible line he was trying to respect and reached out to squeeze Annie's shoulder. "I've been obsessing about letters from my dead wife. I think I win the award for 'most messed up person' in this car."

"This is a strange competition."

"Well, we aren't exactly a normal pair, are we?"

"No." Annie placed her cheek against Luke's hand. "We're not."

They sat in silence for a second, the light pressure of her cheek against his fingers making it nearly impossible for Luke to remove his hand from her shoulder voluntarily. It only lasted a moment, a few strings of breaths inhaled and exhaled before she sighed, sat up, and broke the spell.

The familiar comfort of her company was proving harder to leave than he expected. With one last squeeze, he forced himself to release her shoulder and reach through to the backseat for his belongings. Reemerging through the space between the seats, he passed inches from Annie's cheek. The scratches he'd wanted to kiss three weeks earlier were healed, leaving only faint white lines along her cheekbones and above her eyebrow.

Before he could stop himself, Luke leaned in and pressed his lips to her cheek. It was only for a moment, not long enough to notice the texture of her skin or scent of her shampoo, but it was enough. He sat back, unlatched his seat belt, and opened the car door. "Talk to you tomorrow."

"Tomorrow." She waved, and Luke pushed the door shut.

Luke walked with broad, sure steps toward the entrance to the hospital. Maybe he had been wrong when he told Natalie he could never love again. What he should've said was he couldn't love anyone the same way he loved her.

He entered the lobby through the front sliding doors with a dead cell phone and no idea where Jessie might be. A friendly-looking woman with a plump face sat behind the information desk. She'd know where Luke should go, but what would he find when he got there? What would he say to Neal? His child was lying in bed, terminally ill. This might not be the right time for a confrontation. He'd play dumb—for Jessie's sake he'd pretend he'd never heard of Dr. Neal Townsend, that he wasn't the reason Luke's daughter was buried in some shallow grave somewhere.

CHAPTER 33

The info desk lady turned out to be just as helpful as she looked. Jessie was on the fourth floor in room 482. After a short elevator ride and some helpful nurses directing the way, Luke stared at the maroon plaque with white lettering: **482**. This was the room. He'd hoped to hear voices on the other side of the door, maybe May's bubbly laugh or Terry's monotone, letting him know he'd found the right place.

Instead, there was nothing but the soft whir of an automatic blood-pressure machine, the chugging of a hulking piece of machinery in the corner, and silence. He'd just have to be brave and go in, not knowing what he might walk into. Luke grasped the cold brushed-nickel handle and forced the door open wide into a tidy, neatly furnished hospital room with one bed. In the bed was what seemed to be a sleeping, swollen version of the Jessie he knew. Her skin was stretched so taut, Luke was afraid to touch her in case any gentle pressure in the wrong spot could make her explode.

In a chair at the end of the bed sat Dr. Neal, eyes closed, hands pressed together. His lips moved ever so slightly, maybe praying. Neal looked a lot like his faculty picture from the Eastern Michigan University website—neatly trimmed salt-and-pepper beard, full head of graying hair. Dark circles under his eyes, skin a sallow color almost like he was as ill as his daughter. Luke wanted to hate him, but at that moment he couldn't see Neal as the man who'd given his child to a mentally unstable adoptive mother who hurt her, maybe killed her. He didn't even see a man who'd planned and carried out a complex and at times painful plan as Natalie's confidant and companion. He saw a father with a sick child. Any confrontation with Neal would wait until Jessie was well.

With Jessie asleep and May and Terry nowhere to be seen, Luke started to back out of the room, hoping someone at the nurses' station could help him locate the pair. He took one step back and then another until he bumped hard into the wall. Luke flinched, muffling a gasp, his elbow throbbing. Ignoring the shot of pain, Luke reached for the door handle.

"Ahem." Neal cleared his voice across the room and rubbed his eyes. "Hello?"

Luke swore silently. Small talk with the man he'd been consumed with for the past several months would be difficult. But, standing in the same room with him meant there was no turning back now. All he could hope for was Terry and May to show up and provide a diversion.

"Hi, uh, you must be Jessie's dad." Luke dropped his bag by the door and forced his feet to move him back into the hospital room. "I'm Luke Richardson."

"Oh, yes." Neal sat up in his chair and smoothed his hair. "You called 9-1-1, correct? Your mother just took May down to the cafeteria for a snack."

"My mother?" It was strange to hear anyone labeled as his mother, much less Terry. "Oh, you mean Terry." Luke took two more steps toward Neal. "She's my wife's mother. Was my wife's mother . . . she's my mother-in-law." Forming coherent sentences was turning out to be a problem. Whether it was from the lack of sleep, the emotional trauma of the past twenty-four hours, or the pure fact of who Neal really was, Luke knew he must seem out of it.

"Well, it's nice to meet you, Luke. I'm Neal." He half stood and reached a hand out. Luke took it and gave one firm pump and then backed away, wondering how long he had to stay in the room with an unconscious Jessie and friendly Dr. Neal. "Please, take a seat." Luke glanced around the room. A flimsy gray chair sat on the other side of Jessie's bed. Neal jumped out of his chair and shifted over to Jessie's bedside.

Luke sat in the chair, still unnervingly warm from Neal's body heat. From this angle Jessie's condition came into focus. He couldn't even count the tubes and machines running in and out of her body. It was almost worse than seeing her passed out on the floor in his home. Now the reality of her illness was painfully obvious.

"So, how is she doing?" Luke felt stupid asking. Clearly she wasn't doing great.

Neal rubbed his temples. "Not well." The answer hitched in his throat. "She needs a transplant. She has a few weeks, maybe a month. I never thought . . . I never thought it could happen this fast."

"I'm so sorry." Luke struggled to continue. Neal, who'd already lost his wife, could now lose his only child. "She's a wonderful young woman. I . . . my children . . . we all have come to care for Jessie." Then Luke found himself saying the sentence he'd heard more times than he could count. Perhaps the least helpful sentence he'd ever heard. "If there is *anything* I can do to help, please, let me know."

When Natalie's school acquaintances or the administrative assistant at work said those words, they always sounded empty, like a halfhearted attempt to care. Now he knew—it's what you say when there's nothing you can do to help besides *want* to.

Luke expected to hear an approximation of the answer he always gave in return, something like "I'll let you know" or "We're okay for now, thanks," but Neal didn't say . . . anything. He just nodded and rubbed his beard, like he was thinking of some errand for Luke to run.

"Luke, I . . . uh . . . I wasn't supposed to tell you this way."

There was heaviness to his words that made Luke feel like he always did in Pentwater when he could see thunder and rain clouds developing offshore over Lake Michigan. Something was coming; he could see it, hear it, feel it in the air. He had few choices; he could take shelter, or he could meet the storm head-on.

"Neal." Luke stopped him. "I know."

"Hmm?" He sat up slowly, like a man just woken up from a deep sleep.

"I *know*." He gave Neal a meaningful look, but he didn't seem to catch on so Luke continued. "The letters—I know you sent them. I know you were Natalie's teacher. I know about Maranatha House. I know about . . ." He didn't want to have to say the name—he hadn't said it out loud since finding the scrapbook—but he'd already said too much to go back. "I know about Mallory."

"You know about Mallory?" Neal glanced at Jessie like he wanted to make sure she was still asleep. He tangled his fingers into the neatly tucked sheet on the corner of her mattress. "How did you find out?"

The pity that had been keeping Luke calm and understanding was starting to dissolve. Even with the letters, the order from the florist, even the giant scrapbook detailing the life and death of his first child, Natalie's deception didn't become real until Neal confirmed it with that simple question.

"Not from Natalie, that's for sure," Luke said gruffly, the bitterness starting to escape. "I found a letter from your old boss, Ms. Stephani. It made things pretty clear."

Neal released the sheet and spread his fingers wide, smoothing the wrinkles on the bed. "Ah, yes, Christina and her conscience. Natalie told me about that letter, but I didn't know she'd kept it."

"Well, she did, and I found it. So, what about you, Neal? And your wife? From what I can tell, without you two, my daughter would still be alive." Luke's anger, the anger he worked so hard at tamping down, was building.

"All right, I deserve that." Neal nodded with his whole body and then looked up, meeting Luke's gaze. "You're right: we made a lousy choice. Eva Witling was a very ill woman, and we didn't see that. But to be fair, doctors, nurses, detectives, friends, family—no one suspected. No one."

"Fine," Luke acquiesced. "Fine; you didn't know. But now that we are revealing secrets, maybe you should tell me a little more about your relationship with my wife."

"I loved her," he answered simply. The words burned Luke's ears.

Defeated, the anger left him. He thought he'd want to hit Neal, or at least scream at him, but at that moment of admission, Luke was relieved to finally know the truth.

"How long?" he managed to ask, trying to calculate how many years she'd been living a double life.

"It's not like that."

"Do *not* lie to me, please," Luke begged, suddenly exhausted and feeling more ready to go home and go to bed than to argue. "It's obvious you two had a secret relationship. So, how long?"

"Twenty-three years."

"She was *fourteen*," Luke half whispered, half yelled, forcing his voice down in case Jessie could hear them through her medication. He closed his eyes and rubbed the bridge of his nose. How had pedophile pastor never crossed his mind? "I think I should leave."

"No, for God's sake, no, that's not what I meant." Neal put up his hands in defense and then tapped his forehead as if his hands could summon the right words to say. "I was Natalie's pastor, her professor, and eventually her friend, but I was *never* her lover. And you're wrong. I hadn't seen Natalie for years, *years*, until she found me at Eastern. This was her idea, not mine."

"Well then, pastor"—he said the title like an accusation—"maybe you can tell me the one thing I can't figure out: Why did Natalie lie to me?" Luke's eyes clouded with tears, and his throat was so tight he could force out only one more question. "Why did she have you send those letters instead of just telling me the truth?"

"This wasn't supposed to happen . . ."

"Yes, I know, this wasn't a part of your plan. But it *is* happening like this. Why all the smoke and mirrors? Was it guilt? Was she afraid of me?" This thought was the most painful, and after her letter about the day his mother died, how that one slap had kept her from contacting him for those six years, maybe she thought it was safer to tell the truth when she was dead.

"She had her reasons." Neal shook his head and then slapped his hands on his thighs before standing up. "I'm not *supposed* to be the one who tells you these things, but Natalie couldn't have known any of this"—Neal gestured to Jessie asleep in her hospital bed—"was going to happen. I knew I'd see you here eventually, so I brought this in case . . . in case I found a way to tell you." He walked over to the nightstand and pulled open one of the drawers. It opened with a quiet whoosh, and Neal pulled out a blue envelope and offered it to Luke. "The answers are in here."

The envelope had Luke's name on it, as always, and the back flap read: "The End." It didn't feel like as many pages as he expected, one maybe two. Opening it he knew why. It was another typed letter, two pages single-spaced.

"Did you type this for her?" Luke asked, wondering how to trust a letter written by someone other than Natalie.

Neal nodded. "I did. She was too weak, and she wanted to tell you everything. I just typed what she said, Luke, I swear." There had been a few typed letters. Neal must've typed those too.

"This one was going to be delivered on the one-year anniversary of her death. She thought one year would be enough to prepare you . . ." Neal stopped himself. "But when your mother-in-law called me about Jessie, that you were headed to the hospital with her, I knew the time line would have to change. Just read it."

Luke didn't like the idea of doing anything at Neal's bidding, but he'd waited long enough for the truth. He wasn't going to wait longer out of sheer spite. He looked back at the page full of neat, black lettering and read.

THE END

Dear Luke,

Well, this is it. My final good-bye. It's becoming clear that my time is close, so I'm going to tell you what I've been dying to say (no pun intended) for our whole marriage because you have the right to know. I'm sorry I didn't tell you sooner. I was going to let my secret die with me, and by the time I changed my mind and decided you had a right to know, I knew my death was only a matter of months away. I didn't want to poison the last few memories of me with anger. I guess I'm a coward, but I hope one day you'll understand why I didn't tell you sooner. So, here it goes, my secret.

I had a baby, Luke. Our baby. I was nearly fifteen years old when she was born. I only saw her once. Hours upon hours of pain, months upon months of regret and embarrassment, all that ended when I looked on our daughter's face. She was so beautiful, but had so much hair I thought she might be a mutant. I looked right in her eyes and told her how much I loved her and that her daddy loved her too. I told her we were too young to raise her and that you were so far away. I kissed her twice, once for you and once for me. Then I passed our little girl off to Mrs. Townsend at Maranatha House, the maternity home and adoption agency where I stayed. I prayed she'd be happy and safe. I kept that little girl in my heart every day after that, praying she'd found a new home with wonderful parents who would love her and raise her in a way I wasn't equipped to.

Okay, so why didn't I tell you about her when we met at the University of Michigan? That's a fair question. My reasoning was—she was five and had a new mom and dad, we couldn't get her back, and who knows what you'd think about being a dad. You said you didn't want kids, afraid you'd be like your dad. To be honest, I was a little afraid too after what happened in the shed. By the time I was sure of who you were and who you weren't, we were married. When I got pregnant with Will, I made a plan. I would tell you the whole story after his delivery.

Then I got some horrible news. I found out that when our daughter was only three years old, she "disappeared" from her home and was presumed dead. Remember the Mallory Witling case I was so obsessed about? That was our Mallory.

She didn't live far from us, actually. Just over in Lansing. I had no idea that the pigtailed little girl from the news who'd gone missing from her home during my senior year of high school was our daughter. She'd been reported missing by her parents, who woke up one morning to an empty toddler bed, a pool of blood on her pillow, and no sign of Mallory.

A hunt for the little girl ensued; the whole town pulled together to look for her. But as the investigation went on, Mr. Witling soon brought up concerns about his wife, about her behavior with their first child, who'd died only four years earlier. After exhuming

Mallory's sister's body, it became clear that Mark Witling was right. His wife, Eva Witling, suffered from a psychological disorder called Munchausen syndrome by proxy. She had been making her daughter sick, probably with poison, slowly, to get attention from hospital staff, friends, and family.

With the help of Mark Witling and the evidence from their first child's death, the prosecution was able to get a confession, and Mrs. Witling ended up in prison. It's a small consolation for such a horrific crime. I wanted to go visit her in prison, scream at her, say, "She wasn't even your child!" but I didn't. Instead, I tried to bury my regrets and myself in work and in our growing family. Those were some beautiful years.

Then cancer came into our lives, and I decided to finish up my master's degree. I was going to finish at UM but it was beyond our budget, so I researched a few programs in the area. That's when I saw a picture of Dr. Neal Townsend, associate professor of education at Eastern Michigan. I knew who he was right away—the pastor from Maranatha, he and his wife had helped place Mallory. Suddenly I didn't care about any of the programs, ratings, or even tuition. I knew I had to see him again.

First day in his Math Methods class, and there wasn't even a twinge of recognition from my old pastor. Twenty-odd years and three kids later, I'm sure I looked far different than the fourteen-year-old girl he knew at the maternity house. Then I saw him talking to a girl in the hallway; there was something about her that made me look twice. He looked at her differently than the other students at school, and she bounced when she talked to him. She reminded me of someone. So, I followed her. Yes, I was losing my mind; I'd become a crazy stalker, but I didn't care. I started studying in the same vestibule where she liked to sit and read. Slowly we became friends, and soon I found out this girl, Jessie, was Neal's daughter.

I'll spare you all my secret agent moves, but Dr. Neal, as his students call him, and I became friends, starting with him rescuing me from that confrontation with Tiff. Either way, it wasn't until my most recent, devastating diagnosis that I had the courage to tell him the truth. In return, he told me something I've felt in my heart for a long time: our daughter isn't dead.

Neal told me Jessie's story that day. It actually all goes back to Mr. Witling. Neal said that he showed up one morning on the steps of Maranatha House with three-year-old Mallory in her pj's. Maria, Neal's wife, was working the desk at the time. Mallory was sick, very sick, her kidneys severely damaged from the ethylene glycol, the antifreeze, he'd discovered his wife adding to Mallory's juice cup.

Mark Witling begged her to take the child back, keep her safe from his wife. Maria tried to refuse, encouraged Mr. Witling to go home and call the police, to take the little girl to a hospital, but then looking at the sick child, knowing she could have no children of her own, Maria made a decision that would change half a dozen lives. She took Mallory out of his arms and brought her into Maranatha.

When Maria told the story to Neal, he wanted no part of it. But Maria begged him to give her a day or two to figure out how to help the child without landing her in foster care or as a ward of the state. As sickly Mallory slept between them that first night, the news broke of a missing little girl from Lansing, Michigan. The news story methodically described the blood in the house, the broken screen to her bedroom window, the muddy footprints outside her window. Mark had faked a kidnapping.

So, there it was—they could keep the child, find a way to forge her adoption, care for her physically, emotionally, spiritually, or they could give her back to a family where the mother was hurting her and the father didn't seem strong enough to stand up and fight. So they kept her.

After lying to you for decades, I'm so scared you'll hate me, that the anger I see you fight will take over you and our family. Plus, the selfish part of me wants to die as your beloved wife. I want you to mourn the years we had together, not the years we could've had if I'd told you sooner. I don't regret giving up our daughter; I know it was the right choice given our age and situation. I don't even regret the secrets; I'm sorry, I don't. But I won't keep you from Jessie. Neal has agreed to help. I know some of these letters will be hard for you to read, but I hope others can be a place you can go for comfort. I know you don't believe I exist anymore, that my time on this planet is over, but you're wrong. I live in these letters.

Jessie doesn't know anything beyond the fact that she's adopted. I'll leave it to you and her father to decide what and how much to share. If you ever tell her who you really are, who I was to her, who she really is, please give her my love—my love and my letters.

I'll love you forever.

Natalie

"Jessie?" Luke asked, not trying to stop the tears this time. He'd always known there was something familiar about her. The rest of the letter, the admission of a felony, all the lies and secrets—he didn't care. He'd thought his daughter was dead, and she wasn't.

"Yes," Neal said, sitting again, this time with Jessie's hand in his. "She's your biological daughter. Yours and Natalie's."

"She's *what*?" Terry's shrill voice cut in from the doorway. She pulled the door closed behind her. Fortunately, there was no sign of May by her side. Luke sat frozen in his chair at the end of the bed.

Thankfully, Neal spoke up.

"I'm sorry I didn't tell you." He looked over at Luke. "All of you, but yes, Terry, Jessie is your granddaughter. You might remember my wife better than you remember me. Maria Townsend. We were both much younger then."

Terry's hands shook by her side, her footfalls slow. "You adopted her? You and Maria?"

"Yes, we did." Neal glanced at Luke like he was pleading for him to keep the secret they'd only just shared. Then he stood and helped a dazed Terry to Jessie's bedside. "She's been the greatest joy of our lives."

"I've been looking for her, you know." Terry didn't take her eyes off Jessie. "Maranatha Adoptions gave me the runaround, so I've been saving up for one of those private services. When I lost my baby girl . . ." Terry choked up. "When I lost my Natalie, I knew I had to find her daughter, maybe see a little of Natalie still living in her like I do in the other kids. And now, here she is."

"She's been looking for you guys too," Neal responded, his lips trembling. "She's never had much family beyond me and her mom. A few years after Maria died, she wanted to find her birth parents. I could've told her, maybe I should've, but she's been getting sicker and sicker, and it just never felt like the right time."

"Oh my God, she's so sick." Terry looked at Neal, panicked. "She's not going to die, is she? I don't know what I'd do if she died." Luke cringed at Terry's bluntness. To talk about Jessie's death in front of Neal was cruel.

"They just don't know. Her kidneys have given out completely. She was living on dialysis, but her body is not tolerating it well. Eventually, she needs a new kidney."

"Oh that poor girl." Terry stepped up to the edge of the hospital bed. Terry went to her knees, using the bed to balance. She took Jessie's hand in her own. "I was the last person to hold her, you know, before they took her away. I . . . yes . . . I see it now. A mix of May and Clayton, and maybe my auntie Clara, don't you think?" She reached out, tucked some stray hairs behind Jessie's ear, and looked up at Luke.

"Sure," Luke answered, completely overwhelmed by the revelation, Terry's surprising joy, and Neal's contrition. And what was worse, the child he thought was dead might actually be dying in front of his eyes. "Uh, Terry, where's May?" Luke kept a cautious eye on the door. May couldn't know, not yet. Jessie didn't even know.

"She's just down the hall charming the nurses." She waved Luke off. "What was she like as a baby? May was fussy, but Will was a little angel."

Neal opened his mouth to answer, and Luke was sincerely curious as to what he was going to say since he didn't get Jessie until she was three. A knock sounded at the door, and a middle-aged doctor wearing a white lab coat and dark-rimmed glasses, holding a stainless steel clipboard, walked in. Terry wiped at her eyes, eventually taking off her glasses to get better access, and then used Neal's arm for support to get on her feet.

"Mr. Townsend, can I speak with you for a moment?" The doctor's face was stoic. He looked meaningfully at Luke and Terry, silently inviting them to leave. Luke took the hint and stood.

"Come on, Terry, we should give them some privacy." Luke stood beside her and put out a hand. "Let's go find May." He could read Terry's reticence as she glanced between Neal and the doctor, but after a moment she ignored his hand and headed for the door.

"Yes, that's fine." She seemed to have gathered herself enough to speak normally. "The nurses invited May to 'help' them for a few minutes over at the nurses' station."

As they left the dimmed room and entered the brightly lit hallway, Luke tried to tune out Terry's grumblings about how as Jessie's grandmother she should be allowed to stay in the room and since Natalie was gone she was the closest thing Jessie had to a mother. Instead, he strained to hear the half-whispered conversation between Neal and the doctor. As the door clicked shut, all Luke could be sure he'd heard were the words "transplant" and "terminal."

CHAPTER 34

Luke finished counting the letters again. Fifty-six, fifty-seven, fifty-eight . . . yes, fifty-eight letters filled with Natalie, her words, her stories, her beliefs. He put them all in chronological order, one behind the other, in an oversize shoebox. He'd been counting them compulsively all morning, finding it was a better way to pass time in a hospital waiting room than reading a magazine. This must be what it was like for fathers back in the days before men were allowed in the delivery room. The waiting was unbearable.

When Neal popped his head into the sparsely decorated room, full of the most uncomfortable chairs known to man, Luke slipped the bright-orange lid back on the box. It was time.

"You don't have long, maybe ten, fifteen minutes before they'll come for her, but it should be enough for the basics." Neal took several turns down seemingly identical hallways. It'd be easy to get lost in Detroit General, far bigger and more intimidating than quaint Botsford. Neal wore scrubs today, Luke wasn't sure why, but didn't care to ask. They looked more comfortable than Luke's khakis and button-up collared shirt. Maybe he'd ask for his own pair.

Two more turns, and after passing what Luke swore was the same nurses' station twice, Neal stopped abruptly and then turned to face him. "Thank you for doing this. I know I can't be your favorite person right now, but . . . I have a lot of respect for you. I hope one day we can be friends."

Neal put out a hand, and Luke stared at it for a moment. He'd spent months searching for this man, making up all kinds of stories about who he was and why he was so important to Natalie. The truth was not even close to anything Luke could've ever imagined. And the man *had* raised and cared for his biological child, a child with special medical needs, a child he could've tossed into the same system Luke had floundered through.

Carefully balancing the box under his arm, Luke gave Neal's hand a firm shake. He might not be at the point of liking the man yet, but he certainly could respect him back.

"This is her room. I'll wait out here until they come." Neal pointed to a large metal door, oversize so wheelchairs and gurneys could fit through easily. "Unless you want me to come?"

"No," Luke blurted, faster than would be considered polite. "I think I'll be fine."

"Good luck," Neal said as he held open the door.

Luke hugged the box of letters against his chest. The room was smaller than the one in Farmington Hills. Today Jessie's eyes were open, though turning her head to see who walked in seemed to exhaust her. He hadn't seen her since the revelatory letter from Natalie, but even in her puffy, weak state, there was something that stirred in his chest, the same feeling he had the first time he saw Will, May, and Clayton, the feeling that confirmed this was his child. Luke sat down on an empty chair arranged near Jessie's head.

"Mr. Richardson. I mean . . . Luke . . . hi." Jessie welcomed him weakly, her fingers lifting ever so slightly.

"Hey there, Jessie. How you doing?" Luke flinched, taking in the tubes going into her arms, machines droning beside her. "Stupid question. Sorry."

Jessie looked like she was trying to laugh but could only manage a pained smile. "I've definitely felt better."

"I'm sure you have." He put the box on the floor under his chair, wondering if he'd even find the courage to tell her anything.

"Well, the kids miss you. Um, May says she wants to give you a pedicure after your surgery, when you're allowed visitors and all."

"I can't wait." Jessie's bottom lip, dry and cracked, quivered.

"So, did your dad tell you why I'm here today?"

"Not really." She shook her head ever so slightly.

"Well, it has something to do with your surgery, and he thought you should know before . . ." Oh, this was just too hard. Neal had convinced Luke to speak with her about Natalie because there was more than a small chance that she could die under the knife. He decided to try another approach. "So, uh, your donor. Did your dad tell you where they found her?"

Another nearly unperceivable no.

"She's related to your birth mother, Jessie. She's actually your maternal grandmother."

"My, my birth mom?" Jessie struggled like she was trying to sit up, her breathing becoming more ragged. "You found her?"

The hope in Jessie's eyes stabbed at the place inside Luke that was still raw from missing Natalie. How was he supposed to tell this sick girl that her birth mother had been claimed by cancer, just like Maria Townsend?

"She found *you*, Jessie. Last year, at Eastern. You got to know her very well. She loved you so much." The glowing lights of Jessie's monitors blurred as Luke's eyes filled with tears. As sick as she was, it was clear Jessie immediately understood. Her own eyes glistened too, and her chin quivered.

"Natalie . . . Natalie . . . was my mom?" She asked the question, but Luke could tell she already knew the answer.

"Yeah, honey, she was." Her shoulders shook and Luke rubbed them, worried that if she got too upset, the alarms on one of her machines would go off.

"Natalie was my mom." She said it again, a statement this time. Then her face crumpled. "Why didn't she tell me? I . . . I have so many questions. We could've had some time together. We could've . . ." She trailed off.

Luke sniffed. "I know. I know you do, and I'll answer as many as I can. Your dad knows a lot more than I do."

"Wait, he knew? All this time, he knew?" Luke hadn't considered what would happen if Jessie *didn't* like the revelation.

"I'm sorry, I don't know. I just found out myself. I . . ."

"What about my birth dad, is he dead too? Did he wait till everyone was dead to tell me?"

"Jessie, your birth dad isn't dead. And your dad did what he thought was best for you. Please, don't be upset. I just wanted to see you before you went into surgery. I wanted you to know . . ." This was harder than revealing Natalie's maternity. "I'm your birth dad."

"What?" Her face crumpled. "You and Natalie? You must've been . . . so young." She paused to take a breath before continuing. "Wait, so May is my sister? I have a sister?"

"Yes. A sister and two brothers who adore you, who are worried sick about you. And your grandma Terry, she's your donor."

"Oh my God, I . . . it's so much to take in." She blinked away the tears since her arms were too weak to wipe them off. Luke grabbed a handful of tissues out of the box on the nightstand and wiped her face. "This is a good thing, right?"

"Yeah, I know *I* think it's a good thing."

"I just wish I knew before Natalie died. I wish I could've hugged her just once knowing she was my mom."

"I know. I agree." Luke refolded the tissues and soaked up the last few rogue tears. Jessie's eyes were drooping shut, reminding him of Clayton on the brink of a nap, wanting sleep but resisting it too. Maybe the letters would have to wait. "You just go in there and be strong. When you get out and your brand-new, slightly used kidney starts working then we can fill in all the blanks, okay?"

"Okay," Jessie whispered, leaning her forehead against his hand. "Mr. Richardson?"

Luke chuckled. "Jessie, now you *really* have to call me Luke."

A smile flitted over her chapped lips. "Luke," she said, starting again. He could almost hear her mother's voice in the layers of her whisper. "If I don't come back . . . do you think she's waiting for me? In heaven, I mean."

"I don't really know. I'm not sure . . ." Luke stumbled through his reply. He should lie, like he did to Natalie. He should give his child the comfort she was seeking.

There was a knock at the door and a flood of people came through without waiting for permission. Neal was the last one through the door. Time was up.

Luke opened his mouth, unsure what to say to the daughter he may never speak to again. He didn't believe—not in heaven, maybe not even in God. But then again when he thought of Natalie and of her letters he wondered how she could be gone forever. Natalie had found their daughter once. Maybe she could do it again.

He leaned over the bedrail, his cheek grazing Jessie's damp hair. "If there is any way to find you—she will. I know it." Luke stood up, blinking away the tears in his eyes before Neal could see them.

"It's time." He stood beside Luke and they both watched as a crew of hospital staff unplugged wires, lowered her bed, and pulled up bedrails. "Did you say what you needed to?"

"I think so." Luke smoothed down a piece of Jessie's hair with the same gentle pressure he used on the other kids when they were babies and then stood back so the team could get in position. "I didn't tell her about the letters." He looked over at Jessie, who was struggling to stay awake even with all of the activity in the room. She'd make it through. He knew it. She had to. "I'll give them to her tomorrow."

Luke stood back and let the nurses, doctors, and Neal exit before he grabbed the shoebox and tucked it under his arm. After a few wrong turns and dead ends, Luke finally navigated his way out of the maze of patients' rooms into the waiting room.

His seat was still open, and Luke reclaimed it and placed the box on his lap. Sitting in the barren, chair-lined room gave him a sense of déjà vu. It felt like he'd been in a waiting room since Natalie's death—waiting for a letter, waiting for instructions, waiting to feel something other than sorrow, waiting for May to smile without guilt, for Will to feel like he belonged in their family, Clayton to sleep without a phone in his hands, for Annie to find peace.

Luke settled down lower in his seat and closed his eyes. There wouldn't be news for a few hours. For now, he'd rest. After today there would be no more waiting. Tomorrow they would start living again.

ACKNOWLEDGMENTS

First, I have to thank everyone from the Sarcoma Alliance. So many of you were willing and eager to share your battles with me. You know what it is to face an unknown future—you are fierce warriors, and you are my heroes.

A special thank you to these sarcoma warriors who have passed on and to their family members who continue to support others battling this disease: Beth H. Levy Feigenblatt, Ellen McCaffrey, Kate Caruso, Christopher Hecknauer, Mark A. Cohen, Doug Haro, Peter Tomaras, Glenys Perry, Jenny Miller, Jim Markey, Vanessa Sandré, and Amy Heiter.

Thanks to my wonderful "real-life" writers' group: Joanne Osmond, Paulette Swan, Kelli Swofford Nielsen, Mary Rose Lila, and Deb Brooks. I look forward to our meetings all month. You give me such a safe, comfortable place to share and grow as a writer. I love working with each of you and enjoy sharing our passion for writing.

And my virtual support system—Dennis Maley, J. S. Hughes, Natasha Raulerson, Jimmy Cearlock, and Kalinda Knight—you keep me going on those days when I think I can't write another word. Between word sprints, word goals, critique sessions, and brainstorming, you remind me that writing doesn't have to be solitary.

To Natalie Selbe, you are the reason I started this story. Thanks for brainstorming crazy story lines with me, always being up for a read, and giving excellent feedback. What would I do without you?

To my author friend Lauri Fairbanks, you are a wonderful writer and an even better person. We are on this journey together. Thanks for always keeping me on your to-do list. You are one strong woman.

Authoress Mallory Crowe, you are such a good example of hard work and dedication. Thank you for knowing the right words to say and for putting up with my late-night texts and early-morning panics. You deserve all the joy and success that comes to you.

My agent-mate and friend, Charlie Donlea, how the heck did I get so lucky to find another StringerLit author so close to home? You have talked me off a ledge more than once. Thanks for reaching out and being so accessible. Here is to many more releases, launch parties, and panic-induced e-mails in our futures.

And to J. S. Hazzard—you keep me honest, you keep me real, and I love that about you. Thank you for being you.

Thank you to my lovely and talented critique partner, Maura Jortner—you go above and beyond. How you do so many wonderful things all at the same time makes me believe you must be super-human . . . or have perfected cloning.

Thank you to the author team at Lake Union, including Gabriella Van den Heuvel and Thom Kephart. I treasure all the behind-the-scenes work you do. Seriously, you guys are amazing.

To my second set of eyes, developmental editor Nancy Brandwein, you help me take these stories to a whole different level. I'm eternally grateful for your insights and suggestions. And my copy editor, Cheri Madison, thanks for having some seriously awesome eyes and catching all those details that *my* eyes blur over.

Danielle Marshall, my editor and cheerleader, you can't know how much your drive and skill inspire me. I am so very lucky to have you as a partner in this process.

My wonderfully talented agent, Marlene Stringer, you teach me so much. I can honestly say I am living my dream because of you. Thank you for your hard work and dedication. Your passion for my stories keeps me going.

Thank you to everyone who read and loved *Wreckage*. All of you that took the time to leave me a message on my Facebook page or contact me on Twitter, or send me a nice e-mail—you've been the fuel in my tank. Knowing there are readers out there who want to read more is humbling and invigorating.

To my friends and family—wow. That's all I can say. You've rallied around me, encouraged me, supported me, and high-fived me. I am *your* biggest fan. Thank you endlessly for not getting tired of me talking about books, publishing, and all the ups and downs of writing.

Thanks to my sister, Elizabeth Renda, for reading, learning how to give me excellent feedback, and attending a writing conference with me even though you pretend not to be a writer. Thanks to my brothers and parents for bragging endlessly and embarrassing me only slightly less. I feel loved.

To my kids—so, you got a mom who makes up stories for a living. Right now you think that is pretty cool, and I love that. I hope you always enjoy being creative and using your imagination. Thanks for your love, hugs, and patience. You are a stellar group of little people, and every day I am grateful for the opportunity to watch you grow up.

And to my husband, Joe. This is a fun ride, and I'm glad you are on it with me. Thanks for cheering me on, providing me with snacks, caffeine, and belly laughs right when I need them. I love you.

AUTHOR BIO

Emily Bleeker is a former educator who learned to love writing while teaching her students' writer's workshop. After surviving a battle with a rare form of cancer, she finally found the courage to share her stories, starting with her debut novel, *Wreckage*. A fully recovered "secret writer," Emily now spends her days wrangling four kids while planning out plotlines and writing about the people in her head. She currently lives with her family in suburban Chicago. Connect with her or request a Skype visit with your book club at www.emilybleeker.com.